WALKER'S WAY

— A NOVEL —

WILLIAM GREER

Walker's Way

Copyright © 2020 William Greer

Published by Tidewalker Press
Madison, Wisconsin

Paperback ISBN: 978-1-7347346-0-7
eISBN: 978-1-7347346-1-4

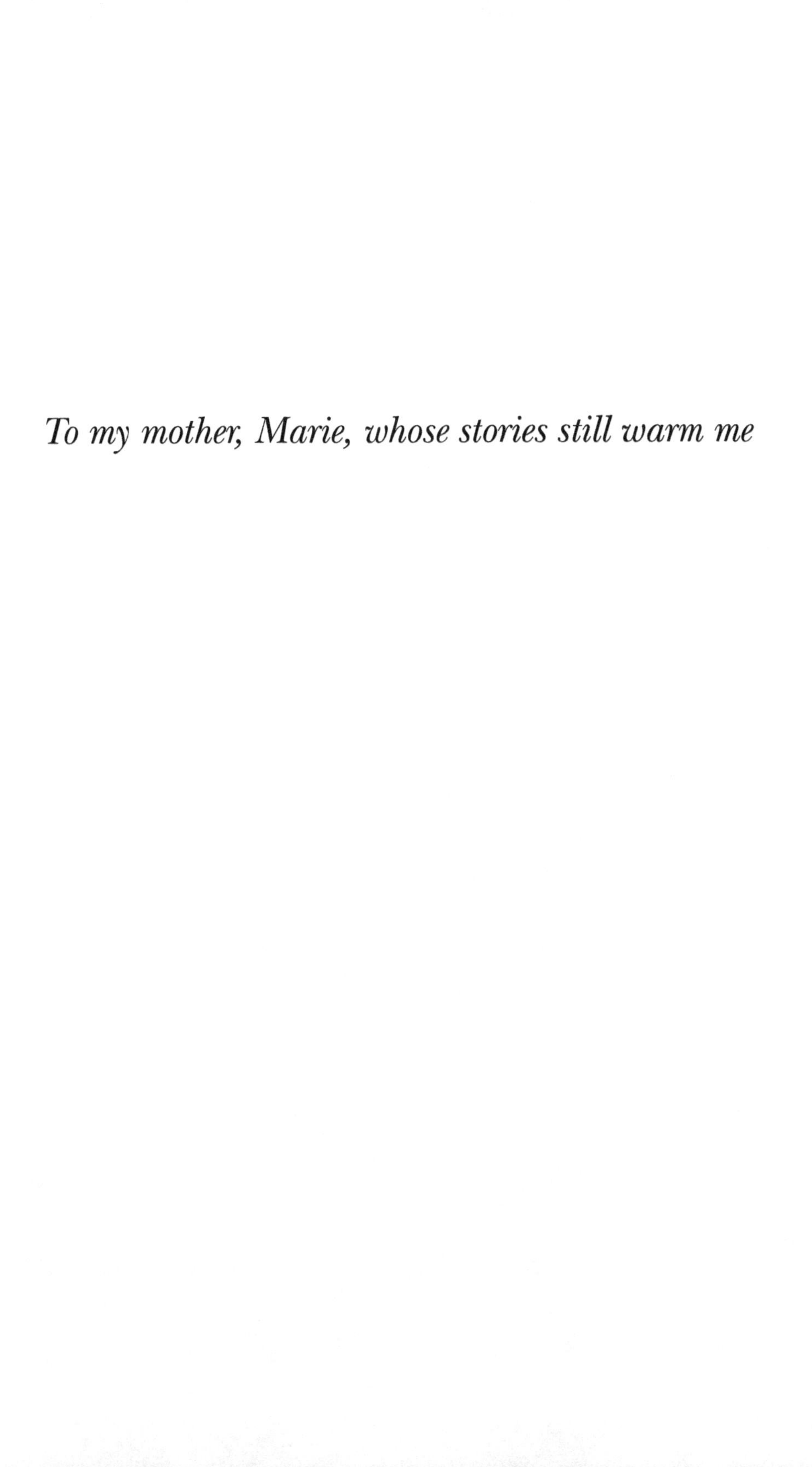

To my mother, Marie, whose stories still warm me

PART 1

"Slow Joe"

1

Joe Walker woke to the smell of hay and horseflesh. The night before, he had bedded down in the stall with his bay gelding, Brandy, as he often did in strange towns. Joe knew that not every place was welcoming to a lone black man. Brandy wasn't bothered by such qualms. He nickered good morning and nuzzled Joe's shoulder. Joe patted his muzzle and scratched behind his ears, a familiar ritual between the longtime trail mates.

It was early May of 1884. The previous day, Joe had ridden into the bustling prairie town of Norfolk, Nebraska, at about sundown. The urgency of his business dictated that he stay only long enough to get some sleep, fill his belly, and ask a few questions. Joe was a bounty hunter of considerable reputation, on the trail of a bad man named Jim Slocum. Joe had pursued his dangerous profession for over a decade because his life had taught him that *truly* bad men rarely stopped themselves. They had to be stopped—by good men.

His resting place was on the edge of town, a rude two-story building with six stalls and a forge on the main floor and a hayloft above. Two of the stalls were occupied, but Joe's presence did not spook the horses within. Joe had had an affinity with horses since childhood. They were comfortable in his presence and he in theirs.

Joe stood and stretched out the night's kinks as he ran a hand over the stubble on his face. Time for a shave. He found a bucket and filled it with water from the trough. His hand mirror revealed a mahogany face with strong, wide features. His broad brow was accentuated by closely cropped hair and close-set ears. His lips were full, covering surprisingly white teeth. His dark eyes made him hard to read and therefore unpredictable.

Joe's ancestors were farmers, hunters, and warriors. Those bloodlines, coupled with his own life experiences, had endowed him with determination, self-reliance, and a fighting spirit. He hummed unconsciously as he shaved, a sound that resembled a purr more than a tune.

After a shave and a wash, Joe put on his boots and vest. Then he reached under his saddle for his most valued piece of outerwear, a well-oiled, nickel-plated Colt Peacemaker with perfect balance, a feather trigger, and the head of a wolf embossed in silver on its handle in homage to the Cherokee clan that had adopted him as an adult. He had had the weapon crafted to his specifications by a New Orleans gunsmith, and it was as distinctive as a calling card.

He strapped on the sidearm reflexively the way other men put on their belt or suspenders. He wore it on his left hip butt first, Texas style. The quality of the weapon and the obvious care it had received suggested that this was a highly prized and essential piece of hardware.

"Good mawnin'."

Joe turned to see the liveryman in the doorway. "Mornin.'"

Joe was grateful that this was a black man. That had made the previous evening's negotiation much easier.

"You sleep okay?"

"Fine, thanks."

"You et yet?"

"Nope."

"I brought you some pone and fatback from the house plus hot coffee if you've a mind."

"Much obliged."

The older man chuckled and shook his head.

"'Twarn't no bother. More'n I could eat. Sometimes my wife ack like she still cookin' for a twenty-year-old."

"You're a lucky man."

"I know. She reminds me every day."

Joe took the proffered vittles and sat down to breakfast. The stable man went over to Brandy's stall. The bay backed away, keeping a wary eye on the stranger.

"Mistuh, that's one fine piece o' hossflesh. I didn't get too close a look last night, but still I could tell he was somethin' special. Sixteen hands and action like runnin' water. I'll bet he can cover some ground."

"You'd win that bet."

"I reckon a man with a mount like that don't look to stay in one place too long." Joe's furrowed brow caused the old man to quickly change course. "I didn't mean to pry into your bizness. No offense."

"None taken. Have you worked here awhile?"

"Yessuh, comin' up on ten years."

"I'm lookin' for a fella who mighta come through here not long ago. A big white man, about my height with light hair and brown eyes, about thirty years old with a scar on his left cheek. He may be wearin' a beard to cover it. Anybody like that come to your attention?"

"He a friend of yours?"

"No, we haven't met."

"But you lookin' for 'im?"

"Yessuh, I am."

The stable man hesitated, carefully weighing his next words.

"Where are my manners? I don't b'lieve we been properly introduced. I'm Henry Johnson."

"Pleased to meet you, Mistuh Johnson. I'm Joe Walker."

"Joe Walker?"

"That's right."

"*Slow* Joe Walker?"

"Some have called me that, yes."

Despite his discovery, the old man could not contain his incredulity.

"How did you get to be Slow Joe Walker?"

Joe smiled for the first time that day.

"Practice," he said.

The liveryman eyed Joe with newfound respect bordering on awe. "I guess there couldn't be two shooters like that in the territory," he said, eyeing Joe's gun. "They say you went up against all three Byles brothers by yourself."

"They say a lot of things, mistuh. Have you seen the man I'm lookin' for? Maybe this will help."

He pulled a wanted poster from his vest pocket. On it was a sketch of a white man with a broad forehead punctuated by knitted brows. His sandy hair fell away from a slightly off center natural part, covering his ears and touching his collar. But for the scowl on his face and the scar on his left cheek, he would have been considered handsome.

The liveryman peered closely at the poster.

"That fella was through here day 'fo yesterday. I fed and stabled his hoss. What does dis here poster say?"

"It says his name is Jim Slocum and he's wanted for robbery and murder."

"Murder! Why, that fella was as friendly as a bible salesman."

"A gator eats by lookin' like a log. Did you see which way he was headed?"

"Yessuh, he rode west. He was ridin' a middlin'-sized sorrel with a white blaze on his forehead. If that helps yuh."

"Very helpful. Here's for your trouble." Joe took a silver dollar from his pocket and gave it to the man.

"Thank you, suh! I don't know if I'm gon' spend this or frame it."

"Spend it. Buy your wife somethin' nice."

And with that, the man hunter saddled his horse and rode after the man who had, so far, eluded him.

2

Joe Walker was a bounty hunter whose tenacity was legendary. He had never failed to bring in an outlaw that he decided to pursue. His skills as a tracker and gunman made him a formidable adversary. The word on the frontier was that, if you were a bad man and you heard that Slow Joe Walker was on your trail, your options were to run, give up, or die. Jim Slocum was unaware that the time was nearing for him to choose.

Walker sat easy in the saddle. The prairie he rode through was a sea of waving green grass recently nourished by spring rains. In the distance, he could barely make out the peaks of the Sierra Nevada Mountains.

Over the years, Brandy's ground-eating canter had become like a rocking chair. Joe's eyes searched the ground in front of him for sign. Someone who was in no hurry had passed this way not long ago. Joe hoped this might be his man. He had been chasing Slocum for nearly a month, getting closer by the day. He climbed down and examined the track more closely. The prints were deep, suggesting a heavy rider. There was a nail missing from the back left shoe. He'd seen this print before . . . Slocum!

Joe was riding south. The relatively flat terrain enabled him to emphasize speed over caution. He topped a rise and saw buildings about three quarters of a mile further on. He drew his Henry from its scabbard and advanced upon the structures at a trot.

Drawing closer, Joe saw the structures were a two-story farmhouse and a good-sized red barn abutted by a corral. The door of the farmhouse stood open.

As he rode into the yard, Joe saw two figures lying on the ground. Dismounting, Joe kept his senses on alert and his rifle at the ready. He knelt and rolled over the body of a bearded man approximately in his midthirties. The man had been shot in the chest at close range and again in the head. Joe could picture Slocum riding in with a smile on his face and malice in his heart, catching the farmer off guard as he had done with previous victims.

Walker went to the second body, about fifteen feet away, and saw that it was a boy of about eleven or twelve. He had been shot in the back and in the back of the head. The two were, most likely, father and son. The presence of female garments on the clothesline and the well-tended flower garden beside the house suggested there was also a woman somewhere.

Joe went to the house, his eyes searching. He stepped on the porch and glided to the side of the front door. He had replaced his Henry with his Colt because it was easier to wield in close quarters.

"Anybody in there? Show yourself. I'm a duly appointed warrant officer on official business. I mean you no harm."

Joe stepped through the door quickly with his gun cocked. The front room was in disarray. The contents of dresser drawers had been emptied on the floor and the cupboard was open. In the second room, he found the body of a woman, naked and tied face down to the bed. Her throat had been cut and, judging by the signs on her body and the bed sheets, she had also been raped. A spontaneous prayer came to Joe's lips.

"Lord help me stop this devil before he kills again." Outside, Brandy gave a warning whinny. Joe went quickly back through the house and emerged on the front porch to see two riders approaching. He holstered his gun and waved to the men as they drew up.

"Nigger, what's goin' on here?" asked the leader, a squat redhead with a full beard and tobacco-stained teeth. He reached for his sidearm as he spoke.

Joe touched the butt of his gun and said, "Go easy, mister. This ain't my doin'."

"Nigger, you got one second to get your hands up or get sent to nigger hell."

Joe's hand remained on the butt of his Colt. His eyes narrowed and his tone turned feral.

"I hear there's a peckerwood hell too. I've sent a few that way."

The man stopped and took a closer look at the man in front of him. His glance flicked to the bodies of the man and boy, and his tone lost its edge.

"That's Richard Scott and that's his son, Billy. We was supposed to go into town yesterday for supplies. When he didn't show, me and Frank come lookin'. What the hell happened here?"

Joe saw the other mounted man start to turn his horse to present his profile to him. Joe turned slightly in that direction.

"I wouldn't do that, mister, if I was you. Better if you and your friend stepped down."

"I'll be damned if . . ."

The farmer's hand dipped toward his holster. Walker's draw was undetectable. One second his hand was hovering over his gun butt. An eye blink later, his colt barked and the stranger's hat flew off as if it had been caught in a stiff breeze. This jaw-dropping speed was, in fact, the reason he had acquired his ironic nickname. The rider's horse reared and the man was dumped unceremoniously in the dust. Joe turned to the other man.

"Now, please step down so we can parlay in peace."

The redhead stepped down slowly, nervously eyeing the tall black man with the uncanny skill with a gun.

As soon as the men had collected themselves, Joe began. "I'm Joe Walker. I'm a warrant officer out of Texas looking for the man who killed these people and a few others to boot."

The redhead said, "I'm Red Murphy and this here's Frank Graham."

Graham put his finger through the hole in his hat. "I heard o' you, mister. Sorry I pulled on you."

"Not as sorry as you might o' been," Joe said pointedly.

He produced the wanted poster from his shirt pocket. "This is Jim Slocum. I believe he's our man. This has his filthy prints all over it. There's a woman inside with her throat cut. She's been used pretty bad too."

Graham turned ashen under his tan. "Oh Jesus, no! That'd be Addie, Dick's wife. What kinda animal is this Slocum, anyway?"

"The kind you don't turn your back on," Walker said. "It looks like he took what valuables and supplies he could find. I was about to look for sign when you two showed up. Will you men tend to the bodies while I look around?" They nodded grimly and walked toward the house.

Joe found boot and hoofprints in the soft earth by the well. Judging by the back hoofprint, it was Slocum's sorrel. There was also a bloody fingerprint on the water dipper. Joe thought, *If I have anything to say about it, big man, the next blood you shed will be your own.*

He turned back to the house. Graham came through the front door followed by Murphy carrying the woman's body wrapped in a blanket. His mouth was set in a grim line.

"If it's the last thing I do, I'll have his nuts on a stick," he said. He placed the woman on the porch between her husband and son.

Walker said, "Come with me." He took them to the well and showed them the tracks and the bloody dipper handle. "It's Slocum, all right. These are his horse's tracks. He's got a day's start on me and he'll be movin' fast after this business, so I've got to get after him. I understand you wantin' his hide, but somebody needs to tend to these folks and then ride to town with the news of what happened here. That'll take another day. If there's a sheriff in town, he'll raise a posse. You might be of a mind to join it. Slocum may already be out of your lawman's jurisdiction, but he'll never be out of mine. I promise you I'll settle up for these folks or die trying."

While Walker was talking, he was filling his canteen from the well. He made a chirping noise and the big bay came obediently to his side for water and a handful of grain. He reached into his saddlebag for a piece of jerky, which he chewed while adjusting Brandy's saddle. His routine completed, he swung into the saddle.

"I'll leave trail markers for your posse. Maybe we'll meet again. Sorry for your loss." With that, Joe kicked the bay, which started south at a pace he could maintain for miles.

Murphy and Graham watched him until he disappeared over the rise then turned to the grim task before them.

3

Try as he might, Joe could not get the picture of the dead woman's body out of his mind. The bloody welts Slocum left on the woman's back sparked memories of how he had acquired the network of scars on his own back. And with those memories came the suppressed ache of shame mixed with anger and grief.

Joe was thirty-eight years old, but a lifetime of duress and duty had seasoned him beyond his years. He had been born in February on a plantation in Benton, Tennessee, the second of four children born to slaves, David and Sarah Walker. Amos was the couples' first-born child, followed by Joseph, Rosemary, and Lillian.

Amos was five years Joe's senior and, as a result, was often charged with watching Joe while his parents were occupied elsewhere. The minute his parents were out of sight, Amos would take a length of rope and tie one end around Joe's waist and the other end around his own wrist. If Joe toddled toward a hot stove, a sleeping dog, or a pie cooling on the windowsill, Amos would give a tug on the rope and Joe would end up on his backside.

Even at an early age, Joe was persistent to the point of stubbornness. He was not about to give up on a goal after a single try, so Amos was kept busy yanking and admonishing. Joe's frustration at being continuously thwarted often brought him to tears, but they were short-lived since they had no effect on his older brother.

As Joe moved beyond toddler stage, he continued to behave as if he and Amos were physically bound together because he followed his older brother everywhere. Amos's attempts at losing him were only partially successful. They were undermined by his mother's constant request that he look out for his little brother.

The dynamic changed the summer after Joe turned eight years old.

One day, Amos and his best friend, John Henry, managed to sneak away from Joe and go to their favorite fishing hole, secluded in a stand of deep woods on the Walker property. They intended to catch a mess of catfish for their respective suppers. Without their knowledge, Joe had followed them from a distance and was watching from the woods, waiting for the right moment to announce his presence. Before he could devise a plan of action, two white men stepped out of the woods on the other side of the pond and headed in Amos and John's direction.

The men were young, possibly in their early twenties. The one in the lead carried a squirrel rifle and wore coveralls, no shirt, and a battered straw hat. His companion was armed and dressed identically but was bareheaded, revealing a shock of corn silk blond hair. The one with the straw hat spoke to Amos and John.

"What you niggers doin' on our property?"

"'Scuse me, suh, but we thought we was on Massa Christopher Walker's land," Amos said.

"Well, you thought wrong. This is my pappy's land, and you niggers are truspassin' and poachin' to boot, by the looks of it."

"Oh no, suh, nothin' like that. We was just lookin'. We'll be movin' along now."

"You disputin' my word, nigger?" the man in the straw had asked. With that, he approached the two boys with his rifle crooked in his arm, his face a mask of menace.

Joe could see that things were about to go bad. Without thinking, he ran out of the woods toward the group. "Amos! John Henry!" he shouted at the top of his lungs. The party turned to look in his direction. "Massa Walker's lookin' for y'all. He said it don't matter that you his houseboys—he gon' peel your hides for goin' off without tellin' nobody. He and the overseer are right behind me. If I was you, I'd ditch them poles and hightail it back to the big house." He looked at the two white men with wide eyes. "Are these gen'men with y'all?"

"Hell naw!" Straw Hat said, wanting to avoid getting in the middle of a confrontation with an angry white landowner and his slaves on the former's land. "You niggers get to steppin'."

"Yes, suh," Amos and John said in unison. They turned and followed Joe back the way he had come. When they gained the cover of the trees, they broke into a run and didn't stop until they reached the field adjacent to the slave quarters. While they caught their breaths, Amos grabbed Joe by the shoulders and looked at him in wonder.

"Jaybird, how'd you come up with that story?" Amos asked.

"I don't know. Once I started talkin', it just made itself up," Joe said. "I couldn't just stand by and watch 'em hurt y'all."

John Henry spoke up, "Joe, you cain't never tell *nobody* 'bout what happened today, you hear?"

"I won't tell nobody," Joe said. As he thought about what might have happened, his voice quavered and he began to cry.

Amos stepped close and put his arm around his brother's shoulder. After that day, they were practically inseparable.

4

Joe's father, David, was the Walker plantation's blacksmith and wheelwright. He was a coffee-colored man, a shade under six feet tall with broad shoulders, a thick chest, and a tapered waist. His arms were corded with veins and heavily muscled due to years of pounding and bending iron. He combed his coarse, straight hair backward so that it framed his face like a pharaoh's nemes.

Despite his place on a higher rung of the slave hierarchy, Joe never saw his father take on airs with anybody. Similarly, Mr. Walker was unimpressed by the words that came out of people's mouths, whether of flattery or good intention. His favorite saying was "Talk is cheap. Deeds make the man."

Next to God, David Walker was devoted to his family, starting with his wife, Sarah.

Joe's mother worked in the "big house," cooking cleaning and tending to the Walkers' children. If her husband was an oak, she was a willow, lithe and supple in physique and personality. Her laughter was spontaneous, like a fountain of joy that started in her belly and burst from her lips. No one who heard it could repress at least a smile. Joe remembered her rocking him to sleep while singing lullabies about the love of Jesus and the promise of heaven. She smelled of soap, vanilla, and hair oil. Joe knew from birth that she loved him unconditionally. And this was confirmed daily in her touch, her words, and her actions.

Joe learned about forging and bending iron and training horses from his father. His father taught him how to shoe, groom, and tend a horse in sickness and health. He taught Joe that horses, despite their size, are prey animals and, therefore, wary and skittish by nature. Joe also learned that horses are herd animals that gain a sense of security from knowing who is in charge. A person provided them that security by treating them with kindness and firmness.

Joe first learned to work with the farm's plow horses and slowly graduated to Mr. Walker's prize racehorses, exercising and training them at the age of nine. As his comfort with horses grew, he spent more time with them, finding that he preferred their company to the company of most humans. He learned to read their moods and respond appropriately. Anytime Master Walker purchased a new horse, he put Joe's father in charge of "gentling" the animal. In time, David routinely entrusted this task to his son.

Joe's second mentor on the plantation was his father's best friend, James. Since the two men acted like brothers, David's children began to refer to their father's close friend as Uncle Jim. Uncle Jim's hair was completely white and he was at least ten years David's senior, but he could work all day in the field without faltering and get up day after day and do it again. No one, including Jim, knew his exact age.

In addition to being a top field hand, Uncle Jim was an excellent wood-carver who made furniture for the Walker mansion and toys for the Walker children. He took Joe under his wing and taught him the fundamentals of woodworking. Joe loved watching the old man's deft movements and trying to imitate them.

Uncle Jim's favorite instruction to Joe was "Pay attention. It saves time and wood."

Uncle Jim's most eccentric talent was storytelling. He was the plantation's griot, and at the end of the day, the slaves would gather at his cabin where he would regale them with tales of that day and of days past, showing them the symbiotic relationship between their lives and the lives of their owners. He was an excellent mimic and could imitate both the black and the white people on the farm, much to the delight of his audience. Joe could still remember Uncle Jim's voice and facial expression changing fluidly as he shifted from character to character.

Even though he was a slave, Joe was content with his life. This all changed one summer day when he was unceremoniously sold away from his family. His last memory of his parents was the sight of his mother lying on the ground in a paroxysm of grief while his father knelt at her side. Joe had to be bound and a burlap sack placed over his head. He howled himself hoarse and received a blow to the head for his trouble. When he came to, he was on a barge on the Mississippi river. At the end of his trip, Joe's life entered a dark valley.

5

It was May of 1856 and Joe had been sold to Jackson Budreau of the New Orleans Budreaus. Budreau was a small, fussy man whose large eyes and thin, cruel lips gave him a reptilian appearance. He came out from the big house to inspect his new property.

"Shawn, get those niggers down so I can take a closer look."

Shawn was the overseer, a burly white man with a bullet head, a scraggly beard, and sloping shoulders. He prodded the shackled slaves out of the wagon with the end of a billy club.

Budreau walked along the line of six, pausing before each man or woman for a closer inspection of teeth, limbs, and genitals. When he came to Joe, he grabbed the boy's chin. Instinctively, Joe drew back. The man slapped him hard across the mouth.

"Don't ever pull away from me boy." He pulled Joe's jaws apart and looked at his teeth. He squeezed his penis and scrotum to the point that Joe felt a wave of nausea.

"This one should be a good breeder," Budreau said.

He turned to walk away when Joe spoke.

"'Scuse me, suh, where is dis?" This elicited another hard slap, which added to the ringing in Joe's ears.

"Don't ever talk to me, boy, unless you're spoken to. Where is this nigger from anyway?"

"Tennessee, suh," Shawn said.

"Well, you're going to have to teach him some Louisiana manners pretty damn quick. Now take these niggers over to their quarters and get 'em squared away."

Shawn led the new arrivals to the slave quarters, several wooden shacks clustered at the edge of the clearing. There were two people in the shack where they were taken, an old man with a twisted leg and a pregnant woman. The rest of the slaves were in the fields. "Cecil, Lula, I got a new crew here. Get 'em squared away. I'll be back in a shake to take them to the fields." With that, Shawn left them.

The old man said, "I'm Cecil. This here Lulabelle. You womens go with her. You mens stay with me."

After the women left, Cecil showed each man the place where he would place his sleeping pallet. "Meals is at sunup, midday, and sundown. The privy is out back and down dat path yonder. We get water from the creek for washin'. From the well for drinkin'."

Joe went cautiously to the old man and raised his hand.

"What you want, young un?"

"Can I ax you a question?"

"What?"

"Where we at?"

"We on Mr. Budreau's plan'ation, boy."

"Where dat at?"

"Why, dat be in Louisiana."

"Which way is Tennessee?"

"What you need to know dat for?"

"That's where my family be."

"Boy, yo family's gone for good. So stop thinkin' about 'em. If you try to get back to 'em, they'll make you sorry you was eva born."

There was a heavy step on the porch and Shawn reentered the cabin. "Let's get to woik, ya'll." He led them to the cane fields and for the rest of the day, Joe was introduced to the backbreaking job of cutting cane. At the end of the shortened day, his back was racked with pain and his hands were blistered and bleeding from grappling with the rough cane stalks. That day was the end of Joe's childhood.

The next day he met Jacob Budreau. Jacob was a Negro boy of thirteen who had light skin, slightly protruding eyes, and thin lips. His resemblance to Jackson Budreau struck Joe like a slap in the face. Despite the differences in their ages, Joe was a head taller than Jacob.

Jacob had learned to avoid the lash and curry favor at every opportunity. In fact, he had earned his way into Jackson Budreau's meager circle of trust. This was probably why he was assigned to teach Walker how to behave himself as a Budreau slave. They first spoke after Walker had endured a severe beating for riding one of the master's horses without permission.

Walker was lying on his bunk with his bleeding back exposed. Bertha, an older slave woman, was applying cold compresses.

Jacob approached the boy. "Is you crazy, nigga? Nobody but the white people rides dem animals. You lucky the massa didn't hang yo' ass."

"I was just trying to work 'im a little bit. He gittin' fat for lack of exercise."

"And what business is dat of yo's? You ain't no jockey. Now listen to me, nigga, and listen good. You do what you's told. Nothin' mo—nothin' less. Massa Budreau done put me in charge of you. So yo mess-ups is my mess-ups. And iffen you get me in trouble, I'll hang you my ownself."

"You ever been to Tennessee?" Walker asked.

"What that got to do with anythin'?"

"That's where I'm from and I need to get back there."

"What *you* need don't matta. Only thing that matta is what Massa Jackson Budreau need. You got that, boy?"

Walker determined from that day that Jacob would not be an ally and resolved to regard him as suspiciously as he did the white people. He was right in his assessment. Jacob became his private guard, watching his every move and alerting the overseer to any transgressions.

Walker spent three days in the "oven," a three-foot by eight-foot tin box, after Jacob reported him for stealing roasting ears from the corn-crib. After Joe's first escape attempt, Jacob disciplined him with thirty lashes. Jacob also came up with the nickname that stuck to Walker for the rest of his days on the plantation, "Jock."

Misery had all but won out over hope in Walker's life, when the war broke out. Budreau's two sons enlisted early, expecting to wrap themselves in glory during a truncated conflict. As the war dragged on, Budreau's fortunes took a turn for the worse, fueled by his profligate lifestyle and the precipitous drop in the price of sugar. He had to begin selling off land and human property. Walker was a piece of the latter.

As a healthy young male, he could still command a good price. Given Walker's recalcitrant ways, Budreau was glad to get rid of him and profit in the end from what had turned out to be a bad investment. He sold Walker at auction to a Virginia farmer. En route to his new home, Walker escaped. He joined the Union army on December 23, 1862 and fought the Confederates with the ferocity of a man with a score to settle.

6

Jacob, for his part, stayed on the Budreau land until the war ended. By then, the plantation had become dysfunctional and Jackson Budreau was a bitter, broken man transformed into a drooling invalid by a massive stroke at the age of fifty-six. Both of Budreau's white sons, Peter and Simon, died in the war. That left Jacob as the only male on the premises who carried Budreau's bloodline, although his chances of benefitting from that relationship were practically nonexistent. He recalled when his mother had confirmed on his fifteenth birthday that he was the master's illegitimate son. She warned him never to speak of this to anybody. Regardless, it was the worst kept secret on the farm that he *and* his sister, Ruby, were Budreau's children.

The white man had had an unrelenting attraction to Jacob's mother, Molly. In fact, he had loved her to death. She died at thirty-six giving birth to his third child, a stillborn breach baby. This placed Jacob and Ruby in the peculiar circumstance of being orphans while their father lived a hundred feet away.

After Molly's death, Jackson Budreau went into a funk. He was often drunk and unshaven at midday. He and Mistress Jean could be heard arguing loudly in the evening, and he let business matters slip. Gradually, however, he returned to himself. It was at this time that he began to pay positive attention to Jacob, praising him in front of the other slaves and taking him along on trips to town to purchase seed, supplies, and sometimes slaves. He even allowed Bertha, the plantation's cook who adopted Jacob and Ruby, to bake him a yearly birthday cake.

Bertha had suffered so much loss in life that her heart had become a stone that she carried to test the limits of her endurance. When she adopted Molly's children, her burden lifted to a degree that she never would have thought possible.

As Ruby approached puberty, she attracted Budreau's salacious attention. Ruby was as sweet and unassuming as Jacob was cruel and conniving. She became close to Joe, as if she were seeking the positive regard she would never receive from her biological brother. Joe soaked up her growing affection like a thirsty sponge. He would carve her tiny wooden horses and birds that she named and placed on the windowsill beside her bed.

Bertha did her best to protect the child, finding some errand for her to do every time she saw Budreau approaching their quarters. He raped her for the first time when she was thirteen. Joe added it to the list of Budreau's sins and vowed he would make him pay.

Jacob was in a quandary. He wanted to protect his sister but he had no idea how to do so against the god of his universe. He watched her lose the innocent glow of childhood and become a harried, frightened animal. She stopped taking care of herself. Her hair was dirty and matted and she smelled. These things seemed only to further inflame Budreau's lust. He impregnated her at age fourteen.

7

"M iss Jean" Budreau, Jackson's wife, planned a special celebration for Jackson's fiftieth birthday. She had invited friends from the neighboring plantations and had spent time making and buying special gifts for her husband. The meal she planned included all his favorites: candied yams, roast pork, turnip greens, okra, shortening bread, and fried chicken. The pièce de résistance was a triple-layer chiffon cake complete with candles.

The evening went off like a charm and Budreau was clearly pleased with the attention and the largesse of his family and friends. When dessert time came, Jean excused herself and went back to the kitchen to light the candles on Jackson's cake. She walked in the kitchen and saw Ruby washing dishes at the sink her protruding belly advertising her condition. Next to her on the cooling board was Jackson's birthday cake. Jean's stomach clinched at sight of the girl, her latest rival. As Ruby dropped a large pot into the dishwater, some suds splashed out and landed near the cake. Joe had just entered the kitchen with an armful of firewood.

"Watch what you're doing, girl!" Jean Budreau screamed. Ruby jumped like a startled deer, knocking the cake off the counter where it landed upside down on the kitchen floor. The mistress's rage was stoked by jealousy.

She advanced on the wide-eyed girl and, grabbing an iron skillet from the stovetop, she swung it in a deadly arc into the side of the girl's head. Ruby dropped to the floor where she lay jerking uncontrollably.

Bertha screamed and dropped to her knees beside the convulsing girl. "Oh Lord no! Baby, is you all right? Don't leave me! Please don't leave me!" She turned to her mistress and for one unguarded moment, the hatred in her eyes was so clear and clean that Miss Jean recoiled in terror.

"What the hell is going on out heah? If you niggers . . ." It was Jackson Budreau. He paused in midsentence at the sight of Ruby on the floor in a puddle of her own blood. He turned to his wife, who still had the skillet in her hand.

"What did you do?" It was at this moment that Jean Budreau swooned. She and the frying pan fell to the floor. Budreau went to his wife and lifted her in his arms. He emerged from the kitchen with her that way. His guests were standing in an anxious knot in the dining room. He smiled wanly.

"No cause for alarm. Jean just got a little ovawrought. I'm going to take her upstairs and put her to bed. I'll be down directly." As he passed his oldest son, Peter, he said, "Clean up that mess back there and keep your mouth shut."

Twenty minutes later, Jackson Budreau returned to the party, apologizing for his wife who had suddenly taken ill. He spent the rest of the evening distractedly opening gifts and receiving congratulations.

By the time the last guest had departed and he rushed to Bertha's cabin, Ruby was dead. Bertha was still rocking the girl in her arms. Joe, Jacob, and several adult slaves stood in attendance. No one had been able to take Ruby away from her second mother. Bertha's eyes were swollen from crying and her usually spotless apron was stained with her adopted daughter's blood.

Budreau approached and said softly, "Bertha, what happened?"

"Ruby knocked yo cake off the counter and Miss Jean hit her wid de skillet." She paused. "My baby's dead over a *damn* birthday cake . . ."

Her voice trailed off when she realized who she was talking to. Budreau apparently decided to let it go.

"Bertha, you got to let us take her now. You heah me?"

He motioned two men forward and they pulled the dead girl from Bertha's now strengthless arms. The shattered cook let out a sound that was a combination sigh and moan and collapsed on the bed. Budreau turned to the men who held the body.

"Get a coffin ready. We'll bury her in the mawnin'." He patted the old woman's shoulder and turned to go.

"Massa?"

"Yes, Auntie?"

"Why y'all hate us so much?" Expecting no answer, she sighed deeply and buried her face in the blanket.

Joe watched them carry Ruby's body from the cabin. His heart felt like a leaden weight in his chest but he knew tears would avail him nothing. He vowed once again that he would someday make the Budreaus pay for all the pain they had caused.

He walked back into the cabin. Bertha was lying on the bed weeping softly. Jacob sat on a stool at the foot of the bed. He was the picture of despair. His shoulders slumped and his hands rested limply in his lap. He too was crying silently.

Joseph approached the boy who had bullied him since almost the first day he had arrived on the plantation. "Jacob, can I do anythin'?"

Jacob looked up. For a moment his face was clouded by conflicting emotions. Then he sprang up from the stool and slapped Joseph hard across the mouth. "Get outta my sight, nigga, or there'll be two funerals tomorra."

Joseph turned and walked quickly from the room, his mouth bleeding and his mind racing. The enmity between them was permanently sealed at that moment.

8

Miss Jean stayed in bed for two days. She was literally sick with grief. Jackson's fiftieth birthday party had been ruined along with her reputation as the parish's finest hostess. All because of a trifling, clumsy slave wench. Barring some kind of social tour de force, it would take her years to regain her status in the community. Never one to overindulge herself, she resumed her household duties after a week of convalescence. She did not suspect that every meal she consumed during her respite contained a gift from Bertha.

Jacob was grief stricken over Ruby's death, but it did solve his dilemma over what to do about Master Budreau's unwanted advances toward his sister. He was all alone in the world now and if he survived, it would be because of his foresight and his cunning. It was patently obvious that the only way to survive was to do nothing that would incite the Budreau's wrath.

For the next five years, he did everything he could to solidify his good standing in his owners' eyes. He breathed a sigh of relief when "Jock" was sold off, allowing him to devote his full attention to his own fortunes. He went from field slave to house slave to "Boss Negro." The civil war broke out when he was nineteen years old, and his fortune followed his father's into decline.

As her social status declined, Miss Jean became a drug-addled recluse. Her fear of the slaves who surrounded her grew large. She ranted about their suspected indiscretions from stealing food to plotting her murder. She would only eat meals prepared by her daughter-in-law, Serena. She slept with a loaded pistol beneath her pillow. Wracked by guilt and fear one winter night in 1864, she overdosed on the laudanum she took for her "female problems." She was buried in the family cemetery next to her sons, another casualty of war.

In the spring of 1865, the Union army "liberated" the Budreau plantation. Jacob and the remaining slaves were set free, but no one told them what to do with their precious freedom. Despite their loyalty, they had become pariahs in their own land. Serena took Jackson and moved back to her family in Ohio, leaving Jacob and the other servants to fend for themselves.

Jacob tried share cropping but found it to be just another form of slavery. He ran away from his landlord, abandoning his debt and his pregnant wife. He tried dock work but found that he didn't have the strength for it. He tried working as a swamper in a saloon but couldn't handle emptying spittoons and cleaning up blood, piss, and vomit on a daily basis. Everything he tried seemed to him to be beneath a Boss Negro's status. After years of struggling and barely getting by, he turned to crime like a long ignored suitor. That's what eventually brought him to Slow Joe Walker's attention.

9

By 1875, Jacob Budreau was working with two thugs named Lenny Ryback and Jerry Weems, robbing people along the highways of east Kansas. Rather than robbing people one at a time, Budreau had proposed that they graduate to stagecoaches and payroll shipments. He staked out the coach between Lawrence and Topeka and learned everything he could about its schedule and security. Then he had Weems ride the stage as a passenger. Satisfied that they were sufficiently prepared, he set up a roadblock about midway between the two towns. When the stage stopped to clear the road, he and Ryback rode out and accosted the driver and shotgun rider.

"Hands up!" Budreau shouted. When the guard hesitated, Budreau fired a shot over his head. The man immediately threw down his weapon. They robbed the passengers and took the strongbox that was carrying the payroll for the Gibson mine. Weems had remained hidden with his rifle at the ready in case anything unexpected happened. The whole operation took twenty minutes and netted $10,000. His partners were ecstatic. Any doubt they had about who should be leading the gang was permanently erased.

They robbed several more stages with mixed results. Either the passengers were relative paupers or the strongboxes didn't contain what they were supposed to contain. So, Jacob decided they should move on to trains. Using the same basic preparation and adding three more confederates, they took down the Kansas City Limited and scored $50,000. Since they had to ride the train to pull off the job, they went in unmasked. Several passengers were able to give their descriptions to the authorities, particularly the black man who seemed to be their leader. Wanted posters were immediately issued for the "Blacksnake Gang."

Walker apprehended Lenny Ryback in Missouri, where he was living the high life on his share of the Kansas City take. Shortly after his arrest, Ryback gave up his entire gang for the promise of a lighter sentence. When Walker heard the name Jacob Budreau, it was all he could do to keep his composure. "What does this Budreau look like?" he asked.

"Light-skinned nigra, five seven or eight, maybe one hundred sixty pounds. Gray eyes. Somebody was dippin' his pencil in the ink well, iffen you know what I mean," he said with a smirk. "Smart as a whip, though. He got us inta the big money."

Walker couldn't believe that his path had again crossed that of his nemesis. He was determined to find Budreau and bring him to justice for his transgressions, old and new.

"Where did you split up with Budreau?" he asked.

"Lawrence," the outlaw said.

"And where were you gon' meet up with 'im again?"

"I dunno what you're talkin' about," the outlaw said, dropping his eyes.

"A man like you don't tear up a meal ticket. You just said Budreau got you inta the big money. I don't reckon you planned on goin' back to slim pickins. Once you and your crew spent yourselves broke, you'd want to hook up with Budreau again. So, where's that s'posed to happen?"

Noting the man's continued hesitation, Walker turned to the sheriff. "This look like cooperation to you?"

"Nope, I guess we'll just lock 'im up and throw away the key like we planned on doin'."

"Wait a minute," Ryback said. "We're s'posed to meet up at a hideout in the Missouri Breaks sometime during the week of August seventeenth. Anybody who don't make it gits left behind on the next job."

"That's over two months from now," the sheriff said.

"Draw me a map," Walker said.

"If you're lyin', you'll do all of your time and every bit of theirs too," the sheriff said.

"I ain't lyin'," Ryback said. He hoped never to see Joe Walker or Jacob Budreau again.

10

Walker arrived at the hideout on August 12. The shack was almost invisible in a dense thicket of scrub pine in the throat of a deep gully. He scouted the shack from cover and, seeing no movement, approached it on foot. He was wearing moccasins to cover his tracks and soften his footfalls. He paused and crouched behind a tree ten yards from the front door. He sat motionless there for a half hour. Then he rose suddenly and ran to the side of the cabin. He peered through the side window and saw that the cabin was empty. He raised the window and stepped through into the cabin. There were bunks against three walls, a stove, a long table, and a cupboard filled with dry goods. He examined the floor. Beneath a worn rug, he found a trap door. He lifted it and saw a short ladder leading to a lower space. Drawing his colt and striking a match, he descended the ladder.

He found himself in an eight-by-ten-foot room with a gun rack, a larder filled with more provisions, and a door that led to a tunnel that ended in a concealed door in an embankment thirty feet behind the cabin. There was a table in the center of the room with a kerosene lamp on it. Finally, in one corner of the room, there was a rough-hewn cabinet. It concealed a safe with a combination lock. Walker left the cabin exactly as he had found it. Time to lay his snare.

Budreau arrived a day later. He was a cautious man and that dictated that he be the first to arrive at the hideout. He approached the cabin with his gun drawn. Though he saw no sign of occupancy, he called out, "Hello, the cabin!" There was no answer. He dismounted and walked to the front door. The ashes he'd left on the doorstep were undisturbed. He went into the cabin and found it as he had left it. He returned to his horse and led him around to the stable behind the cabin where he unsaddled him and gave him some fodder.

Budreau returned to the cabin carrying his gear. As he entered the room, he sensed danger, but before he could react, Walker stepped from behind the door and struck him on the back of the head with his blackjack, knocking him unconscious.

When Budreau came to, he was cuffed with his feet bound, lying on one of the bunks. Seated before him was a man who looked familiar but whose name he could not place. He observed these things through slitted eyelids while remaining motionless.

Despite his subterfuge, the stranger said, "You can sit up now."

He pushed himself erect. "What're you after, mistuh?"

"I'm after you, Jacob."

"Do I know you?"

"You tell me."

Budreau stared at the stranger and in his dark eyes, he saw a resolve that took him back fifteen years. "Jock? Jock Budreau? Is that you, nigga? What the hell do you think you're doin'?"

"The name is Joseph—Joseph Walker," Walker said.

"I don't give a damn what you callin' yourself these days. Turn me loose before I forgit maself."

"I'm takin' you in for robbin' the Kansas City Limited."

"You think you a lawman, nigga? Show me a badge."

Walker took a wanted poster from his pocket and showed it to Budreau. "I'm a duly appointed warrant officer and I'm takin' you in for robbin' the Kansas City Limited."

"A goddamn bounty hunter. I'll be damned. Look, if it's money you want, I can match that bounty and you won't have to worry about how you gon' get me to the nearest jail house with my gang on your trail."

"It ain't about the money. You keep goin,' you gon' kill somebody, and I cain't have that."

"I'm gon' kill somebody all right. I'm gon' kill *you*, nigga. Now get ova here and cut me loose."

As a horse wrangler, Walker knew the importance of establishing who is in charge between man and beast. Likewise, as a bounty hunter, Walker's life literally depended upon his ability to dominate his captives physically and psychologically. He could tell by Budreau's words and demeanor that he still thought of him as the young boy he had bullied on the plantation. Walker had to disabuse him of that notion straight away to forestall trouble down the road.

Walker stood up and went to the bunk, where he removed Budreau's handcuffs and untied his feet. "You betta not have stole none of my stuff. Where's my gun?" the outlaw asked in the tone one would use with an errant child.

"It's in your bedroll," Walker said.

Budreau retrieved his colt and put it in his holster.

"You betta check your loads," Walker said.

Budreau spun the chamber, saw that the gun was fully loaded, and reholstered it. He continued talking while he went through his saddlebags. "Now, if I was you, I'd hightail it out of here befo—" He turned and saw Walker standing in front of the door with his arms folded. "What's this, nigga?" He demanded.

"It's you and me, Jacob. Mebbe for the last time. The only way you get out o' here is over me."

Budreau dropped his hands to his sides and his face became an unreadable mask. "I don't want ta have ta kill you boy," he said.

Walker's voice was ice dipped in poison. "You yella-bellied bag o' wind, I'm sick of your noise. So eitha unbuckle that gun belt or fill your hand." Walker needed Budreau to know that, if crossed, he was a deadly adversary.

Budreau, who had survived most of his life by reading people, was convinced. He reached down slowly with both hands and unbuckled his gun belt. "No need for bloodshed," he said lamely.

"Go back over there and put them cuffs on," Walker said.

Budreau went to the bunk, retrieved the handcuffs, and put them on. For the time being, Walker had established that he was the one in charge, whether or not Budreau was bound. He hoped Budreau's belief in his dominance would last until he got him safely behind bars.

"Now what?" Budreau said sullenly.

"Now we hit the trail."

"Might be better to get a fresh start in the mornin'."

"And give your boys some more time to git here? I don't think so," Walker said.

"As soon as they see I'm not here, they'll be on yo trail, and them boys is first-rate trackers," Budreau said.

"If they was first rate trackers, they wouldn't be robbin' trains," Walker said.

Walker filled Budreau's saddlebags with provisions. He found $2000 dollars in cash in a money belt in one of the bags.

"This money is probably stole, so I'll turn it in with you."

"Sho' you will," Budreau said with a smirk.

Walker took Budreau to the stable and saddled his horse. Back in the front yard, he made a chirping sound and Brandy came trotting out of the trees and stopped in front of his master, head up and ears pricked. With the sun glinting off his coat, he looked like a bronze sculpture.

At the sight of the bay, Budreau gave a low whistle of appreciation. "Looks like you finally found the hoss you was lookin' for, boy."

"Let's go," Walker said.

"Ain't you gon' take these cuffs off?"

"Nope. Now climb up. Daylight's wastin'."

Walker headed for the nearest town, Fort Benton. That evening, he and Budreau camped on the trail. After supper, Budreau drew Walker into conversation, hoping for an opening.

"What happened to you afta you got sold?"

"I run off and joined the Union army," Walker replied.

"You fought for the Yankees?"

"Right up to Appomattox. What about you?" he asked Budreau.

"Never could get away. Funny, I spent most of my life as a slave and now you takin' me in to be locked up for pretty much the rest of it." Budreau paused. "Don't seem like somethin' one black man oughta do to anotha one."

"Takin' what ain't yours ain't a way to stay free, Jacob."

"Ain't much a nigga can do to get ahead. White man sees to that. I ain't a cold-blooded killer like you, so my chances at the good life is slim. Joseph, I know you holdin' all the cards heah, but if you could see yo way clear to lettin' me go, I promise you I'll never commit another crime in life. You know, I got a wife and baby girl back in Louisiana. I was just tryin' to raise a stake that would give us some kind of life as a family. I couldn't save my motha or my sista. Looks like I ain't gon' be able to save my wife and baby neitha." He put his head in his hands and sighed heavily.

Walker said, "Can I trust you, Jacob?"

"That's for you to decide, brotha. All I know is we been hatin' each other for a long time. It just don't make no sense to me no more."

Walker was silent for a time, staring into the fire. Then he said abruptly, "I need to sleep on it."

"Suits me. Much obliged for at least thinkin' on it."

Walker damped down the fire. He spread out his bedroll and summoned Brandy, who came and stood directly over him. "Watch," he said to the big bay.

"What's that, your guard hoss?" Budreau asked.

"If you try to get away, he'll wake me up, and if you come near me, he'll stomp you to death. See you in the mornin'." With that, Walker rolled himself into his blankets and went to sleep.

The next morning, Walker and Budreau ate breakfast with minimal conversation. Finally, the outlaw could stand it no longer.

"Well, what's it gon' be?"

Walker walked over to him and removed his handcuffs. "I reckon both of us have spent enough time in chains. I figure that two thousand in your wallet should stake you to a new start."

Budreau let out his breath and an incredulous smile spread across his face. "Brotha, I don't know how to thank ya. If there's ever anythin' I can do for you, just ask."

"You can do two things," Walker said. "Go straight from here on out like you promised and take care o' your family. That's the real treasure."

Budreau was effusive "I will or die tryin'."

Walker tossed Budreau his saddlebags and then his gun belt. He turned to gather his own gear and heard the familiar click of a hammer being drawn back.

"Hands up, Jock! And turn around real slow."

Walker did as he was told.

Budreau's smile was genuine this time. "Well, look at the big bad bounty hunter who thought he could bring in Jacob Budreau. You may be faster'n me and bigger'n me, but when push comes to shove, you're still just a ignorant field nigga. I figure my stake plus yours will just about finance my next job."

"There's nowhere you can run where I won't find you," Joe said.

"I know," Budreau said. He pulled the trigger and it clicked on an empty cylinder. He rapidly pulled the trigger three more times with the same result. His eyes grew wide with dawning realization.

"Always check your loads," Walker said. He reached under his shirt and produced a .44 pistol. "Drop the gun and put up your hands."

Budreau was beside himself. "You double dealin' black bastard. I should've killed you when you was a whelp."

Joe walked to Budreau and tossed the handcuffs to him. They struck him in the chest and fell to the ground. "You know what ta do," he said.

Budreau picked up the handcuffs and put them on. Joe approached closer, his gun steady. He made sure the cuffs were secure and stepped back.

"How did you know what I'd do?" Budreau asked.

"I didn't. That's why I unloaded your pistol last night. I was fixin' to let you go on accounta yo family. All you had to do was get on your hoss and ride away. Instead, you tried to kill me for what was in my pockets. You too dangerous to let go, so I gotta take you in."

When they reached the outskirts of Fort Benton, Budreau made one final attempt to avoid his fate. "Listen, I know you don't give a damn about me, but if you send me to prison, you'll be sentencin' my family to a life that's one step away from slavery."

"I been thinkin' on it," Walker said. "If you tell me where yo family's at, I'll take 'em your stake and tell 'em what happened to you. You got my word on it."

"I knew you would find a way to get yo hands on my cash," Budreau said bitterly.

"I ain't gon' give 'em your cash," Walker said. "I'm gon' give 'em your bounty and look out for 'em. So just tell me where they at and you won't have to worry."

Stymied by Walker's unassailable sense of duty, Budreau elected to tell the truth. His next words came in an angry torrent. "Nigga, I don't know where my family's at. I left 'em five years ago. They may be dead for all I know or care."

Walker looked at him as though he were regarding a new kind of reptile. "Well, I reckon that's that," he said.

Walker placed Budreau into the custody of the Fort Benton sheriff. He collected his bounty and gave the sheriff his map to the outlaw hideout. Before he left the sheriff's office, he and Budreau had one more exchange at the latter's request. The outlaw drew close to the bars and practically spit his words in Walker's direction.

"You sending me to hell, Walker. But I swear I'll survive it, and when I get out, I'm gon' kill ya. As the devil is my witness, I'm gon' kill ya.

Think about that every day and every night, and one day, I'll be there to keep my promise."

Walker's eyes bored into his enemy's, and they showed no fear. "If we ever meet again, one of us *is* gon' die. You've used up all your chances with me. The next time I send you to hell, it'll be permanent."

They tried Jacob Budreau for train robbery and stage robbery. Ryback's testimony virtually sealed his fate. He was sentenced to fifteen years of hard labor on a Missouri chain gang. In other words, he was sentenced to hell on earth. What Joe didn't know was that nine years into Jacob's sentence, he accomplished something that no one had ever accomplished. He escaped.

11

Walker's mind was jolted from the past back to the present by the wink of the sun off metal or glass from a grove of cottonwoods twenty yards off to his left. Reflexively, he flung himself out of the saddle as a rifle's report shattered the still afternoon air. He lay still as death in the tall grass. His gun was already in his hand.

"Brandy, git!" The bay took off in the direction they had come. Seeing his remount headed for the hills, Slocum grabbed up his horse and set off in pursuit. As he neared the fallen rider, he raised his rifle for the kill shot. Walker suddenly rolled, firing three shots in rapid succession. The first shattered Slocum's elbow and the next two took him in the chest. He tumbled backward off his horse and lay still in the grass.

Walker walked to Slocum with his colt trained on the outlaw's prostrate form. He rolled Slocum on to his back. The outlaw was still breathing but fading fast. His last words came through a froth of blood.

"Who are you?"

Walker took the wanted poster from his pocket and showed it to the killer. He leaned closer and said, "Justice."

Walker gave a high piercing whistle and Brandy came galloping across the plain and stopped in front of him. The bay gave a nervous snort at the smell of fresh blood. Walker mounted and retrieved Slocum's horse.

Joe noticed that the animal was limping due to a missing shoe on its left back hoof. Not wanting to make the damaged mustang bear Slocum's full weight, Joe cut two sturdy saplings to make a travois, using Slocum's lariat and blanket to make the stretcher. He also cut a patch from Slocum's leather vest to make a temporary boot for the horse's unshod hoof. If he travelled slowly, this arrangement should work until he reached a homestead or a town with a sheriff.

The next morning, a cool wind blew from the direction of the mountains. Walker had just broken camp beside a stream swollen by spring rains when a group of riders approached from the east. It was the posse from Norfolk, including Red Murphy and Frank Graham.

The two men were more than happy to see the bounty hunter. They had told everyone of Walker's promise to them at the Scott homestead, and they were gratified and proud to see he was a man of his word and that he was capable of a task at which they might have failed.

"I see you got the sumbitch," Graham said, extending his hand.

Walker grasped the man's hand. "It was touch and go for a minute. You fellas are a might outside your range."

"As long as we kept findin' your trail markers, we felt like we had to keep comin'."

"Even if we ended up at the gates of hell," Murphy added. "I reckon Richard and Addie and young Billy can rest easy now." He spat in the dust beside Slocum's body.

Walker turned to a square-set, beetle-browed man with a badge on his chest. "I'm warrant officer Joe Walker, and that's Jim Slocum, who's wanted for robbery and murder in Texas and now in Nebraska. Here is a wanted poster that backs that up."

"Mr. Walker, I'm Sheriff Ben Grigsby. I've heard of you and it appears, in this case, that the man matches the reputation. You have my thanks and the thanks of my town for what you done here. If you come back to Norfolk with us, I'll see that you're paid what's owed you."

They strapped Slocum to his sorrel, whose foot had healed sufficiently, and the posse turned back toward Norfolk with Graham and

Murphy flanking Walker like sentinels.

Walker was tired but satisfied with the job he had done. He would rest a day or two in Norfolk and then he and Brandy would hit the trail for Texas. Later he would take another assignment and set off after another bad man. These men had cheated the law. Walker, for reasons that had little to do with fortune or fame, would hunt them down and make them pay. His first steps on the path to retribution occurred when he was just seventeen years old.

PART 2

Brothers in Arms

12

Joe Walker rolled over and stretched in his bunk. The brassy alarm of reveille still rang in his ears. It was followed by Sergeant Jeremiah Adams's robust breakfast invitation.

"We stopped servin' breakfast in bed just before ya'll got here. So if you want to eat, you better get your asses out o' those bunks and down to the mess hall double time."

It was October of 1863 and Joe was a seventeen-year-old recruit in the Union cavalry. He was a youth of some sturdiness due to a lifetime of forced labor. His face was leonine in nature with a broad brow, a long, wide nose, and a chiseled jaw. The latter gave him the appearance of perpetual determination. It was only when he smiled, revealing even, white teeth, that the grim aggregate of his appearance was relieved. He wore his coarse hair long, adding to his lion-like appearance. On the verge of manhood, Joe's physical attributes were only beginning to emerge. If he survived the coming ordeal, he would likely be a man to be reckoned with.

Months earlier, he had escaped after his master, Jackson Budreau, sold him to another slave owner. En route to the new farm, his captors had run into a Union patrol and had scattered for their own survival. Joe took the opportunity to escape. He moved north, avoiding capture and seeking purpose for a life he had never truly owned.

When he heard about President Lincoln's call for colored troops in the aftermath of the Emancipation Proclamation, he joined the Union army. In doing so, he joined thousands of black men and boys who enlisted to help wrest their freedom and the country's soul from the grasp of slavery. He got in because he was big for his age and because the North needed every able-bodied man it could muster to overthrow a surprisingly fierce and determined Confederate insurgency. They were three years into the conflict and its outcome was still uncertain.

Joe's service was motivated by revenge and loss. He relished the idea of meeting the slaveholders with a weapon in his hands and comrades at his side. Also, he hoped against hope to be somehow reunited with his family who were still enslaved in the heart of the South.

Joe pulled on his uniform and headed for the mess hall. He was stationed in Kentucky as part of the Fifth Colored Cavalry. This hastily formed "colored regiment" was made up of ex-slaves, freedmen, and a handful of white officers and non-coms under the leadership of Colonel James Brisbin, an officer with aspirations of rapid advancement and enduring glory. As a cavalry man, Joe was delighted to be allowed not only to care for his mount but to train and ride him as well.

As he walked, the grass crunched under his boots due to a thin covering of frost deposited the night before. Joe, who had been raised in the deep South, was still acclimating to cold weather. He pulled his coat tighter around him and hurried toward the warmth of the mess hall, a squat wooden building in the middle of the fort.

He stepped into the shuffling line of half-awake soldiers and grabbed a tin plate that was subsequently filled with corn bread, molasses, fatback, and beans. He grabbed a steaming cup of coffee to wash it down. Surveying the hall, he spied his first real friend in the unit, Holata Turner, and slid in beside him at one of the long tables.

"How do you always manage to beat me to the chow line?"

"The same way I manage to beat you at everything else," Turner said.

"You must not be woke yet, talkin' like that to me. You need a slap upside the head to bring you to?"

"Eat your breakfast while you still got some teeth."

After this exchange of pleasantries, both men fell to and finished in time to go back for seconds, which was their wont. They were both from poor circumstances, and the army's material and financial largesse were still a source of wonder to them.

They shared a love of horses, and both showed aptitude for riding and training that drew them to the cavalry. A healthy respect and genuine liking had developed between them. Holata was the first Indian Joe had met other than his mother, a so-called "black Indian" because of her mixed lineage. He walked with the pigeon-toed stride of many of his people and carried himself like a chieftain, though he was only five years older than Joe.

Shortly after they had arrived on post, the men were issued mounts. Because of their skill with horses, Joe and a hulking ex-slave named Jim Boseman were charged with taking the edge off the mostly unbroken animals. One day, Joe cut out a four-year-old Morgan gelding named Buck. The horse was dark brown, deep chested, a little over fifteen hands high with two white stockings on his hind legs. It turned out his name was well deserved because he was skittish and prone to biting and bucking. Joe was unaware of these characteristics the first time he attempted to ride Buck. He reached out to pat the horse's muzzle and received a nip for his trouble. Joe withdrew his hand quickly and massaged his smarting fingers. Some onlooking recruits greeted this incident with raucous laughter. Boseman led the crowd. "Look like the cowboy done met his match."

Joe ignored the group and took Buck's reins, mounting him smoothly. The horse stood quietly for a moment and then exploded into a bucking frenzy. Joe stayed on until he lost a stirrup and was tossed high in the air. He landed on his belly in the dust. The laughter from the bystanders was loud and unrelenting.

"That boy gon' have to walk to the fight unless we can find a tall sheep or a cow for 'im to ride," Boseman said. He was in fine form.

Boseman, who had been a slave on a Virginia plantation, fashioned himself the best wrangler at the fort and resented that Joe had been given equal status though years younger than him. "Look here, boy. You gotta teach 'im who's boss. Jus' like Massa used to teach you." With that, he fetched a length of knotted rope, grabbed Buck's dangling reins, and began beating the horse about the head and neck.

Joe was off the ground like a rocket. He grabbed Boseman's shoulder and spun him around. The next blow of Boseman's lash fell across Joe's shoulders. Joe waded in and punched the big man flush in the mouth. He could feel teeth beneath his knuckles and blood gushed from the giant's battered lips. With a roar, Boseman bull-rushed him and carried him backward to the ground. Boseman weighed well over two hundred pounds. He pinned Joe with his weight and pulled a straight razor from his pocket.

"Now I'm gonna see if you can breathe without a nose."

The blade arced up, glinting in the sun, but before it could descend, one of the onlooking recruits stepped in and grabbed Boseman's wrist in a grip that made the bull wince in pain. The man was a leaner version of Boseman himself—tall and muscular with a hawk nose and piercing black eyes.

"Stay out of this, Injun, or you'll be next," Boseman snarled. Instead of loosening his grip, the stranger twisted Boseman's wrist more cruelly until the big man dropped the razor with a yelp of pain. He retrieved the weapon and stepped back. Throughout this episode, his expression had remained unchanged. It was as though he were engaged in a mundane act like pouring a cup of coffee or whittling a stick.

"No need to kill a man over a horse," he said.

Boseman was massaging his wrist and glaring at the tall Indian. "This ain't over. You can bet your bottom dollar, redskin. This ain't over," Boseman said through swollen lips. Joe's unexpected ally looked at Boseman as though measuring him for a shroud and tossed the razor between the big man's legs.

"Let's finish it then," he said in a voice that made you glad to be anybody but Boseman. Boseman looked at the razor and then looked up at his adversary, whose air of expectation was palpable.

"What the hell's going on here?" It was Sergeant Adams approaching across the parade ground. Boseman quickly pocketed the razor and the Indian extended his hand to help him to his feet.

"Just a little training mash-up, Sergeant," the tall man said. "This cayuse done managed to throw both our wranglers back to back." He made a show of brushing dust off Boseman's shoulders.

"In case y'all misunderstood, this is the US cavalry. We break the horses. They don't break us. Now get to work before I find somethin' else for you to do," Adams said, shaking his head in either bemusement or disgust before turning toward headquarters.

That was how Buck became Joe's mount and Holata Turner became Joe's best friend. Turner was a full-blooded Seminole Indian who joined the Union army for reasons similar to Joe's. His people also chafed under the assaults on their freedom of southern rule, and they were historical allies of black slaves.

Holata's wife, Opal, a black woman, had been stolen by slave catchers and sold to a plantation owner. When he tried to buy her back, he was threatened by the owner and nearly beaten to death by his henchmen. Bereft of all hope, Opal hanged herself in her master's barn. Two nights later, Holata drifted like smoke into the big house and killed the man with his bare hands. He fled, taking his sorrow and his rage to the military.

Boseman never took the opportunity to brace Joe or Holata in a fair fight. Instead, he bullied his fellows into ostracizing the two of them. This exclusion strengthened the bond between the friends. They ate, rode, and trained together. Joe shared his horse-gentling secrets with Holata, and Holata taught him the finer points of knife fighting and hand-to-hand combat. Joe had never held a gun, much less fired one. Holata had been hunting with bows and rifles since he was a child.

Joe soaked up weapons training like a sponge—because he was a soldier, his life depended upon it. He learned to load and fire accurately the Enfield muskets they were issued. He wondered how they would be able to load these unwieldy weapons from horseback. When he asked

Sergeant Adams, he was told that a fighting man uses whatever weapon is at his disposal. He found the Colt 44 army-issue sidearm another matter. With practice, the revolver transformed from an unfamiliar weight in his hand to a tool he learned to use with deadly proficiency.

Joe spent his free time working with Buck. He stopped the horse from biting by bringing Buck a treat every time he approached him. He had Holata do likewise. Twice a day, he groomed the Morgan until his coat gleamed like satin. During these sessions, Joe talked to Buck about anything that came to mind.

The gelding gradually came to associate Joe's hands and the sound of his voice with positive experiences. Because of Joe's gentle technique, Buck developed the ability to sense his presence from a distance, so he would routinely begin dancing in his stall and neighing expectantly seconds before the young trooper came into view. For his part, Joe greeted the gelding the same way each time they met: "Yo, Buck, I got you."

Joe invariably accompanied this salutation with a small treat, a scratch behind the ears, or a pat on the neck. After Joe gained Buck's trust, riding him was easy. Joe used his hands, subtle knee pressure, and the sound of his voice to guide the powerful animal. In time, to the casual observer, they would seem to be connected telepathically.

Sometimes, when nightmares robbed Joe of sleep, he would leave his bunk and go to Buck's stall where he would lay down literally at the animal's feet. With Buck standing guard, he would often find the rest that had eluded him in the midst of his fellows. Subsequently, they would carry this ritual into the field. By the time boot camp was over, Joe and Buck were more than rider and mount—they were partners.

Six weeks after arriving at Fort Bainbridge, Joe was declared ready to fight for the country that viewed him, at best, as a stepchild. He and the Fifth Cavalry mobilized to support Colonel Brisbin's forces, who were marching to Virginia to engage the rebels.

Joe's feelings on the day he left the fort were a mixture of anticipation, pride, and anxiety. He was a soldier about to take part in a righteous cause. His chances of surviving this adventure were unknowable, but he had a premonition that the pain and loss he had suffered to date were just a prelude to what lay ahead. As he rode out of the fort with his comrades, he wondered if he would ever see it again. Holata rode to his left, and the two briefly exchanged a glance of solidarity and resolve. One anchoring thought kept repeating in his roiling mind. *Here we come.*

13

Joe and the ninety-nine other troopers of the Fifth rode east to Prestonburg, Kentucky, to join Major General Burbridge's forces. The Union camp consisted of hundreds of tents in orderly rows on roughly a square acre of flat land, flanked by a tributary of the Big Sandy River. The tents were large enough to accommodate four men each, and most had been draped in animal skins to stave off the cold. The soldiers had dug fire pits in front of their lodges to cook game and heat coffee. They were mostly veterans of a brutal war who had lost comrades on an almost weekly basis. They had heard about the colored troops made possible by Lincoln's Emancipation Proclamation, but they had little patience for unproven "coloreds" who could turn out to be more of a liability than an asset.

When they arrived at the camp, Joe got his first taste of Yankee hospitality. The men of Burbridge's company stood in rows as the colored cavalry rode in. They hooted and whistled in derision at the sight of the black soldiers. Joe could hear isolated comments from his soon-to-be comrades.

"*This* is what we been waiting for?"

"Old Abe musta lost his mind."

"Hey, boy, careful you don't fall off that horse."

Joe stared straight ahead. Sgt. Adams had prepared them for this reception. *Most of these boys grew up in the lap of slavery, and they ain't gonna respect you until you earn it.*

Someone threw a dirt clod that struck Buck's flank, causing the horse to momentarily break formation. Joe's hand went instinctively to his holster. "Easy, Little Brother. Don't let 'em rile you." It was Holata who rode at his side. His face was a bronze mask but his eyes were busy. Seething, Joe soothed Buck with his voice and hands. They pulled up in columns before the assembled officers of the Kentucky Brigade. Colonel Brisbin dismounted and saluted smartly.

"Colonel James Brisbin and the Fifth Colored Cavalry reporting for duty, sir."

Major General Stephen Gano Burbridge was a tall, pale, goateed man. His wide forehead, high cheekbones, and aquiline nose gave him an aristocratic bearing. He returned Colonel Brisbin's salute. "Welcome, Colonel. We have prayed for your swift arrival. Please take your troops to the campsite east of the river where they can attend to their needs and those of their mounts. After you have encamped, please join us in the officer's tent."

They rode back through the gauntlet of jeering soldiers to their campsite across the river. Unlike the white troops, their camp was just a barren field. They were divided into three groups: one to set up a picket line for the horses; one to forage for game, edible roots, and berries; and one to go to a thicket of poplar trees a mile beyond the river and chop firewood for the cooking fires. As soon as they had completed these tasks, the men gathered to discuss the day's events.

Henry Simmons, a squat, barrel-chested recruit with an incongruously high voice, summed up what they were all thinking when he said, "I'm gonna feel a might nervous with the rebels in front of me and these boys in back o' me."

"A peckerwood don't change his stripes just 'cause you put 'im in a blue uniform. I trust 'em about as far as I can throw that mule over yonder," Boseman said.

There were general murmurs of agreement. At that point, Sergeant Adams stepped forward from the edge of the group. "I believe you judge a man by his actions, not his words. Those boys are Union soldiers just like us. They took an oath, and because of that oath, they've been killin' their own kith and kin for nigh on to four years now. When the time comes, I expect they'll stand with us, and any man under my command who don't stand with them is lookin' for a bullet or a court martial."

Sergeant Adams would have been the result if you could have convinced a grizzly bear to wear a man's clothes. His legs were like curved tree trunks, and you could have hung an oxen yolk across his shoulders. From his head to his toes, he was virtually covered with dense, curly brown hair. He had been born one of fifteen children on a hardscrabble farm in west Kansas. At the age of sixteen, he left home to seek his way in the wide world. In the ensuing years, he was a buffalo hunter, a sailor, and a constable in a small town in northern Pennsylvania. When the war broke out, he enlisted in the Union army because he was a lawman who didn't particularly like the idea of kowtowing to a bunch of traitors.

After the sergeant said his piece, the crowd dispersed. Joe and Holata walked together. Joe said, "The sarge may be right, but right now, I trust you and my company. I'll fight with them white boys because that's what I'm s'posed to do. But I'll hold off on trustin 'em until they show me somethin'."

Holata nodded and said, "You speak of trust, battle, and honor in the same breath. This is the way of a warrior. There might be hope for you yet, Little Brother."

The next day, Sergeant Adams told them they would be heading to Saltville, Virginia, to destroy the salt works there, thus eliminating a prime link in the rebel supply chain. The troop moved slower in the company of the infantry and its equipment. Each evening, the companies retired to their separate camps, offering little opportunity for fraternization.

After a ten-day march, they arrived on the outskirts of the city and prepared to face an overmatched confederate force that had been hastily mustered to protect it. The rebels were a mix of regular army and guerrilla fighters. Some were in full uniform and some wore only the rebel kepi with coveralls and homespun work shirts. They varied in age from young boys whose muskets were taller than they were to grizzled old men. Their faces were lean and their eyes burned with a mixture of fury and resignation. They were dug in and desperate.

Burbridge decided to first soften up the enemy's battlements with his artillery. The sound of the cannonade caused Buck to dance in place and snort nervously. Joe patted his neck and awaited orders.

The rebels returned fire with their own cannons. Soon the space between the two armies was a field of smoking craters—lurking pitfalls for any mounted soldier. Burbridge sent his infantry next. They ran toward the rebel line yelling like demented banshees.

The rebels fired in deadly volleys that precipitously thinned the ranks of the charging men. Joe heard Colonel Burbridge's deep voice over the din ordering the Fifth to conduct a flanking maneuver to support the infantry. Colonel Brisbin drew his saber, stood in his stirrups, and ordered the unit forward. Joe kicked Buck and felt the horse respond to the call for action that ended his jitters. They surged forward in a compact phalanx, sabers gleaming and bugles blaring. They wheeled and approached the rebel line from the east, forcing the enemy to divide his fire and offering some relief to the advancing infantrymen.

Joe was in the belly of the beast called war. To his left, a soldier took a round through the eye that blew out the back of his skull like an over-ripe melon. To his right, Henry Simmons was thrown backward from his horse, his arms thrown wide as if welcoming death. The air was filled with the sound of muskets, artillery, and the screams of the wounded men and horses. In the midst of this maelstrom, he tried to maintain focus and courage. When he could see the faces of his enemies, he raised his preloaded musket and fired at the line. He reholstered the now useless weapon and drew his revolver. At this range, he heard shots whizzing past his head and the oaths of friend and foe alike.

As they approached the rebel front, their adversaries turned and retreated into the woods. The Yankees gave a shout of triumph at the sight and rushed into the grove in pursuit of their enemy. The trees slowed the advance of the cavalry and the Union foot soldiers surged ahead.

Given his superior numbers, Burbridge had devised a battle plan that was bold to the point of recklessness. The Confederate commander's plan, by contrast, was deliberate and tactical. He played the fox to Burbridge's hound. So it was that when the Union soldiers emerged from the woods, they were met by a force of a thousand men coming over the hillside in a pincer movement.

Joe saw the Union infantry engulfed by a sea of gray and prepared to die well.

Colonel Brisbin rallied his troops around the infantry and had his bugler sound retreat. Both of Joe's guns were empty, so he used his saber to engage the rebel cavalrymen. He slashed with abandon at the men in gray, unleashing a fury that had been building his whole life. One of them cut his rein and he had to turn Buck with his knees to head back in the direction they had come. He grabbed his horse's mane and made for the woods.

He bore down on a redheaded union soldier who was running in the same direction. The foot soldier clasped his right elbow with his left hand to avoid jostling a wounded shoulder. Joe pulled up and offered his hand and an empty stirrup to the man, who swung awkwardly up behind him. They reached the cover of the trees closely pursued by the Confederate cavalry. Joe weaved among the trees, searching for reinforcements, his companion hanging on literally for life. Suddenly, the man stiffened and fell backward from a bullet to the back of his head. His death grip pulled Joe from the saddle. When he fell, Joe's head hit something hard and he blacked out.

When Joe came to, the battle had washed over him and he lay in a slaughter ground of dead and wounded men. Not knowing where the enemy was, Joe climbed a tree to reconnoiter and wait for darkness. An hour later, from his place of concealment, he witnessed a small squad of rebels moving among the fallen soldiers. Judging by their outfits, they were irregulars. They were systematically robbing the dead and dispatching the wounded.

One of the men approached a slightly wounded Union soldier, who raised his hands in surrender. The rebel pulled his sidearm and shot him in the head. Another soldier joined him as he searched the body. "Anythin' good?"

"Nonaya business."

"Did you have to kill 'im?"

"You know what the captain said. All niggers and nigger lovers die where they lay."

The squad moved on, leaving Joe the lone sentinel in a nascent slaughterhouse. After dark, Joe climbed down from his perch. He loaded his pistol and retrieved another from one of the dead men. After slaking his thirst from the stream that ran through the copse, he headed toward where he presumed the Union army would be. Overhead, the stars shone like chips of ice against the blackness of the night sky. Joe's head was aching and he was bone tired now that the adrenaline of battle had left him.

He was walking briskly, not knowing how far he would have to travel before dawn. He stumbled over something in the darkness. Reaching out to right himself, he touched a cold face covered with a sticky wetness. A gasp escaped his lips and he jerked his hand away, overcome by an atavistic dread. He heard the sound of hoofbeats in the darkness. *Was this death finally come to claim him?*

Joe exhaled in relief as Buck emerged from the gloom, whinnying a welcome. He caught the horse's reins as though they were a lifeline. The sight and touch of Buck calmed Joe immensely. "Yo, Buck, it's good to see you, boy. Looks like the Lord spared us both today." He climbed into the saddle. "Let's see if we can find the troop and get back in this."

For the next two days, he eluded rebel patrols and staved off hunger until he overtook his unit en route to the Kentucky border. After reuniting with what was left of his troop, he reported directly to General Burbridge and Colonel Brisbin. He told them what he had seen and heard on the deserted battlefield.

Burbridge said, "This is the work of Champ Ferguson and his guerrillas. The word is that they even butchered our boys in their hospital beds. Those curs have slaughtered soldiers and noncombatants indiscriminately since the war started. As God is my witness, I'll see that son of a bitch hanged. I still can't understand how they beat us so handily when we outnumbered them two to one."

"It was the Enfields, sir. It's almost impossible to load and fire one on horseback. With the muzzleloaders, our men are forced to rely on short-range weapons, placing themselves at higher risk," Brisbin said diplomatically, omitting Burbridge's ill-conceived battle plan.

Joe added his two cents. "Puhmission to speak freely, suh?"

"Go ahead, trooper."

"What the colonel says is true, suh. I only fired my rifle once during the whole battle."

Brisbin continued, "We need to requisition Spenser repeating rifles for our men like the Pennsylvania units have."

"I'll do whatever it takes to beat these devils. I plan to go back to Saltville and complete my mission or die trying," Burbridge said.

Joe left the meeting with the commanders and rejoined his unit. He was anxious for news of Holata, who was not among the men who had greeted him. His inquiries revealed that no one had seen his friend since the battle. Knowing the fate of captured colored troops, Joe had to accept that Holata was gone. The loss of his friend affected Joe more deeply than he could have anticipated. His life had been riddled with loss: home, family, friends, and now a spiritual brother. He consoled himself with the thought of Holata and Opal reunited in heaven. Again the southern establishment had robbed him of something of inestimable value. He was prepared to die to balance the scales.

14

It was mid-December and the Fifth Cavalry was headed back to Saltville, Virginia. This time, Major General Burbridge's division was part of a three-pronged brigade commanded by General George Stoneman. Despite the military setback at the first Battle of Saltville, the colored troops had acquitted themselves well and were now considered reliable forces by their white commanders.

The battle had also strengthened the bonds within the Fifth. The petty rivalries and intrigues that had consumed them during training had melted in the heat of war. They now knew that they would lay down their lives for each other. They were brothers in arms. Sergeant Adams was a casualty of the first Saltville battle, but the things he had taught them about duty and solidarity stayed with them for the rest of their lives.

General Stoneman had no intention of underestimating the Confederates on this second engagement. He had assembled ten thousand battle-hardened soldiers to accomplish his mission. He sent General Gillem's brigade to attack first. The men were fresh off a successful engagement in Marion, Virginia, against a determined rebel division who surmised their ultimate destination. Holata rode with Gillem's men. The familiar environs and the memories they evoked put him in a deadly mood. Under his breath, he said the warrior's prayer: "Today is a good day to die."

They swept into the rebel ranks like a prairie fire. Their Spencer repeating rifles allowed them to shoot twenty rounds a minute, and they fired until the battlefield was a smoking cauldron. Under this onslaught, the rebels retreated, giving ground inch by grudging inch.

From the right flank came a Confederate cavalry unit—five hundred screaming demons bent on breaking the Yankees' front. But Stoneman was prepared. He launched Burbridge and the Fifth and, in a matter of minutes, purgatory turned to hell.

Joe guided Buck with his knees and fired his Spencer at the advancing riders. Ironically, now that he had the long-range weapon, he wanted to be among them. Moments later, he got his wish. The two units clashed and resorted to sabers and sidearms. Instead of his Colt, Joe had a Bowie knife in his left hand. Holata had taught him to fight with the short and the long knife together.

He parried the saber stroke of a rebel horseman and drove his knife into the man's tricep. When the rebel's arm dropped, Joe slashed his jugular with his saber. He heard a shout of rage behind him. He spun Buck around to face a charging bull. The man leapt from his horse and knocked Joe to the ground. Joe tried to stab him, but the rebel clamped his wrist in an iron grip.

"You killed my brother, you black son of a bitch!" The man was literally frothing at the mouth. He grabbed Joe by the throat and began to squeeze the life out of him. Joe's vision went gray. Suddenly, the man went limp and Joe could breathe again. Five yards away, Jim Boseman lowered his smoking pistol. He nodded at Joe. Joe nodded back and ran to Buck. He swung into the saddle, drew his Colt, and reentered the fight.

By the time the rebel bugler blew retreat, Joe was bleeding from half a dozen wounds. Fortunately, none of them were serious. Stoneman sent in his second division of cavalry, and the rout was on.

Having smashed through the rebel defenses, their approach to Salt-ville was steady. Joe noted that the green hills and heavy tree cover gave way to a small cluster of buildings, most of them made of stone and wood. These were the saltworks.

They destroyed the boiling kettles and evaporating sheds and blew up a portion of the adjacent Virginia-Tennessee railroad. They took prisoners—mostly regular army. The bulk of the marauders had run like the cowards they were. General Stoneman had ordered that all Confederate prisoners be treated humanely and, for the most part, they were.

Joe went to the infirmary, where they treated his wounds. From there, he went to see about Buck. When he arrived at the horse's stall, he saw a tall figure standing in front of it, stroking Buck's muzzle and speaking quietly to him. As Joe approached, the man turned and recognition hit Joe like a thunderbolt.

"Holata!"

"Little Brother?"

The two men ran to each other and embraced. Holata literally lifted Joe off the ground in a hug that aggravated his fresh wounds. But that had nothing to do with why Joe was crying. "I thought they killed you," Joe said.

"I thought they killed *you*," Holato echoed.

Joe wiped his eyes. He could barely believe them. But there, standing in front of him, was Holata Turner, the man he regarded as a brother. The only family he knew he had for sure. He had a thousand questions, but they could be summarized in one sentence. "What happened to you?"

So they sat together on a bale of hay for the next hour under Buck's watchful gaze and brought each other up to date. Holata's story amazed Joe with the courage and ingenuity he showed behind enemy lines.

15

Holata Turner's horse had been shot from under him in the retreat from Saltville. As the animal fell, Holata instinctively freed his feet from the stirrups and landed rolling. He came to his feet unharmed, but a charging rebel cavalryman sought to change that. Holata ducked the man's saber blow and shot him as he wheeled his mount to reengage. Holata set off for the woods at a dead run. The distance in the open was roughly a hundred and fifty yards. Holata's ground-eating stride was narrowing that distance rapidly. A rebel infantryman intersected his path and fired his musket point-blank. Miraculously, the gun misfired. Holata cut him down and grabbed his sidearm.

Firing his pistols at anything in gray, he reached the edge of the forest and plunged beneath the shelter of the trees. Once there, he ran zigzagging from tree to tree. He could hear the whiz of bullets and the exclamations of men killing and dying. But the thing that sent a chill through his blood was a glimpse of Buck, riderless and running free.

He veered from the path of his retreating comrades and found a downed tree to lay behind. Though this was a good day to die, he would try to avoid that fate, if for no other reason than to avenge his brother. Holata discovered that the tree he was hiding behind was hollow, so he crawled inside and drew branches and leaves over the opening behind him. From his place of concealment, he heard the rebel marauders come and carry out their grisly mission on his fallen comrades.

When night fell, Holata climbed from his refuge and surveyed his surroundings. Dead union soldiers littered the woods. Many were missing shoes, teeth, and ears. A number of trees had been splintered or felled by musket shot or cannonballs, and a faint whiff of gunpowder remained in the air.

Holata set out in the direction he knew the rebels would pitch camp, near grass and water. He heard the sounds of the camp before he saw it, nickering horses and the relieved laughter and banter of men who had faced death and walked away. Victory had made them careless. There was but a single sentry guarding the horse herd. Holata slit his throat and stole a mount. At a safe distance, he mounted the horse. He used the tricks his father taught him to hide his trail and then headed west to find his unit. His mood matched the night—bitter and cold.

Before Holata could reach his division, he encountered the brigade of Brigadier General Alvan C. Gillem. Holata told the general and his command group what he had seen in terms of the Confederates' atrocities, troop numbers, and location. When he finished his report, the general regarded him with unconcealed admiration.

"Excellent work soldier. With a few thousand like you, I could end this business in a week. I need a man like you to fight and scout for me. So you are temporarily reassigned to this brigade. Are you ready to dance with the devil again, soldier?"

"Ready and able, sir," Holata had said, saluting.

16

When Holata finished his story, Joe asked, "How long you gon' be with Gillem?"

"Hadn't thought about it. But I suppose I'll have to ask for a transfer now so I can get back to nurse maidin' your raggedy behind."

"Don't do me no favors," Joe said suppressing a smile. "Where you bivouacked?"

"East of town. You?"

"We're to the north."

"I'll ask General Gillem to let me go back with the Fifth now that this campaign is over," Turner said.

"What you gon' do if he say no?"

"Ask again."

They rose and shook hands, having regained their manly composure.

"I'll see you soon, Little Brother."

"See you soon, Big Brotha." It was the first time Joe had allowed himself to acknowledge the meaning of the sobriquet.

The next day, Private Holata Turner returned to the Fifth Cavalry with orders that explained his prolonged absence. Among his transfer papers was a commendation for "exceptional valor" from General George Stoneman. No one was happier to see Holata than Joe Walker.

He shadowed the tall trooper for the rest of the day and listened proudly as Holata reluctantly told the story of his time under General Stoneman's command. News traveled fast in an army camp, and it wasn't long before they learned of Holata's commendation. It was then they realized how much he had downplayed his role in Stoneman's campaign.

17

Joe and Holata served together until the war ended in April 1865. During that time, Joe learned to be a man—more precisely, a man of discipline and honor. The brothers' last campaign was at Appomattox. There, they were once again witnesses to history. After General Lee's surrender, Joe and his company watched as the old lion passed on his white charger, Traveller, who had become nearly as famous as he was. In the end, Lee and his confederates' willingness to champion the devil's cause had led to the devastation of a region and the death of over six hundred thousand men.

A month later, Joe and Holata mustered out of the cavalry. They felt strange in their mixture of civilian and military garb. There was much they could have said to each other, but they were not men of that ilk.

"You will always have a place in my lodge, Little Brother," Holata said, clasping Joe's hand and holding him with his raptor's gaze.

"Thanks for everythang," Joe said, his voice suddenly growing husky.

Their bond sealed, they rode away toward their separate destinies. Holata had found purpose in the midst of chaos. He planned to return to his people and help guide them to their rightful place in a unified nation. Now that Joe was a free man in a free country, he intended to find what was left of his family and spend the rest of his life making up for lost time. He almost lost his life in pursuit of that goal.

PART 3

Freedom

18

For the first time in his life, Joe Walker was a free man. He had been born a slave and had escaped slavery only to enter the Union army that opposed it. Now at the age of nineteen, he was a seasoned veteran of the most brutal conflict in American history. He had a face sculpted by physical and emotional privation. His broad brow over-arched brooding brown eyes leached of all boyishness by the horrors of slavery and war.

A slight rain was falling and he was riding Buck through the Tennessee countryside. Horse and rider seemed ideally suited to each other. Joe held the reins loosely in his left hand and used them like a telegraph wire to talk to his mount. Buck's ears cocked back at Joe's slightest utterance, further enhancing their communication. Their bond had been forged in battle where each had trusted the other with his life. Besides his fighting prowess and his manhood, Joe's most treasured legacy from the US cavalry was the horse he rode.

Joe was in search of the family from whom he had been separated as a child. This required him to return to Tennessee, a state in the very heart of the war-ravaged South. He knew the plantation where he was born was outside of a town called Benton. He and his father used to accompany his master, Christopher Walker, there to pick up supplies.

He subsequently learned that Benton was in Polk County, Tennessee.

The country he rode through was lush and green. The rain-cooled air carried the perfume of azaleas and phlox, among other native blossoms. The grassy plain was dotted with maple, walnut, and sweet gum trees. The road ran abreast of a clear, gurgling stream in which Joe could see moving fish. To the east, the Blue Ridge Mountains loomed like shrouded sentinels. As a child, he had taken these surroundings for granted, but after living in the sweltering heat and humidity of Louisiana cane country, he felt like he had entered paradise. If his family was still alive and together, Joe was convinced they would be in Tennessee.

As he rode, he encountered groups of displaced black people carrying their belongings on their backs. Freedom was a new and puzzling concept to them. Their faces were studies in wonderment, elation, and fear. Joe stopped one man and his family on the road. The man was short, balding, and powerfully built with a scar on the left cheek whose pull gave him a kind of permanent smirk. He pulled a cart that contained the family's meager possessions. A woman and three young children traveled with him.

"Scuse me, suh. My name is Joseph Walker. Just got out the army. Where ya'll headed?"

The stranger eyed Walker with a wariness based on hard experience.

"Pleased to meetcha, Mistuh Walker. My name is Matthew Rawlins and this is my *wife*, Caroline."

Joe noted his emphasis on the word "wife."

"We's headed nawth."

"Howdy, ma'am," Joe said touching the brim of his hat.

Mrs. Rawlins was half a foot taller and fifteen years younger than her husband. She wore a long blue dress faded by many washings. A pair of men's shoes peaked from beneath the hem of her dress. Even though she wore her long headscarf Bedouin style, it did not conceal her satin skin, curvaceous lips, and sparkling eyes. She looked at Joe, and the fear in her eyes made him think she recognized the tiger chained inside him.

In a voice whose calmness bordered on resignation, she said, "We ain't got nothin' worth takin'.'" She drew her children closer to her.

"No, ma'am. You mistake me. I'm just a soldier headed home, hopin' to find someone who bears my name." He punctuated his speech with a smile. Her wary look relaxed a bit, and Joe hoped she saw the thing that kept the tiger in check.

"Like I said, we's headed nawth," Rawlins repeated. "These white folks down heah ain't used to losin', and soon as the Yankees leave, they gon' take all they spite out on us. If you was raised down heah, you knows dat. Mr. Lincoln done freed us. But he ain't told us what's next. I hear there's work for a able bodied man in the nawth. Dat true?" he asked with a note of entreaty in his voice.

Joe knew that false hope was better than no hope at all. "I heard the same. There was lots 'o good men killed in this wah. I reckon somebody's gotta step in and pick up the slack."

The man smiled the way a desert wanderer would who had just been told there was an oasis over the next dune. "You right as rain, son. Yessuh, right as rain."

Joe looked at the three children who accompanied the couple. Their eyes were unnaturally bright and their faces gaunt. He dismounted. "Mr. Rawlins, I wonda if you could help me out with somethin'?" He reached into his saddlebag and retrieved a folded piece of paper. Rawlins walked over to stand beside him. "Do you have any idea where the Christopher Walker plantation is from here? I got this map but it don't show much detail."

"Walker—Christopher Walker? I'm 'fraid, I cain't help ya, Mr. Walker. We ain't from 'round heah," Rawlins said.

It was the answer Joe had expected. He put the map back in his saddlebag. When he turned around, he held a side of bacon and a tin of biscuits he had purchased that morning. "Take this for your trouble," he said, proffering the rations.

"I cain't take your food, son."

"You got furtha to go and mo' mouths to feed than I do. Look, Mr. Lincoln is way up in Washington, so we gotta look out for each other for now and maybe for quite a spell. Besides, these woods is full o' game and I'm a crack shot."

Matthew Rawlins took the food and wiped his eyes with his sleeve. "I reckon the wah ain't killed *all* the good mens," he said.

19

Joe Walker arrived in Polk County nine years after he left it as a frightened child bound and hooded in a slave wagon. His mind flashed back to that day and he was flooded with feelings of rage, fear, and sadness. He remembered his days on the Budreau plantation where he was taken after being separated from his family. The suffering and humiliation he endured there nearly broke him. His love of horses and his hatred of the Budreaus sustained him through his coming of age.

He had been a cauldron of rage when he joined the Union cavalry. His fantasy was to face Jackson Budreau and his sons on the battlefield and kill them all. The Civil War slaked his bloodlust by teaching him the fragility and value of life. During the war, he also met men of all colors who treated him as a brother and showed him how to acquit himself with dignity and honor. Now a grown man, he sought every man's birthright: freedom, family, and a home of his own.

He rode into the town of Benton at midday. The dusty main street was lined by a general store, a saloon, and a combination blacksmith shop and livery. A freshly painted church stood at the end of the main street. As a child, Walker had listened to the hymns that the good Christians sang there on Sunday morning before returning to the weekday business of fostering human bondage.

He reined in before a square building across from the saloon that advertised itself as the sheriff's office. He brushed the dust from his frock coat and trousers before entering.

The sheriff was seated behind a large wooden desk facing the door. He was a man in his fifties with thinning gray hair and a bushy mustache. His faded blue eyes narrowed at the sight of Walker. "Can I help you, boy?"

Walker returned the verbal slight by staring the white man directly in the eye. "I'm lookin' for the Walker plantation. Is it still around heah?"

"Who wants to know?"

"My name is Joseph Walker and I used to live there."

Realization dawned in the sheriff's eyes. "Oh, you used to live there, did ya? I don't recall any darkies being in the Walker family."

"Me and my family were Mistuh Walker's slaves. I'd like to inquire about their whereabouts. I thought it would be best to approach 'im in the company of the law sose to avoid any trouble."

The sheriff's expression of open hostility deepened. There was a certain type of white man who preferred a black man to be one or two rungs down during every encounter, and the sheriff was apparently that type of man. His blue eyes practically sparked with resentment. His thin lips pressed tightly together, and Joe knew he would receive no accommodation here.

"Well, ain't you the educated nigger? Where'd you learn all them big words, boy?"

"Sheriff, I was wonderin' if you would be willin' to ride out with me to the Walker plantation, if there still is a Walker plantation."

The lawman was relentless. "I asked you a question, nigger." The sheriff had unknowingly poked the tiger one time too many.

"I got all my education in the army," Walker said, holding the other man's gaze until he dropped his eyes.

The sheriff saved face by saying, "Well, I got better things to do than to escort the likes of you all over the goddamn county. The Walker plantation is ten miles south of town."

Walker's attempt to go through channels had foundered on the bigotry and self-importance of a small town official. He would have to proceed on his own.

When Walker exited the sheriff's office, he was confronted by a group of townsmen standing on the sidewalk. A rangy fellow with a pockmarked face and a droopy left eye stepped in front of Walker. He wore a Confederate army jacket with sergeant stripes still on the sleeve and was undoubtedly one of the many bitter war veterans forced to live under a regime they had sacrificed much to defeat. He was armed with a big Colt that he wore waist high on his right side.

"Hold up there, nigger. Where you think you're goin'?"

"Headin' out of town," Walker said. He stepped toward Buck at the hitching rail.

"Where you'd get that hoss, boy? He got a US brand on 'im. That means he belongs to a Yankee. Now as much as I hate Yankees, I hate nigger hoss thieves even mo."

Two men stood abreast of the Reb, clearly backing his play. The one on the right, Joe guessed, was in his mid to late twenties. He had bulging eyes, a receding chin, and a prominent overbite, giving him a rodent-like appearance. His face was framed by greasy black hair. He was armed with a Colt revolver, also worn high on his right hip. The one on the left was older and thicker through the body. He wore a sweat-stained blue work shirt and coveralls. His wide leather belt contained an ancient Colt across his belly and a scabbard with a bone-handled hunting knife on his left hip. With his beetle brows and hanging jowls, he resembled a bulldog.

Rat Man said, "Mebbe he'd 'fess up with a hot poker up his ass." This brought a hoot of approval from the crowd.

Bulldog took a menacing step toward Joe. At that moment, the sheriff stepped out of his office.

"Caleb, what's goin' on heah?"

The Reb said, "We 'bout to arrest a hoss thief that was right under yer nose, Ben."

"This man ain't no hoss thief."

"But he ridin' a Union hoss!"

"That's 'cause he was a Union soldier."

"Git outta here," Caleb said in disbelief.

"Judgin' by his boots and sidearm, I'd say US cavalry," the sheriff said.

"If this coon was a horse soldier, then I'm a wet nurse."

"Be that as it may, you men better step aside. This boy ain't broke no laws that I'm aware of. He's just in these parts lookin' for his kin who used to belong to the Walker family. I just told 'im how to get out there."

A look of surprise came across Caleb's face. "But ain't no . . ."

"Mind yer own business, Caleb," the sheriff said sharply.

Caleb looked like a dog that had just had his bone snatched away. "So you're one of them backstabbin' biscuit-eaters who turned on them that took care of you your whole worthless life. Well, your day is comin,' boy. The real white men in this country are gon' rise up and take it back, and then your high-and-mighty days will be ova for good. If I was you, I wouldn't let sundown ketch me in Polk County." With that, he grudgingly stepped aside, followed by his two heel hounds.

The sheriff turned to Walker. "So long, boy. I hope you find what yer lookin' for." The sheriff's message was clear: *Get out of my town.*

Walker stepped through his would-be apprehenders and mounted Buck in one fluid motion. He backed the big Morgan with his face to the crowd for two wagon lengths and then turned and rode away.

20

Walker realized the sheriff had put a target on his back and turned him loose. He checked his loads and urged Buck into a ground-eating canter. An hour later, he arrived at the Walker plantation. The road to the main house was bordered by sawtooth oak trees. Walker remembered gathering acorns beneath this canopy to feed to the master's horses. The once carefully tended grounds were covered with weeds, wild flowers, and saplings. The picket fence surrounding the front yard was missing in some places and leaning in others. The once fertile cotton fields were now barren, gone to seed and fodder. As he approached the house, he could see all the first floor windows were broken and weeds had overtaken both the front yard and Mrs. Walker's pampered flower garden.

Joe had spent the happiest days of his young life on this plantation. Though he was a slave, he was surrounded by a loving family and a supportive community. He recalled his mother's loving touch and her laughter and his father's valuable lessons in self-comportment, loyalty, and hard work. His older brother, Amos, was his protector and role model, and Joe had tried to do the same for his younger siblings. The hope he had allowed to flourish on his trip to the homestead was flickering, and with its departure came an almost physical sense of loss.

Despite the signs of abandonment, he sat his horse before the verandah and hailed the house. "Anybody to home?" He dismounted and went to the front door where he knocked loudly. No one responded. He knocked again.

"Ain't nobody in there."

Joe whirled, gun in hand, to face an old black man who raised his hands high and blurted, "Don't shoot, son! I ain't armed!"

The man before him was ancient for a colored man. He was the color of a roasted coffee bean. He had a full head of hair and a full beard, both snowy white. He wore a coarse shirt made from flour sacks and patched wool breaches held up by rope suspenders. His head and feet were bare. Despite his age, his arms were corded with muscle, his voice strong, and his back straight.

"Who are *you*?" Walker asked.

"Name's Jim Walker. I lives heah."

Walker's eyes widened in amazement. "Unca Jim? Unca Jim? Is that you?"

"Yeah, it's me. Do I know you?"

"It's me, Joseph—Joseph Walker. David and Sarah's boy!"

"Joseph? Oh Lawd, Joe?" The old man lowered his arms and held them out.

Walker was suddenly a nine-year-old boy again, and he ran to his elder and embraced him with such force that the old man was almost knocked off his feet. They were both crying unashamedly and neither seemed to want to end the embrace. Finally, Jim held Joe at arm's length.

"Boy, we thought you was lost, cradled in the bosom of Abraham. But heah you is a full-growed man and the spittin' image of yo daddy. Praise the Lawd! Praise him!"

"Unca Jim, where is everybody?"

"Well, son, dat's a story that takes some tellin'. Let's get outta the sun fuhst."

He led Walker away from the main house toward the slaves' quarters. Joe remembered this cluster of rude shacks as his refuge from a larger, more complicated world. He saw the cabin where he had been born and marveled at how small it was. The door stood open as if the last residents had left in a hurry—as indeed they had. Uncle Jim went to shack near the end of one row. He opened the door and revealed a six-by-eight-foot room with a dirt floor, a sleeping pallet, a table, a chair, and a potbellied stove.

"You hungry, son? I got some hash and a pot of chicory coffee on the stove."

"I'll take some of that coffee," Joe said, knowing it would be rude to refuse the old man's hospitality entirely. After Joe had his coffee in hand, he returned to the point of his visit. "Unca Jim, can you tell me where my family's at?"

"I hate to be the one to tell you dis, but dey's all gone."

"Gone where?"

"Dat's what I got to tell ya, but I cain't do it quick 'cause it didn't happen quick." He lit a corncob pipe with a brand from the stove. "After you got sold down the riva, yo mama was sick with grief. She stopped laughin'. She stopped singin'. She lost interest in just about evathang. She was scared to let her otha chirren outta her sight. She watched 'em like a mutha hen from sunup to sundown. She barely slept and some-times forgot to eat. She worked like a dog to keep on Massa Chris's good side in hopes he wouldn't sell no mo' of her younguns. Seems like she got old and sad ova night.

"In the winter of '58, the flu went through this plantation like boll weevils through a cotton field. Everybody at the big house got it and they passed it on to us. Your mama nursed Mrs. Walker and her chirren round the clock. But when she got the flu herself, there wa'n't nobody to nurse her. We did what we could, but pneumonia set in and she died that winter along with your little sister, Lillian."

Walker felt as though he had been kicked in the stomach. The thing that had sustained him through his exile was the thought of how his mother would respond when she saw him again. Now to learn that she and his sister, whom they nicknamed "Lil Bit" because of her delicate frame and quiet nature, were both dead within weeks of each other was more than he could bear. He put his head down on the rough table and wept like a child. Uncle Jim placed a hand on his shoulder and squeezed it gently.

"I'm sorry, boy. Sorry to put this pain in yo heart on top of what mus' already be there. I wish to heaven dat dis was the last hard thang I had to tell ya, but it ain't."

Walker looked up and saw the sadness in the old man's eyes. He wiped his own eyes and took a long breath. "G'won, tell the rest," he said.

"The only thang yo' daddy loved mo than you chirren was yo' mama. He was cut to the quick when she died, but he squared them big shouldas and went back to carin' for his family. The next summer, a hoss he was shoeing kicked 'im in the head and kilt him. Nobody who knowed David Walker could quite believe that he got hisself kilt by a hoss. But I believe he felt kinda torn 'twixt this life and the next. We buried 'im next to yo' mama. I'll tell a man, yo' daddy was like a brother to me." Jim took a rag from his pocket and blew his nose loudly. But he wasn't through wringing Joe's heart.

"When the wah broke out, Massa Chris joined the Rebs and got hisself kilt at a place called Shiloh. When Mrs. Walker got the news, she neah 'bout lost her mind. She took to her bed for a week. The other massas' wives come and took care 'o her till she come back to herself.

"Miss Betty didn't know nuthin' about runnin' a workin' cotton farm, so she put the plan'ation and all of us up for sale. The man who bought it was named John Poteet. He was from up nawth and had an idey that he could make him some money in the cotton business. Some folks thought Mr. Poteet was a Yankee spy, so they give 'im the cold shoulder right off. Other folks was mad that he swooped in and bought a prime piece a land right out from under they noses. The upshot was he was pretty much on his own from the git-go. But Massa Poteet wan't heah to make friends.

"The fuhst thang he did was hire a' overseer name o' Lucas Tull. Boss Tull was a natcha bone slave driver. He could get a hunnut pounds a cotton a day outcha gran'mamma and he'd beat you neah to death for jes rollin' yo' eyes. That fuhst yeah, he got a full crop in for Massa Poteet, even though they started behind eva'body else. After the harvest, Massa Poteet threw a big party for his neighbas and dat pretty much killed all dat spy talk.

"Life got so hard aroun' heah that yo' brother, Amos, lit out. They caught 'im and brung 'im back in chains. Massa Poteet decided to make a zample outta him, so he had Boss Tull whoop 'im bloody in fronta all o' us. Then he put Amos in the hot box for a week. Nobody run after dat."

Joe looked down at his hands and saw that his palms were bleeding where his nails had dug in. Uncle Jim continued his story.

"Soon, eva'thang was goin' Massa Poteet's way. He put mo' land to plow and bought mo' slaves to work it. He started courtin' Massa Finley's daughter and they got engaged. He put up a new barn and hired a second overseer and set back to take his ease. But like the Bible say, God was vexed by his 'niquity.

"The Yankees come that spring. Dey hit our county from two sides, killin' and lootin' as dey went. We heard the cannons and the gunfire gittin' closer by the day. One mornin', while I was sweepin' the front poach, a rider come in. It was Massa Finley's son, Shawn. He said the Yankees had just hit they place and would be comin' to Massa Poteet's next. His daddy sent him to warn us but he had to get back to his place and make a stand with his fam'ly.

"Massa Poteet told Boss Tull to go tell us slaves to run hide in da woods until he sent for us. Then he locked his doors and loaded his guns. I followed Boss Tull to the cabins. I reckon he knowed the game was up, but it was against his breedin' to set slaves free even for a short spell. When he got to our quarters, he just started shootin' people. He kept firin' till his gun was empty. While he was reloadin', Amos hit 'im in the back of the head with a rock. Then he hit him ova and ova agin till he was dead.

"I gathered the folks and told 'em the Yankees was on us and to run hide in the woods. We hid out till the shootin' stopped and we saw the soldiers leave. Then we went back to the big house. Massa Poteet was hangin' from an oak tree in the front yard. There was a sign aroun' his neck (T-R-A-I-T-O-R) but nobody could read it.

"The Yankees had picked the place clean. After we buried our dead, we didn't know what to do. That's when Amos spoke up. He said he was headin' out befo' the white folks come and chained us up again. He grabbed what food and supplies he could find and hit the woods on the run. After dat, everybody scattered. Steel yo'self, Joseph. One of the ones Tull kilt was your sister, Rosemary.

"After that day, I neva expected to see dis place again. I stayed on the move for 'bout a month but I wan't headed nowhere. When we got freed, I ended up comin' back heah thinking I'd hire myself out. That was six months ago. Nobody done come to claim this land, so I been livin' heah waitin'. Reckon mebbe I been waitin' for you. The lawd works in mysterious ways."

The old man cleared his throat and folded his hands, having discharged an onerous task with grace and compassion. Joe was battered by feelings of sadness and rage. The tiger inside him wanted to tear flesh and spill blood, but the only one in front of him was Uncle Jim, the closest thing to family he had.

Finally, he asked a question that released them both from the quagmire of regret. "Can you show me their graves?"

The old man nodded. "Come with me," he said, standing up from the table.

He led Joe down an overgrown path to a small cemetery about one hundred yards from the slave quarters. There, about thirty handmade markers stood in untidy rows. Joe noticed that the grass was cut and the markers were maintained. He figured this was Uncle Jim's work. Uncle Jim led him to a section with four graves in it. Each of the graves was carefully maintained with markers of shaved pine. Each marker had a unique carving on it. One had a horse's head, a second had an angel, the third had a rose, and the smallest one bore a lily.

Joe knew who was responsible for this homage. He embraced his companion and said, "Thank you."

"They woulda done the same for me," Uncle Jim said.

The two stood by the cluster of graves in silence for a minute. Then the older man said, "I'm gon' go back to the cabin now. Give you some time with yo' family." Uncle Jim squeezed Joe's shoulder and moved off.

As soon as Jim was out of sight, Joe knelt by his parents' graves and poured out his heart. "Mama, Daddy, it's me, Joseph. I'm sorry I didn't make it back before you passed. I tried my hardest, but the devil got in the way. I know you two are together in heaven and that's where I'll see you again. Thank you for all your love. Thank you for my life. I promise to live it in a way that will make you proud."

For Joe, speaking to his parents, albeit posthumously, brought back memories of his time in their care. He remembered his mother's infectious laugh and the feel of his father's big hand on his shoulder in a moment of pride. They had made him feel special in a world that regarded him as little more than a mule. What he had hoped would be tears of joy at their reunion were tears of sadness instead. Still, they served a purpose—closure.

Joe was snatched from his reverie by the sound of gunshots behind him. He leapt to his feet and ran toward the all too familiar summons.

21

Uncle Jim's mind was on other things when he reentered the slave compound or he would have sensed the presence of the three white men who stood in front of his cabin.

The tallest one drew his weapon and motioned Jim forward. He was wearing rebel gear and something was off about one of his eyes. "Come heah, boy."

Uncle Jim paused, weighing his options, his eyes darting. The tall man cocked his pistol and pointed it at Jim's chest. "I said, get yo black ass ova heah."

Uncle Jim walked forward, bent over and feigning a limp. "Yassuh, boss," he said, painting a confused smile on his face. "I didn't quite heah ya. I'm a might deef in one ear."

"You ain't gon' have ta worry 'bout that much longer," the white man said. "Where's the nigger that belongs to this hoss?" He pointed at Buck.

"I don't know, boss. I just got heah myself."

"So that stuff in the cabin don't belong to you?"

"Nawsuh, I'se just passin' through lookin' for woik."

"Listen, boy, that hoss is stole and we gon' hang the man that stole it. Now you can tell us where he is or you can hang in his place. You got five seconds to make up yo' mind. One . . ."

Uncle Jim knew he was done one way or another. His only concern was to keep Joe from walking into an ambush.

"Three—four . . ."

"Hold on, boss. I'll tell you where he is if you'll do somethin' fo' me."

"What's that, boy?"

Uncle Jim drew himself up to his full height and his eyes turned to obsidian chips. "Kiss my black ass!"

The defiant words hung in the air crackling with the rage of a man who had suffered the countless indignities of slavery. Caleb Swenson, the bully from town, fired his gun reflexively, and Uncle Jim crumpled to the ground. Swenson kicked the black man and shot him two more times despite his fending hands.

It was then that Joe ran into the clearing. He saw everything clearly, instantly—the Reb from town flanked by Rat Man and Bulldog, the smoking gun in the Reb's hand, and Uncle Jim's fallen body. The tiger was loose.

Swenson turned toward Joe, a sneer of recognition on his face. He raised his gun and aimed it at Joe. Swenson said, "Drop that—"

Joe shot him in the heart. Joe fanned the hammer of his Colt, and Rat Man and Bulldog crumpled to the ground in mid-draw. He reloaded his gun as he advanced across the clearing to confirm what his killer's instinct had already told him. The trio's waylaying days were over. The dead men's names were Caleb Swenson, Billy Ray Rogers, and Homer Watson, but Walker wouldn't learn that until much later.

Joe went to Uncle Jim and knelt at his side, gently taking him in his arms. Miraculously, there was still a flicker of life in the old man's body. Uncle Jim moved his lips and Joe leaned close to hear.

"Y'aight?"

"I'm a'ight," Joe said.

The old man was fighting for each breath now. He squeezed Joe's hand with his remaining strength and whispered his last word. "Free."

Joe felt as if he had lost his father all over again. He placed Uncle Jim in his family's section of the colored cemetery. He made a cross out of slats from the garden fence. With his knife, he carved an inscription.

JAMES WALKER
BORN A SLAVE
DIED FREE
JUNE 18, 1865

Joe knew that his chances of getting a fair trial in Benton were nonexistent, so he buried the three white men in the cornfield. The loamy soil made for easy digging. He unsaddled their horses and took them to an isolated meadow near the edge of the farm. A stream ran through it where he and his father used to go fishing. By the time they were discovered, he would be long gone. Back at the compound, he picked up his shell casings and wiped out his tracks. Then he led Buck back through the tall grass to the main road.

Everyone in Joe's family was gone now in one way or another. He had put some ghosts to rest, but he was still unsatisfied. It was time for him to find out if freedom was worth all he had sacrificed for it. He mounted Buck. The Morgan danced beneath him, eager to be on the trail again. He set out at a brisk trot and rode until he came to a crossroads. There he made a decision that charted the rest of his life. Walker rode west.

PART 4

Into the West

22

Joe Walker rose each morning with the sun at his back and lay down each evening with the sun in his face. He was heading west. Buck could not cover enough ground to free him from the things he had seen and done before his twentieth birthday. A fortnight ago, he had left Tennessee looking over his shoulder for likely pursuers. He had just killed three men, albeit in self-defense, but that mattered little because they were white men. His plan was to put some distance between him and the scene of the showdown. Once he settled somewhere, he would decide his next moves.

His worst fears about his fugitive status were confirmed when he spied a wanted poster nailed to a tree on the outskirts of Memphis. The poster contained information in a format with which Joe would become all too familiar.

Beneath the script was a sketch of a scowling coal black man with long, coarse hair, close-set menacing eyes, wide nostrils, and thin lips. The resemblance to a gorilla was striking.

Joe took down the wanted poster. He waited until sundown and rode into Memphis under the cover of darkness. He found two more posters on buildings along the main street and took them both down. He left Memphis without speaking to a soul.

His hard-won freedom was suddenly at risk. He had hoped that by leaving Tennessee, he could outrun the reach of the law. Later, a bounty hunter named Jim Carson would put that hope permanently to rest.

Once he crossed the Tennessee border into Arkansas, Joe's thoughts turned to the future. He had heard there was land to be had in the great west and neither the color of a man's skin nor lack of cash would be a hindrance to acquiring some. The caveat was wresting and holding it from the Indians. He had never had a place he could call his own and that had left an ache inside him that nothing—not war, not vengeance, not the patina of freedom—had been able to fill.

On his fifteenth day on the trail, Walker spotted a line of wagons on the horizon. He was moving into Indian territory and figured now would be a good time to hook up with somebody. He followed the wagon train in no particular hurry. He was uncertain of the reception he would get but hoped that another pair of hands and another gun would be welcome. That night, he camped in a grove of poplars a mile away from the circled wagons. The next morning, he shot a whitetail. While he was dressing out the deer, a man rode into his camp from the wagon train. He was a tall, muscular man whose light skin, reddish hair, and freckles suggested mixed parentage. He wore a two-gun rig over a fringed buckskin jacket. Instead of boots, he wore knee-length moccasins. His face was shaded by a flat brimmed hat with a feather in the band. The stranger reined his horse and regarded Walker calmly. Lifting his hand, he offered a salutation.

"Mornin'. I saw your fire last night and heard you shootin' this mornin'. Figured I'd come over and say 'howdy.'"

"Mornin'. Figured somebody'd come callin'. I'd like to join y'all if I could. I'm a good hand with horses and I can help fill the cook pot," Joe said. "Join me for breakfast?"

"Thank ya kindly, but I just ate. Name's John Parker. I'm the scout for that wagon train yonder. Where you headed?"

"West," Walker said.

"Where you from?"

"Back east."

The scout smiled. "You don't have a lot to say, do you, Mistuh . . . ?"

Joe hesitated a beat and decided to use his real name, a decision that had profound consequences.

"Name's Walker . . . Joseph Walker."

The scout's eyes widened at this and he took an even closer look at Walker.

"My daddy used to say, 'Talk is cheap. Deeds make the man,'" Walker said by way of explanation for his taciturnity.

Parker's smile broadened and he relaxed visibly. "We got a Walker on the train and it sounds like you and him may have the same daddy."

Of all the things that could have come out of the man's mouth, nothing could have surprised Walker more. He practically gaped. "What's this man's name?"

"Amos . . . Amos Walker."

"Amos? You sho' his name is Amos?"

"It was when I left this mornin'," Parker said.

"Mistuh Parker, it don't matter if you let me join yo' train or not. I got to speak to that man."

"What's yo' business with Amos?"

"Family business, I believe," Walker said, and for the first time, he smiled.

Walker broke camp with haste and they rode toward the now moving wagon train. He tried to keep his rising hopes in check but to no avail. By the time they pulled abreast of the slow-moving wagons, he felt like he had swallowed a handful of live grasshoppers. Parker rode to the front of the thirty-wagon train and held up his hand. A dark-skinned man of medium height wearing a black frock coat and matching hat came forward. Joe noticed that colored people also occupied the wagons.

"This is Mr. Justin Ross, the wagon master," Parker said.

"Name's Joseph Walker," Walker said and extended his hand.

The man took it in a powerful grip. "Glad to meet you, Mistuh Walker."

"Mistuh Walker wants to join the train," Parker said.

"Do you have any capital, son?"

"Capital?"

"Money to buy a spot on the train," Ross said.

"How much does it cost?"

"A hundred dollars."

"I'm afraid I ain't got that. Could I work my way?"

Parker said, "Can I speak to you a minute, Cap'n Ross?" The two men stepped aside and engaged in quiet conversation.

Captain Ross turned to a boy seated beside his father in one of the wagons. "Noah, run git Mr. Walker and bring 'im up here." The boy leapt down and ran back along the line of wagons. "We'd certainly make better time without craning our necks to keep sight o' you. That's a fine hoss you got there," Ross said with an appraising glance at Buck.

"He was my cavalry mount," Walker said, laying another card on the table.

"What outfit?" Ross asked.

"Brisbin's Fifth Colored," Joe said.

The wagon master looked at him with new respect. "I was with Stoneman's Brigade at Saltville. I'll tell a man, you boys was some fightin' fools."

Noah returned leading a tall man with a bushy head of hair and a bristly black beard. He had a puzzled look on his face. Despite his beard and the streaks of gray in his hair, Joe recognized his older brother immediately. He dismounted and ran to the big man and grabbed him by the shoulders. "Amos! Amos! It's me . . . Joseph."

The man looked at Joe as though he had taken leave of his senses. Then recognition dawned in his eyes. "Jaybird? Jaybird! Is that you?" No one other than his father and his brother had ever called Joe "Jaybird."

Walker nodded, tears welling in his eyes.

Amos took his brother in his arms and held him like his life depended on it. "I thought we lost you, boy. Thank God. Thank the Lord." Once their initial emotions were spent, Joe and Amos held each other at arm's length and noted the changes that time had wrought in each of them. Amos marveled at the young lion before him whose air of quiet assurance spoke volumes about the man he had become. Joe saw the brother who had teased him mercilessly at times but had come to his defense the minute the older boys tried to bully him. Amos taught him to fish with his bare hands and to shoot out a squirrel's eye with a slingshot, how to pick cotton and track game and, regrettably, how to make his daddy swear and his mama cry. Next to his father and his Uncle Jim, Amos was the man Joe had wanted to be.

The devil-may-care light that had always shone in Amos's eyes had been all but extinguished by loss and pain. It had been replaced by grim determination. Like Walker, he had been robbed of his childhood and his family. He had witnessed and caused death. His body was a monument to endurance with a corded neck, a scarred torso, and large, calloused hands meant for breaking and tearing. Though he was only twenty-six years old, his hair and beard were already streaked with gray. Despite the passage of time, both men saw the child the other had been and were briefly transported back to a happier time.

Amos wiped his cheek with the back of his hand. "Looks like the devil didn't get his way with all of us, little brotha."

Amos's use of the term "little brother" took Walker back to the war and his bond with Holata Turner.

"I guess not," he said, mimicking his brother's wiping gesture.

"I couldn't quite see what the Lord had planned for me. Now I see it plain," Amos said. He smiled, and Joe caught a glimpse of the adolescent from whom he had been separated.

"Does that mean I can come with you where you're goin'?"

"Same ol' Jaybird," Amos said with a loud snuffle. Amos put his arm around Joe's shoulders and turned him to face the people.

"Folks, this heah's my little brotha, Jay—Joseph. Me and him ain't seen each other since he got sold down the river when he was a boy. That's what all this carryin' on is about. He the only family I got left. He's comin' with me to Kansas."

With that pronouncement, the question of whether Joe would join the company was settled. All eyes were on Joe and he felt self-conscious in the spotlight. He nodded at the crowd that had gathered around them.

"Anything you wanta say, little brotha?"

Joe removed his hat and began haltingly. "I been trying to git back home since the day I was sold. Amos being heah kinda makes this home. I'd like to join up with y'all if ya'll'll have me." Having revealed more vulnerability than he intended, Joe lowered his head and cleared his throat.

They came forward en masse to hug his neck, shake his hand, and slap his back. Joe was overcome with a sense of belonging. It was the first time in his life that he had been part of a community of free black folk. Perhaps here he could lower his guard and reclaim some of the carelessness of youth. It was the beginning of the fresh start he had hoped to find in the west.

When the welcome party dissipated, Amos led Joe to his wagon. It was twelve feet long, eight feet high, and four feet wide and pulled by a six-mule team. In the bed of the wagon were farming tools, pots and pans, a large chest, a table, and some chairs. There was a water barrel lashed to one side of the wagon and a vegetable bin lashed to the other.

"Well, this is home for the time being," Amos said.

Joe stared in amazement. "Where'd you get the money to buy all this?"

"It's a long story. I'll tell you later," Amos said.

That night they feasted on venison, yams, corn bread, and roasted grasshoppers dipped in honey. They washed it all down with corn liquor. Sated, Amos turned to his pipe. He packed the bowl with homegrown tobacco and lit it with practiced movements. Joe had never taken up the use of tobacco, but the aromatic smell of Amos's pipe took him back to his childhood when his father would end his meals with the same ritual. "All right, Jaybird, start talkin'. What happened to you?"

Joe then told his brother the story of his days on the Budreau plantation, his escape from slavery, and subsequent enlistment in the Union army. The part he hated telling most was the murder of "Uncle Jim," their closest family friend.

Amos involuntarily exclaimed upon hearing the news. "Aw, nah! Not Unca Jim. He never hurt a soul in his whole life. Them murderin' sons of bitches. If I had 'em here, I'd kill 'em with my bare hands."

"They're already in the ground," Joe said with a matter-of-factness that made Amos regard his younger brother with something akin to envy.

"I buried Unca Jim in the colored cemetery with our family. He died protectin' me. He was three times the man as him that killed 'im."

Joe came to the part of his story that he would just as soon omit, but he did not want to place his brother at risk without fair warning. He told Amos about the wanted poster and his status as an outlaw. He looked at his brother with sadness in his eyes, aware of what he might have to give up.

"I should'na brought this to yo' door. I guess my feelin's got the best of me. If you say 'Ride on,' I'll be gone in the mornin'."

Amos looked at Joe with the same incredulous expression Joe recognized from their childhood after he had said or done something incredibly stupid.

"Jaybird, are you out of your cotton-pickin' mind? You think I would send you away right after the Lord just sent you back to me? You and me are guilty of the same crime. I killed the bastard that shot Rosemary for the same reason that you killed the bastards that shot Unca Jim. The only difference is that you got a price on your head and I don't. Anybody that comes for you is gon' have to go through me, 'cause you and me is all the family we got. And them's my last words on the matter."

Joe's sense of relief was inundating. He hadn't realized how much he dreaded losing Amos and having to face an uncertain future alone. His mind raced with thoughts of love and gratitude. In the end, he simply said, "It's settled then. We go on together."

They sat in silence for a while, basking in the bond each had thought was lost forever.

Presently, Joe's curiosity resurfaced. "So you was gon' tell me how you put your stake together so quick?"

"Massa Poteet had a safe behind a paintin' on the wall in his bedroom. I guess he didn't trust them southern banks. Rosemary was workin' in the house and saw him go into it one time when he thought he was by hisself. She told me about it. After the Yankees raided the place and killed Poteet, I went back and took a pickax to that safe. Guess what was in there?"

"Money?"

Amos leaned in and whispered conspiratorially, "Five thousand Yankee dollars and this." He pulled a pouch on a thong from inside his shirt and poured a diamond ring into his palm. "I guess this was gon' be for Miss Finley when they got married. I used a chunk of that cash to buy my wagon and mules and a place on this wagon train. Some more of it went for supplies and weapons. I still got enough left to homestead a piece of land in the territories." He looked intently at Joe. "Half of everything is yours."

Joe knew there was no use objecting to this offer. He would have done the same were their positions reversed. Instead, he extended his hand to his brother and they shook on it.

23

Day after day, the line of wagons moved west. They made between ten and twenty miles a day depending on the weather and terrain. They rode through flat lands covered in golden grass higher than a tall man's waist. There were trees of every variety—poplar, cottonwood, oak, ash, maple, and plum. These groves provided the settlers with firewood, fruit, nuts, and shade. They crossed the Red River and kept moving west. The prairie was teeming with wildlife from grasshoppers to buffalo.

Joe lost count of the different kinds of birds he saw. When he exhausted his knowledge of the ones he knew, he amused himself by giving unfamiliar varieties made up names, such as "yellow head," "speckled breast," and "white wing."

Joe became a fairly competent teamster driving his brother's wagon and he relished the time with Amos to reminisce and plan for the future. Joe had spent little time in the company of women and children. He was bemused by the curiosity and fearlessness of the children on the train. Indeed, everything from wasps' nests to prairie dog holes were an invitation for closer inspection.

There were several girls around his age. Their whispers and shy glances in his direction were oddly unsettling. One girl in particular caused his cheeks to warm and his thoughts to spin. Her name was

Christine Archer. By plying Amos with questions, he learned that she was seventeen years old and from Louisiana. Her father, James, was a carpenter who intended to build a home of his own somewhere west of the Mississippi. Her mother, Mabel, and younger brother, Ethan, completed the family. Christine's presence at Sunday morning worship caused Joe to become a regular attendee. After one such meeting, Amos introduced him to the Archers.

"This here's my brother, Joseph. He fought for the nawth during the war. Helped drive them Johnny Rebs inta the swamp and helped us git free," Amos said with more than a little pride in his voice.

Joe removed his hat and shook Mr. Archer's hand. He nodded politely to Mrs. Archer. "Ma'am." At the same time, Christine gave him a smile whose beauty and brilliance made him blush. He hoped it was unnoticeable.

"Son, I thank you for your service. You and Amos must come to supper tonight," Mr. Archer said. His voice was the deepest bass Joe had ever heard.

"We wouldn't want to be a bother, suh," Joe said.

"No bother whatsoever. We'd be honored to have ya'll," Mrs. Archer said, squeezing Joe's forearm after the manner of mothers everywhere.

"Knowin' what you can do with a fryin' pan and a Dutch oven, you don't have to ax me twice, ma'am," Amos said. This solicited a smile from Mrs. Archer that was clearly the author of Christine's version.

"It's settled then. See y'all at our camp this evenin' for supper," Mr. Archer said.

The day Joe had spent hiding in a tree from rebel marauders seemed shorter than the rest of that Sunday. By suppertime, he had brushed his clothes, his hair, and his manners to the point of tedium. When Joe and Amos approached the Archer's wagon, they were delighted by the smell of cooking meat and fresh-baked bread.

Mr. Archer came forward to greet them smiling around a corncob pipe. "I hope you boys brought yo' appetites, 'cause Mabel done outdone herself."

Mrs. Archer turned from the pot she was tending to chime in. "It's just Sunday supper," she said wiping her hands on her apron and placing them on her generous hips. "You two look like you could use a proper feeding."

Joe extended the bouquet of prairie flowers he had picked earlier. "For you, ma'am," he said.

"Why, *Joseph*. Thank you kindly, dear. Your mother would be so proud of the young man you've become."

Joe was so moved by her words that he forgot to mention the flowers had been Amos's idea, and his big brother generously let him take sole credit for the gesture.

Christine emerged from the Archers' wagon, and Joe's breath caught in his throat. She was wearing a pink gingham dress with her long silken hair arranged in a single French braid that hung to her waist. This was festooned with a pink ribbon. She had replaced her traveling shoes with a pair of pink slippers. She glanced shyly at the two visitors, still a stranger to her own beauty.

Amos said, "I swear, Miss Christine, if you ain't the prettiest flower on the prairie."

She smiled and gave a slight curtsy. "Thank you, Mr. Walker, but surely you haven't seen all the flowers yet."

"I've seen enough," Amos said, and they exchanged a look that spoke volumes.

The truth struck Joe like a thunderbolt. The looks, nods, and smiles he had thought were for him had been for his brother. He suddenly didn't know what to do or say. He stood in a cone of embarrassment while events flowed on around him.

He was brought out of his reverie by Amos loudly calling his name, "*Joseph*, Mr. Archer is talkin' to you, boy." Joe started back to attention and looked at Mr. Archer, who had a bemused smile on his face.

"I said, how have you been enjoyin' your time with the train, son?"

"Uh, just fine, suh. It's a comfort to have good, trustful people around you when you're movin' into strange territory. Matter of fact, I ain't felt this safe since I was back with my unit during the wah."

"Strange to feel safe in the middle of a war."

"It all depends on who you with, suh," Joe said.

Mrs. Archer deftly changed the subject. "Enough talk of danger and war. Let's have our meal and get better acquainted."

A tuneless whistle floated on the air, and Ethan appeared with an armful of firewood. "Wood Man! What'd I miss?" he asked.

"Nothing. Now wash those hands and come to the table," his mother said.

Ethan Archer, at eleven years of age, was a font of energy and preadolescent "devilment." He took every opportunity to pester his sister, just to see her aggrieved response. He was a natural athlete, already a perennial winner in contests of strength and speed with the other boys on the train. His laugh or whistle usually preceded him into most situations. He delighted in showing off—doing spontaneous handsprings, shooting at various targets with his slingshot, or just mugging at his sister behind his parents' back. After the manner of boys his age, he believed the world was his oyster.

Mrs. Archer had prepared a feast of roasted quail, mashed potatoes, asparagus, and biscuits and gravy.

After his second slice of apple pie, Joe leaned back with a sigh of satisfaction.

"Ma'am, that may be the best meal I've had since I left home."

"Just plain old down-home cooking," she said, her voice warm with gratitude.

"You sure you don't want another piece of pie?" she asked with a mischievous twinkle in her eye.

"Not if you don't want to have to stitch me back together." This brought a laugh from the entire table. In this humble setting, Joe felt the weight of years of care slipping from his shoulders. This experience mirrored his memory of meal times before his family was shattered by the dictates of avarice and slavery. His upset over

Christine's choice of suitors was salved by the balm of a newfound feeling of security.

After the dishes were cleared away, pipes lit, and cups filled, they exchanged background stories. The Archers were creoles from northwestern Louisiana. Mr. Archer was a skilled craftsman whose services as a carpenter and furniture maker were highly sought after. He saved his meager earnings for years in anticipation of one day buying his freedom. During that span, he met and married Mabel. She was as industrious and ambitious as he. A skilled cook and seamstress, she became the designer of choice for local mistresses who needed a handmade christening dress or a replica of a ball gown they had seen in a catalogue. She also became known for her "specialty" cakes that graced local sideboards on birthdays, anniversaries, and other special occasions. She, too, had saved her earnings to purchase her freedom.

When the war ended, the Archers used the money they had originally saved to buy their freedom to buy their way west. Against law and custom, Mrs. Archer had been secretly taught to read by her mistress, who was a schoolteacher from Kansas. Consequently, Christine and Ethan could read, write, and figure. Christine conducted literacy classes in the evenings for the children of the camp and any adults who wanted to learn. Her beauty and brains made her a mate that any man would be proud to share his life with. Joe felt a fresh pang of envy for Amos if he should be the one to win her hand.

With some prodding, Joe talked about his time in and out of uniform. He excluded the killing he had done to survive and spoke instead about the camaraderie and code of honor he had found in the service and his joy at finding his brother after finding their home laid to waste.

By the time they finished talking, the stars were out and the fire was fading. Ethan had already turned in with little urging from his parents. They stood and said their good-byes, bonded now by shared bread, shared knowledge, and shared hope. When Joe extended his hand to Mrs. Archer, she ignored it and wrapped him in a breathless hug, rocking him gently from side to side. At length, she stepped back.

"Do come back and see us again, dear," she said, wiping the corners of her eye with her apron.

"Yes, ma'am. I sho will. Thank you for *everythang.*"

Amos and Mr. Archer had been engaged in quiet conversation to one side. They shook hands and returned to the group. Amos took Christine's hands in his. "Thank you, ma'am, for one of the best evenings of my life. I hope to see you again right soon."

"I look forward to it," she said.

Joe took his leave from Christine with a polite, "Thank you, ma'am."

Back at their wagon, Amos was still giddy with the possibilities the evening had unveiled. "Jaybird. Did you know you just mighta met my future wife?"

"I kinda guessed that might be the case," Joe said.

"I been trying to work up the nerve to ask her daddy if I can come courtin' since I first laid eyes on her, but you saw her—you heard her. What she want with a field nigga like me? Right? But tonight I decided to throw my cards on the table. And she looked like she might be interested. Didn't she?"

"She didn't get dolled up like that for me," Joe said, tasting the irony in his words. "But ain't but one way to find out for sho. My ol' sarge used to say, 'Losers wish. Winners do.' You best stake yo' claim befo' somebody else moves in. You ain't the only single man on this train, ya know."

"I'm way ahead of ya, boy. I told Mr. Archer tonight I want to talk to him tomorra about an important matter. Our daddy didn't raise no cowards. Havin' you back and hearin' what you been through made me realize that. If her daddy say no or she don't want nothin' to do with me, at least I tried. I swear, Jaybird, since you come back, everthang is as clear as day to me."

Amos lay down, wrapped himself in his blankets, and in a matter of minutes was snoring loudly. Sleep did not come as easily to Joe.

24

As soon as they made camp the following day, Amos washed himself and put on his Sunday-go-to-meeting coat. He had shaved his bushy beard, making him look years younger. Finally, he brushed his hair back and put on his Sunday bowler.

"How do I look?"

"Like wife bait."

"Wish me luck."

"Luck."

Two hours later when Amos returned, the answer to his request was written all over his face. His shoulders drooped, his feet dragged, and his freshly shaven countenance bore a frown. Joe felt a stab of anger at Mr. Archer for failing to even give his brother a chance at fulfilling his dream.

"Well, what did the ol' bastard say?" Joe asked.

"The ol' bastard said . . . YES!" With that, he grabbed Joe and danced him around the campfire, howling like a man possessed. Once again, Amos had surprised Joe with a playful side he thought was a thing of the past.

"He said yes! By Jim, he said yes! Jaybird, I swear I ain't been that scairt since the slave catchers was on my trail. But I stood in front of 'im and said my piece. Told him that we Walkers was men of our word, and I promised him I would never mistreat or disrespect his daughter."

"So what did he say to that?"

"He said him and Mrs. Archer had talked about it and they allowed that I was a man to be trusted. They'd seen the way the other men, even the older ones, looked to me when direction was needed. He said they'd also seen the way Christine looked at me, and they felt like she might have some feelin's sim'lar to mine. Can you imagine that, son? Finally, he said they seen the way I treated you who I hadn't seen in ten years, and that let them know that family came fuhst with me and that if Christine was to someday become a Walker, I would stand by her to the death. We shook hands and I asked him if Christine was to home."

"Boy, once you get up a head o' steam, you don't stop do you?" Joe said.

"I didn't wanta lose my nerve. He called Christine and she come out the wagon lookin' as fresh as the mornin' dew. Mr. Archer told her I had somethin' to say to her and that's when I almost bolted, but I knew I didn't wanta have to hoe that row again. So I axed her if she was up for a walk. We went down by the creek and I told her that her daddy had give me permission to come courtin'. You know what she said then, Jaybird?"

"What?"

"She said, 'Come ahead.' I felt like I was full o' sunshine. We kept talkin' about this and that. It didn't matter to me. It was the fuhst time we been alone together, and I just soaked it up like a biscuit in molasses. Finally, she said, 'We better get back.' Then come the best part of all. On the way back to the wagon, she took my arm. Lawd, I wished their camp hadda been in Missouri."

Amos finished his story with a satisfied grunt. His face was that of a man who had just been told that he had inherited a gold mine. Joe's joy on Amos's behalf was tinged with sadness. The brother he had just found was about to be partially taken away.

25

As they moved deeper into Oklahoma's Indian territory, the wagon master sent John Parker ahead to survey the territory and give warning if he sighted hostile Indians. Joe began riding out with the scout on these patrols primarily out of boredom. He enjoyed being the first to see new territory. The prairie was like an ocean that teemed with vegetation and wildlife. Parker was a man of few words, but his size and strength garnered him much respect. Once when a wagon broke its wheel in a dry wash, Parker placed his broad back under the wagon bed and lifted the conveyance while the owner changed the wheel. At first, Walker and Parker, both solitary men, were uncomfortable in each other's company. But over days of riding together, the ice thawed.

One evening, Joe invited Parker to join him and Amos for supper, and thereafter this became a regular occurrence. Often it was just Joe and Parker at supper, as Amos was off courting Christine. So it was, in bits and pieces, that Joe learned Parker's story.

John Parker was born a slave on a plantation in western Kentucky. His master, who was also his father, freed him after John saved his life at some risk to his own. After he received his manumission papers, Parker immediately left Kentucky and settled in Springfield, Illinois. There, he pursued occupations that included ditch digger, farmer, bartender, and stage rider. He met and married his wife, Lucille, in Illinois. She was a schoolteacher who taught him to read and write, pastimes that he enjoyed immensely. When she became pregnant with their first child, he was as happy as a man could be this side of heaven. Then when she and the child died in childbirth, he sank into a pit of despair, drunkenness, and self-pity.

When the war broke out, Parker enlisted in the Twenty-Ninth Colored Infantry, hoping the Confederates would do quickly what he had been trying to do slowly. Instead of taking his life, the army saved it. Through shared struggle and sacrifice, he regained his dignity and sense of purpose. He rose to the rank of sergeant and earned the Medal of Honor for his exploits at the Battle of Chaffin's Farm. After the war, none of his previous occupations seemed suitable. Instead, he formed a partnership with Justin Ross and they began guiding black settlers west in pursuit of the dream of land ownership. They had made two successful trips to date.

Their shared war experience helped create an unspoken bond between Joe and Parker. Joe treated him with the deference and respect owed a superior officer.

One day when they were scouting about five miles ahead of the train, they ran across the trail of a large group of riders. The horses were unshod, leading Parker to tell Joe they had crossed the track of a war party. The trail led northwest, and Parker suggested they follow it for a while to see if they could catch sight of those who had made it. Riding swiftly, they soon came to a rise in the ground. Topping that rise, they saw the party about a mile away across a flat expanse of prairie. It numbered between seventy and eighty riders.

Parker immediately dismounted and Joe followed suit. The scout took a telescope from his saddlebag and trained it on the group ahead. Parker whistled softly. "Comanche war party," he said, handing Joe the glass.

Joe took the telescope and got his first view of "wild" Indians. The men rode two or three abreast. They were adorned in war paint, leather leggings, and breechclouts. Their bodies were studies in lean muscle and sinew covered by almond-colored skin. Most wore feathers in their hair. They carried rifles, bows, and lances.

The Comanche were, arguably, one of the most feared Indian tribes on the western frontier. They took no side in the Civil War, instead using the opportunity to raid towns and settlements in Texas and Oklahoma left defenseless while the US Army was occupied elsewhere. In order to protect their culture and homeland, they formed alliances with the Apache and Kiowa tribes to resist the westward movement of the white man. Their principle chief, Quanah Parker, was a skilled warrior and diplomat who fought the United States Army to a standstill and then negotiated an honorable peace.

As Joe rested his gaze on the glistening back of one warrior, the man turned his head and stared straight back at him. He raised his hand and the column stopped. Joe and Parker slid back into the cover of the tall grass, but their attempt at concealment was too late.

About ten warriors turned their mounts and came toward them at a gallop. They caught up their horses and beat a retreat back the way they had come. Shortly, the Comanches topped the rise and caught sight of their quarry. With a wild whoop, they came on.

Realizing their plight, Joe spurred Buck to greater speed and pulled his Colt from its holster. The Comanches had fanned out and were riding low over their horses' necks, whooping incessantly. They would have to get closer for their weapons to be effective. Therein lay Joe and Parker's only advantage.

The Indian ponies were fleet and rock ribbed. Buck probably could have outdistanced them over a long haul, but Parker's mount was no match, particularly under the big man's weight. They crossed a shallow stream with a copse of trees on the other side. Parker rode into the trees and dismounted. Joe followed suit, pulling his Spencer from his boot. The line of warriors drew closer. Joe could finally see their faces. These were fighting men.

Joe raised his rifle, slowed his breathing, and set his sights on the torso of one of the approaching Comanches. He awaited Parker's command to fire. Instead of a verbal command, the big scout fired his rifle and knocked one of the Indians from the saddle. Walker fired and another warrior fell. He levered another shell into the chamber and fired again with the same result. To his right, Parker was also firing deliberately. Return fire from their attackers caused them to seek cover.

The Spencer rifle was a deadly weapon in the right hands. Joe and Parker were military-trained marksmen. Under their deadly fire, the Comanches were forced to turn back to the other side of the stream where they took cover behind a hillock. Five of their companions lay dead or dying. Soon, one of the men left the group and rode back in the direction they had come.

"Goin' for reinforcements," Parker said.

"Yeah. I don't reckon we can hold off the whole bunch."

"Time to skedaddle," Parker said.

"Which way?"

"North. We cain't afford to lead 'em back to the wagons," Parker said.

"How 'bout one of us goes north and the otha one goes west. That way, they have to split up to follow us. After we either shake 'em or kill 'em, we circle back to the train," Joe said.

Parker looked at Walker with quiet admiration. "See ya back at camp," he said extending his hand.

Walker shook his hand and they retreated into the trees, where they mounted their horses. The remaining Comanches were caught by surprise when Walker and Parker broke from the trees headed in different directions. Two took out after Parker and two followed Joe.

Joe urged Buck into a gallop both to put distance between him and his pursuers and draw them away from Parker. When he could no longer see the two following warriors, he slowed to a canter. He was moving through unfamiliar territory, and he didn't want to run into trouble while ostensibly fleeing it. The terrain was still mostly flat. He came to a stream and allowed Buck to drink, and then he rode into the stream and followed it for a half mile before exiting on the opposite side. He knew this maneuver wouldn't stop his pursuers, but it should slow them down. It might also cause them to split up, which suited his plans precisely.

He rode approximately a hundred yards from the streambed, dismounted, and, using his saber, cut out a swath in the prairie grass. He had Buck lay down in the depression. He put his back to the horse's haunch and waited, his rifle across his knees. About a half hour later, a lone figure rode into view, closely checking the ground for sign. Joe crouched in the grass and waited. The Comanche spotted Joe's tracks from where he exited the stream and decided to follow them far enough to ensure it was not a false trail. When he got to within a stone's throw of Joe's hiding place, Joe stood up and trained his rifle on the man.

"Hold up!"

The Indian raised his rifle and fired blindly. Walker fired simultaneously. He heard a bullet whiz past his head. His shot hit the Comanche in the chest and he toppled from his horse. Walker walked over to the brave and turned him over. The man was still alive but fading. He reached convulsively for the hatchet in his belt. Walker raised his rifle for the coup de grace but the brave succumbed with a convulsive shudder before it was necessary. Walker took the Indian's tomahawk, thinking it might come in handy down the road.

"Now, where's your partner?" he said to himself.

Joe mounted Buck and rode back the way he had come, his eyes searching. He was in no mood to run from one man. A quarter of an hour later, he spied his second adversary riding toward him on the opposite side of the stream. The brave was of indeterminate age. He was muscled like a mountain lion, strong and sleek. He sat his pony with the bearing of a prince, and as he came abreast of Joe's position, he turned to face his enemy and issued a long blood-curdling yell. This was the Comanche war cry that would strike terror in the hearts of countless settlers over the next fifteen years.

Joe could have drawn his Spencer and dropped the man in his tracks, but warrior blood also coursed through his veins. Instead, he drew his saber from the scabbard affixed to his saddle and held it out at arms length in the attack position. The Comanche raised his war lance in similar fashion and, as if on cue, they charged each other across the narrow stream. As they closed, Joe leaned to the side to avoid the lance's blade while slashing at the brave's torso. The Comanche blocked the blow with his shield and they completed their first pass unscathed.

The Indian screamed his defiance and raised his lance. Joe twirled his saber like a baton. They charged again. The brave hurled his lance and it struck Buck squarely in the chest. The Morgan let out a cough of pain and fell to his knees, throwing Joe over his head into the water. He came up stunned and sputtering just in time to catch the Comanche, who leapt from his horse into Joe's arms. Joe grabbed the Indian's knife hand, and they strained against each other in the knee-deep water.

Joe used a wrestling maneuver Holata Turner had taught him. He pushed with all his strength against his adversary, and when the brave pushed back with equal force, Joe suddenly ceased his resistance and leaned forcefully backward while placing his right foot in the Indian's midsection. The warrior's momentum, aided by Joe's thrusting foot, carried him over Joe's head in a somersault onto his back. Joe drew the tomahawk from his belt and struck the Comanche in the sternum with such force it lodged in the bone. The man gave an agonized bellow and reached convulsively for Joe's throat. Joe struck the grasping hands away, clasped his hands around the brave's throat, and forced his face under the water. The Comanche thrashed and beat at Joe's arms trying to break his grip, to no avail. Joe choked the man while looking into his eyes. Even after the life left those eyes, he continued to squeeze. He was aroused from the red mist that enveloped him by a gurgling neigh from his horse.

Buck was laying on his side at the edge of the stream, the war lance protruding from his chest. His mouth and nostrils were oozing blood. It was a mortal wound. As Buck strained to lift his head clear of the water, Joe hurried over, lifted Buck's head and placed it in his lap.

"Easy, boy. I got you." This was a mantra he had recited countless times before they rode into battle. It had its usual calming effect on both of them. Buck rolled one eye in his direction and nickered softly. Joe stroked his muzzle with a tenderness that contrasted sharply with his recent battle rage.

"Don't worry, son. I'm gon' fix it. I'm gon' fix it now." Aware that he was still surrounded by enemies, Joe pulled his knife. Covering Buck's eye with his palm, he drove the blade into the horse's heart. Buck shuddered once and then lay still. Only then did Joe remove the lance from Buck's chest. He broke it across his knee and flung it into the tall grass. He dragged the Comanche warrior from the water and covered his body with grass and branches. When he was finished, he washed the blood from his hands in the tepid water of the shallow stream.

26

When Joe and Parker failed to return from their scouting foray, Amos wanted to take out a search party immediately. Justin Ross tried to convince him to wait.

"It's almost dark. Parker has stayed away over a day before, usually lookin' for water. Give 'em till noon tomorrow and if they ain't back, we'll go lookin'," he said.

"I cain't wait, Justin. It'd drive me crazy. That boy is all the family I got. I'd never forgive myself if he was out there hurt or in some kinda trouble and I was sittin' here twiddlin' my thumbs waitin' for daylight," Amos said.

"All right, but if you run into Injun trouble, don't try to handle it by yourself. Come a runnin'."

"Yessuh." Amos saddled a horse and took two day's worth of provisions, two pistols, and his rifle. He rode out at sunset. He rode until he couldn't see the trail anymore. He made camp in a cottonwood grove that provided both shelter and concealment.

The next day he was up at dawn and moving west. At midmorning, he spied the Comanche war party. They were about three miles away and moving fast. If they were the reason Joe and John hadn't returned, there was little hope of their survival. He spun his horse and headed back to warn the wagon train. He rode hard, trying not to imagine what his brother would have suffered at the hands of wild Indians. If the Indians had seen him, they would follow him home, but that couldn't be helped. The people on the train had to be warned.

His horse was lathered and breathing hard when he saw the wagons on the horizon. Shouting and waving, he came on. When he was about a thousand yards out, three riders separated from the wagon party and rode in his direction. Justin Ross, James Archer, and a farmer named Roscoe Williams met Amos, their faces concerned.

"What is it, Amos?" Archer asked.

"Injuns! Headed this way! Circle the wagons!"

As they rode back to the wagon train, Amos briefed them on the size and distance of the war party. The three men passed the word to their companions that an attack was imminent. The settlers positioned the wagons in a circle with the livestock inside. They filled the spaces between the wagons with mattresses, barrels, and chests. Justin Ross issued a weapon to every adult who could shoot. The settlers had diligently practiced these maneuvers well before arriving in Indian territory. When their preparations were completed, they settled down to wait. Christine had come to Amos's side.

"Are you sure you're all right?" she asked.

"Yeah."

"What about Joe?"

"I don't know." The dejection in his voice said otherwise. She took his hand and squeezed it in both of hers. He took what comfort he could from the gesture and thanked God again that, of all the men in the world, she had taken a shine to him.

When the settlers' preparations were completed, as if on cue, the Comanches rode over the horizon. They came on in a long, even line, brandishing their weapons above their heads and emitting blood-curdling war cries.

Their leader was Chief Iron Jacket, veteran of a hundred skirmishes. He wore a feathered war bonnet and a Union army jacket. He was, by any measure, a fine-looking man with a broad brow, straight nose, high cheekbones, and sculpted jaw. His dark brown eyes were windows to an exceptional intellect and a fiery spirit. Next to Quanah Parker, he was the most notorious and feared warrior on the plains.

Justin Ross's calm voice eased Amos's nerves.

"Wait for my command to fire. Don't expose yo'selves. Remember, they may try to burn the wagons, so be ready."

Five hundred yards out, the Comanches split into two phalanxes. One veered to the right and the other to the left. As the riders approached, Amos leveled his Henry rifle at the group and waited for a target to emerge. He turned to look at Christine, and an unrelated thought popped into his head. "If we get out o' this in one piece, will you marry me?"

Without hesitation, she said, "It would be my pleasure," and gave him a look that put a razor's edge on his determination to survive.

There were four Sharps rifles on the train, including Ross's. He had positioned these "snipers" at various points within the circle. When the Comanches were roughly twenty yards away, Ross gave the command to fire. The air was filled with the sound of gunfire and the smell of gun smoke. Indians spilled from their horses all along the charging fronts. The Comanches immediately began a circling maneuver around the wagons, launching a steady barrage of arrows and bullets.

When the Indians began circling, Amos began firing at the horses rather than the men. He saw the man to his left go down with an arrow through his shoulder. Christine ran to his aid. He kept firing, trying to make every shot count.

Ross was still shouting orders, his voice having taken on a new urgency. "Steady now! Lead 'em! Lead 'em! Shoot the horses! You women, help the wounded!"

A horse reared and neighed in pain, an arrow protruding from its rump. A young boy ran to comfort the animal and was shot in the back. A woman ran to the child and took his limp form in her arms, rocking him back and forth, her face contorted with grief. A Comanche charged the wagons and jumped his horse over the barricade. Amos shot him and he pitched from his horse. He leapt up and charged the nearest settler before a dozen shots rang out and he fell for good.

Thirty minutes into the battle, Iron Jacket raised his lance and the Indians retreated. The settlers let out a lusty cheer that was cut short when the Comanches broke off their retreat just out of rifle range.

The plains Indians were successful for decades against the larger, better-armed United States Army for two reasons: one, they knew the territory like the back of their hand, and two, they didn't engage unless they had the advantage of numbers or surprise. They rarely fought for fighting's sake. Iron Jacket had paused to weigh the risks and rewards of pursuing this engagement. The wagon train wasn't going anywhere.

The settlers used the respite to tend to the wounded, remove the dead, and take some nourishment. Ross knew another test was coming, and he did his best to prepare his people.

"You folks did good. We gave 'em a nose full of needles. Now they got to decide if takin' this train is worth the price they gon' to have to pay. I figure they'll make one more run at us. So get ready to fight for everything you came out here to claim. Remember, they're horse soldiers, so killin' a horse is near 'bout as good as killin' a man."

The second attack started with a group of braves riding close enough to shoot fire arrows into the wagons. Several of them caught fire, and while the settlers were dealing with this, Iron Jacket launched his next assault. Forty or so archers fired arrows in a rainbow trajectory that brought them down behind the settlers' defenses. The hail of arrows wreaked the desired havoc. Humans and animals were randomly wounded or killed. Amos pulled Christine under a wagon with him. The settlers' nerves were beginning to fray under Iron Jacket's multi-tiered assault.

Iron Jacket raised his lance and the main body of warriors charged the camp. The settlers responded with desultory fire. Ross's Sharps rifle boomed, and one of the Comanches threw up his arm and tumbled into the grass.

"Shoot 'em! Shoot 'em, goddammit!"

The settlers responded by firing in unison with deadly accuracy. The Comanches once again began moving in a circle around the wagons, but this time the circle was tightening. One group of assailants fired bullets and another continued to fire arcing arrows. Most of the settlers had taken cover under their wagons, but this limited their view of the field of battle. One after another, warriors were breaching the circle. The settlers shot the first few interlopers but then the combat devolved to hand-to-hand. Amos shot one Indian in the stomach and rose to meet another who charged, tomahawk in hand. The fury of the Comanche's assault drove Amos back against the wagon. The brave raised his hatchet to split Amos's skull. Christine shot the Comanche in the back before the axe could descend. Amos grabbed her pistol, placed her behind him, and prepared to keep his promise to her father.

In the distance, Amos heard an incongruous sound. It was the ringing staccato of a trumpet followed by a volley of fresh gunfire. At a shouted signal from their chief, the Indians who had breached the circle turned and rode back to their comrades. Amos pulled Christine back under a wagon, from which vantage point they saw a cavalry troop comprised entirely of black men descending on the Comanches like a grass fire in a high wind.

Iron Jacket led his warriors in retreat with the soldiers in furious pursuit. One rider broke off from the pursuing troop and rode toward the wagon train at breakneck speed. He was not in uniform and rode an Appaloosa stallion recently acquired as a spoil of war. He rode through a break in the circle caused by a smoldering wagon and reined his horse so hard that the animal practically sat on its haunches.

Amos saw his brother leap from the saddle and turn in a circle, his Colt drawn. Amos crawled from beneath his wagon with Christine in tow and ran to Joe and embraced him.

Joe returned his brother's embrace. "I was afraid I'd be too late," Joe said. "I was afraid . . ." He broke off and just let the relief wash over him.

"You made it, boy," Amos said, holding Joe at arm's length. "When I saw them Injuns, I thought I'd lost you all over again." He peered closely at Joe. "Not a scratch. Not a scratch. Thank Jesus!"

They were interrupted by a grunt from behind them. Joe spun around and drew his Colt in one fluid motion. The Comanche whom Amos had shot in the stomach was struggling to sit up, a pistol in his hand. Joe shot the man and he collapsed backward.

He went over to examine the body and saw the man was wearing John Parker's two-gun rig. Sadness and rage welled up inside him as the fate of his friend was fully confirmed. He unbuckled the holster from the Indian's waist and handed it to Amos.

"Damn! Damn!" Amos said, shaking his head.

Joe surveyed the scene around him. People were dumping water and dirt on burning wagons to extinguish them. Several people lay still on the ground while others were having their wounds attended by friends. Captain Ross moved from wagon to wagon, offering words of solace or encouragement. People spoke in hushed tones as if they were uncertain how to behave under these unfamiliar circumstances.

By the time they had verified their casualties and extinguished the remaining fires, a squad of cavalrymen rode back into camp. They were led by Sergeant Ishmael Stanhope, a five-foot-ten-inch bull of a man with walnut-colored skin whose head and face—except for a bristling gray-streaked mustache—were both cleanly shaven beneath his slouch hat. He dismounted and walked over to Walker.

"Are your people all right, Corporal?" The fact that Walker no longer wore the uniform mattered little to Sergeant Stanhope.

"Most of 'em, Sergeant," Walker said.

"Iron Jacket and his cutthroats are runnin' like scared rabbits, but now that we got 'em in our sights, I guarantee ya, there's gon' be a reckonin'. The captain sent me back to escort you folks out of the territory."

"Much obliged, Sergeant. Sergeant Ishmael Stanhope, this is my brother Amos and this is our wagon master, Justin Ross," he said indicating the men standing to the right and left of him. Ross stepped forward and offered his hand.

"Sergeant, you and your men are a sight for sore eyes. I don't think we woulda lasted much longer without your help," Ross said.

"Well, it was lucky we ran into young Walker while we was huntin' Iron Jacket. He told us your outfit was directly in that scoundrel's path, so we come lickety-split. Looks like you folks gave as good as you got heah today. But rest assured that what y'all started, the Tenth Cavalry will finish."

They loaded up the wagons and prepared to move on. Behind them, they left a charred wagon frame and five fresh graves. In one of them lay the carpenter and family man, James Archer.

27

Two weeks later, they crossed the border into Kansas. Their destination lay in the northeast corner of the state. Sergeant Stanhope's orders were to return to his base, Fort Scott, once he had escorted the wagon train across the border. Ross decided to accompany the troop to the fort so the train could resupply itself for the final leg of its journey.

In the weeks since the Indian raid, Amos had spent the bulk of his time consoling and caring for James Archer's family. He drove their wagon now while Joe attended to his. Christine and her mother leaned on each other for emotional support. Their tears were frequent and unexpected like summer rain. Ethan became silent and withdrawn. His twelve-year-old insouciance seemed to have perished along with his father. Amos let the boy have his grief but kept him engaged with life by assigning him a myriad of mundane tasks. From time to time, he sent the boy to keep Joe company in his wagon.

Joe did his best to entertain the lost child. He let him drive the team and taught him horse lore. After a time, Ethan came to ride with Joe of his own accord.

In search of fodder for conversation, Joe told Ethan about his boyhood on the Walker plantation and how that life abruptly ended.

In a way, Joe's loss mirrored Ethan's, and he hoped the boy would feel a connection based upon that fact.

One day, out of the blue, Ethan asked, "Do you believe in heaven?"

"Yes, I do."

"Do you believe my daddy is in heaven?"

"If anybody is in heaven, your daddy is."

"So if I go to heaven, I'll see him again?"

"Yep."

"So, how do I get to heaven?"

Joe paused a moment. He chose his next words carefully. "Believe in God, don't lie, don't steal, and don't hurt nobody who ain't tryin' to hurt you or people you care about."

The boy pondered this awhile. Then he said, "I wish I could see my daddy now."

"I know how you feel, but you got a lot of livin' to do yet. But mebbe you can take some comfort in knowing that he can see you."

"He can?"

"Uh-huh. Just like my daddy and mama can see me. Everyday, I try to do somethin' to make 'em proud. Do you know what I think makes them mos' proud?"

"What?"

"When I try to help somebody," Walker said.

After that exchange, Ethan's mood seemed to take a turn for the better. First his smile returned from hiatus, followed by his laughter and then his curiosity.

One evening, Joe joined Amos and the Archer family for supper. Upon seeing Joe, Mrs. Archer came to him and put her arms around him and gave him an enveloping hug. "Thank you for bringing our Ethan back to us," she said with tears in her eyes.

Joe was discomfited by the depth of her emotion. He tried to make a joke to break the spell. "Yessum, he hadn't gone far."

That evening, Ethan demonstrated his old appetite and an attitude toward his sister and mother that was both empathic and protective. With Walker's help, he had taken a decisive step on the road to manhood.

28

They arrived at Fort Riley in mid-August. The sight of the fort took Joe back to his time in the military. The fort occupied roughly an acre of land that included barracks, a stockade, the post's exchange, and the company's headquarters. The yellowish buildings were made of native limestone. The American flag flew above the headquarters and also from a twenty-foot-high lookout tower at the front of the enclave.

There were teepees outside the fort, occupied by so-called "tame" Indians who traded with and worked for the army in various capacities. The air was filled with the odors from their cooking pots. Joe noted that the Indians moving between the teepees and back and forth from the fort proper were unarmed.

The fort was the home of the Seventh Cavalry, 250 soldiers under the command of Lt. Colonel George Armstrong Custer. While there, the black settlers repaired damaged equipment and replenished their depleted larders.

The entire train's spirits lifted within the security of the fort's barricade. Amos had waited as long as he could, so two days after they arrived, he asked Christine to be his wife. She said yes and they were married by the fort's chaplain. When Amos gave Christine the diamond ring he had confiscated from John Poteet's safe, her eyes shone as bright as the gem itself. The wedding party that ensued was a further balm to the settlers' battered morale.

The next day, Joe's head was throbbing from his first hangover. He was glad he did not have to sit on a jostling wagon seat for twenty or so miles that day. He was finishing his second cup of coffee when Amos came to his wagon carrying an object wrapped in an army blanket.

"Well, if it ain't the newlywed," Joe said with feigned seriousness. "I'm surprised you even left your quarters today."

"Well, I had to bring you your birthday present," Amos said, holding out the blanket. Joe hadn't celebrated his birthday in a dozen years, and the fact that Amos remembered it the day after his nuptials brought a lump to his throat. He unwrapped the blanket and within its folds found a brand new Henry repeating rifle and two boxes of cartridges.

"This is too much," Joe said, not trusting himself to say much else.

"You already saved my life twice. If you gon' make a habit out of it, I want you to have the best weapon possible. Besides, I got a lot of catchin' up to do on yo birthdays."

Joe went to his brother and embraced him. Momentarily, they patted each other's backs and stepped back self-consciously. Joe took the rifle, upon which he would rely in countless future situations, and placed it in his wagon. When he returned, he had the Comanche tomahawk in his hand. "I missed a lot of yo' birthdays, too, so here's somethin' for you," he said holding out the war hatchet. "It saved my life. Maybe someday it'll save yours."

Amos tucked the tomahawk in his belt. "I best be gittin' back to my wife." He savored the words like a man tasting vintage wine. As Amos left Joe's camp, he passed Ethan coming to it. "Mawnin', Ethan."

"Morning, sir."

Joe greeted the boy in turn. "Hey, young buck. You et yet?"

"Hey, Mr. Joe. Yep, I et, but if you ain't, I'll join you for manners sake," Ethan said, mimicking Joe's rough grammar.

"That's mighty kind of ya," Joe said with a smile.

After breakfast, they went for a ride. Joe was taking every opportunity to work the Appaloosa, whom he had named Dice because of his spotted coat. The stallion was worthy of a chief with his arched neck, intelligent eyes, and effortless gait. Joe put him through his paces, using the subtle tactile language of horse and rider. Ethan did his best to keep pace on the small roan he was riding.

Five miles outside the fort, they stopped to give the animals a rest. Ethan took this opportunity to flex his curiosity. "What is Amos to me now?"

"He's your brother-in-law."

"And what are you to me?"

"Same as before—your partner."

"Partner?" Ethan sounded disappointed.

"We look out for each other and share our grubstake. And if one of us ever gets in trouble, the other one will come a runnin'. A man can have a passel of brother-in-laws, but he only has one or two good pards in life," Joe said.

Ethan's look of disappointment was replaced by one of dawning realization. "Partners," he said softly.

29

They left Fort Riley feeling fortified in body and spirit. The two-week journey to Atchison County was uneventful. They joined a growing contingent of black settlers who were homesteading in and around Atchison, Kansas, a small town in northeastern Kansas located along the Missouri River. Since Atchison had the distinction of being settled largely by black folk, it offered Joe a sense of security and belonging that carried over from the wagon train. "Captain" Justin Ross left them in Atchison, with many a heartfelt "good-bye" and "Godspeed," to return east to form another wagon train.

Joe, Amos, and the Archers went right to work putting down roots. Using the cash he called "Poteet's inheritance," Amos purchased 250 acres of land on the outskirts of town. On it they built a "proper" house of milled lumber that would accommodate their blended family. It was two stories high with a parlor, pantry, and kitchen on the first floor and three bedrooms on the second floor. With the help of their neighbors, they also raised a barn to accommodate their livestock. They finished their building just in time for winter.

During the first snowfall, Joe and Amos stood in their front yard, faces upturned to the unfamiliar precipitation.

"Ain't this one of God's miracles, Jaybird?" Amos said, letting a few flakes fall on his tongue.

"I reckon so," Joe said, extending his hand for a similar anointing.

"What d'ya you think Mama and Daddy would say if they was here now?"

"They'd say, you done right by all of us," Joe said.

Amos put his arm around Joe's shoulders and they stood in silence, giving thanks for the providence that had led them safely through the wilderness to this place—their home.

During that first winter, they occupied themselves with various pursuits, some old, some new. Amos built furniture, hauled stones for a fireplace, and planned his spring itinerary. Joe found work assisting the town smithy. And Christine took a job teaching at the local school where Ethan was promptly enrolled. Mrs. Archer busied herself keeping house and cooking and sewing for the family.

The hardships of the trail were exchanged for the mundane concerns of domestic life. Joe grew accustomed to home-cooked meals, clean sheets, and sleeping without a gun near his hand. He, too, took advantage of Christine's tutelage and began to envision a day when his work would not necessarily involve toil and sweat.

When spring came, they dug a well, planted a large garden, and sowed their "cash crops"—an acre of corn, an acre of oats, and two acres of wheat. Amos also bought a rooster, a dozen hens, two hogs, and a milking cow. Tending the livestock and the garden became Ethan's chores, although Joe helped him with the animals and Mrs. Archer loved working in the garden. Under her watchful eye, the plot yielded a multitude of fresh vegetables that enriched the family's diet and flowers that brightened their surroundings with rainbows of color and delightful fragrances. Joe provided fresh meat for her various savory recipes.

On one particular day in the middle of summer, Joe took his Henry and went in search of venison. There was a dense wood bordering their property, a dark cluster consisting of mostly sycamore and white pine, where Joe had found both small and large game in abundance. The air was damp with humidity, and Joe's cotton shirt stuck to his body. He paused and took a drink from his canteen.

He rode Dice into a clearing and left him long tethered to a tree, contentedly munching grass. Proceeding on foot, Joe kept a sharp eye out for game sign.

Deeper in the woods, Joe was surprised by a horse that burst out of a grove and ran directly toward him. As the panicked animal bolted past him, Joe noticed that it was bleeding from wounds across its chest. He levered a round into his Henry and ran in the direction from which the pony had come.

Five minutes later he heard the roaring of what could only be a big bear. Joe parted a curtain of low-hanging pine branches to see an Indian with his back against a tree facing a huge black bear that advanced on its hind legs. The man's left arm was bleeding profusely, and he uttered a chant that was both defiant and resigned. The Indian was a shade under six feet tall and the bear towered over him. Joe fired and hit the bear in the back. The animal turned, dropped to all fours, and charged his new assailant. Joe fired round after round, trying to control his breathing.

The bear kept coming and Joe kept firing. Eight feet away, the brute stumbled then rose on his hind legs and staggered forward. Joe pulled the trigger and the hammer clicked on an empty chamber. Discarding his rifle, Joe pulled his Colt and fanned the hammer, watching tufts of fur fly from the animal's chest and stomach. The bear dropped at Joe's feet with a final ferocious grunt.

Joe retrieved the Henry and reloaded. He prodded the bear with his foot, rifle at the ready. The animal remained motionless. He approached the wounded man while reloading his revolver. The man had slumped to a sitting position with his back against the tree. At Walker's approach, he sheathed his knife and raised his hand in a salute.

"Peace, my brother. It seems I owe you my life. The bear would have taken me. I was already singing my death song. I am William Adams of the Wolf Clan."

"What tribe?" Walker asked, remembering his last encounter with red men.

"Cherokee," the man said.

Walker's grandfather on his father's side had been Cherokee. He holstered his revolver and knelt next to the wounded man. "Can I look at that arm?" Walker asked.

"Yes."

Walker pulled back the bloody sleeve to reveal Adams's forearm, which was clawed to the bone and pouring blood. He opened his canteen and washed the wound. Then he removed his neckerchief and tightly wrapped it around Adams's arm. Adams grimaced but made no sound as Joe cut away his sleeve to fashion a sling.

"We got to get you to a doctor," Walker said. "There's one in Atchison."

"My horse?"

"Probably halfway to Texas by now," Walker said.

He helped Adams to his feet and placed the Indian's good arm over his shoulder. He began walking them back toward the place he had left Dice. Halfway to their destination, Adams passed out. Joe slung him over his shoulders and trotted on. He cursed himself for having tethered Dice.

By the time he reached his horse, Joe's shirt was streaked with red. Dice neighed nervously at the smell of blood. Joe soothed him with his voice and hands and then wrestled Adams onto Dice's back and climbed on behind him. Joe kicked Dice's flanks and they headed for town.

Thirty minutes later they arrived at the doctor's office, a neat one-story building in the center of town. Adams was semiconscious and singing again. Joe lifted him down and carried him into the office.

"Dr. Peters! Dr. Peters!"

Martin Peters, a bespectacled middle-aged white man with thinning blond hair and a pleasant open face came from the back room with a half-eaten sandwich in his hand.

"Doc, this man got attacked by a bear. He's lost a lot of blood."

"Bring him in here. "

Walker lifted Adams in his arms and carried him into the doctor's examining room where he placed him on one of several beds covered with white sheets. The doctor was already washing his hands.

"I'm going to have to stitch dose vounds and I don't haf time to sedate him, so you're going to haf to help me keep him still."

Walker sat at the head of the bed and held Adams's bicep while the doctor sutured his tattered forearm. Adams uttered sporadic grunts of pain, and sweat broke out on his face, but otherwise he was compliant.

When the operation was finished, Adams said, "Thank you," and then lay back and closed his eyes.

"I guess dey don't call dem the civilized tribe for nothing," Dr. Peters said.

Back in the outer office, Joe asked, "What now?"

"Now, ve vait and see. If dat arm becomes infected, he could lose it and a lot more."

The next day, Joe came by the doctor's office to check on William Adams. He noticed there were three horses tethered to the hitching post that sported blankets instead of saddles. He proceeded to the door and knocked. Dr. Peters opened the door and a smile wreathed his pleasant face.

"Vell, speak of the devil . . ." he said. "Come on in, Joseph. Dere is a man here who is very anxious to meet you."

There were two Indians in Dr. Peters's office. Judging by their clothing and features, Joe surmised they were Cherokee. One was about Joe's height with a lithe, sinewy build. The other was three inches shorter and built like a wrestler. Their smooth skin and pitch-black hair made it difficult to guess their ages. Just then, another man came out of the infirmary with his arm around William's shoulder. The resemblance between them was obvious. The older man left William's side and advanced on Joe with his hand extended.

"Mr. Walker?"

"Yessuh."

"I am William's father, Chief Joseph Adams and your eternal benefactor."

He grabbed Joe's elbow and then his hand in a grip that placed the backs of their hands facing each other's chests, adding to the young man's discomfort. Joe had merely come to look in on his new friend.

"Pleased to make your acquaintance, suh," Joe said, not sure exactly what a benefactor was. William stood in the background, smiling at Joe's abashment.

"When William's horse returned without him, we feared the worst. But he's alive because of you. I owe you a debt I can never repay, but you must let me try," the chief said.

"There's no debt to repay, suh. Things just kinda happened all at once. In that situation, anybody woulda done what I did."

The chief ignored Joe's disclaimer. "When William is able to travel, you will come to our village for a visit and we will show you how the Wolf Clan treats its allies."

Joe was smart enough to know that it would have been the height of insult to decline the chief's offer. So he gave his assent. After all, it was only one visit. Thus began his introduction to the Wolf Clan.

30

The Cherokee were one of the five so-called civilized tribes. They had their own spoken and written language, producing almost universal literacy among the people. Most of them also spoke English or French, having been proselytized by European missionaries for over a century. Indeed, Chief Joseph spoke five languages. The Cherokee were divided in their allegiance during the Civil War. The Wolf Clan sided with the Union.

After the war, Chief Joseph accompanied a contingent of Cherokee leaders to Washington to take part in peace negotiations. A grateful nation granted his clan the land, water, and mineral rights to eight hundred acres in the Arkansas River basin along the Kansas-Colorado border.

The first time he visited William's village, Joe was impressed by its size. He was met a mile outside the gates by a welcoming committee comprised of William, Chief Joseph, and ten braves. They approached him with shouts and hands raised palms outward. William broke away from the crowd and rode to Joe's side, smiling broadly. He reached out to Joe and they clasped forearms.

"Welcome, brother! You are truly a man of your word."

"I told you I'd come," Joe said, smiling.

Chief Joseph rode up with his remaining entourage. "Joseph, my friend, we have eagerly awaited this day. You are our most honored guest. As long as you are among us, my lodge is your lodge. Tonight we will feast and become better acquainted. Tomorrow there will be more feasting and games."

He led the group back to the compound. The village and its confines covered five acres and were occupied by about five hundred people. They lived in wikiups, circular huts about twenty feet in diameter consisting of a wooden frame covered with long grasses and brush. A fifteen-foot outer wall surrounded roughly sixty of these dwellings. In the middle of the compound was a longhouse for communal gatherings.

The people had heard of Joe's exploits and they gave him a hero's welcome. Men, women, and children ran to greet him, some of them literally skipping. The nearness of the crowd and the cacophony of their voices caused Dice to dance nervously. Joe patted the stallion's neck and made the chirping sound that served to soothe or summon him.

After Joe was given a tour of the village, he joined the tribe in the longhouse for a repast that included venison, buffalo tongue, baked potatoes, pemmican, and honey cakes. During the meal, his education about the Wolf Clan began.

The Wolf Clan (Aniwaya) was the largest of the seven Cherokee clans. The wolf was regarded as a protector by the Cherokee people and, therefore, members of the clan were expected to defend the tribe at all costs. The war chief was usually selected from the Wolf Clan. Chief Joseph was, in fact, the war chief of the Cherokee nation and had represented them at the peace talks in Washington, DC, after the Civil War.

After supper, Joe sat and smoked with the men of the tribe. He was relieved to find himself among comrades at arms. He told them about his recent sojourn as a US cavalryman, his life as a slave in Tennessee and Louisiana, and his journey west with the Ross wagon train. The Indians sat in rapt attention as he recounted his history. Joe saved the most intriguing revelation for last.

"According to my daddy, his grandfather on his mother's side was a Cherokee Indian."

A wave of murmurs rippled through the crowd.

Chief Joseph leaned forward. "Joseph, tell us about this man."

"I don't know much about him otha than his name, Richard Gray Horse."

The men gave a collective gasp, and Chief Joseph stood up and grasped Joe by the shoulders.

"Ah-ni-sa-ho-ni! You are Bear Clan!" Apparently, Gray Horse was a well-known surname and identified Joe's forebear as part of the clan known variously as the Blue Clan, Wild Cat Clan, Bear Clan, or Panther Clan.

So it came to pass that, after many retellings, the story of Joe's encounter with the black bear took on a supernatural dimension, wherein he was transmogrified into a bear to kill the bear that attacked William. He was, therefore, believed to possess "strong medicine." Consequently, Joe was treated with the respect afforded a medicine man.

What Joe had intended to be a two-day visit to the village turned into a weeklong stay. He and his hosts engaged in storytelling, shooting, wrestling, and riding contests. Joe, a skilled rider himself, marveled at the horsemanship of the Cherokee warriors. He saw braves perform feats with lance and bow while riding bareback that he had no hope of duplicating. The Cherokee were equally impressed by his skill with a gun and with his saber. When it came to wrestling, Joe learned that height and weight were no advantage.

One evening at the communal meal, Joe noticed a stunningly beautiful woman attending Chief Joseph and a swarthy man seated beside him. She was about Joe's age with raven-black hair that hung to the middle of her back. This glorious veil was complemented by a dusky rose complexion, high cheekbones, and a full mouth that turned up slightly at the corners. The deerskin calf-length dress she wore was embellished by her curvaceous body. Joe stared at her as one might stare at a rose in the desert.

Joe leaned over to William, seated beside him, and asked sotto voce, "Who is that?"

"That is my cousin Martha. She is the chief's niece and the tribe's medicine woman. She, along with you and Dr. Peters, is the reason I'm alive today. Would you like to meet her?"

Before Joe could reply, William called out to the young woman. "Martha, please come and meet our guest. He is asking about you."

Joe kicked William under the table and William responded with a quizzical look while shrugging his shoulders.

She came to the place where Joe and William were seated and stood in front of them somewhat self-consciously.

"Martha White Horn, this is Joseph Walker, the man who saved my life."

Martha inclined her head as though addressing an elder. "It is an honor to meet you, Mr. Walker. My family is forever in your debt."

"Ma'am, your hospitality has already paid any debt you mighta owed," Joe said, drinking in her appeal with his eyes and ears.

The two of them were suddenly out of words but kept staring at each other.

William interceded. "Maybe you'll meet again under less formal circumstances."

"It would be a pleasure," Joe said, emphasizing the last word.

Martha smiled and nodded and returned to her duties.

Joe spent the rest of the meal sneaking glances in her direction and plotting ways he might contrive to speak to her again.

When Joe prepared to leave on the seventh day, William came to him leading two horses, a palomino filly and a black stallion, both three years old.

"A gift for you," he said, holding out the reins.

Joe nodded and took the leads. "Thank you," he said. He had been expecting this. He pulled his telescope from his saddlebag and handed it to William. "A gift for you," he said.

William accepted the telescope with a grunt of appreciation. "You must come again. There is still much for us to say and do."

"I'll be back. Count on it. Thank y'all for your hospitality," Joe said.

"Thank you for my life."

Joe rode away. Now that the formalities were out of the way, he was already looking forward to his next visit.

31

True to his word, Joe became a regular visitor to the Cherokee village. That summer and fall, he and William developed a friendship that bordered on brotherhood. Joe learned to speak and read the Cherokee language. He also learned to shoot a bow, throw a knife or a tomahawk, ride bareback, and track game. When Chief Joseph suggested he become a member of the clan, Joe agreed without hesitation.

The initiation rite involved a protracted ceremony in a sweat lodge where Joe went without food or sleep until he had a vision that would guide his steps for the rest of his life. Joe sat in the sweat lodge wearing only a loincloth. He took deep inhalations from a medicine pipe laced with peyote. As the smoke filled his lungs, he felt light-headed and nauseous. He leaned to the side and vomited, emptying his stomach. The men in attendance chanted sonorously while pouring water over heated stones to produce steam. Sweat poured from Joe's body, adding to his sense of weightlessness. His vision blurred and his ears buzzed as though he were in a hive of angry bees. Hours passed.

Outside the sweat lodge, village life went on unabated. At dinnertime, Joe's stomach began to growl. He was given a thin broth that tasted of chicken. The drumming and chanting continued. Joe could not remember a time without their accompaniment. His very nerves thrummed with the incessant beat.

At some point in the night, Joe experienced the sensation of observing himself from a position above his head near the top of the lodge. He could see his glistening body and those of the medicine men around him beating their spirit-summoning drums. And then Joe was no longer in the lodge. Instead, he stood on a misty plain surrounded by skillfully carved totems with human bodies and animal heads—bird, bear, puma, wolf, deer, and raccoon. Two of the totems were fully human. One was a woman with long, intricately braided hair. The other was a man whose skin was the color of red paint. Before his astonished eyes, the figures came to life and began dancing in a circle, their feet creating a hypnotic drumming on the packed red earth. Their eyes burned yellow and red like smoldering embers. Staring into those eyes, Joe was transported back in time.

Joe awoke in a dark place. He smelled the stench of feces, vomit, putrefaction, and unwashed bodies. He was chained hand and foot and was unable to sit up or roll over. He heard the beating of waves against a wooden hull and smelled the briny odor of the sea. He heard lamentations in a dozen languages. The dancing beasts had transported him to an inner circle of hell, and he feared he would remain there for eternity. But then, suddenly, he was jerked back in time again to find himself walking beneath a scorching sun in a line of shackled black men, women, and children. They were marching through golden grass dotted by trees that rose like knotted sentinels on an endless plain. Joe saw elephants, giraffes, and zebras—animals he recognized from his alphabet primer—and strange doglike creatures with sloping hindquarters, spotted fur, and pointed ears.

The men who were their drivers were also black and goaded them with lash and club. They wore leather skirts, along with metal bracelets around their biceps and ankles. Their faces were scarred with symmetrical tattoos. Joe felt the hot lick of a lash across his shoulders.

"Move, dirt digger," one of his captors said.

Joe tore his eyes away from the arresting sights around him and quickened his pace. His feet were swollen and bleeding, and his throat was parched with thirst. He looked up and saw vultures circling slowly in a cobalt sky. Before he could complete this trail of tears, the drumming started, the sky went dark, and he was transported again.

This time, he awoke to find himself moving in a semicircle of warriors who were armed with spears and shields. They were advancing toward a grove of thorn bushes and chanting in a low chorus. There were low growls coming from the grove. As they approached, Joe stepped out of the line and moved alone into the bush with his spear and shield raised.

As he moved further into the grove, the growling intensified and, suddenly, he was confronted by four hundred pounds of charging feline fury. Joe's mouth became as dry as dust and his heart drummed in his chest. As the lion leapt, he stepped forward and thrust the blade of his spear into its chest.

Joe's perspective shifted and he was observing the scene from above. He saw the lion knock him over and then turn to close for the kill, raking at the spear protruding from its chest. The lion charged again and Joe used his shield to ward off its teeth and claws while plunging his short spear into its throat. Blood suddenly poured from its nose and mouth. The cat coughed once and fell to its knees then rolled on its side where it lay twitching. Joe raised his fist and gave a triumphant shout.

Joe looked into his ancestor's eyes and felt the chain that linked them across generations. He felt the spirits of his African forebears pour into him like rainwater into a cistern. In that moment, his purpose in life became clear to him—*survive.*

Joe felt a whirling, sucking sensation as if he were caught in a maelstrom but instead of water, people and events swirled around him. He caught glimpses of births, deaths, feasts, and battles all involving people who shared his blood. And then he was transported a third and final time.

When he awoke, he was once again within the familiar confines of the sweat lodge, his journey complete. They brought him food and mare's milk and wrapped him in blankets before taking him out into the autumn air. The people treated him with reverence, for he was newly returned from the spirit world. It took another day for him to become fully reoriented.

After his vision quest, Joe became an adopted member of the Wolf Clan. He had entered the spirit world and communed with his ancestors. As a result, he felt rooted in two continents. The Great Spirit had given him an incredible gift. How he would use it was yet to be determined.

32

When Joe wasn't at the Cherokee village, he was helping Amos work the farm. They planted and harvested their cash crops and managed to break even from their sale that year. Joe saddle broke the two horses William Adams had given him and gave the filly, Sunshine, to Christine and the stallion, Shadow, to Amos. Both were taken aback by his generosity and tried to refuse, but Joe would have none of it.

"Y'all are my family. Besides, I cain't ride but one horse at a time."

Amos was too busy to properly exercise Shadow, so that task often fell to Ethan, who was more than happy to oblige. Under Joe's tutelage, the boy became a skilled and patient horseman. After Joe told the family about his and Amos's probable membership in the Bear Clan, the boy began to accompany him on his trips to the Cherokee village. He was restrained with the Indians at first, but his curiosity eventually overcame his shyness and he became a part of the cohort of young aspiring warriors who constantly challenged each other in games of strength, speed, and endurance designed to hone their survival skills.

As a result of this regimen, Ethan gradually lost his boyish physique and took on the lean, muscular build of the Cherokee boys. He adopted their dress, their speech, and their youthful arrogance. The Cherokee called him "E-ton" and treated him like one of their own.

Joe was living a life he could not have imagined as a youth. Instead of one family, he had two. His hard work put money in his own pocket, not some master's, and no man held sway over him. He even relaxed his vigilance concerning pursuit from the east. One feature, however, caused him discomfiture.

Christine had grown into a beautiful, vivacious woman. Her skin was as soft and lustrous as brushed velvet, her figure was firm and voluptuous, and her smile was the harbinger of unfathomable delights. Her sense of humor, kindness, and lack of pretension only served to magnify her physical beauty. Amos loved her madly and unconditionally, and Ethan's teasing thinly veiled his doting affection. That left Joseph to mediate an argument between his head and his heart. The more he tried to ignore his sister-in-law's charms, the more they were made evident to him. At times, he found himself staring at her involuntarily. Sometimes she would be staring back, then they both would avert their eyes as if on cue.

The times they were alone together were the best or the worst, depending upon whether his heart or his head was in control. He accompanied her the first time she rode Sunshine. By then, the spirited filly was already bonded to Christine. This was due to Christine's habit of grooming her daily and feeding her treats at the drop of a hat. They rode across their property and into a wide meadow that was dotted with wild flowers. It was a perfect summer day, and Christine could not contain her delight.

"Oh, Joseph, she's just perfect for me. Her gait is like sitting in a rocking chair, and she's as gentle as a lamb. How did you know we'd be so good together?"

"Two pretty ladies. Why wouldn't ya'll get along?"

"No, seriously," she said blushing.

"Seriously, all I did was saddle break her. You won her trust. That's why you're good together."

They dismounted and walked to a giant oak tree. Christine was wearing wool trousers with rolled cuffs, a blue gingham shirt, and a wide-brimmed Stetson hat that protected her exquisite face from the sun. The wind and activity of the ride caused her to glow like a lit candle. Joe pretended to check her rig in order to divert his attention from the vision in front of him.

"This stirrup length suit you?"

"It's just right," she said. She sat down with her back to the tree trunk. Joe sat down beside her. A blue jay scolded them from a high branch and then flew off to less-crowded environs. Chipmunks and lizards scurried in the grass. A red-tailed hawk circled high above. Joe noticed all these things, though Christine appeared to be oblivious.

Christine closed her eyes and took a deep breath. "The air out here is different from back home—dry and clean, like it's been scrubbed. Joe, I hope you won't think less of me for saying this, but, in spite of everything, I'm glad we came west."

"Me too," Joe said. They sat in silence, enjoying the day and the respite from care.

Apropos of nothing, Christine asked, "Have you been studying your lessons?"

"Yes, ma'am."

"How many times do I have to tell you not to call me ma'am. I'm not your auntie."

"Yes . . . Mrs. Walker."

Christine sighed in exasperation, which brought a smile to the corners of Joe's mouth. "Have you been reading the Bible I gave you?"

"Uh-huh, but a lotta them words don't quite fit my tongue."

"Well, just sound them out the way I taught you. There's no hurry."

"Yes, Christine."

This student-teacher banter kept their minds off other, riskier dialogues.

Nevertheless, Joe changed the subject. "Seems like new folks are comin' in every day, black and white. Chief Joseph said he had to run some squatters off Cherokee land last week. They didn't take too kindly to it. The army's supposed to see to it that that don't happen, but I guess they're spread pretty thin."

"Do you think the Cherokee could lose their land?"

"According to the treaty they signed in Washington, it's theirs as long as the sun rises, the wind blows, and the river flows. If somebody tries to move 'em off it, there'll be hell to pay. Pardon my language."

"Oh, I've heard much worse," she said with a smile. "If it came to a fight, who would you side with?"

"I guess I'd have to side with my blood," Joe said.

Christine pondered this for a while. "I hope it doesn't come to that."

"Me too."

Squinting and shading his eyes, Joe looked up at the sky. "Well, I guess we best be headin' back before they send out a search party."

A brief look of disappointment crossed Christine's face before she said, "I guess you're right."

Joe stood up and extended his hands to help her. She took them and rose gracefully. For a moment, they were close enough for him to smell the soap she had washed with that morning and the lilac water she had applied afterwards. They teetered on the brink of an unspoken desire. Then, as if by mutual consent, they stepped back. Joe released her hands and she brushed off the seat of her pants. She abruptly turned, went to Sunshine, and mounted without a look in his direction. Joe followed suit and they rode back home. Little else passed between them for the rest of the day.

33

After the interlude in the meadow, Joe purposefully avoided being alone with Christine. He spent as much time as possible at the Cherokee village to avoid further temptation. He and William hunted and fished all over the reservation. The bond he was establishing with William—and, through him with the Wolf Clan—gave him a feeling of security for reasons that were not altogether apparent. If, someday, his past caught up to him in the form of men who sought to put him behind bars or in the grave, it would be good to have a sanctuary that was outside the jurisdiction of the United States government.

One day when they were returning from a three-day excursion, they came across a group of settlers camped in a canyon on the western edge of the reserve. It was apparent that the settlers had plans to stay. They had already felled trees for permanent structures that were outlined by stakes in the ground. William was adamant that they nip this invasion in the bud, so they approached the encampment with the intention of peacefully ushering the interlopers off Cherokee land.

When they approached the camp, three men came forward with rifles rested at port across their forearms. Joe assessed them with a warrior's eye. The one on the right was middle sized and lean with shoulder-length blond hair and a scraggly beard. He wore a rebel kepi.

His face reminded Joe of a starving ferret. The one in the middle was heavyset with a broad chest, round belly, and tree stump legs that ended in a slew-footed stance.

The man on the right was short, redheaded and doing his best to look menacing, though his darting eyes and bobbing Adam's apple betrayed him. His chest-length beard was streaked with tobacco stains. In addition to the rifles, each man packed a handgun. Two of the men wore their Colts in conventional fashion. The ferret-faced one wore his butt forward.

Hiding in the wagons behind them were three dough-faced women and a passel of children ranging in age from toddlers to adolescents. William held up his right hand, palm outward in the universal sign of peace.

"Hello, folks. I am William Adams, son of Chief Joseph Adams of the Cherokee Wolf Clan, and it seems that you are about to make your homestead on Cherokee land by mistake."

The burly man said, "Our map says this land is outside Injun territory."

"Your map is wrong. This is part of the land of the Cherokee Wolf Clan ceded to us by the president of the United States."

"You say," the burly man replied.

William kept his voice even but Joe saw the muscles tighten in his jaw. "This matter can be decided by a trip to the surveyor's office in Atchinson."

"Well, why don't you make that trip and come back with some proof that this is yo land?" the burly man said.

"I know this is our land. I would suggest you make the trip," William said, his voice no longer accommodating."

"I didn't come all the way from Alabama to be cheated out of what's mine by a buncha redskins," the big man said. His jaw jutted but his tone suggested indecisiveness. Joe began to envision a peaceful resolution to their dispute.

Then the blond man spoke up. "Why don't you and your nigger friend git to steppin' befo we have to bury y'all on this land."

Joe could feel the tiger rousing. He looked the lean man squarely in the eye and said in a voice that would eventually become as recognizable as a calling card, "You wouldn't be the first to try."

The man's upbringing caused him to ignore the warning in Joe's voice. All he saw and heard was a black man back-talking a white man. He swung his rifle up to take aim.

Hours upon hours of gun practice had turned Joe's brain, eye, and hand into one extended organ. He drew and fired before any one else could move. His first bullet went through ferret face's shoulder, causing his weapon to discharge into the ground. Joe fanned his Colt, and his next shot shattered the stock of the big man's rifle. His third bullet snatched the hat from the little man's head. The settlers threw up their hands in unison.

Joe turned to look at William, who was staring at him with naked awe, his hand still on the butt of his pistol. "Ya'll best git on," Joe said.

Indeed, there was no further argument. The settlers packed up their wagons and their wounded and moved on down the trail. Joe and William pulled up their building stakes and made sure their campfires were extinguished before resuming their own journey.

That night after they made camp, William, who had seen Joe shoot only with rifle and bow, could no longer contain his curiosity. "How did you learn to shoot a pistol like that?"

"Practice."

"Practice! I practice. Hell, everybody out here practices. But to draw and hit three targets from horseback at fifteen feet in two eye blinks—that just ain't natural, brother," William said.

Joe nodded. "I've always—"

Dice neighed loudly and pawed the ground. Before Joe could react to the stallion's warning, a shot rang out and he felt a hammer blow to his back. He pitched forward and hit his head on a rock. The last thing he remembered before losing consciousness was the sound of gunfire and William's war cry.

34

Joe came to on a pallet in a Cherokee wickiup. A young woman knelt with her back to him, tending something on a small fire. When Joe tried to sit up, he felt an electric jolt of pain along the right side of his body that elicited an involuntary groan.

The woman turned and he saw it was Christine. Her face was drawn and her eyes puffy and red. She came to him and took his left hand in both of hers. "Joe, you've come back to us. Thank God."

She bent and gently kissed his forehead. If not for the pain that coursed through him with each breath, Joe would have thought he was in heaven.

"Christine. Where am I? How'd I get here? What are you doin' here?"

"Easy, Joseph, one question at a time. You're in Chief Joseph's lodge. William brought you here. And I'm here because—where else would I be?"

"Where's William?"

"He and Amos went after the men who ambushed you."

"How long have I been out?"

"Two days on and off. Dr. Peters came all the way from Atchison to treat you. He said the bullet should have killed you but it hit one of your ribs and then ricocheted through your side and lodged in your arm. He said William's immediate medical attention saved your life. I guess the two of you are even now."

As if on cue, Dr. Peters entered the wickiup, carrying his medical bag. At the sight of Joe conscious, a broad smile wreathed his round face. He greeted Joe in his accented English. "Joseph, it is goot to see you back in der land of der living. It is amazing vot dedicated nursing care can do." He nodded to Christine, who flushed at his acknowledgement of her devotion.

"Doc, thanks for savin' my life. I owe you."

"Don't tank me. Tank Gott and Villiam Adams. All I did vas remove a bullet and set some bones."

"How long am I gon' be laid up?"

"Two or three months depending on how goot a patient you are."

"No way, doc. I gotta catch up with William and Amos." Joe attempted to sit up and felt a lance of pain along his right side that caused him to lie back with a groan.

"No, Joseph, your only job now is to rest and regain your strength. You are among friends and they vill provide you vit excellent care. Villiam and Amos are more dan capable of taking care of demselves."

Joe had no choice but to follow the doctor's orders. Over the next two days, he patiently submitted to Christine's ministrations and Ethan's endless questions. He gradually managed to sit then stand on his own.

On the third day, the war party returned. Joe noted with relief that William rode at the head of the troop. He looked for Amos, a lump of concern growing in his stomach.

William dismounted and walked to Joe and hugged his friend, which caused Joe to groan involuntarily. "I'm sorry brother. I, of all people, should know your wounds are far from healed," William said.

"No bother. I'm just glad to see you back in one piece." He noticed that William's shirt was slashed across the front and there was a bloodstain along the tear. "I see you got cut," Joe said, indicating the bloody gash.

"Yeah. I geed when I shoulda hawed. Nothing to worry about."

"Jaybird!" Amos was coming on the run. "Jaybird! I knew you'd pull through."

Joe's relief was palpable. Seeing his brother's headlong approach, he held up his hand to protect his injured side, but to no avail. Amos grabbed him in a modified bear hug, which elicited a yelp of pain from Joe. "Ow!"

"Oh, my fault. Sorry." Amos immediately curbed his enthusiasm, at least physically. "I didn't know whether to stay with you or go with William. Christine told me to go, that she'd hold down the fort on this end. I figured there wasn't much I could do here but wait, and I wasn't in a waitin' mood. You know what I mean? So I went with William to find the murderin' sumbitches that bushwacked you. So—it seems like ever'thang worked out all right?" His face was a study in conflict.

"I'da done the same thing," Joe said by way of removing any lingering doubts Amos might have had about the choice he made.

"We caught up with the bunch that shot you. Their bushwackin' days are over," Amos said with grim satisfaction.

Joe knew his brother had a tigerish side, but he had never seen it before. This was the man who had killed to obtain his freedom—the man who, no doubt, would kill again to keep it.

That night, despite his wounds, Joe sat with the tribal council to hear the story of William's foray. In the deliberate, ritualistic manner of the Cherokee storyteller, William recounted the following tale.

After he left Joe at the village, William and Amos and ten braves picked up the ambushers' trail and followed it to a large settlement west of the Arkansas River. There were about twenty-five wagons in the group and they, like the smaller group that William and Joe had encountered, had begun the process of putting down stakes. William noticed that the three wagons he and Joe had ushered off the Cherokee reservation were among this group.

There were approximately thirty fighting men in the party. William waited for sundown. When the camp was finally quiet, he and his party moved in, scattered the horses, and set half a dozen wagons on fire. The panic this maneuver created caused the settlers to divide their forces. A group of men went off on foot to catch the stampeded livestock. Amos and a party of six warriors ambushed them, killing them all. They circled back to the camp where William and the remaining braves were attacking the wagons.

William had charged the defenders, and the fighting was hand to hand. The settlers put up a desperate fight, and three Cherokee warriors lost their lives.

Two white men surrendered. One of them was the bearded redhead William and Joe had encountered previously. The other was a hulking, pockmarked fellow with shoulder-length hair in his midtwenties.

When William went to disarm them, the big man drew a knife and slashed him across the chest. William drew his own knife and motioned the man forward. The fight was brief. When it was over, William took the redhead's guns and unloaded them. Then he sent the man back to his party to shepherd the women and children. He made him promise that neither he nor any of his party would ever return to Cherokee land under penalty of death.

Joe was nearing the limit of his physical endurance by the time the story ended. He excused himself and returned to his wickiup, where he tried to sleep. The pain along his right side made sleep nearly impossible, so he reviewed the events of the last week, particularly the part where he allowed himself to be bushwacked and the people who subsequently placed themselves at risk on his behalf. Before finally drifting off, he thanked God for the safe return of both his brothers.

35

Joe awoke with a start, reaching for his gun. The action caused bone to grate against bone along his injured rib cage, and he gasped with pain. He had been dreaming, and in his dream, a giant albino wolf with pink eyes and yellow fangs was leaping for his throat. His instinctive response was like a hot poker to his nervous system. His forehead beaded with sweat, and he tried to take short, shallow breaths to ease the pain. Effortfully, he rose to his feet and went to the water bucket in the corner of the wickiup. He drank deeply, cupped his palm, and splashed his face. He lifted the flap of the wickiup and stepped outside.

It was several hours to dawn. The crisp night air cooled his skin and calmed his nerves. The sky was a canopy of stars. Looking north, Joe spotted the cluster of stars called the Drinking Gourd, the beacon of runaway slaves. Joe started walking. He reached the corral, where a guard accosted him.

"Kagiyusdi?" (Who is it?)

"Joe Walker," Joe said.

Recognizing the black man, the brave grunted and continued his rounds. Joe went to the corral and chirped. A familiar shape emerged from the other side of the enclosure. Dice nickered a greeting and came to Joe. Joe stroked the stallion's muzzle and patted his neck.

"How you doin', fella? Thanks for savin' my bacon. I guess it'll be a while before we go ridin' again. But I'll make sure you get your exercise. They feedin' you okay?" Dice snorted as though he understood Joe's question.

"How about I hunt up some rutabagas or carrots tomorra? I know you'd like that." Since he was a boy on the plantation, Joe had found the company of horses to have a calming effect upon him. As he looked into an uncertain future, he felt momentarily anchored and hopeful in the stallion's presence.

Joe returned to his wickiup just as the sky was turning pink. He figured he might as well start his day. He began the daunting ritual of dressing and washing himself left handed. By the time he finished, the sun was up and the camp was bustling. Chief Joseph stopped to see him. After inquiring about his health, the chief raised a utilitarian but awkward topic.

"Joseph, judging by your appearance, you need someone to cook for you and bathe you until you can do so for yourself. I will send someone around."

Joe was caught off guard. "That won't be necessary, Chief. I can manage."

"You don't have to manage. What kind of host would I be if I allowed you to starve and rot under my roof?"

Joe understood that this was a rhetorical question. He was trying to guess who the chief might send to attend him when William dropped in. His greeting was irreverently fraternal.

"Still loafing, I see. How long is it going to take for you to recover from those scratches?"

"If anyone knows how long it takes to recover from scratches, it'd be you," Joe said.

They laughed at each other's jabs, and William sat down to visit a spell.

Joe took the opportunity to ask a question he had harbored since coming to a week ago. "Now that it's just the two of us, tell me how you got us out of that pickle back at our last camp. I thought we were goners."

"To tell you the truth, I did too. There isn't much to tell. It was cussedness and luck that saved us. The first bit of luck was when they tried to bushwack us—whoever had a bead on me missed. I still pretended I was shot and rolled out of the firelight. From cover, I could see that they were advancing slowly in a half circle. They must've heard about your talent with a gun and were taking no chances. I moved to flank them. I took the man on the end of the line with my knife and then used his gun to shoot another one.

"I started yelling and shooting, moving quick as I could from place to place in the shadows. I wanted them to think there were more than two of us. It must've worked because they panicked and broke ranks. I shot another one as they were retreating, and I think I wounded one as they were riding away. One of the men I killed was that black-haired, husky son of a bitch who braced us at the settlement.

"As soon as I was sure they had lost their stomach for a fight, I came back to you. That's when luck stepped in again. You were still breathing. I treated your wounds the best I could and headed back to the village with you on a travois. The rest you know."

William's simple recounting of a deed that would be celebrated by his clan for generations further marked him as a man of courage and humility. Most men would have been proud merely to be acquainted with such a man. Joe had the privilege of calling him "brother."

Joe said, "I reckon we're even now."

"Yes, my debt of honor is repaid. I no longer need to feel humble in your presence."

"That's what you call humble?"

They looked at each other and laughed out loud. They continued to talk about mundane things, enjoying each other's unstressed company until a female voice from outside the wickiup intervened.

"Mr. Walker, may I come in?"

Joe looked at William with a puzzled expression.

"Do you usually leave your guests standing on your doorstep?" William said with a mischievous grin.

Joe stood up and said, "Come in."

Martha White Horn entered the wickiup. "Excuse me, Mr. Walker. Chief Joseph asked me to make breakfast for you and see if there was anything else you needed." She blushed at the double entendre.

William chose that juncture to take his leave, knowing it would increase Joe's discomfiture. "Well, I guess I'll get on and let you two have your breakfast. Good morning, Martha," he said, nodding to his cousin.

"Good morning, William," she said with a smile that had the effect of polishing silver.

After William left, Martha prepared breakfast and said, "Please eat your food before it gets cold."

Joe's breakfast consisted of scrambled eggs, bacon, cornbread and molasses, and coffee. He hadn't realized how hungry he was. Martha sat patiently while he cleaned his plate. He realized, belatedly, that his appetite had overshadowed his manners. "Thank you, ma'am, for goin' to this bother for me. This was one of the best meals I've had in I don't know when."

"It was no bother at all. It's a way for me to say thank you for what you did for my cousin William. And please call me Martha."

"Well, Martha, William has settled all accounts on that score. And please call me Joseph."

"Not in my uncle's eyes. Besides, you are our guest and we do not expect our guests to fend for themselves, even when they are fully able." The young woman had the carriage and mannerisms of a princess, and Joe was inclined to submit to her will just as he had been similarly inclined with her uncle.

"Yes, ma'am."

"Now there is the matter of your face."

"Pardon?"

"Is it your wish to grow a beard?"

"No, ma'am. I just ain't got the hang of shaving left-handed yet. Last time I tried, I almost cut my throat," he said with an anemic smile.

"Then I will shave you."

"Maybe one of the men could take that on."

"If the chief wanted a man to do it, he would have asked one. Instead, he made it my job. If I neglect it, I will be punished."

"No, I wouldn't want that."

"Good. Do you have a razor?"

"Yes, ma'am."

Joe dutifully retrieved his shaving materials from his saddlebag and handed them to Martha. She built a fire and set water to warm over it. While the water heated, she sharpened Joe's razor.

"You look like you've done this before."

"Yes, my father is a hairy man, and he lets me shave him sometimes because he has stiffness in his fingers. Dr. Peters says it's arthritis. Besides my mother, I'm the only one he lets shave him."

When the water was heated, Martha poured it into a basin and soaked a clean towel in it. She then applied the warm towel to Joe's face. The sensation was blissful. Joe's face was irritated from ingrown hairs and coarse stubble he had been rubbing absent-mindedly throughout the day.

Once the steam had softened his beard, Martha applied soap to it. The touch of her hands and her scent were setting off hormonal alarms in Joe's body. He focused on the intricate patterns of a spider web in the corner of the wickiup to distract himself. The sound of the scrape of the razor across the planes of his face was familiar and soothing.

Martha took her time and did the job as well as any barber could have. When she finished, she stepped back and admired her work. She held up Joe's mirror for him to see the results. He was pleased to see his lean, clean-shaven face staring back at him from the mirror. It helped him, psychologically, to feel like himself again.

After the shave, she cut his hair using scissors and a comb. She trimmed his hair until she could comb it easily backward and forward. Joe's next look in the mirror revealed a young man who, except for his eyes, could have been Martha's age mate.

"Thank you, ma'am. This makes more of a difference than you know. What do I owe you?"

"There is no charge for this. I'll help you with grooming until you no longer need my help. It is my honor to do so."

Her sincerity caused a lump to rise in Joe's throat. "I won't forget your kindness," he said.

"I'll be back later with dinner. I'll also bring you some clean clothes and help you get a bath."

"Ma'am?"

"Chief's orders," she said with a smile. Before he could protest further, she gathered the dishes and was out the door.

True to her word, Martha returned with his midday meal. Afterwards, instead of bathing him, she took him to the sweat lodge where he languished for the better part of an hour. After his pores were cleansed, she gave Joe a blanket and drove him by buckboard to a minor waterfall on a tributary of the Arkansas River. The sparkling water cascaded some twenty feet down a rock face, creating a liquid growl that muted all other sounds. Martha gave him a bar of soap and indicated the waterfall.

"You can wash yourself here. I'll be back by the time you're finished."

Joe bathed under the refreshing spill, taking care to scrub his privates. When Martha returned, he was drying off on the riverbank. She handed him a shirt, breeches, and moccasins that fit surprisingly well. She redressed his wounds, applying a healing salve. Her touch was deft and expert so Joe felt a modicum of pain.

She rubbed some of the ointment on the old lash marks on his back. This probably had no medicinal effect but Joe was extremely moved by the gesture. Finally, she reached into her basket and handed him a large apple.

Joe bit into the fruit and savored its tart-sweet flavor. "Well, I guess I could die now and figure I hadn't missed much."

"Not under my care," she said with a smile.

They rode back to the village. On the way back, she told Joe more about herself. She was the daughter of Chief Joseph's sister, Tessa. She lived in her parents' lodge with her two younger sisters. In addition to her culinary skills, she was a medicine woman. She had used the time Joe was bathing to gather some medicinal roots and herbs from the surrounding woods.

Dr. Peters had heard of her talent for healing and took every opportunity to instruct her in white man's medicine and plumb her knowledge of Cherokee healing lore. She even assisted him in his office from time to time.

Of everything he learned about Martha on that ride, Joe was most interested in the fact that she was still under her father's roof. This raised his hopes to new levels, and he began to hum quietly to himself.

Martha heard his self-serenade and asked, "Are you feeling better?"

"Right as rain! Yes, ma'am, Right as rain."

"Good. My uncle will be pleased."

"I don't know how I'm gon' repay him or you for your kindness."

"You are our guest and our benefactor. No payment is necessary."

They rode on through countryside drenched in sunshine and perfumed by the scent of a dozen varieties of prairie flowers. Joe didn't know how it was possible to feel like you'd known someone you'd just met for your entire life. He sneaked every opportunity to glance at Martha's profile and her posture on the wagon seat. He felt lightheaded, not altogether because of his wounds.

36

Joe's days during his healing process were divided into two categories—time spent with Martha and time spent in her absence. Two days after their initial meeting, Amos and Ethan came to see him. Ethan was beside himself with joy and relief to see his mentor and adopted uncle. He was a veritable font of questions.

"Are you all right?

"Yep. Just a little nicked up."

"Where did they shoot you?"

"In the back."

"When are you comin' home"

"Don't know yet."

"We thought you would be comin' back with us today," Amos said, frowning.

"Chief Joseph wants me to stay here under the care of his healers until I'm out of the woods. It would be an insult to refuse."

"Christine ain't gon' be very happy to hear that. She was planning on takin' care of you herself," Amos said.

Joe was glad that he didn't have to deliver his message to Christine in person. "Break it to her gentle. Shouldn't be no more than a couple o' weeks. I'm sure she's got enough to do."

"Can I stay here with you? School's out," Ethan said.

"No, with me laid up, Amos's gon' need you at the farm."

Joe felt a modicum of guilt concerning his ulterior motive for keeping his family at a distance. But he told himself that God would not have given him this opportunity to get to know Martha if He did not want him to take advantage of it.

Amos moved on to other matters. "I brought William a skinning knife, a keg of sorghum, and some salt pork to say thank you."

"Much obliged," Joe said. He was deeply appreciative of Amos's gesture on his behalf.

William joined them and was greeted warmly by the trio. He and Amos had established a tighter bond since facing danger together.

"Just the man I was lookin' for," Amos said, standing and extending his hand.

"Greetings, Amos, Eton. It has been too long since your last visit. The sight of you gives me great pleasure and surely must be like medicine to Joseph. My father is tied up with other matters but sends his greetings as well."

"We came to take this hombre off your hands, but he tells us your father is set on him staying put till he's all healed up. So, out of respect, we'll leave 'im here till Chief Joseph says he can go."

William gave Joe a calculating look. "Thank you for honoring my father's wishes," was all he said.

Amos gave William the gifts he had brought. William thanked him gravely and left with his bounty. A short time later, he returned carrying a buffalo robe and a hand-carved wooden pipe. These he presented to Amos.

"Please accept these gifts as a sign of friendship," he said.

Amos started to protest but a look and an imperceptible shake of the head from Joe silenced him. "Thank you, my friend," Amos said instead.

After the exchange of gifts, they had a meal that Martha prepared and served. Upon being introduced to the young woman and told of her responsibilities regarding his brother, Amos could not keep himself from taking a dig at Joe. "Now, I see why you ain't all that anxious to come home. Good vittles, a warm lodge, and a pretty nurse makes a man want to stay put even if he's being missed somewhere else."

Customarily, Joe would have taken the bait and come back with a jab of his own. But Amos's comment had hit close to home, and he was reluctant to draw further attention to it. "I reckon I'll be back in time for hayin'," he said.

"You reckon so, Miss White Horn?" Amos asked.

"We will do what we can to make it so, Mr. Walker," Martha said.

"I guess I can count on it then. Thank you for your service to Joseph. We won't worry knowing that he is under your special care." Having needled his brother enough, Amos prepared to take his leave. "Well, we best be hittin' the road, if we want to get home fo' dark."

He and Ethan said their good-byes, promising to check in on Joe again soon. Amos sent Ethan to hitch the team and load up the wagon. Martha accompanied him. When they were alone, Amos turned to his brother and said, "That's one handsome woman there, Jaybird. You lucked out gettin' her for a nurse. Too bad you ain't gon' need nursin' too much longer."

Joe said, "That's why when she's through bein' my nurse, I hope she'll consider bein' my wife."

37

Joe's life had been one long fight for survival. He now desired something he could not take by force of arms or will—Martha's love. The prospect of filling the emptiness inside him with her love and companionship was so daunting that it literally made him lightheaded. During their times together, he was constantly engaged in two conversations, the one on his tongue and the one in his head. The latter was the more urgent and necessary but he could not bring it forth. This duplicity was utterly foreign to him, and he grew more desperate and distracted as time passed and his body healed.

He discussed his dilemma daily with Dice. And if the stallion could talk, he certainly would have had well-reasoned advice for Joe. In the end, the answer was as simple as falling off a log.

After Joe's morning baths, he and Martha had taken to going for walks together. She usually did some ingredient gathering during these excursions. She told Joe about the medicinal qualities of the herbs, barks, and roots she collected, and he was a willing pupil if for no other reason than it allowed him to spend more time in her company. His arm was no longer in a sling and his ribs were almost completely healed at this juncture. Their walks usually took place in the woods that abutted the river where he bathed.

Martha paused, stooped, and picked some flowers with purple/pink petals and a thistlelike cone in the center. "This is the coneflower. It's good for colds and the flu. I grind it and make a tea. Aren't they pretty?" she said.

Not as pretty as you, Joe thought.

At another point, she paused and picked bunches of blackberries. "Their juice helps with joint pain. I give this to my father for his arthritis."

I wonder if your father would give you to me?

She picked some daisies.

"What are those good for?" Joe asked.

"I just like the way they look and smell, Joseph," she said, handing him the flowers.

Joe smelled the daisies and nodded. "Nice." He picked more daisies and made a bouquet that he handed back to her. *This is my heart.*

Smiling, she accepted his gift and put one of the flowers behind her ear.

"What do you think?" she asked, posing.

"Pretty as a picture," he said.

As they continued their walk, she casually took his hand and his heart soared. They came to a meadow and sat on a downed tree.

Joe summoned his courage and took both her hands in his. "Martha, I need to say somethin' to you while there's still time."

"What is it, Joseph?"

"When I left Tennessee, I coulda rode in any direction. There weren't no chains or oaths bindin' me anymore. But God told me to head west. Now I know why. Because he knew that's where I'd find you. I have to tell you now that I love you and if you don't feel the same way about me, I'll ride on. But if you do, I want you to be my wife and share the rest of my life. This may not be the right way to ask you, but my heart tells me it's the right time. So, will you have me?"

Martha was staring at him intently, her eyes alight. The expression on her face seemed to be a mixture of joy, relief, and wonder, as though she had been waiting for this moment. Joe noticed that her hands were trembling.

Martha leaned forward, took his hands, and said, "Yes, my darling, I will be your wife and share your life. It is what I have wanted since I first saw you in the council lodge. You were so strong and handsome and when you spoke, I heard the goodness in your heart. When you got shot, I asked my uncle if I could care for you, because it was a chance to be near you. Forgive me for being so bold."

He kissed her then. Her lips were soft and yielding. He felt her heart beat like a fluttering bird against his chest and her fingers caressed the back of his neck, telegraphing her love and her desire.

They folded into each other and, in doing so, forgot where they were perched. They fell backward off the log and into the grass. Joe felt a twinge of pain, but it was drowned by his joy at having, miraculously, won his heart's desire. He let out a whoop that was part exultation and part relief.

Hearing this, Martha was alarmed. "Joseph, did I hurt you?"

"No, darlin'. I think you just healed me," he said and kissed her again.

On the way back to the village, they talked about their future in the manner of two people who had just been freed from prison.

"You must ask my parents' permission to marry me," Martha said, holding his arm as if she feared he would disappear.

"Do you think they'll say yes?"

"They want what every parent wants for their daughter—a man who will take good care of her and make her happy."

"Well then, I reckon I'm that man." He began to hum a tune with no name.

When they got back to the village, Joe went looking for William. He could not wait to share his good news and see his friend's reaction. He found William at his lodge.

"Is there something on your mind, Joseph?" William asked.

"I just asked Martha to marry me and she said yes." Joe somehow felt that saying the words to another person would ensure he was not dreaming.

William rose, went to Joe, and embraced him. "It's about time," he said with a broad smile.

William's response surprised Joe. He thought he had been careful to conceal his feelings for Martha for fear of being rejected and subsequently ridiculed. "You knew?"

"Everybody in the village knew. We just wondered if you were going to make your move before Martha either lost interest or died of old age."

"I'll be damned. Why didn't you say somethin'?"

"Because Martha would have gutted me with a dull deer antler. She wanted you to come to this conclusion in your own way in your own time."

"Well, I'm through wastin' time. She said I've got to ask her parents for permission to marry her. How do I do that?"

"Well, you send an emissary to request a meeting with her parents."

"What's an emissary?"

"A go-between. I would be pleased to act as your emissary," William said. "When you go to the meeting, you should wear your best duds and be on your best behavior. Also, you want to bring a gift as a token of your respect."

"What kind of gift?"

"Food—venison or buffalo is good. You introduce yourself and tell them who your people are. Give them the gift and ask for Martha's hand. Don't expect them to answer right away. They may want some time to think about it. And although the White Horns speak English, you should conduct this meeting in the Cherokee language out of respect for tradition."

"Will you help me with that part?"

"It would be my honor, my brother."

Joe practiced his speech while William paved the way.

Three days later, he was prepared to approach Samuel and Tessa White Horn to ask for their daughter's hand in marriage. At dusk, Joe approached the White Horns' wickiup. It was located in a clump of trees near the center of the village.

He was dressed in his Sunday trousers and frock coat. His freshly laundered shirt was of white linen and his boots shone like mirrors. Tessa White Horn was a statuesque woman in her early forties, although she looked much younger. Joe saw instantly where Martha got her beauty and flawless skin. She favored Joe with a smile of greeting that raised his hopes for a successful outcome. Samuel White Horn was a man about six feet tall. Joe had first seen him being attended by Martha at the evening meal during Joe's first week in the village. His face featured piercing brown eyes, a curved beak of a nose, high cheekbones shadowed by nascent stubble, and a cleft chin. He wore his thick black hair in two braids that ended at his belt line. When he spoke, his voice was deep and arresting.

"I have heard much about you and your bond with the Wolf Clan. Welcome to our lodge, Joseph Walker."

"Thank you, suh. It is a honor to be heah," Walker said. He removed a venison haunch wrapped in butcher's paper from his rucksack. "Please accept this gift as a token of my respect."

Mrs. White Horn took the package. "Thank you. That's very considerate of you."

Martha and her sisters came forward to greet Joe. Ten-year-old Celia was a plump miniature of her mother with a shy smile and eyes that glistened with vitality and good humor, while fourteen-year-old Meredith was gangly and reserved with her father's sharp features and brooding eyes.

Joe said, "So these are the sisters I've heard so much about. Martha didn't tell me how pretty ya'll were." This elicited a spontaneous giggle from Celia and an eye roll from Meredith.

Martha was looking at him in a way that made his heart skip a beat. "I hope you will get to know them a lot better," she said, her voice filled with hidden meaning.

"I look forward to it," Joe said, holding her eye just long enough to share the unspoken sentiment.

After a few more pleasantries, they sat down to eat. Mr. White Horn sat at one end of the table and his wife at the other. Joe sat beside Martha on one side and the girls sat together on the other. The meal consisted of venison, corn, sweet potatoes, and fresh bread. They washed it down with sweet tea. Joe thought he would be too nervous to eat, but Mrs. White Horn's culinary skill overcame his anxiety and he found himself asking for seconds.

When the meal was finished and the dishes cleared away, Mr. White Horn turned to the business at hand.

"Martha, why don't you take your sisters out for a walk. You can take care of the dishes when you get back."

"Yes, Father." She gathered Meredith and Celia and ushered them toward the door."

"Will Joseph be here when we get back?" Celia asked.

"Yes. Now git," Mr. White Horn said.

When the young women had left, Mr. White Horn lit his pipe with a brand from the fire. He took several preliminary puffs before settling back and regarding Joe solemnly. Despite his relaxed posture, his piercing eyes focused on Joe as though he were peering down the barrel of a rifle. Joe nervously licked his lips and tried to remember his speech.

"Mr. Walker, I believe you've come here tonight for a purpose. Why don't you tell us what's on your mind?"

Joe began slowly reciting, in Cherokee, the speech he had practiced for days.

"Mr. and Mrs. White Horn, I am Joseph Walker, son of David and Sarah Walker and great-grandson of Richard and Molly Gray Horse. I am descended from a member of the Bear Clan and a blood brother to William Adams of the Wolf Clan. I come here today to ask for your daughter Martha's hand in marriage." Joe swallowed and waited for a response.

"And what would you offer my daughter besides your hand?" Mr. White Horn asked in English.

"I am a hard worker and a straight shooter. You can ask those who know me well if that ain't true. Soon, I will be a landowner, and I plan to build a house on my land and fill it with a lovin' family. If Martha becomes my wife, I will honor her and protect her all the days of my life."

"Do you love Martha?" Mrs. White Horn asked.

"Ma'am, to me, loving Martha is like breathing. It's the easiest, most nat'ral thang of all, but if I was to stop, I'd die."

"So you plan to live off the reservation?" Mr. White Horn asked.

"Yessuh. But we would come back often."

"Martha has never lived off the reservation. What if she didn't like it?" Mr. White Horn asked.

"Well, suh, I've lived on and off the reservation. Both suit me. So I don't figure I'd have a problem making a home with Martha where we both would feel comfortable."

Mr. White Horn nodded and puffed on his pipe.

"Did you ever meet your great-grandfather, Richard Gray Horse?"

"No, suh."

"Did you ever see a picture of him?"

"No, suh," Joe said, wondering where this was headed.

"So, for all you know, he might not even exist."

"All I have is my mother's word," Joe said.

Ignoring this, Mr. White Horn said, "So you might have some Cherokee blood, but the only ancestors you can be certain of are coloreds—slaves."

Joe felt gall rising in the back of his throat. He had lived out from under the shadow of prejudice for just long enough that he was caught off guard when it raised its ugly head in these heretofore benign surroundings. "I have no problem with that. I was a slave myself. It was not a life we chose. It was forced upon us."

"The Cherokee have never been slaves and never will be. It is not in our nature."

Joe felt the tiger rousing. Though he knew his next words might doom his marriage to Martha, he could not let this insult to his family and his race go unanswered.

"The white man stole the Cherokee's land, drove you across the country like cattle, and forced you to settle in wild country. Still, when the wah broke out, many Cherokee fought and died to protect the white man's property. After the wah, the whites gave y'all pieces of worthless land and told y'all to stay put and that's exactly what y'all did. A man don't have to be a slave to ack like one."

Realizing what he had done to his prospects, Joe decided to leave before creating more carnage. "I reckon that about does it for me, suh. Please say good-bye to your daughters for me." Joe rose to leave, wishing that, just this once, he could have kept his big mouth shut.

"Joseph, wait. Sit back down, please," Mr. White Horn said. "Forgive me for pushing you to this point, but I had my reasons. As man and wife, you and Martha will have a harder time than you would if she were Negro or you were Cherokee. She is determined to marry you, and there is nothing I can do to stop her short of tying her to a tree for the rest of her life. You plan to take her into the wide world away from the safety and security of the tribe, so I had to know if you have the grit to stand up for her and for yourself. I am satisfied you are a man of courage and honor. Tessa, what do you think?"

Tessa White Horn, who had watched their previous exchange with a pained look on her face, spoke now. "I think we owe Mr. Walker an apology for any harm or insult we may have done to him or his family. This final cruel test was my husband's idea. I went along with it because I love my daughter and because I secretly hoped you might fail. But we are the ones who failed for not trusting Martha's judgment. You are every bit the man she said you were, and I would be proud to have you as my son-in-law."

"I guess that does it then." Mr. White Horn stood, walked to Joe, and extended his hand. "Welcome to the family."

Joe took a deep breath and tried to take in what had just happened. One minute his world was crashing down around him and the next he was floating on a cloud. He had thought himself prepared for every possible test of his fortitude and fidelity, but the White Horns' gambit had caught him completely off guard. He grasped Mr. White Horn's calloused hand and shook it. Mrs. White Horn joined them and clasped their joined hands in hers, smiling and crying at the same time.

"Joseph, don't say a word to Martha about this. She would never forgive me. Oh, and one other thing. Just so you know, I fought for the Union," Mr. White Horn said.

"I know, suh. I was just tryin' to shame you the way you shamed me."

"No harm done. Let's have a drink to celebrate the occasion."

He went to a cupboard and took out a bottle of brandy and three glasses. He poured two fingers of liquor into each. Holding his glass aloft, he made a toast. "To family," he said and clinked glasses with Joe and his wife.

"To family."

"To family."

The hard liquor made Joe cough involuntarily, much to his embarrassment. Mr. White Horn clapped him on the back. "I can see you're not a drinking man."

"No, suh, 'fraid not."

"Well, son, Tessa would say that's another point in your favor, and I can't say I disagree."

"Father, may we come in?" The girls had returned from their walk.

"Yes, you may."

Martha and her sisters entered the lodge in a flurry of anticipation. Martha looked at her mother, who gave her an affirming smile, and then to her father, who merely nodded his head. she let out a shriek of joy and ran to Joe and leapt into his arms.

Joe spun her around twice before checking himself. He set Martha on her feet and stepped back, looking at Mr. White Horn. "Excuse me, suh."

"I guess it's okay since you're betrothed."

"What does 'betrothed' mean, Mama?" Celia asked.

"It means they're going to be married, dear."

It was Celia's turn to let out a shriek of her own. She and Meredith ran to their sister, grabbing her hands, and the three of them danced in a giggling, babbling circle. "Girls! Quiet! You'll wake the whole village," Mr. White Horn said with mock consternation.

With difficulty, the sisters restrained themselves verbally, but their body language remained exuberant. "When is the wedding, Mama? Can I get a new dress? Where are Martha and Joseph going to live?"

"Celie, please. We will decide all those things in good time. For now, all you need to know is that Mr. Walker asked to marry Martha and your father and I said yes."

"Hooray!" Celia ran to Joe and gave him an unselfconscious hug that caused him to wince in pain.

"Celie! You're hurting Joseph," Meredith said.

"Oh!" Celia stepped back and gave Joe a look of concern.

"It's all right, darlin'. My ribs are still just a little bit sore."

"All right, you've pestered our guest long enough. I'm sure he and Martha would like some time alone. You two get started on those dishes," Mrs. White Horn said.

Reluctantly, Celia released Joe's hand and followed her sister to the dishpan.

Joe took Martha's hand and they left her parents lodge. Once outside, Joe and Martha walked to the corral as he had done by himself so many times. There he poured out his heart now that its desire had been granted him. "Martha, will you have me for your husband?"

"Yes, you know I will."

"I promise you I'll love and honor you till the day I die. I'll treat your flesh and your spirit just like they was my own. Wherever we go, whatever we do, we'll face it togetha. God has blessed me, first with freedom and now with a partner to share it with. I'll try to be worthy." He took her in his arms and kissed her as though they had all the time in the world.

38

The next day, William asked for a full report on Joe's meeting with Martha's parents. Joe recounted the events of the previous evening, leaving out the bitter exchange between him and Samuel White Horn. He concluded by saying, "So now that I got her parents' permission, we gon' get married."

"You don't waste any time do you?" William said.

"Slavery taught me that time is precious and family is everythang. I'm gon' marry Martha and start a family with her while there's still time."

"Well, there are some things you should know about Martha before she becomes your wife."

"Like what?"

"Like marrying Martha will make you famous overnight and you'll probably have to share her with the whole village."

Joe said, "You betta explain yo'self."

A look came over William's face. His eyes lost focus and his voice took on a guttural singsong quality. It was the same look Joe had seen the night in the council lodge when William told the story of the fight with the settlers who shot Joe. It was the look of a man about to tell a story.

As a child Martha would find injured animals in the woods and bring them home to nurse them back to health. She rescued squirrels, rabbits, chipmunks, birds, and an occasional lizard. Often her efforts were unsuccessful and she ended up burying her patients in the yard, accompanied by appropriate ritual and sadness.

Her most exotic and infamous charge was a baby red-tail hawk that had fallen from its nest. Martha, as was her wont, picked up the bird and brought him home. Curiously, Martha had no fear of animals, nor they of her. She fed the bird with scraps of meat from the family's larder and kept it in a fur-lined basket next to her bed. She named it Hawk. She talked and sang to Hawk constantly, and the bird responded as though he understood. Soon he was riding her shoulder wherever she went.

When Hawk became strong enough to fly and fend for himself, Martha released him. It pained her to see Hawk fly away, but her heart told her he was meant to be free. She had barely begun to adjust to Hawk's absence when he swooped down out of the sky one day and landed on her shoulder. He stayed with her for the rest of the day. Hawk became Martha's constant companion. He went off on daily hunting forays, often returning with a rabbit or a quail that he dropped at Martha's feet. These went into the cook pot.

When it came time for him to mate, Hawk and his mate built a nest high in the branches of a cottonwood tree within sight of the White Horn's lodge. With the responsibilities of parenthood, Hawk was less available to Martha, but he checked in with her everyday.

The red-tail hawk is a protector animal and, therefore, is sacred to the Cherokee people. Anyone who harmed Hawk or his family would have been immediately killed or ostracized. Consequently, Hawk's offspring patrolled the village freely, keeping it free of rodents, lizards, and snakes.

Martha's association with a sacred animal imbued her with mystic powers in the eyes of the tribe. Many believed she and Hawk exchanged spirits and she was able to fly long distances and see through his eyes. At a young age, she became known throughout the nation as a powerful medicine woman and was often summoned to other villages to attend their sick and wounded. The Cherokee called her A-gay-luh Ta-wo-di (Lady Hawk).

William ended his story by saying, "About a year ago, Hawk disappeared. As the days turned into weeks and the weeks into months, Martha came to accept the fact that he was gone. She built an altar for him at the base of the cottonwood where he nested. She would often go there at sunset to meditate. When you came to the village, she experienced a strong connection to you. She came to believe you were the vessel of Hawk's spirit. To prove this, she had to get to know you. Your injury gave her the chance to do just that."

Joe sat in silence, digesting what William had just told him. He deciphered the clues that had been right in front of him since he first set eyes on Martha. The people of the village treated her with the deference due to an elder or a chief. The laying on of her hands had brought him both physical and psychic relief. The "glow" that he had attributed to her physical beauty was the powerful aura associated with her supernatural gift. No wonder her parents were loath to see her leave the village. "She made me think she was just a simple medicine woman," he said finally.

"She made us promise to keep A-gay-luh Ta-wo-di a secret. She wanted you to meet Martha White Horn first."

Joe got up abruptly and headed for the door.

"Where are you going?" William asked.

"I got to talk to Martha," Joe said.

He found Martha at home alone. She was tidying the lodge while her family was occupied elsewhere. Her welcoming smile faded as she saw the look of concern on Joe's face. "What's wrong?" she asked, matching his expression.

"We need to talk," Joe said and took her by the hand. "Why didn't you tell me who you really are?

Martha did not try to dissemble. "I'm nineteen years old, and no man has come to court me because they are all afraid of A-gay-luh Ta-wo-di. You knew nothing of Lady Hawk, so I knew if you came to love me, it would be for who I am inside. Forgive me for deceiving you. I was planning to tell you everything today."

Joe asked a question he was dreading the answer to. "If we get married, what will happen to Lady Hawk?"

"She will spend the rest of her life trying to make you happy," Martha said.

"But your people need you," Joe said.

"Once we are married, you will be my people and I will be yours. The Great Spirit showed you to me in a dream and told me you would be the only man I would ever love. Everything else, we will work out together. If only you will have me."

Martha was looking at Joe with a sincerity that tightened his throat and caused his heart to stutter. She gripped his hand in both of hers as though she feared he would be snatched away suddenly—permanently.

"Yes, A-gay-luh Ta-wo-di, I accept you body and soul and I'll love you all the days of my life."

He took her face in his hands and kissed her eyelids to stop her tears and then her lips to stop his own.

39

There was only one thing left for Joe to do—inform his family of his wedding plans. When he was finally able to ride again, he saddled Dice and headed for Amos's farm.

The air was crisp and clean, cooling Joe's skin and raising his spirits. He was wearing a fringed buckskin shirt and leggings, a gift from the White Horns.

Dice gamboled like a colt. It had been some time since he had had a decent run. Fat gray clouds to the east suggested the possibility of an afternoon rain. Joe was as close to carefree as his past would allow.

As Joe came within sight of the homestead, Amos rode out to meet him and greeted him warmly.

"Jaybird! I knew that was you when I seen that Appaloosa. We was just about to come back and check on you. You must be feelin' shipshape to make this ride."

"I feel good, big brotha. Mighty good!"

"I guess that Injun medicine did the trick, huh?" he said with a knowing smile.

"You could say that."

Joe could hardly keep himself from blurting out his news but he wanted to wait until the family was assembled and the time was right.

They rode to the farmhouse where Joe became the center of a circle of love and thanksgiving.

Mrs. Archer, who hadn't seen Joe since the accident, gave him a hug that radiated maternal concern. "Joseph, you scared me half to death. They wouldn't let me come see you. All I could do was wait and pray. It seemed so long. I don't know what I would have done if . . ." Her voice trailed off.

"I'm sorry to've been such a bother, Mama Mabel. But, as you can see, ain't no cause for worry. I been in good hands all the time, thanks to my friends and your prayers. I rode over here today to get my last dose of medicine—this right here," Joe said, giving her a squeeze.

Mrs. Archer reluctantly released him from her embrace. She wiped her eyes with her apron and immediately assumed the role of surprised hostess.

"You're staying for supper, of course. Lord, I don't know what I can put together on such short notice. Ethan, go get me some yams. Christine, catch two of them fryers and wring their necks. Amos, I'm going to need some more firewood. Then fetch me a ham from the smokehouse."

"What about me?" Joe asked.

"See to your horse and wash the trail dust off you. Supper will be on the stove by then. That'll give us time to catch up on what's happened over these last few months."

"Yes, ma'am," Joe said, smiling at how easily he fit back in to his family's bosom.

Events proceeded as Mrs. Archer had dictated, and while supper cooked, the family sat on the porch and visited. Joe could not help but notice that Christine rarely took her eyes off him to the point it caused comment from Amos.

"What's the matter darlin'? Do you think he's a ghost? Come supper time, you'll see how real he is."

"It's been all we could do to keep her from ridin' to the village and draggin' you home," Ethan said.

"Ethan, shut up. I just thought Joe would do better with proper nursing and familiar surroundings," Christine said.

"From what I could see, Joe had first-rate nursin'. What was the name of that gal who was tendin' you, Jaybird?" Amos had deliberately set the stage for the news he suspected was coming.

"Her name is Martha, and she's the kindest, sweetest person you're ever gon' meet. She brought me back to health and she helped me to see there's more to life than workin' and fightin' and eatin' and sleepin'. There's buildin' and dreamin' and laughin' and lovin'. We found out that even though we're from different worlds, we want the same things. I couldn't feature goin' on without her, so I asked her to marry me and she said yes."

The words had poured from him like water from a sluice, and the group was silent for a second as they sunk in.

Mrs. Archer was the first to respond. "Joseph, you've found your soul mate. That's wonderful news!" She came to him and gave him his second prolonged hug of the day.

"Congratulations, Jaybird! Take it from me—you'll never regret it. Right, Christine?" Amos said, clapping him on the back and turning to his wife for confirmation.

Christine stood up and ran into the house.

"What's gotten into her?" Amos asked.

"Probably heard a pot boiling," Mrs. Archer said. "I'll go help her check on supper."

Joe's senses were sharpened by war and outlawry. He thought he heard sounds that had nothing to do with a pot boiling coming from the recesses of the house.

A short time later, Mrs. Archer returned to the men on the porch. "Christine was right. The yams were boiling. Time to drop that chicken in some hot grease. Joe, you look like you lost some weight. Don't worry—we'll put some meat on your bones before your wedding day."

At that point, Christine came out the front door. She looked flushed but composed. Joe noticed that she exchanged a pregnant look with her mother.

She went to Joe and took his hands in hers. "Joseph, I'm so pleased to hear about you and Martha. I can't wait to meet her. I wish you two every happiness." She rose on her tiptoes and kissed his cheek.

"Thank you, Christine." The words came nowhere near expressing his gratitude and his relief. The last obstacle between him and happiness had been removed.

"You men folks talk. We women have to finish cooking," Mrs. Archer said. She put her arm around Christine's waist as they walked to the front door and whispered something in her daughter's ear.

The meal that followed was seasoned with tension for Joe. He sensed a subtext that cast a pall over the gathering. It dampened his enjoyment of Mrs. Archer's excellent meal.

After supper, Amos and Joe retired to the front porch where the former promptly lit his pipe.

"Man, I'm so full I could bust," Amos said.

"Me too. If I ate like this every night, I'd be near 'bout as big as that rain barrel over yonder."

"To tell the truth, I've had to let out my belt a coupla notches. I been tryin' to push back from the table without hurtin' Ma Mabel's feelin's. But tonight was a special occasion. My little nappy-headed brotha is gon' get married. Who'da thought it?" He playfully punched Joe's shoulder.

"I told you what I was plannin' to do."

"Yeah, but I thought you'd take your time. Start to courtin'. Get to know her. Bring her around to meet the family. You know, like Daddy used to say, 'Measure twice, cut once.'"

"That was the plan I had in my head, all neat and proper, but my heart had a different notion. I knew she was the woman for me from the minute I laid eyes on her. I cain't explain it. It was like God spoke to me."

"And you didn't have no choice. That was the way it was for me with Christine," Amos said, nodding.

Joe felt a pang of guilt for the feelings he had harbored toward his brother's wife. *Thank God for finding Martha.* "I wanted y'all to meet her, but I didn't want to spring everything on you at once."

"And you wanted to make sure there wasn't gon' be no problems," Amos said.

"Yeah," Joe said, alerted by a change in his brother's tone.

Amos stared at Joe in a way that made him uneasy. "Well, there's nothin' preventin' you from bringin' her for a visit now, is there?" he said, holding Joe's eyes for several beats.

"Not a thing," Joe said, emphasizing each word. "When would be a good time?"

"How about y'all come for supper next Saturday?"

"We'll be here. Thank you," Joe said. His last words were heartfelt.

Amos said, "I'm glad you found what you were looking for. I guess you just needed to look in the right place."

A familiar feeling came over Joe. It was the feeling of having dodged a bullet. "I think I'll stretch my legs a bit," he said.

"Go 'head."

Joe walked to the newly built two-story barn and went inside. The smell of fresh hay and livestock was comforting. He forked some hay into Dice's stall. While the horse munched fodder, he told him about the day's events.

Joe left the barn and walked the circuit of the smokehouse, the woodshed, and the outhouse. His stride was casual but his eyes were vigilant. Some habits lasted a lifetime.

When he returned to the house, Amos had just about finished his pipe. "Is the perimeter secure, soldier?"

"Yessuh," Joe responded by rote.

"I'm kinda tired. I think I'll turn in. See you in the mawnin'," Amos said.

"'Night."

The next morning, Joe was up with the sun. He wolfed down a breakfast of ham and eggs, buttermilk, and cornbread. Standing on the porch afterward, he hugged Mrs. Archer and Christine, thanking them for their kindness. He then went to his brother and tentatively extended his hand. Ignoring Joe's hand, Amos grabbed him in a bear hug. "I'll see you Saturday. Tell Martha I'm a hugger."

Ethan had saddled Dice and brought him around to the front of the house. Joe went to Ethan, took the reins, and hugged him, surprising them both. "Much obliged. You know, you're the only one besides me that he'll let get close enough to saddle him."

He swung into the saddle and pointed Dice west, waving to his family as he departed the yard. The next time he came to the farm, it would be in the company of his bride-to-be. As he set out that morning, he felt a heightened sense of urgency to get back to her.

40

Two hours into his ride, Joe saw a lone horseman approaching from the opposite direction. Joe recognized William Adams and a sense of foreboding washed over him. William's face was painted black and his hair was cut raggedly to shoulder length. When they were feet apart, William raised his hand and Joe reined Dice to a halt. Without preamble William said, "Joseph, I come bearing terrible news. Martha is dead."

"What?"

"Our beloved Martha is dead." He emitted an involuntary wail and his eyes filled with tears.

Joe heard a rushing sound and he swayed in the saddle. Had not William grabbed his shoulder for support, he would have fallen to the ground. He tried to somehow undo William's words. He imagined he was still back in bed at the farm and this was a bad dream. He would wake soon and start his day. But his mind could not long support the healing fantasy. A look at William's ravaged face and reality came rushing back like a runaway train.

"No! No! No! You wrong. I just left her the day fo' yesterday and she was fine."

William's next words were like acid, each one eating a hole in Joe's heart. "She went out herb gathering. When she didn't come back by sundown, we went looking for her. We found her in her favorite meadow. A rattler bit her. The wound was in her neck so death came quickly."

Recounting the story had refreshed William's grief. He started to cry again but controlled himself with difficulty. "I came to fetch you. The White Horns are delaying the burial until you come."

Although Joe wanted to lie down and die, the prospect of seeing Martha one last time galvanized him. He straightened in the saddle and said to William, "Let's go."

They rode like highwaymen fleeing the scene of a crime and reached their destination in record time. As they entered the village, they heard the sound of drums and of women wailing. This haven of comfort and security now felt to Joe like the anteroom to hell. They rode straight to the meeting lodge. Joe dismounted and entered without ceremony.

Inside the log house, Martha's body rested on a low platform. She was dressed in her finest clothes. Her long hair was braided and bedecked with ornaments and her skin was painted vermillion. The platform was surrounded by a group of grieving women. Joe parted the crowd and knelt next to his betrothed. He took Martha in his arms and attempted to turn back time.

"I'm heah now, darlin'. Your Joseph is heah. You can come back now. I won't let nothin' hurt you. I promise."

The stiffness and coldness of Martha's body confirmed for Joe that his true love now resided irrevocably in the spirit world. He felt a hand on his shoulder and turned to look into the grief-ravaged face of Tessa White Horn.

"You made it, Joseph. I know she would want you to be here. Now she can rest in peace."

Joe stood and took Mrs. White Horn in his arms. She allowed him to embrace her with her arms at her sides. It was as though her loss had drained all but a flicker of energy from her. She, too, had cut her hair and there were fresh knife wounds on her arms.

"God bless you for thinking of me. I'll never forget it. I loved her with everythin' I had. I was gon' make her my wife. My family was lookin' forward to seein' us wed. They woulda loved her and ya'll. I shouldna waited so long."

Joe had many regrets. One of the most prominent was that he would never get to call this woman "Mother."

They held Martha's funeral the next day. Her final resting place was a wooden scaffold on a hill in the open air where her spirit would be free to float on the breeze and ascend to the stars. Among the valuables they placed with her were her herb basket, her favorite comb, and Joe's cavalry insignia.

Dr. Peters stood among the mourners. He had covered his face with soot that was now streaked with tears. As the tribe was singing the death song, a red-tailed hawk flew over the crowd and perched on one of the posts of the scaffold. This set off loud ululations from the women and war whoops from the men.

The grieving ritual continued for four days with the women gathering at the burial site to weep, wail, and chant death songs each morning. The men paid their respects individually.

Joe knew his family would be worried when he and Martha failed to appear at the agreed-upon time, but he could not tear himself away from Martha's side. He spent hours at a time sitting next to her gravesite, professing his love and his regret. This was his punishment for the sin of coveting his brother's wife.

On the fifth day, Mr. White Horn joined him. Together they commiserated and reminisced about Martha. Mr. White Horn's hair had new streaks of gray, and his beard had grown to a bushy mat covering the lower half of his face, a rare sight on an Indian. He and Joe chanted songs to express their grief and honor Martha's life. In the depths of despair, they tried to comfort each other.

"She was the best woman on God's green earth. You should be proud of the daughter you raised," Joe said.

"She was my pride and joy, but I was worried that she was carrying too much weight on her shoulders for one her age. After you came into her life, I saw that weight melt away. You made her happy." Mr. White Horn squeezed Joe's shoulder and left to go back to his remaining family.

Rather than comforting Joe, Mr. White Horn's words stoked his grief. On the outside he was still, almost paralyzed by remorse, but on the inside, he was a mad wolf howling at a crimson moon. He picked at the food that the village women brought him and went for days without washing or shaving.

On the sixth day of his vigil, Amos and Christine arrived. Joe was gaunt and dirty with a full beard and wild, matted hair that stuck out like a nappy corona around his skull. Christine went to him and gave him a hug despite his stench.

"Joseph, dear. I was so sorry to hear about Martha, God rest her soul. We knew something must be wrong when you didn't return to the farm. We're here as long as you need us."

Amos joined them. "Jaybird, if I could lift this off you, Lord knows I would. But like the Good Book says, 'The Lord will never give us more burden than we can bear.' You got to be strong and trust Him."

Joe regarded him with weariness born of despair. "I did trust Him and look where it got me. Ya'll shoulda stayed home. Ain't nothin' you can do heah for either one of us."

"That's just the grief talking," Christine said. "You'll feel better if you get some food and rest. Why don't you come on back down to the village and let me fix you something?"

"I already ate and I ain't tired," Joe said. "If you wanna take care of somebody, take care of your husband. I just wanna be left alone. Is that so hard to understand?" Christine's lower lip began to tremble but she did not succumb.

Amos interceded. "Christine, why don't you go on back to the village and get dinner started. Joe and me will be along directly."

Christine nodded and walked away, grateful for the reprieve. Once she had departed, Amos turned to his brother. "You know who you remind me of?"

"No, who?"

"Mama, after you got sold. She cried and cried. Daddy couldn't comfort her. I couldn't comfort her. She had lost her baby boy and she came to the conclusion some way that it was her fault. She stopped laughing and joking and tellin' her stories. Instead, she snapped at us for the least little thing. I thought I had lost you and Mama both. You know what brought her back?"

Despite himself, Joe had to ask. "What?"

"Lillian got real sick—some kinda croup. I remember her coughin' all night and Mama bathin' her with cool cloths to keep her fever down. She would feed her chicken broth and Lil Bit would bring it right back up. It was touch and go for about a week. One night I heard Mama prayin'. She promised God that if He let Lil Bit live, she would stop grievin' over what she lost and try to 'preciate what she had. Lil Bit's fever broke that night and she came back to us. So did Mama. Now, she never came all the way back, but she tried her hardest to keep her promise.

"I know you hurtin' now. I been there. When Mama and Daddy died, I wanted to give up, but I was the head of the family then and I had to look out for Lillian and Rosemary. So I pulled myself together and carried on the best I could. You're a fighter and whatever got you through losin' yo' family and fightin' in the wah, you got to call on that to get you through this. Otherwise, it's all been for nothin'." He paused to let his words sink in. "All this talkin' has made me hungry. So, let's go eat."

Joe followed him down the hill. It turned out that he was hungrier than he thought he was. He cleaned his plate twice. After supper, he could barely keep his eyes open and went immediately to bed.

Joe woke in the middle of the night to the sound of someone calling his name, *Joseph.* He rolled out of his blankets and moved toward the voice that was coming from outside the wickiup. He stepped into the yard and followed the summoning voice to Martha's burial site. When he reached the scaffold, he saw the origin of the summons.

Martha stood at the base of the scaffold. She was transformed into a phantasm from another world. Her dress and moccasins were white and they literally glowed in the darkness. She wore a headdress shaped like a hawk's head, and russet-colored wings extended from her shoulder blades.

He wanted to run to her and take her in his arms, but his feet were rooted to the spot. "Martha, is that you?"

Joe tried to look into Martha's eyes but saw only empty sockets. He felt the hair stand up on the back of his neck and his skin pebble with goose bumps.

"Yes, my darling, it's me. I've come to tell you that I will always love you and to ask a favor that only you can grant."

"I love you too. I don't know how I'm gon' go on without you," he said.

"Joseph, you have to let me go. Your grief is so strong that it is holding me between this world and the next. The Great Spirit has granted my wish to speak with you one last time. I want to tell you that my death was not your fault. It would have happened even if you had been by my side. The Great Spirit had numbered my days just as He has numbered yours. Now, I go to live in the spirit world. Nothing can harm me there. You are still part of the world of the living. It would be wrong for you to try to be in both places at once. Live your life. When your time is ripe, Yo-ho-wah will call you and we will see each other again. Go to sleep now and let me live only in your dreams."

When Joe awoke the next morning, he felt as if a burden had been lifted from his shoulders. He felt more refreshed than he had since Martha's passing. He attributed it to Amos's revelation about his mother, a solid meal, and a good night's sleep. In fact, he was hungry again. But first, he needed a bath and a shave.

41

When Amos and Christine returned to the farm, Joe went with them. His heart still ached but his head was clear. It was time to get back to living. He threw himself into the routines of farm life like a man trying to build a shelter between storms. From sunup to sundown, he harvested crops, cut hay, milked cows, mended fences, and shoed horses. When he went to bed, he was asleep almost before his head hit the pillow. Amos remarked that having Joe back was like he'd hired two new hands. He and Ethan tried to keep up, but they were working for necessity not salvation.

Despite his wounds, Joe had struggled with guilt during his protracted stay at the Cherokee village. He knew that Amos's ambition was to build a fortune that he could pass on to his children, as white men routinely did. Joe also knew that his brother was counting on his help to accomplish his dream. In a way, Martha's death had freed him to recommit his energy and ambition to his brother and the farm.

They made their second good crop in a row and once again were able to put some money aside. They decided to use what they had laid by to purchase more land and livestock to work it. There were fifty prime acres to be had right next door.

That night at supper, Amos couldn't control his exuberance. "Watch us now, Jaybird. When we get that extra acreage planted next spring, we gon' be on the gravy train with the throttle wide open." He grabbed Christine and danced her in a circle around the kitchen.

She pretended to be put off by her husband's antics. "Watch out, Amos. You're going to break something. You know how you get," she said, her voice filled with good humor.

"It ain't what's out here that you worried about. It's what's in here," he said, patting her stomach.

Joe almost spit out his coffee. "What you say, Amos?"

At the sink, Mrs. Archer let out a squeal that belied her age.

Amos turned to his brother, beaming like a searchlight. "Well, I guess this is the first chance we've had to tell you, Jaybird. YOU GON' BE A UNCLE!"

Joe practically leaped across the kitchen and grabbed Amos and Christine in a single embrace. Mrs. Archer joined them in a group hug, and the four of them jumped up and down like they'd lost their senses.

"You rascal! How long y'all been keeping this a secret?" Joe said, playfully punching Amos's shoulder.

"Dr. Peters made it official last Monday," Christine said.

"That old faker told me he was out here to see me," Joe said.

"Well, he didn't wanna spill the beans," Amos said.

"I knew there was something different about you, and then I told myself it was just all the fresh air and sunshine and feeling relieved to have Joe back home. I should have trusted my instincts," Mrs. Archer said, pinching her daughter's cheek and then kissing it for good measure. Her eyes were brimming with tears. "My baby's going to have a baby."

That made Christine cry, and just before Joe and Amos could join in, Ethan came through the front door with an armful of firewood.

"What's the matter?" he asked, fearing more bad news.

Amos turned to the boy and said tentatively, "Well, we was just tellin' Joe and Mama that we gon' have a baby."

Joe looked at Amos's face and realized he was uncertain how Ethan would respond to this news.

Ethan went and put the wood in the woodbin beside the stove. Then he turned and ran to Amos and threw his arms around the big man's waist. The boy's face was hidden in Amos's chest, but his shoulders were shaking uncontrollably.

Amos held Ethan while tears streamed down his face. The other adults were equally moved. After all they had endured to get here and stay here, the promise of a new life in this new place somehow made it seem worthwhile.

With the baby coming, they needed more room. They added two more bedrooms to the house. One would serve as a nursery and now Joe and Ethan each would have his own room. They built a stable to house additional livestock and expanded the root cellar. They accomplished all this before the snow flew. It was late September. Come spring, they would be ready to hit the ground running.

Winter came and they busied themselves moving snow, hauling wood, mending harnesses, sharpening tools, and caring for the livestock. Christine rounded into motherhood and shone with an inner light that warmed the entire family. Amos and Joe planned the spring planting process and crop rotation. Joe and Ethan sharpened their hunting and tracking skills under winter conditions. Ethan bagged the Thanksgiving turkey with a single arrow and blushed with pride when Joe extolled his marksmanship to the family.

The first blizzard came during the week of Christmas, and they spent the holiday around a freshly cut fir tree and a blazing fire. Joe gave Christine and Amos a cradle he had made himself and kept hidden in the barn. Mrs. Archer got a new apron and a new bonnet. Joe gave Ethan a Cherokee bone-handled hunting knife in a leather scabbard. The boy immediately put the tool on his belt.

At fifteen, Ethan had shed the loquaciousness and selfishness of childhood. The men he most admired spoke when there was something to say and otherwise let their actions do most of the talking. He absorbed instruction like a sponge, whether it came from Joe and Amos or the men at the Cherokee village. He was as lithe and quick as a cheetah with a steady gaze and a strong grip. Hardship, aptitude, and necessity had pushed him to the brink of manhood. Time would take care of the rest.

After all the gifts were exchanged, Amos said, "I think there's one more in the back there."

Ethan reached in under the tree and retrieved a large package wrapped in paper. "It's for you, Uncle Joe," he said, handing Joe the package.

Joe unwrapped the package. Inside was a beautifully colored woolen Indian blanket. Joe unfolded the blanket and saw that it was covered with pictures woven into the fabric with brightly colored thread. He spread the blanket out on the floor and stood over it to get a better view.

One scene showed a creature with the head of a bear and the body of a man fighting a bear while another man lay on the ground behind him. The two combatants were engaged in a deadly embrace, jaws wide and eyes blazing. Joe recognized this mythologized version of his rescue of William, wherein he took on the form of the totem animal of the Bear Clan to save William's life.

Another scene showed a colored man walking hand and hand with a Cherokee woman. They walked beside a river with a waterfall in the background. A red-tailed hawk was perched on the woman's shoulder. Joe felt a lump rise in his throat at this depiction of his courtship of Martha.

A third tableau was of a burial scaffold with a woman lying on it with her arms folded across her breast. Poised above her was a red-tailed hawk with a writhing snake in its talons. The woman's face was painted vermilion.

Below this scene was a picture of a beautiful hawk-woman dressed in white with wings outstretched, rising into the clouds above the burial scaffold. Men and women stood at the foot of the scaffold gazing up at this apparition. Among them was a tall black man with outstretched arms lifted toward the departing angel.

Joe was overwhelmed by the significance of the gift. The blanket was tangible proof of his enshrinement into the folklore of the Cherokee Wolf Clan. It assured him he would always have a place in their midst. He picked up the blanket as though he were handling a priceless artifact and carefully began refolding it.

Joe felt hot and cold at the same time. His breath quickened and his vision was blurred by unshed tears. Meanwhile, a host of bittersweet memories flooded his mind, each seeking priority. He was brought back to the present by his brother's voice.

"William said this is a gift from the Wolf Clan and you would know what it means," Amos said.

"It means everything," Joe said softly. "I have to put it away. Excuse me."

He took the blanket and went to his room. He sat on his bunk, holding the gift and allowed his emotions to flow unchecked. When his feelings subsided, he put the blanket in the locker at the foot of his bed. In the years to come, it would become his shield against the elements, as well as against self-doubt and loneliness.

42

Jim Carson was hunting his favorite game, the kind that walked on two legs and passed as human. Before the war, he had been a slave catcher. He had gained a reputation for ruthless efficiency. Once Carson took up the hunt, it was said it was just a matter of time before "the nigger was back in the field."

After the South lost its war of independence, he assumed that he would have to make his living as other men made theirs, some spirit-numbing endeavor that hid his considerable talent like a light under a bushel. But then he had discovered bounty hunting and realized everything was going to be all right.

His new profession frequently gave him the option of bringing in his prisoners dead or alive. He preferred the former when dealing with members of the Negro race. He relished the pursuit of black felons because it provided him with the best of both worlds.

He had come across a wanted poster for Joe Walker almost a year ago in Mississippi. The amount of the reward and the color of Joe's skin made it an irresistible challenge.

Carson then began the methodical business of man hunting. When it came to his calling, he was as crafty as a fox, as persistent as a bloodhound, and as deadly as a snake. He got his first lead when he overheard a conversation in a Memphis saloon in which a wagon master recounted the tale of two long-lost brothers who were reunited on his wagon train and eventually saved the train from an attack led by one of the fiercest Comanches on the frontier. The brothers' names were Amos and Joseph Walker. Carson learned further that the wagon train was headed for Atchison, Kansas. The trail was heating up.

When he arrived in Atchison, he inquired about the Walkers, explaining that he was an old family friend. He was promptly directed to their farm on the outskirts of town. Now, at long last, he would get his first view of his quarry.

He rode into the front yard of the Walker farm. He was impressed by the spacious house, the new outbuildings, and the large, well-tended garden.

Mighty fancy for a bunch of niggers, he thought.

A stunning young woman came out of the house to meet him. She was of mixed race with an exceptional face and figure.

She'd be a good breeder if you was into that kinda thing, Carson thought.

Christine asked, "May I help you?"

Carson put on his most ingratiating manner. "Yes, ma'am. Is this the Walkuh farm?"

"Yes, it is," Christine said, shading her eyes to get a better look at him.

"Are your menfolk at home?"

Christine hesitated. "Is there something you wanted?"

"Well, I'm an old friend of Joe's. We were in the same brigade together during the wah." He had done his research.

"And your name is?"

"If I could just speak to Joseph a minute. Is he to home?"

This time, his voice was more salt less honey. At that point, a boy of about fifteen or sixteen years old came out of the barn. He moved with the pigeon-toed grace of an Apache, and he was carrying a hatchet.

"What is it, Christine?" he asked.

"This gentleman is looking for Joseph."

"He ain't here," the boy said.

"When do you expect him back?"

"I don't think that's any of your business, mistuh," the whelp said.

Carson dropped all pretext. He drew his gun and covered the boy. "Put down that hatchet, boy, and come over heah with yo' hands in the air. Mind yo'self—you wouldn't be the first nigger I killed."

Ethan dropped the hatchet and approached Carson with his hands raised. Suddenly, Christine turned, crouched, and dived through the front door. Carson fired twice. One bullet whizzed past Christine's head, shattering a vase of flowers on the living room table. The second bullet splintered the doorframe.

Carson was off his horse in an instant and running toward the house. He reached the door and took a calculated risk, entering the house without pausing. The parlor was empty so he proceeded to the kitchen— empty too. He heard a sound from the second floor and ascended the stairs two at a time.

In one of the bedrooms, he found Christine ramming shells into a Spencer rifle. Somewhere a baby was crying. He stepped to her and clubbed her in the temple with the barrel of his Colt. She dropped senseless. He stooped to retrieve the rifle and shells.

"Leave my sister alone, you son of a bitch!"

Carson spun around, intending to finish the boy. Instead, he felt an exploding pain in his chest. Ethan had hurled his hunting knife with practiced ease, and his aim was deadly. Carson dropped to his knees, clutching at the handle of the knife. His expression was a mixture of pain and disbelief. After hundreds of conquests, he was meeting his end at the hands of a boy with a knife. He tried to lift his Colt but his heart literally was not in it.

43

Joe and Amos had taken Mrs. Archer to the apple orchard they had planted on their new property. There, the three of them fertilized and watered the twenty or so young fruit trees. The work went smoothly because of their camaraderie. They were about to have lunch when they heard the sound of gunfire coming from the direction of the main house.

"That was a Colt," Joe said, moving automatically toward Dice.

"Stay with Mama!" Amos shouted as he ran to Shadow, swung into the saddle, and took off at a gallop toward the house. Joe looked after his brother, his face painted with indecision.

Seeing his dilemma, Mrs. Archer said, "Go help your brother. I'll be fine. I got my rifle."

Joe said, "Stay here until I come for you or you hear me fire three 'all clear' shots." Then he ran to Dice, vaulted into the saddle, and followed his brother.

When Joe overtook Amos, his brother glanced at him reprovingly. Joe shrugged as if to say, "I couldn't help it." There was no way he was going to let his brother face possible danger alone. With no words exchanged, they proceeded to the task at hand.

As they approached the farmhouse Joe saw a strange horse in the yard. They drew their pistols and separated. Amos approached the front of the house and Joe circled around to the back.

Joe heard Amos call out from the front of the house.

"Christine, Ethan, are you in there?"

Using this diversion, Joe quietly entered the house through the back door. He heard voices coming from Ethan's room and moved toward them.

Then Ethan yelled, "Amos, is that you? Come here. We need you."

Joe came through the bedroom door fast and low. Christine was sitting on Ethan's bed with a bloodstained bandage around her head. She was holding her daughter, Emily, trying to comfort the child. Ethan was sitting beside her with a rifle across his knees. With Joe's unexpected entrance, he raised the gun reflexively.

"Hold on, Ethan. It's me. What happened heah?"

At the same time, Amos called from the parlor, "Where y'all at?"

"Upstairs, Amos," Joe said.

Amos came through the door, holding his gun. At the sight of Christine, he uttered an expletive, moved to her side, and took her in his arms. "Baby, what happened?"

"I'm fine, Amos. Just a headache, that's all." At that moment, Emily began to fret, and Christine momentarily turned her attention to the child.

"Somebody better tell me what happened heah. We heard shots," Amos said.

Ethan said, "A man came looking for Uncle Joe, but he wouldn't say why. When we wouldn't tell him where you were, he pulled a gun on us. He almost killed Christine and then he hit her in the head with his gun . . ."

"A man did this to Christine? Where *is* the muthafucka?" Amos said.

"He's in Joe's room. He's dead. I killed him."

Ethan leaned forward and vomited on the floor. With that, he started to tremble uncontrollably. Christine handed Amos the baby and took her brother in her arms, rocking him gently.

"It's all right Ethan, honey. You couldn't help it. He would have killed us all. You saved us. Thank you for me and for little Emily. We love you."

After Ethan composed himself, he led them to Joe's room where he showed them Carson's body with a blanket thrown over it.

Joe peered closely at the dead man. "I ain't never seen this fella before," he said.

Amos retrieved Carson's wallet and removed the contents. "Says here his name is James Carson and he's a warrant officer out of Virginia. Take a look at this, Jaybird," Amos said, handing him the wanted poster Joe had hoped never to see again.

Joe studied the paper with grim realization. His past had finally caught up to him. He folded the poster and put it in his breast pocket.

"What is it?" Christine asked.

"The devil has come for his due," Joe said.

He went back through the house to the front porch. There he fired three shots into the air to summon Mrs. Archer. Her frightened and wounded children sorely needed her mother's touch. He led Carson's horse to the barn and put him in a stall. Next, he went back to his room where Amos had rolled Carson's body in the blanket Ethan had thrown over it.

"Look what I found under his shirt," Amos said, holding up a canvas money belt. When they counted the cash and coins inside, the amount totaled $891. Amos held the small fortune in his hands. "This money could practically get us all the way to where we want to go, Jaybird, and he sho' ain't gon' need it where he's goin'. Whatcha think?"

Joe had forged a code of conduct over twenty-four years of hardship, discipline, victory, and loss. Certain events would cause him to bend that code. But in that moment, as in so many moments to come, he was not prepared to break it. He drew his next words from that ethical reservoir.

"It was necessary for Ethan to kill this man. He didn't give 'im no choice. But it ain't necessary for us to rob 'im. I think if we took this money, it wouldn't put us ahead. It would set us back—quite a ways."

Amos considered this and said, "You right." He put the cash back into the money belt and replaced the belt around Carson's waist.

When they searched Carson's saddlebags, they discovered handcuffs and leg irons among the usual items. They hid the restraints in the woodpile.

"I guess we got rid of everything that might point to his true line of work," Amos said. They bound Carson's body in the blanket and placed it in the root cellar until they could decide what to do with it. Then they rejoined Ethan and Christine and made them tell every detail of the events of that morning. Mrs. Archer sat with an arm around each of her children. When all was said and done, Mabel Archer said a prayer, thanking God for protecting her children and calling on his continued favor in the future. She then busied herself preparing a late lunch for everyone.

Joe signaled Amos to follow him outside. Once they were on the porch, he led his brother to the barn for a private talk. There he began with what both he and Amos were thinking.

"We cain't let Ethan take the weight for this."

"You right. That means we got to make this fella disappear pronto," Amos said.

"No, I tried that back in Tennessee and look where it got me. There may be people in town who know this fella was askin' about me or even that he rode out this way. So what we gon' do is put this on me. Here's our story. He came here to do a robbery. Heard we had some cash put aside. You and Ethan and Mama were away tending the orchard. He rode up all friendly like and got the drop on me and Christine, but I ducked into the house looking for a weapon. He shot at me but missed. He marched Christine into the house at gunpoint and threatened to kill her if I didn't show myself. I didn't have no choice but to lay my rifle down, but just then Christine broke away from him. He caught her and clubbed her with his gun barrel. That gave me the chance to throw my huntin' knife. That's it—self-defense plain and simple. We just need to get rid of the reward poster and Carson's papers and take him into the marshal's office."

"Yeah, that could work. Except for one thing."

"What's that?"

"You ain't takin' the fall. I am. Ethan's my responsibility," Amos said.

"So is Christine and Emily and Mama. I don't have any of that responsibility and I'm already a wanted man. Use your head heah, big brotha. There's too much at stake not to. People in these parts know us and trust us. Carson's a stranger—a dead stranger. Besides, you couldn't make that knife throw to save your life."

Rather than renew his argument, Amos went to his brother and embraced him. "Let's go tell the others. They ain't gon' like it anymore than I do, but it's our best selection."

By dint of much persuasion, they convinced everybody to go along with Joe's version of events. They strapped Carson on his horse, and Amos and Joe left for Atchison to report the attempted robbery.

They road into Atchison and proceeded to the marshal's office. Marshal Burt Sayers was a tall, stoop-shouldered black man whose laconic manner was belied by the steel in his gaze and the lightning in his mind. He walked with a limp, courtesy of a bullet in his leg he had received in an altercation with a drunken cowboy early in his career. He was seated at his desk reading the paper when Joe and Amos entered his office. He self-consciously removed the reading glasses that were perched on his nose and asked, "How can I help you boys?"

After hearing their story, the marshal said, "I'm gon' have to go out to your place and take a look around."

So they turned around and rode back to the farm accompanied by the marshal and Dr. Peters, who came along at Amos's request to examine Christine's head wound. Dr. Peters also examined the body of the deceased and determined that he had died of a single knife wound to the heart and that the knife had entered his chest perpendicularly rather than at an upward or downward angle.

Once the marshal viewed the damage done by Carson's bullets and verified Christine's injury, he was satisfied as to the truth of Joe's story. "My boy, Harold, was one of the ones that directed that hard case out here. I sure am sorry for all the devilment he caused. I reckon folks will be more particular in the future about jawin' with nosey strangers. Anyway, my report is goin' to say self-defense while preventin' a robbery. I don't think there'll be an argument from anybody. Now, I have to find out who this fella is—or I should say *was*. Considerin' the amount of cash he had on him, I wouldn't be surprised if he doesn't have a record a mile long."

Dr. Peters and Marshal Sayers left, having offered the benefit of their respective professional opinions. Christine would be fine and Joe was in the clear.

Before leaving, Marshal Sayers had one final question. "Is Ethan all right? Didn't see much of 'im today."

"He's taking this kinda hard, as you might expect, almost losin' his sister and all," Joe said.

"Of course. Well, he's a plucky youngster. I'm sure he'll bounce back. Ya'll take care now. I'll be seein' you."

That evening at supper, their mood was one of subdued relief. They were co-conspirators, bound to a lie for life—a necessary but burdensome evil. Joe had an uneasy feeling. Marshal Sayers was bound to keep digging until he found something. That was his nature. That helped him to make up his mind.

44

After the dishes were cleared and the baby put down, Joe said, "I need to tell ya'll somethin'."

They resumed their places at the supper table. Joe took the crumbled wanted poster from his pocket and placed it on the table in front of him. Then he told his family the story behind it. When he finished, Christine said, "Well, it's over now and we can get back to our lives."

Joe said, "No, it ain't over. Matter of fact, it's just gettin' started. Carson was the first but there'll be others behind him like hounds on a scent. That's why I got to leave."

"You ain't gon' do no sucha thing," Amos said with finality. "You's with family and that's where you gon' stay. We discussed this back on the trail, rememba? We beat this one—we'll beat the next one, if there is a next one."

"I'm sorry, big brotha, but this ain't your decision. It's mine. Do you think I could live with myself if somethin' happened to any of y'all 'cause o' me? I let my guard down and Carson surprised me. I won't let that happen again. Besides, it's just a matter of time before one of these posters comes across Marshal Sayer's desk, and I'd rather face a hundred bounty hunters than that man. So, I'll be ridin' out in the mornin'."

"Joseph, where will you go?" Mrs. Archer asked, her face a study in shock and sorrow.

"I don't know, Mama. But even if I did know, I wouldn't tell you. To keep livin' free, I got to become a ghost. If I ever clear my name, I'll come back to y'all, and I promise you won't be able to drive me away with a stick."

"I'm goin' with you," Ethan said. "This is all my fault anyway."

"It ain't your fault. Carson wouldn'a been here if it wasn't for me, and he wouldn'a almost killed you and Christine if it wasn't for me. I'll take that to my grave. Besides, do you think we went to all this trouble so you could become a outlaw along side o' me?"

"But you said we were partners," Ethan said, his voice trembling.

"Yes, I did, and we are. But you know who our other partner is? Amos. And right now, he needs you to take my place as his right-hand man. You got to help him take care of the family and the farm—same as I was plannin' on doin'. Knowin' that you're heah by his side will help me to rest easy wherever I am. You a man now. Make me and your daddy proud."

After the talk, Joe went out in the night to try to clear his head. He walked down to the stable and went to Dice's stall. The stallion welcomed him with a nicker. Joe gave him a piece of carrot and rubbed his muzzle. "I guess we got some rough trail ahead of us, boy. You up for it?"

Dice's ears pricked forward at the inflection in Joe's voice. He pushed his head into Joe's chest, asking for another treat. Joe heard a footstep behind him and whirled, drawing his knife.

"It's just me," Amos said. He walked over to Joe and stood next to him. At his approach, Dice moved to the far side of the stall.

"I guess your mind is made up then?"

"'Fraid so."

"Well, you'll be needin' this." He pressed $200 in cash into Joe's hand.

"What's this?

"Just somethin' to tide you ova till you light somewheres."

Joe handed the money back to Amos. "Keep your money. I got savin's of my own, and if I need money, I know how to work for it. You got a farm to run and five mouths to feed. Keep your money."

"But you gon' need . . ."

Joe interrupted him. "Let's not waste time havin' a argument you ain't gon' win."

"Well, ain't there nothin' I can do for you, ya stubborn mule?"

Joe smiled and said, "Yeah, live to be a hundred."

"I will if you will," Amos said, grabbing Joe and giving him a hug reminiscent of their reunion. They walked back to the house with Amos's big hand resting on Joe's shoulder.

Alone in his room that evening, Joe was wracked with indecision despite his show of resolve at the supper table. He lay on his bunk reviewing his options on an endless loop. There were hunters coming. To elude them, he must become smoke in the wind. The question was which wind to ride. He could head west and prolong his freedom or head back east and try to clear his name. Stymied, he took the Cherokee blanket from his footlocker and wrapped it around his shoulders. He finally fell asleep fully clothed.

That night, Martha White Horn came to him in a dream for the second time. She took him in her arms and flew him to a place where he was able to commune with his ancestors who had lived and died to bring him to this point in his life. He was the fulfillment of their dreams, the vessel of their hopes, and the bearer of their blood. They gathered in a circle around him—hunter next to farmer, warrior next to slave, African next to American—and told him in their various voices that no matter what path he chose, they would share it with him. They closed around him and touched him with their hands and their minds, and he finally knew peace.

He awoke the next morning with a clear head. For better or worse, his course was set. He changed out of the clothes he had slept in, washed, and went to breakfast. Mrs. Archer had made blueberry griddlecakes, scrambled eggs with diced peppers, and thick slices of honey-cured ham—all Joe's favorites.

When he was finished, Joe said, "Thank you for a meal to remember."

She leaned over and kissed his forehead. "Take care, my darling, and come back to us when you can."

He gathered his things from his room, looking around to fix it in his memory. When he came out the front door, Dice was already saddled and waiting.

Ethan handed him the reins. "I fed and watered him, and there's some jerky, some beans, and a ration of oats in your saddlebags."

"Thanks, pard." He shook the boy's hand and then pulled him into a rough embrace.

Christine came with Emily and handed him the baby. Joe kissed her gently, taking in her baby smell. Emily grabbed his nose and gurgled good-bye. He handed her back to Christine, who gave her to Mrs. Archer.

 Christine came to Joe, put her arms around his neck, and kissed his cheek. "Stay safe. Your family loves you," she said.

Joe put another memory in the bank. Finally, he went to his brother. Tears were streaming down Amos's face.

"No matter where you go on this earth, know that you got a brotha who loves you and would lay down his life for you." They embraced, and the feel of his brother's arms around him was like provisions for the trail ahead.

Joe finished packing his saddlebags, tied on his bedroll, and placed the Henry in its boot. Then he swung into the saddle. He said, "I'll be back. Take care of each other." He wheeled Dice and rode away. He didn't look back. He didn't have to.

PART 5
Black Wolf

45

Joe Walker's first view of the Rocky Mountains almost took his breath away. The Smokies and the Blue Ridge Mountains of Tennessee were just foothills by comparison. He had never seen or imagined an entity that touched the earth and the clouds at the same time. He reined Dice to a halt and took in the mind-boggling spectacle.

"That fella back in Wichita sure wasn't lyin' when he called 'em God's knuckles," he said to his mount. "What kinda man you reckon it takes to live up there? I reckon we gon' find out."

He prodded Dice and they set off toward the mountain range. Joe Walker was a fugitive. With the stroke of a pen, some anonymous magistrate had changed his identity, separated him from his family, and dimmed his future prospects. Despite his circumstances, however, he was determined to maintain a code of conduct that would prevent him from sinking to a moral level from which there could be no return.

He had made a fateful decision before leaving his home in Kansas that he would choose freedom over retribution. And so, he had taken the trail west away from the scene of his alleged crime. There was a thousand dollar bounty on his head, and it ensured that men who were desperate, greedy, or both would hunt him to capture or death.

He sought surroundings that would help even the odds against him. In the open, he would see them coming.

It was May, but there was snow on the mountains and a chill wind blew from their direction. He pulled his sheepskin parka up to his chin and rode on. By sundown, he still had not reached the foothills. He made camp in an aspen grove beside a gurgling stream. Seated by the fire, he reviewed the events of the last year.

After leaving his family in Kansas, Joe had headed west and crossed the border into Colorado. Not knowing who might be tracking him, he intended to lay low and not draw attention to himself. Unfortunately, his code kept interfering with that plan.

The first time was in Cheyenne Wells. He was working in the livery stable. One night, he overheard three drunken cowboys accosting a woman on her way home from church. It didn't help matters that she was black and they were white. He intervened and they objected—strenuously. He avoided using his gun or his knife but, nonetheless, his assailants suffered a broken jaw, a concussion, and a severely bruised kidney. He moved on.

The next time was when he was working as a ranch hand on a spread outside of Pueblo, Colorado. His trail mates wanted to hang a Crow Indian who had stolen and butchered a beef to feed his starving family. Joe offered to pay for the cow, but the cowboys were not interested in a bloodless solution.

The foreman, Hank Jacobs, in particular, kept the fire burning. "This redskin's gonna hang. The only question is whether you're gonna hang with 'im, boy." He flung a rope with a noose at the end over the limb of a cottonwood, and the other hands dragged the protesting native forward.

Joe moved between the men and the tree. "I say we take him back to the ranch and let Mr. Lipscomb decide what happens to 'im," he said.

Jacobs stepped forward, his hand on the butt of his Colt. "Out here, I'm the boss, so you got to the count of three to get out of the way, boy. One . . . two . . ."

Joe waited until Jacobs started his draw then he shot him in the shoulder. He had drawn and fired before Jacobs could clear leather.

"Uhhh! You shot me! You black bastard!"

The other cowboys were eyeing Joe with wariness and respect.

"Everybody stand easy." Joe's tone was conversational, as though he were asking for another cup of morning coffee. He motioned the Indian forward and cut the ropes binding his wrists.

"Git goin'," Joe said.

The man stood still, unable to decide if it was safe to turn his back on Joe.

"Go!" Joe said, this time gesturing with his hand.

"Ahóoh," (Thank you,) the man said in Crow.

"You'll pay for this, Horn," Jacobs said.

"We'll let Mr. Lipscomb decide."

He mounted Dice and rode back toward the ranch, leaving the disgruntled group of ranch hands standing in a clump muttering to each other.

Joe told his story to the ranch owner, as did Jacobs. John Lipscomb sided with his ramrod and promptly fired Joe. He took the price of the butchered cow out of Joe's last paycheck.

As Joe was leaving the bunkhouse for the last time, Jacobs confronted him. "This ain't over, Horn. You and me're gonna meet again, I promise you that."

Joe, who had taken the last name "Horn" to conceal his identity, had had enough of this man's prodding. "We can settle this right now, Jacobs."

"You know I cain't shoot with this arm."

"Well, we can go left-handed then. Don't make no difference to me," Joe said.

Jacobs held Joe's gaze briefly then lowered his eyes. "See, I told you he was a killer," he said to his companions before retiring to his bunk with a sullen but defeated expression on his face.

Joe left the ranch house headed east, but when he got out of sight, he turned west again. After that incident, Joe decided it was best if he stayed as far away from the usual haunts of men as possible. That was when he decided to try his hand in the mountains.

46

Joe had heard there was a living to be made in the Rockies trapping beaver and fox. He bought the necessary gear along with winter clothing in a general store in Platteville, Colorado. He also purchased a pack mule and a Sharps rifle. He followed the Colorado River toward its source and watched the landscape change from prairie to forested slopes and grassy meadows surrounding pristine alpine lakes. The countryside was teeming with awakening life after the protracted winter. The air was exhilarating, laden with the smell of pine needles and wild flowers. Joe's lungs were working overtime to adjust to the altitude. Physical chores like chopping wood or tracking game left him winded. Yet he was more at peace than he had been since leaving Kansas. The absence of human companionship, rather than depressing him, caused him to relax and take emotional inventory. His heart and body had sustained significant scars in the last year, and he needed some solitary time to heal.

The rigors of farming and ranch work had turned Joe into an imposing physical specimen. He moved with the grace of a panther and had cultivated uncanny skill with a rope, a knife, and a gun. Dice had gotten over much of his skittishness and had become a reliable cow pony. Together they were an expert team, capable of earning their keep from the Colorado River to the Rio Grande.

Joe found a location for his permanent homestead in Wyoming in a valley of the Big Horn Mountains at about six thousand feet above sea level. There was a clear stream running through the valley and stands of pine, ash, and birch for timber. There was abundant wildlife and a large beaver pond at the valley's western end. Joe selected a site that was sheltered from the north and west and began the process of building a cabin.

He chopped down trees and hauled them to the site with the help of his pack mule. He laid his foundation and built his walls to the desired height. His experience building the house that he and his family shared in Kansas and helping to build and repair lodges in the Cherokee village came in handy now.

His days were filled with hard work and his nights with dreamless slumber. He had not experienced such a period of tranquil rest since being sold down the river as a child.

After a month's labor, he had constructed a ten-by-twenty-foot cabin with a one-hundred-square-foot sleeping loft. He chinked the walls with mud and covered the roof with sod. He built a bunk for himself, a table, two chairs, a supply chest, and a gun rack. He had purchased a potbellied stove in the town of Lovell along with dishes and cooking utensils. When his cabin was completed, he attached a lean-to for Dice and the pack mule that would provide them with warmth and shelter during the winter months.

After building his cabin, Joe scouted the area for his future trapline. He surveyed the banks of the beaver pond and game trails in the forest frequented by foxes, mink, and snowshoe rabbits. These animals attracted larger predators, including wolves, lynxes, and mountain lions whose pelts were also valuable. He had no trapping experience, so he decided that he would go slowly and learn the trade by which he hoped to support himself.

In his exploration of the countryside, Joe had also discovered the tracks of unshod horses. This meant that he was not alone in the valley, but he convinced himself that, given the abundance of game, there was no need to concern himself with a few native hunters. His sojourn with the Cherokee had fostered in him feelings of empathy, if not brotherhood, with the red man. In time, he was certain to encounter his neighbors, and then he would begin the process of establishing the basis for peaceful coexistence.

One morning, Joe had just finished breakfast when he heard the sound of horses approaching the cabin. He went to the front door and looked through the rifle port. About a dozen mounted Indians were riding into his front yard. Judging by their dress and the length of their hair, they were Crow. They reined up, and the apparent leader hailed the cabin. "Kahée." (Hello.)

Joe pushed his rifle through the gun port.

The speaker raised his hand palm outward and spoke in English. "We come to talk. Show yourself."

The tone and inflection of his voice suggested he was used to being obeyed. He was of average height with a body that was lean and muscled. His long hair was tied back and brushed his pony's rump. His features were sharp. The blade of his nose bisected high cheekbones, which sloped to a rugged chin. He wore a stuffed crow on his head, a fringed buckskin shirt, and leggings. His lance was decorated with crow and eagle feathers. Everything about him spoke of freedom and virility.

Joe decided it would be demeaning to speak to such a man through a slit in his door. He opened the front door and stepped into the yard, his rifle in the crook of his arm.

"I am Heap of Crows, war chief of the Mountain Crow. This valley—Crow land. You no stay here."

"I am Joe Horn and I come in peace," Joe said. "I came for fur. Don't plan to stay long."

"This valley is Crow hunting ground," Heap of Crows said with a sweeping gesture. "You go—now!"

Joe thought, *If only they'd come before I got my cabin built and my garden planted. I woulda pulled up stakes and moved on—no problem. But now it's too late to start over somewhere else before the snow flies.*

The Crow were a proud people. Over a sixty-year period, they had seen their land encroached upon by both native and white interlopers. The Cheyenne, the Sioux, and the Arapahoe were their fiercest Indian enemies, and they were at constant war with these tribes. The Crow were fewer in number than their enemies who frequently joined forces against them, so their defeats outnumbered their victories. With each major defeat, their holdings diminished.

The Big Horn Mountains were prime trapping territory and also held sacred significance for the Crow tribe. The systematic incursion of enemies bent on stealing their land had made them almost fanatical in its defense. Joe was unaware of this history and the imminent danger it placed him in.

Joe surveyed the group in front of him. They were armed with bows, hatchets, and lances. He could drop at least six of them before he backed through the cabin door. After that, it would get dicey. The tension in the air was palpable. Then one of the riders separated from the group and pointed at Joe, talking rapidly.

"Two Lances say you saved his life," Heap of Crows said.

Joe looked at the warrior next to Heap of Crows and recognized the man he had saved from the cowboys on the Lipscomb spread.

Two Lances dismounted and walked over to Joe. He pointed to his chest and said, "Ne-sko-mo-ne. Ahóoh."

Joe asked Heap of Crows, "What's he sayin'?"

"He say he is Two Lances. Thank you for his life."

"Tell 'im he's welcome."

Heap of Cows spoke to Two Lances. The brave looked at Joe and nodded. He stepped forward and offered his hand. Joe and he clasped forearms. Instead of returning to his comrades, Two Lances stepped over and stood beside Joe. Heap of Crows spoke to Two Lances in Crow. Joe could not understand the words but their tone was clear to him. His odds had just improved.

Heap of Crows appeared to be considering his options. Finally, he said to Joe, "You stay until the planting season returns. Hunt. Trap. Fish. Then you leave or you die."

He repeated his message in Crow for his men's benefit.

Joe said, "I'll do as Heap of Crows says. You have my word."

Two Lances nodded and gave a grunt of acceptance. He rejoined his fellows and mounted his horse.

Heap of Crows gave Joe a parting look that said, "Don't test me." Then he wheeled his pony and rode away, followed by his entourage.

Joe watched them until they disappeared over the rise. Then he turned and went back into his cabin.

47

After the Crows' visit, Joe loaded all his weapons and filled his canteen and water bucket. He believed Heap of Crows was a man of his word, but he didn't know who else might come calling and didn't want to be caught off guard a second time.

After two weeks went by without incident, he began to relax somewhat and resumed his normal routine. This involved tending his garden, adding to his woodpile, and filling his larder with salted and jerked meat. To save ammunition, he did most of his hunting with a bow. This required patience and skill and gave him a feeling of deeper connection to his prey and their environment.

Once while tracking a herd of elk, he crossed paths with a Crow hunting party. The men surrounded him and then dispersed when their leader spoke to them. He rode up to Joe and raised his hand in a gesture of greeting. He was dressed in a bleached buffalo robe, fringed deerskin leggings, and calf-high moccasins. He spoke to Joe in Crow. "Ku-maa-leek." (We are leaving now.) Then, he and his party rode on. Apparently the word had gone out that Joe was not to be interfered with.

Joe found the elk herd in a high mountain pass. A cold wind blew out of the north, and Joe could see clouds of steam rising from the elk's muzzles. The herd was taking advantage of grazing the frost-seared grass before it disappeared altogether. There were about a dozen cows and one big bull in the herd who lifted his magnificent head every few minutes to sniff the air for signs of trouble. Joe counted twelve points on his rack of antlers.

Joe dismounted downwind and began a slow approach on his belly through the tall grass. He had drawn to within a hundred yards of the herd when Dice began to snort and stamp behind him. Joe was perturbed by this display, as it meant he would likely lose his opportunity for a shot.

Just then, a grizzly bear burst from the cover of the trees and approached the herd at a ground-devouring run. The bull trumpeted a warning and the herd turned as one and began running in Joe's direction. The grizzly overtook a cow and her calf and felled the calf with one stroke of its giant paw. The remaining elk ran past Joe, oblivious to any threat he posed as he crouched in the grass. The bear had paused at his kill and was disemboweling the calf with its claws and teeth.

Joe began to slowly back way from the feeding animal. Unfortunately, the calf's mother foiled his undetected escape. Unlike the rest of the herd, she approached the feeding grizzly, bellowing forlornly and essaying mock charges. The bear paused in his feeding and growled at the cow. When she did not retreat, he rose and advanced toward her in a shambling run.

Joe was caught between the grizzly and the grieving mother. He notched an arrow in his bow and waited. When the bear was twenty yards away, he caught Joe's scent and stood up on his hind legs, growling and snuffling.

Joe waited until the last possible moment. Then he stood up and loosed his arrow. It pierced the grizzly's chest, eliciting a bellow of pain. Joe shot a second arrow that lodged a hand's breadth from the first. Then he turned and ran.

The grizzly dropped to all fours and pursued Joe at a dead run. A race between a man and a grizzly bear was hardly a contest. The bear was swiftly overtaking Joe when Dice appeared seemingly out of nowhere. His attachment to Joe had somehow overcome his fear of a mortal enemy. Without breaking stride, Joe grabbed the pommel and swung into the saddle.

Dice needed no urging to reach top speed. Still, the grizzly held its own and drew to within yards of the fleeing stallion. Joe pulled his rifle from the boot and fired three quick shots at the pursuing behemoth. The third shot entered the bear's right eye and he dropped like a load of bricks. Joe slowed Dice and turned in a wide circle, approaching the downed grizzly. He raised his rifle for a kill shot but it was not necessary.

For the second time in his young life, Joe had survived an encounter with a bear. He approached the downed animal with his rifle cocked and aimed. Upon close inspection of the animal, Joe realized how fortunate he had been.

The bear was a giant of his species, weighing close to a thousand pounds, Joe estimated based upon its girth and length. The signature hump across his shoulders was a ridge of fat and muscle. His claws were four-inch-long lethal crescents, black at the base and light brown at the tip. Blood and brain matter trickled from his wounded eye. His fall had driven Joe's arrows deep into his chest.

Joe said a prayer of thanks and began to dress the huge animal. This kill would supply him with food, fat, and clothing for months to come. The grizzly's fur was soft and thick and had a wild, clean smell—dried pine needles rubbed with cinnamon.

He looked up at the sound of approaching horses. The Crow hunting party were approaching at a gallop. They surrounded Joe and the bear, shouting and raising their fists in the air. Apparently, they had witnessed Joe's exploit and were paying tribute to his skill and bravery. Joe raised his own fist, unsure of what else to do.

The leader dismounted and said something in Crow to Joe. Though Joe did not understand his words, the man's newfound respect for him was apparent. The Crow extended his hand and the two men clasped forearms. The other hunters began a singsong chant and rode in a circle around Joe and their leader.

Afterward, they skinned and dressed the bear and built a travois to carry the meat back to Joe's cabin. Joe retrieved a haunch of bear meat from the travois and offered it to the Indians. Nodding, the leader removed a bone-handled skinning knife from his belt and gave it to Joe. Joe accepted the knife and said the one Crow word he knew.

"Ahóoh." (Thank you.)

"It-chiik." (Good.) Then the brave pointed to his chest and said, "Co-kan-you-son-ne." (Feather in His Hair.)

Joe repeated the man's name, "Co-kan-you-son-ne." And then pointed at his own chest and said, "Joe Horn."

"Joe Horn," the brave said and nodded.

This time the parting between Joe and the Crow hunting party was genuinely amicable. That night Joe added an apple to Dice's ration of oats and gave him an extra long rubdown. The stallion had saved his life at the risk of his own, and the bond between them was now unbreakable.

Joe celebrated his survival with a supper that included a bear steak, baked sweet potatoes, corn bread, and asparagus spears. He washed it all down with cold, sweet tea. Before retiring, he thanked God for prolonging his life and prayed for the health and happiness of his family. His sleep was deep and undisturbed by guilt or regret.

48

Winter was approaching. The high mountain passes were already covered with snow, and there was a scrim of ice on the surface of the water barrel each morning. Joe had set his trapline with the help of Two Lances and Feather in His Hair. The two Crow warriors had become his hunting companions and frequent guests after the incident with the grizzly in the high pass.

Due to their association, Joe was learning Crow and they were picking up English. They communicated adequately with a mixture of words and sign language. This was the way Joe had learned Cherokee. The Crow braves helped him lay out his trapline based on their extensive knowledge of the game trails in the valley. When the snows came, these would yield a bounty of mink, fox, rabbit, beaver, and ermine sporting their valuable winter coats.

One evening, the three men sat around Joe's table cleaning the turkeys they had shot that day. Joe's cabin was a warm refuge from the howling October wind. The big grizzly's hide covered one wall, helping to stop the wind's penetration between the cabin's mud-chinked logs. The wood stove in the center of the room glowed cherry red and threw off a corona of heat that enabled them to work in shirtsleeves.

Two Lances broached the delicate subject of Joe's promise to Heap of Crows. *"You are set for the winter, but what will you do in the spring?"*

"I'll move on," Joe said.

"Where will you go?" Feather In His Hair asked.

"I don't know."

"Maybe you could ask Heap of Crows to let you stay. We would back you up," Two Lances said.

"I gave my word. I won't go back on it."

They sat in silence, pulling feathers from the turkey carcasses.

"This is woman's work. You need a woman. Come to our village. There are single women there. Pick one. We will vouch for you," Feather in His Hair said.

"I can't ask a woman to come with me when I don't know where I'm going. Besides, I have a woman."

"Where is she?" Two Lances asked.

"She's dead."

"A dead woman is no good to you," Feather in His Hair said.

"I'm still mourning."

"I understand," Feather in His Hair said, sensing Joe's distress.

"How long will you mourn?"

"I don't know. Until my heart says stop, I guess," Joe said, making the signs for sadness and time passing.

Feather in His Hair changed the subject. *"I saw grizzly tracks up near the divide this week—a big one."*

"Oh yeah?"

"If we go back up there, maybe we could find him. And maybe you could race him."

"Kiss my ass," Joe said and threw a handful of feathers at Feather in His Hair.

The brave retaliated, laughing loudly. While Joe was engaged with Feather in His Hair, Two Lances executed a flanking maneuver. Soon, the three young men were rolling on the cabin floor, laughing and tossing feathers until they looked like reincarnated turkeys. When the hijinks were over, Joe felt cleansed of another vestige of pain. His sides ached but in a good way. They cleaned up and had dinner, carefully avoiding all weighty subjects.

The snows came in November, bringing single digit temperatures with them. Joe worked his trapline and prepared his pelts for sale. By spring, he would have a cache of prime-quality furs that would bring a handsome price at the trading post in Laramie. He was totally acclimated to the high altitude and could walk for miles in snowshoes. He usually wore a wolfskin coat, deerskin pants, and boots and gloves made of rabbit fur. He had made a pendant of one claw from the bear he had killed and wore it around his neck.

On his first visit to the Crow village, Joe was surprised by its size. Located in a bowl-shaped valley on the opposite side of the mountain from Joe's cabin, the village consisted of a cluster of about one hundred teepees. There was a crystal-clear lake about a mile in diameter adjacent to the village. The bluffs surrounding the encampment were covered with lodgepole pine, aspen, and spruce trees.

The triangular teepees were roughly twenty-five feet tall, fifteen feet at the base, and made of buffalo skins and prairie grasses stretched over a wooden frame. They were decorated with paintings of humans, animals, and birds, most notably crows. Interspersed among the dwellings were wooden frames used for drying skins in the summer and freezing meat in the winter. There was a large corral containing the tribe's horses. They looked strong and swift—bred for hunting and battle, no doubt.

Riding between Two Lances and Feather in His Hair, Joe made a striking figure, covered in animal hides with his black skin, long kinky hair, and full beard. The people of the village regarded him as they would an apparition. Most had never seen a black man before, let alone one dressed and armed like Joe.

He met the chief of the Mountain Crow, Long Horse, and gave him a gift of tobacco. The chief reciprocated with a peace pipe. After breaking bread, he smoked and powwowed with the men. Two Lances repeated the story of how they met, and Feather in His Hair told the story of how Joe killed the grizzly singlehandedly.

Then Long Horse spoke. Heap of Crows translated, though Joe caught most of the meaning. "Long Horse say Black Wolf is a strong warrior and hunter—friend of the Crow."

Joe said, "Ahóoh," and added the sign for friend.

Long Horse insisted Joe stay the night at the village, and Joe accepted.

Joe stayed in Two Lances's teepee with him and his wife, Aiyana, and his son, Kitchi. Aiyana had been pregnant with Kitchi when Two Lances killed John Lipscomb's steer for food.

Kitchi was an inquisitive toddler with his mother's eyes and his father's smile. At first, he was shy in Joe's presence, clinging to his mother. But when Joe produced a piece of rock candy from his pocket, it was too much for the boy to resist. He tentatively moved forward and took the proffered treat from Joe's hand. The die was cast. By the time it was his bedtime, Kitchi had to be pried, protesting, from Joe's lap.

After Aiyana put him down, she came back to sit with Joe and Two Lances.

"He is usually not that way with strangers," Two Lances said.

"He knows a brother when he sees one," Joe said, smiling. He asked a question that had been nagging him since his meeting with Chief Long Horse. *"Why did Heap of Crows call me Black Wolf today?"*

"O-ne-mok-tan is your Crow name. Feather in His Hair gave it to you. It is a good name. It fits you. You are fierce like a wolf and your skin is black," Two Lances said.

"O-ne-mok-tan," Joe said, imitating Two Lances's pronunciation. *"How did you get your name?"*

"Once on a buffalo hunt, I threw my lance at a bull. It stuck in his side, but he turned and charged me. He gored my horse and knocked me to the ground. Then he charged me again. I ran and pulled another lance from the side of a dead buffalo. My second throw was true. The bull died at my feet," Two Lances said.

"Not only can't I imagine doing that, I can barely imagine anybody else doing it either," Joe said, shaking his head in wonder.

"No harder than facing a grizzly on foot," Two Lances said.

"I was lucky."

"So was I."

Aiyana moved next to Two Lances and spoke quietly in his ear. He nodded and she rose and went to a chest next to the wall of the teepee. She took a snow-white buffalo robe from the chest, brought it to Joe, and placed it in his arms.

Joe was caught completely by surprise. *"What is this for?"*

"Aiyana knows what you did for our family. When I told her you were in the valley, she started working on this robe for you. It is to say thank you," Two Lances said.

The robe was as soft as down and bleached as white as an ermine in winter.

"I will treasure this gift for the rest of my life and thank you from the bottom of my heart," Joe said, bowing deeply to Two Lances's young bride.

Aiyana took his hand in both of hers and spoke from her heart. *"Because of you, I have a husband and my son has a father. You will always have a home with us."*

When Joe understood her meaning, the blood rose to his cheeks and he was thankful for his beard.

"E-wash-chek, Ayóoh," Joe said and squeezed her hand before releasing it.

49

A snow squall moved in that night, so Joe ended up spending several days in the Crow village. By the time he returned to his cabin, he had to dig his way in. He made a fire and put water on the stove for tea.

He had learned more about the Mountain Crow during his prolonged stay. They made a living primarily by trapping and hunting. They traded their pelts for money at the Hudson Bay post in Laramie. They were the sworn enemies of the Lakota (Sioux), and the two tribes engaged in raids and skirmishes along the South Dakota/Wyoming border, stealing horses and taking scalps during the summer months.

Long Horse had succeeded Walking Bear as the chief after the latter was killed in a battle with the Sioux the previous spring. He was a young chief, looking for the opportunity to make a name for himself. Heap of Crows, the war chief, would figure prominently in those plans. Together they would, no doubt, make a pair to be reckoned with.

Joe felt glad to be back in his own place. He had become unused to being around crowds, and his celebrity status at the Crow encampment had worn on him considerably. The next day, he went out to clear his traps. In his absence, he had netted two beaver, a fox, and four rabbits. One trap was sprung. It contained a severed rabbit's foot and was surrounded by wolf tracks.

Price of doin' business, Joe thought. He reset the trap and moved on.

That evening, Joe removed, scraped, and cured his pelts. The cache of furs in his locker was growing satisfactorily. If his luck continued, by spring he could anticipate a handsome return on his labor. The meat he didn't intend to eat he returned to the forest where it would be quickly consumed by nature's hunters.

He developed a routine of walking or riding his trapline by day and curing his hides at night. This was interspersed with household chores—cooking, sewing, and maintaining his cabin. When Two Lances or Feather in His Hair visited, he would take a break to go hunting or ice fishing. The winter passed in this desultory fashion. Joe was snowed in for a week on one occasion. He took the time to write a letter to Amos letting him know he was still alive and still free. He would post it in the spring when he traded his furs.

Writing the letter made Joe think of his family and the one-way nature of any communication between them. He wondered about Ethan's development. He must be quite a young man by now. And little Emily was probably already walking *and* talking.

The thought of never seeing Christine's smile again or feeling the warmth of Mama Mabel's hug also weighed on his heart. Most of all, he missed his brother and the bond they had reestablished during their time together. The relative solitude of a mountain man's life had been what he needed a year ago. But it was not the life for him. He sensed he was destined to live his life and make his mark in some other manner. So he reopened the letter and added a postscript.

Before I left I told you you would see me again. The only way for that to happen is if I find a way to clear my name. I did not do the thing they say I did. I got to go back and face the men who put a bounty on my head. They may beet me. They holding all the aces. But I will trust in God and the truth to set me free. I

been hiding behind a mask for too long. But I will not die with a mark on my name. Pray for me. God willing the next time we see each other we will both be free.
Your Loving Brother,
Joseph

Once again, Joe was putting himself in harm's way to do the right thing. This time, he was about to place his trust in a justice system that had never served his people. He had cheated death many times in his young life. Never had he felt so unprepared for the contest. Yet he moved forward with a calmness born of faith and fortitude.

When spring finally came to the mountains, Joe welcomed it along with all the other beleaguered inhabitants. The sun warmed the frozen slopes, and new grass and flowers covered the mountain meadows. Joe no longer had to break through the scrim of ice on the surface of his water barrel each morning.

The stream in front of his cabin practically sang as it made its way down the mountain. Everywhere the forest animals were tending and teaching the offspring they had brought into the world. The wheel of life had turned again.

He stepped out of his cabin one morning to see three riders approaching. As they drew closer, he recognized Heap of Crows, Two Lances, and Feather in His Hair. He invited his visitors in and placed water on the stove for tea.

While they were waiting, Heap of Crows revealed the reason for their visit. "It soon be planting season," he said in English.

"Yes, I'm planning to leave soon," Joe said in Crow, mildly annoyed that the chief felt he needed to remind him of his promise.

"You don't have to leave. You may stay as long as you like. Black Wolf is brother to the Crow," Heap of Crows said.

Joe was caught by surprise but recovered quickly. *"I am proud to be brother to the Crow, but I have to go. I have something to take care of back east. It is a matter of honor."*

"When honor calls, a man must answer. When will you return?"

"I don't know. I have a brother in Kansas who may need my help."

Feather in His Hair and Two Lances were silent during this exchange. This was not the way they had expected this conversation to go.

"What about your cabin and your trapline?" Feather in His Hair said, trying to forestall the inevitable.

"The Crow can use my cabin anytime they want. And I want you to have my traps."

Stymied, Feather in His Hair turned to Two Lances for support.

Two Lances's words offered small comfort. *"You are like a brother to me. If you needed me, I would walk through fire to help you, so I understand the call of your own blood. You must go now, but I believe we will meet again. The Great Spirit has bound us together."*

Realizing this might be their last time together, the men said their good-byes. Heap of Crows took the war hatchet from his belt and handed it to Joe. Joe went to his war chest and retrieved his bowie knife and gave it to the chief. Heap of Crows removed the knife from its sheath and took in the distinctive shape of the blade with a grunt of approval.

Feather in His Hair removed an eagle feather from his hair and handed it to Joe. *"This is strong medicine. May it protect you as it has protected me."*

Joe removed his bear claw pendant and gave it to Feather in His Hair. *"May this protect you as it has protected me."*

Finally, Two Lances removed a pouch from his belt and handed it to Joe. Inside was a gold nugget about the size of a robin's egg. *"These yellow stones are very valuable to the white man. Maybe you can use it on your journey."*

Joe went to his gun rack and removed his Sharps rifle. He brought it back to the table and placed it in Two Lances's hands. *"May it never fail you,"* he said.

There was little else to be said. They drank tea, smoked, and parted ways.

Three weeks later, Joe was packed and ready to go. He looked at his humble cabin one last time and rode away.

Two Lances and Feather in His Hair had offered to escort him to Laramie. Though it was unnecessary, he was glad for their company.

He sold his furs at the trading post for the remarkable sum of $825 and then sold his pack mule for another $40. He bought supplies and ammunition for himself and trinkets, beads, and rock candy for Aiyana and Kitchi, courtesy of Uncle Joseph. Having successfully completed their business, he and his companions rode back the way they had come.

At the edge of the Crow lands, he parted ways with Two Lances and Feather in His Hair. Their good-bye this time was brief and unsentimental. He was proud to know these men—proud to have earned their respect and friendship. In a way, they had brought him back to himself. He had entered the mountains as Joe Horn, but he was leaving as Joe Walker. It would be either the name on his acquittal or the one on his tombstone.

PART 6

In the Valley of the Shadow

50

It had been a while since Joe Walker had attended church. His knees brushed the back of the pew in front of him, and he was hemmed in on both sides by congregants in their Sunday best, adding to his discomfort. Given the places he had seen and lived recently, it was hard for him to imagine that God preferred these environs.

He was attending the Sunday service at the Ebenezer Church of The Holy Redeemer in Ebenezer, Tennessee. It was a wooden building painted white with an eight-foot cross attached to its peaked roof.

Inside, a wide center aisle with wooden pews on both sides led to a dais on which stood a pulpit of shaved maple wood with a carving of praying hands on its front. Behind the pulpit was a chair with a tall back and cushioned seat, giving it a throne-like appearance. The "throne" was flanked by two standard-size chairs. All three were painted gold.

A six-foot carved wooden crucifix was attached to the wall behind the pulpit. The church's windows were glass, covered by filmy white curtains that let in light and air while maintaining the congregation's privacy. Joe was struck by such opulence in a building owned by colored people.

The congregation rose to sing the opening hymn, "A Mighty Fortress Is Our God." Joe added his baritone to the mix and prayed that the choir director would end the rendition after a verse or two. His prayer went unanswered. At least it was an opportunity to stretch his legs. After the last verse was sung, the congregation resumed their seats and a boy of about fifteen rose and delivered the scripture reading. Joe took out his Bible and followed along.

The congregation was all black except for a white man seated on the dais next to the minister. The scripture reader delivered his text from Galatians 5:1. "Stand fast therefore in the liberty wherewith Christ hath made us free and be not entangled again with the yoke of bondage."

The words caused a lump to rise in Joe's throat and his breath to quicken. It was if God were affirming that the impossible mission he had undertaken was, indeed, the right and necessary thing to do. In recent months, he had ridden over seven hundred miles to come to this particular place.

He had come to see the man who sat next to the white man on the dais—the man who rose after the scripture reading and stepped into the pulpit with an air of quiet authority. His slender build was accentuated by his dark clothing. He had mahogany-colored skin, a high forehead, arching brows, and piercing brown eyes. His beard was neatly trimmed and his hair was professionally barbered as well. His manner and speech were those of a teacher. His voice had a rhythmic singsong quality that he used to great effect as he warmed to his subject. His name was Samuel Johnson.

"Welcome to God's house. No matter what you seek, it is within God's power to grant it to you. The scripture says, 'I was glad when they said unto me, let us go into the house of the Lord.' We ought to be glad this morning. We ought to be rejoicing that we can set aside our burdens for just a little while and lean on the everlasting arms of Jesus."

There were shouts of "Amen!" and "Praise Jesus!" from the congregation. Reverend Johnson continued his sermon.

"Though you may not share our religious convictions, you are welcome here. Though you may be an outcast from the haunts of men, you are welcome here.

Though your heart may be burdened with the shackles of sin, you are welcome here!

"Our text this morning is from Paul's letter to the Galatians. It speaks of both the reward and the cost of freedom. As colored people, we are well aware of this subject. God, in His mercy, has lifted the yoke of slavery form our necks and led us into the 'Promised Land.' But there are still many miles to travel before we can rest. We must make ourselves worthy of God's gift of freedom by educating ourselves, fortifying ourselves spiritually, and assuming our rightful place as productive citizens of the *United* States of America!"

"Amen!" "Get that education!" "Preach!"

"Read your bible! After the Israelites left Egypt, they wandered in the wilderness for forty years. Then when they got to the 'Promised Land,' they had to fight the Canaanites to possess it. The path to freedom is never easy. God made it that way for the Children of Israel, and he makes it that way for us today. Why? So we never take freedom for granted."

The Reverend Johnson spoke for a full hour on the topic of freedom, weaving the story of the Israelites and the Africans who were shanghaied to America into a seamless example of God's magnanimity toward his children. He gave examples from his own life. Although he was born a free man, his father taught him early on that freedom for a black man in America was as elusive as a feather in the wind. Once it was grasped, it must be secured with determination, ambition, and solidarity. He closed with a return to the New Testament.

"As God's people, we cannot be free until we turn over our lives to him. He said in Matthew 11:28, 'Come unto me all ye who labor and are heavy laden and I will give you rest.' Aren't you ready to lay your burdens down? Aren't you ready to be truly free? There is only one answer, 'Yes, I surrender all to my Lord and Savior, Jesus Christ!'"

The choir rose and began singing "Rock of Ages." Several people came down the aisle to surrender their lives to Jesus or to rededicate themselves to his service. The congregation rewarded them with shouts of "That's right!" and "Thank you, Jesus!"

When the woman next to him rose to join the supplicants, Joe followed her and exited the church. He welcomed the fresh air and sunshine after the close quarters of the building. He had found his man. Now it only remained to enlist his aid.

51

The following morning, Joe paid Reverend Johnson a visit. The preacher had an office in town from which he conducted his other businesses. Before entering, Joe read the sign at the door.

SAMUEL L. JOHNSON, ATTORNEY AT LAW
LICENSED REAL ESTATE AGENT
OFFICE HOURS: MONDAY–THURSDAY
8 AM–4 PM

The one-room office had a large rolltop desk against one wall. A four-by-six-foot bookcase occupied another wall. A coatrack was in the corner by the door, and there was a short bench and three chairs for visitors. Each seat had a handmade seat cushion. A spittoon was located beside the door. Samuel Johnson was seated behind the desk whose surface was covered with official-looking papers, notepads, and open books. On the wall in front of him was a county map with colored pins stuck in various locations. A third wall contained Johnson's law and real estate licenses, as well as an insignia from the Ninth United States Heavy Artillery Colored Troops. There was a three-foot wooden partition across the room with a gate in the middle that separated the waiting area from Johnson's workspace.

Reverend Johnson pushed back from his desk and rose to greet his visitor. He was dressed much the same as he had been on the previous Sunday in a dark three-piece suit—whose jacket now hung on a second coatrack beside his desk—and a black string tie with a white shirt. His boots were polished to a high gleam. He approached Joe and asked, "May I help you?"

"Yessuh, I'm lookin' to hire a lawyer."

"And what is this pertaining to?"

Joe's look of puzzlement caused him to rephrase his question. "Excuse me. What is this about?"

"I'm plannin' to turn myself in for a crime they say I did in Benton six years ago, and I want somebody to stand for me in court."

"And what crime are you charged with?"

"Murder."

Sam Johnson's eyes opened wide, and he stared at Joe with a mixture of surprise and apprehension.

"I didn't do it," Joe said hastily. "I mean, I did kill some people, but it was in self defense."

"I'm afraid you've come to the wrong person, Mister. . . "

"Walker. Joe Walker." Joe said, extending his hand.

Sam Johnson tentatively shook Joe's hand. "I'm Samuel Johnson."

"I know who you are, Reverend Johnson. That's why I'm here," Joe said.

"I don't understand," Johnson said.

Joe asked a question he already knew the answer to.

"Are you the Samuel Johnson who was the chaplain for the Ninth United States Heavy Artillery Colored Troops?"

"Yes. I was with the Ninth. But what's that got to do with this?"

"It all fits together, suh, but I need time to tell it. Would you give me just a half hour of your time? I'll pay for it. If you don't want to take my case after that, I'll leave you alone."

Joe saw the lawyer debating with himself internally, and then he made a decision that would have profound consequences.

"Have a seat, Mr. Walker. Something tells me you have a worthwhile story to tell."

Johnson opened the gate and invited Joe to sit in one of the office chairs. He rolled his chair to a place where he could hear and observe Joe closely.

Now that the opportunity to make his pitch had arrived, Joe felt conflicted. He was about to reveal facts to a stranger that could get him hanged, but at the same time, he knew if Johnson could be convinced to take the case at all, it would be the truth that would convince him.

Joe told his story from the shootout with the three townsmen and his decision to bury their bodies and ride on rather than face an all-white southern jury. He told the tale of his settling with his family in Kansas and the fateful arrival of the bounty hunter that reaffirmed his outlaw status. He talked about his initial decision to keep running but how that was altered when he encountered a group of noble and principled men in the Big Horn Mountains who had unknowingly shamed him into reclaiming his own sense of honor.

"I decided that for better or worse, I would come back and face the law and try to clear myself. I didn't have the faintest notion how I was gon' do that though. So I did what I always do when I'm stumped. I let God take the reins. He led me to Sedalia, Missouri, where I met a man named Ben Jackson. He owned the livery stable there. After I stabled my horse, he invited me to dinner with him and his family. Turns out, Jackson was an artilleryman in the Ninth United States Heavy Artillery. I was with the Fifth Colored Cavalry during the war. Those heavy artillery boys saved our bacon more'n once. We got to swappin' stories, and Jackson told me about the unit's chaplain whose name was Samuel Johnson."

Johnson's eyes suddenly lit with understanding. "Ben Jackson? Sergeant Ben Jackson? You met Sergeant Ben Jackson in Missouri?"

"Yessuh, I did."

"Ben Jackson was one of the bravest men I ever met—black or white. He would have walked through hell and back for his troops. Once I saw him snatch a burning fuse from a live cannonball that would have wiped out half his platoon. 'Big Ben' Jackson, helluva soldier! Oops! Excuse me, Lord."

The reverend looked at Joe apologetically for his verbal lapse, causing Joe to relax for the first time since they met. He continued his narrative.

"Jackson told me how much faith the men had in you. They wouldn't go into battle unless you had prayed over 'em. Said they called you 'the Shepherd.' And when it came to guts, he said they were all pretty impressed with what you were packin' in that department too. Didn't matter if there was enough lead in the air to build a statue, you went where you was needed, carryin' nothin' but a Bible, a cross, and a canteen. All that was interestin', but it didn't amount to a hill of beans compared to what was comin'. Out of curiosity, I asked Jackson if he knew whether you had survived the war, and he said last he heard you were in Nashville preachin' and practicin' law. I never kissed a man but I come darn close that day.

"I left Sedalia bound for Nashville. The folks in Nashville told me you had moved to Ebenezer. I came to your church on Sunday and here today. Tell me, Reverend, what are the odds that I would meet Ben Jackson in Missouri and he would tell me about you, the only black lawyer in Tennessee, where I'm wanted for murder? Benton is less than two day's ride from here. If you don't see God's hand in that, you're in the wrong line of work."

Johnson pulled out his pocket watch. He and Joe had been talking almost an hour. "Well, Mr. Walker, I was right—you did have quite a story to tell. And don't worry. You won't have to pay for my time today. Your chances of retaining your freedom are slim, but they become nonexistent if you did do the murders you are charged with. I have decided to take your case on the condition that you always tell me the truth and nothing but the truth. From now on, if I ask you a question and you can't answer it truthfully, don't answer it at all."

Joe looked Johnson in the eye. "I swear on my mother's grave that I killed those men in self-defense after they gunned down my friend who was unarmed and meant no harm to 'em. I am willing to stake my life on the truth, but if you don't trust me, then I cain't trust you. So what's it gon' be?"

After a moment, Reverend Johnson extended his hand and they shook hands. Joe felt a little less desperate—a little less hopeless. If he failed in the coming battle, there would be someone to tell his side of the story for posterity.

The reverend said, "I've done a lot of lecturing and preaching about black people earning their freedom. You have fought for yours on the battlefield and are prepared to fight for it in the courtroom. The least I can do is stand with you."

"That's really all I need. My ol' sarge used to say the only thing more dangerous than a battle-tested Union soldier is two of 'em." Joe's bold words sounded hollow, even to his own ears. Truth be told, he would rather face bullets and bombs than the ordeal ahead.

52

After his meeting with Reverend Johnson, Joe rode back to his camp on the outskirts of town. He had found an abandoned shack in a clearing in the woods and had moved in surreptitiously. He tethered Dice in the backyard and allowed him to graze. Now that he had moved one step closer to incarceration, he had to put his affairs in order. He planned to enlist Reverend Johnson in helping to prepare his will. Although he might come through his trial without being found guilty, the chances were slim. He had prepared himself mentally for the possibility that these were his last days of freedom and life. Consequently, he set to writing letters to his family.

He wrote to Amos, Ethan, and William, explaining his decision to each man and asking for their prayers and forgiveness for deciding to ride this trail without them. He sealed and addressed the letters and placed them in his saddlebag. He would ask Reverend Johnson to mail them in the event of his death.

Writing the letters and planning his will put Joe in a somber frame of mind. To lighten his mood, he went out back to work with Dice. As he looked at the handsome stallion with his proud bearing, black head and neck, and spotted rump, Joe marveled again at the remarkable circumstances that had brought the two of them together. He had no doubt it was the Lord's work.

The Appaloosa knew over a dozen verbal and nonverbal commands now, including kneeling, rearing, and lying down upon command. Joe put him on a long lead and exercised him until his coat gleamed with sweat. Periodically, he dropped the lead and directed Dice with his voice or hands alone. He rewarded Dice's successful efforts with pieces of apple and carrot. After the session, Joe wiped the stallion down and groomed him until his coat was clean and dry. As was his wont, Joe shared his thoughts with the horse to clear his head and settle his nerves.

"I'm about to walk into the lion's den, son. I was halfway hopin' Reverend Johnson would say no, so I woulda had a excuse to turn around and ride back the way I come. But it looks like the Lord has set a path for me and, just like ol' Jonah, I cain't run away from it. If I go down, I'm gon' ask the reverend to set you free in that valley we come through on the way here. You know the one down by the border near Brownsville with the wild mustangs in it and all that sweet grass and clean water. I reckon you'll do right fine down there."

He rested his cheek on Dice's neck and breathed in his horse smell. It was a smell he had come to associate with freedom and safety and it comforted him now in his moment of doubt. Dice nickered softly and nudged Joe's shoulder with his muzzle, as if he sensed his master's distress. They had ridden many difficult trails together and were still a team. Death had brought them together. It would take death to separate them.

Joe showed up promptly for his nine o'clock appointment with Lawyer Johnson the following morning. He had had a restless night and readily accepted the cup of coffee the counselor offered him. Once Joe was settled, Johnson said his piece.

"Mr. Walker, I was carried away by your courage and your faith yesterday, but before we go on, I need to make sure you understand what you're up against. You will be tried by a white judge, prosecuted by a white prosecutor, and heard by a white jury in a town in the deep

South. Your chances of acquittal are almost nonexistent. I have seen innocent black men go to the gallows for much less than you have done. The best advice I can give you as your advisor and your admirer is to ride back to Kansas and forget this whole business."

Joe looked at Johnson for a long time. His resolve had taken a severe blow from the lawyer's unvarnished assessment of his chances in the courtroom. Maybe Johnson was right. Maybe he was on a fool's errand and should walk away while he was still able to do so. Nevertheless, he should at least pay the attorney for his time. He reached in his inside pocket for his wallet. When he brought it out, Feather in His Hair's eagle feather came along with it and fell on the desk.

The sight of the emblem reminded Joe of his mission and of the men to whom he had given his word. "Mr. Johnson, I intend to ride to Benton and turn myself in. I understand if you think it's a lost cause. But right now, it's the only cause I got. So thank you for your time." Joe rose to take his leave.

"Hold on, Mr. Walker. If you're going to Benton, I'm going with you. I just wanted you to know what we're getting into. So now that that's settled, let's get down to business."

Joe sat back down with an overwhelming feeling of relief. At least he would not have to walk the path ahead alone.

"Let's start with the matter of my fee. There will be none. I plan to take this case on a pro bono basis. That's a fancy Latin term that means I'll work for free. And before you start objecting, let me tell you that I feel it is my duty as a Negro and as a Christian to help you, and I would be equally dishonored if I were to profit from your conviction or your acquittal," Johnson said.

"I get your drift. But I came here for justice, not charity. So either you let me pay you for your work or I walk out that door and go this alone," Joe said.

It was clear to Johnson that Joe was not bluffing so he capitulated. "All right, you win, but I set the fee and that's that."

"Deal. How much?"

"One dollar."

"That ain't fair, Reverend."

"Fair or not, it's what you agreed to and either you're a man of your word or you're not. Which is it?"

They maintained their give-no-quarter faces for the appropriate interval. Then Joe grinned and Johnson followed suit.

"I reckon I got the right lawyer after all," Joe said. "Let's get to work."

They sat down at Johnson's desk. He took out a legal pad and pencil.

"Now I want you to go over in detail everything that happened the day of the shootings. Don't leave out anything, no matter how unimportant you might believe it to be."

Joe told his story with frequent interruptions from Johnson. Johnson's questions caused him to remember details that had originally slipped his mind, and together they pieced together the events of that June day some six years past.

53

Joe was headed back to Benton in the company of his newly hired attorney. At Johnson's suggestion, they stopped at the Poteet plantation to view the scene of the alleged crime. Joe was surprised to see the antebellum big house was gone and in its place was a sprawling two-story frame house of brick and wood. As they rode into the yard, a large mongrel dog came out from under the porch barking raucously, alternately revealing a lolling red tongue and sharp teeth.

A black man dressed in coveralls and a muslin shirt stepped out on the front porch. He was middle-aged and solidly built, and a briar pipe sent rills of smoke around his balding head. He was holding a shotgun. "Shut up, Jake!" he said to the mutt, who immediately stopped barking but remained on alert. "May I help you?"

Finding the place occupied caught Joe off guard. He hastily began to improvise. "Yessuh, we was lookin' for the owner."

"I'm the owner. What can I do for you?"

"Suh, my name is Joseph Horn and this is my friend Reverend Samuel Johnson. We're on our way to Benton on business. The man who used to own this place also owned me and my family. I wonder if you would mind if we looked around for my people's graves? I would like to pay my respects."

"There's an old cemetery back there in the woods behind the barn."

"Yessuh, I know. My family is buried there. I promise not to disturb anythang."

The man's expression and tone softened. "My name's Shelby Washington and I don't reckon it'd do any harm. Go head. Take your time. When you get through, come on up to the house. We'll give you something to cut the trail dust."

"Much obliged," Joe said, once again struck by the difference between white and black hospitality in the deep South.

He led the way to the cemetery where he and Johnson examined the graves of the deceased members of Joe's family.

Joe noticed that the grass was cut and all the markers were upright. He went to Uncle Jim's grave, and the events surrounding the old man's death came flooding back. His eyes stung with tears as he knelt beside the wooden marker he had made. "I'm back, Unca Jim—back for justice. Sorry it took me so long."

Johnson paid special attention to Uncle Jim's grave, taking out his notebook and making an entry.

Joe found his parents' and sisters' graves and stood over them and said a silent prayer, asking each to lend him strength and courage during the coming trial. Next, Joe showed Johnson the scene of the shootings, which was now occupied by Washington's barn and outbuildings, and pointed out where he and each of his assailants had been standing when he shot them. Finally, Joe showed his companion the field where he had buried the bodies. Instead of corn, it now contained soybeans.

"I turned their horses loose in a meadow on the east end of the property. I was tryin' to buy as much time as possible so I could put some distance between me and this place. Lookin' back, it was probably the wrong thang to do, but I didn't believe I'd get a fair shake from that sheriff or the townfolk."

"A Negro stranger who fought for the Union, you figured right," Johnson said.

They headed back to the house. Upon seeing them a second time,

Jake gave a few half-hearted barks that said, "I've still got my eye on you."

Mr. Washington opened the front door and invited them inside. Though they were eager to be away, they could not refuse his hospitality. "Did you find your people?" Washington asked.

"Yessuh. Thank you."

The living room was spacious and comfortably furnished with a couch, table, and stuffed chairs. There was a large handwoven rug that covered the center of the floor space and two end tables with kerosene lamps on either side of the couch. The walls featured paintings of pastoral landscapes and a picture of Abraham Lincoln. A portrait of Shelby Washington and a woman Joe presumed was his wife hung over the fireplace. Joe had been inside only one other home of this quality owned by a colored person, and that was the one he and Amos had built in Kansas.

Washington motioned them to the table. "Ya'll have a seat," he said.

A plump, middle-aged woman came in from the kitchen, bearing a tray that contained iced tea and cookies. She was light skinned with gray eyes. Her long hair was braided and coiled in a bun on the back of her head. Joe noticed that she was wearing high-button shoes under her store-bought dress and that she was the woman in the portrait. Joe and Reverend Johnson stood and removed their hats.

"Gentlemen, this is my wife, Sarah. Sarah, this is Mr. Horn and Reverend Johnson. They're on their way to Benton on business."

"Ma'am."

"Ma'am."

"So pleased to make your acquaintance gentlemen," Mrs. Washington said. "Here's a little something to tide you over until you get to town." She placed the tray on the table, stepped back, and smiled, revealing gapped front teeth. "I'll leave you gentlemen to your man talk and refreshments. Let me know if you need anything." Mrs. Washington returned to the kitchen, patting Mr. Washington's shoulder affectionately in passing.

"This is quite a place you have here," Johnson said.

"Yeah, I bought it at auction about four years ago. It was a steal because of the bad history connected to it.

"What bad history?" Joe asked.

"The first owner got shot. The second one got hung, and then shortly after the war, three men were murdered right here on this property by an outlaw named Joe Walker."

Joe and Johnson exchanged a glance.

"The locals think the place is haunted."

"What do you think?" Johnson asked.

"I've lived here for nearly four years and the scariest thing I've seen is my neighbor's cross-eyed daughter. But then I'm not subject to the local superstitions. I was born a free man in upstate Illinois. Went all the way to the twelfth grade. When I was thirty-five, I started a small freight business in Cairo. The war was very good for business, and I put aside some savings. After the war, I sold the company at a handsome profit and moved down here. When I got here, I bought as much land as I could lay my hands on. Now, besides this place, I own the boarding house, the blacksmith shop, and the general store in Benton." Washington sipped his tea and sampled a cookie. He was obviously a man who was very pleased with himself. "Mr. Horn, you said you had some business in Benton. May I ask its nature?"

Johnson looked at Joe and gave a barely perceptible shake of his head. Joe had taken Washington's measure and judged him to be more friend than foe, so he gave him only a slightly veiled response. "Legal business. I've got an old account to settle."

"Sometimes those can be troublesome," Washington said, looking at Johnson, who shifted in his chair and quickly changed the subject.

"Who's the sheriff in Benton these days?" Johnson asked.

"John Colby."

"How long has he been sheriff?"

"About three years now. He was elected when Ben Staley retired."

"What kind of man is Colby?"

"A white man. But he got himself elected by promising that he would treat everybody the same. So far he's done about as well as could be expected. But I don't think he'll last more than one term."

"Why not?"

"Because I'm grooming a Negro candidate to run against him in the spring. You see, whoever controls law enforcement controls the laws. We've got to take advantage of having the vote. There are more coloreds in Benton than there are whites. If we get to the polls on a regular basis, we can run this county."

"You, sir, are a man of the future. I wish I could take your wisdom and sprinkle it like water upon the thirsty minds of Negroes throughout the South. I am currently teaching at an industrial institute in Ebenezer, Tennessee. It would give me great pleasure to have you come and share your inspirational ideas and example with our students," Johnson said.

"I'm too busy *doin'* to teach right now, Reverend. But if I fail to elect my man in the spring, I will seriously consider taking you up on your offer," Washington said.

"Well, Mr. Washington, we've taken up enough of your time. We best be gittin' on," Joe said.

Johnson wrote his name and address on a piece of notepaper and gave it to Washington.

"I hope we'll meet again. It has been a singular pleasure making your acquaintance."

"Same here," Washington said, extending his hand. Johnson took it enthusiastically. They said their goodbyes and thank-yous to Mrs. Washington and prepared to take their leave.

Washington had one more exchange with Joe as he and Johnson sat their horses in the front yard, preparing to depart. "You know, I've been over every inch of that colored cemetery and I didn't find one marker with the name Horn on it."

"I expect not," Joe said.

Shelby Washington lit his pipe and took a long puff. "No sir, not a single Horn—quite a few Walkers though. I hope you're able to settle your account in Benton, son."

"I intend to or die tryin'," Joe said.

Washington lifted his hand in farewell and the two men rode out of his yard and headed toward town.

54

Joe and Reverend Johnson rode down the main street of Benton, Tennessee. The town had grown since Joe was last in it. There were more buildings and more people. The sidewalks were full of people going about their business—quite a few of them were black. Joe's sense of déjà-vu was muted by these changes.

The sheriff's office was in the same place, but it was now a two-story brick building. The windows on the second floor were barred. The houses of the people who lived and worked in Benton radiated from the main street.

Adjacent to the jail was an imposing two-story brick building with four white marble columns. The image of blindfolded lady Justice was carved into the building's façade. This was the courthouse, a building that Joe had never had cause to enter. That would soon change.

Directly across from the jail was a large two-story frame building on the opposite side of the main street. The sign on the front of the building said:

BENTON BOARDING HOUSE

SHELBY WASHINGTON, PROPRIETOR
INQUIRE WITHIN

Johnson said, "Let's stop here for a minute."

They went inside and approached the desk clerk, a black man in his midtwenties wearing a starched white shirt, bow tie, and red suspenders. He looked strangely familiar to Joe.

"Good afternoon, sir. How can I help you?"

"Yes, I need a room," Johnson said

"Yes, sir, for how long?"

"I'm not sure. Can I rent by the week?"

"You certainly can. That'll be thirty-five dollars. Meals are included, of course." Johnson took the cash from his wallet and slid it across the desk. "Would you like a receipt?"

"Yes, please."

The young man filled out the receipt and handed it to Johnson with a practiced smile. "Would you please sign the register, sir?"

Johnson signed the hotel register.

The young man looked at Johnson's signature. "I have rooms on the first or second floor, Mr. Johnson. Which would you prefer?"

"I'd like something on the second floor facing the street if possible."

"Yes, sir. Room number nine, upstairs and down to the end of the hall. Here's your key. Supper is served at five thirty in the dining room right through there. Enjoy your stay. Let us know if there's anything you need."

He turned to Joe. "And for you, sir?"

"I've made other arrangements," Joe said.

The young man nodded politely.

Joe and Johnson mounted the stairs. They went down the hall and Johnson unlocked his room. It was ten feet by twelve feet with a bed, chair, writing desk, and nightstand. The bedspread and linens were scrupulously clean. There was an area rug on the floor that showed signs of wear but was also swept clean. There was a water pitcher and washbasin on the dresser that had a decent mirror for shaving. Finally, there was a wardrobe in the corner with hangers for his clothing.

Johnson looked out the window and nodded with satisfaction. "I'll be able to see anybody who goes into the jail from here," he said.

They left the boarding house and took Dice and Brommy, Johnson's brown roan, to the livery stable that was located at the south end of the main street between a freight office and the stagecoach depot.

The young liveryman was the twin of the hotel clerk. Johnson remarked on their striking resemblance. "May I ask your name, young man?"

"Yes, sir. I'm Meshach Washington."

"I think we just ran into your brother at the hotel up the street."

"Yes, sir. That would be my brother, Shadrach."

"Well, I guess all you're missing is an Abednego," Johnson said, smiling.

"That would be our older brother. He runs the general store," Meshach said without missing a beat.

"You wouldn't be Shelby Washington's boys?" Joe asked.

"Why, yes sir, we are."

"We met your pa this mornin'."

"And what might your name be, sir?"

"My name is Walker, Joseph Walker," Joe said, glad be done with subterfuge once and for all.

"And I'm Samuel Johnson," Johnson said. "Your mother and father were kind enough to offer refreshments to me and Mr. Walker when we stopped at their place on the way into town this morning. They should be proud to have raised such courteous and industrious sons. Are there more of you?"

"Eight boys and two girls, sir. Shelby Jr. works at the bank. Ben, Peter, and John help Daddy on the farm, and Cheryl and Cassie are still in school. We're not sure where Luke is. Last we heard, he was working on a cattle ranch outside of Abilene. If you don't mind my asking, what brings you to town?"

"Legal business," Johnson said.

Meshach's manners trumped his curiosity. "Well, good luck with that, sir," he said, taking the horses' reins.

"Hold up a minute," Joe said. He went to Dice and placed his arms around the horse's neck. He stepped back and turned to Johnson. "Let's go."

They left the stable and walked over to the jail.

As they stood on the sidewalk in front of the jail, Johnson said, "This is the last chance to change your mind."

Joe said, "Let's git it over with."

They entered the building. A squarely built man with sandy hair, jug ears, and bright blue eyes sat behind a desk in the middle of the room. He regarded Joe and Johnson with a look that mixed curiosity and suspicion. Two strange black men could mean trouble.

"What can I do for ya'll?" he asked, putting aside the newspaper he had been reading.

Per prior agreement, Johnson did the talking. "Sheriff, I am Samuel L. Johnson, attorney at law, and this is my client, Joseph Walker. Mr. Walker is here to turn himself in in response to an outstanding warrant for his arrest."

"What's he charged with?"

"The charge is murder, sir." Johnson took out the wanted poster Joe had been carrying with him since he took it off Jim Carson's body some two years previously. He placed it on the desk in front of the lawman.

The sheriff stared at the poster and then sprang to his feet, drawing his gun and training it on Joe, who raised his hands high.

"Sheriff, there is no need for violence of any kind. My client is unarmed and is surrendering voluntarily," Johnson said.

"Step back from the desk and keep your hands up!" Colby said in his no-nonsense voice. Joe did as he was told. The sheriff called out to an unseen companion, "Jason, come out here quick!"

A rangy man with a shock of brown hair and slightly protruding dishwater colored eyes hustled in from the back room. He still carried a broom in his hands. On seeing the sheriff with his gun out covering a large black man, he dropped the broom and drew his own weapon. "What in the blazes is goin' on here, John?"

"Got us a prisoner here, Deputy, and I wanna make sure we keep 'im. You, get over to that wall, put your hands on it, and spread your legs."

Again, Joe did as he was told.

"Sheriff, this is entirely—"

"Shut up, mistuh, or you'll be next. Jason, pat him down," the sheriff said, gesturing at Joe with his gun barrel.

The deputy searched Joe for weapons and contraband, finding none. "He's clean, sheriff."

"All right, take him back and lock him up and be careful."

The deputy marched Joe to a suite of three cells in the back of the room. He locked Joe in the middle one. "Sit down and shut up!" he said to Joe, having suddenly found his courage.

Joe did as he was told. His expression was placid, but his heart was racing and his mouth was dry as cotton. What had possessed him to place himself in the hands of these men? He felt like a wolf in a trap. How would he be able to tolerate weeks or months of this?

On the verge of panic, Joe remembered something Johnson had told him on the way into town. "They will try to break you, make you feel like the slave you used to be. If they succeed, all is lost. Remember you are not a slave—not an animal, even if they put you in a cage. And remember that I am with you and I will fight for your life as if it were my own. My job is to win the battle in court. Your job is to win the battle in your mind."

Joe's breathing slowed and his calm returned like a misplaced blanket. The warrior's instinct that had seen him through countless battles rose up from his subconscious. It spoke to him now. *If they come for you, they must risk themselves. Ready yourself.* Joe sat down on the bunk and let his lawyer work.

"Sheriff Colby, as I was about to say, my client is here voluntarily. He has surrendered because he is innocent of the crime of which he is accused. I am his legal representative and as such I will monitor his treatment while in your custody. If he is harmed in anyway, I will hold you and the city of Benton responsible," Johnson said.

"Who the hell do you think you're talkin' to, boy?"

"I'm merely affirming that Mr. Walker is an American citizen with the full protection of the US Constitution at his disposal. And you, as an officer of the law, are sworn to uphold that constitution. Today is the beginning of his plea for justice. I need to know what to expect from you and your deputy as his guardians."

"Nobody needs to tell me or my deputy how to do our jobs. Least of all you." His tone now was more petulant than bellicose.

"Good, we have an understanding. Now that Mr. Walker is in custody, he has the right to a speedy trial. I would ask that you contact Judge Carstairs at the circuit court and schedule an initial appearance. I intend to make the same request. Here is a copy of my credentials. I think you will find everything in order. Now, I would like time to confer with my client, please."

Sheriff Colby read through Johnson's papers, taking his time. When he was satisfied with their authenticity, he turned to his deputy, who had watched his exchange with the Negro lawyer with something bordering on incredulity. "Jason, take Mr. Johnson back to see his client but search 'im first."

The deputy patted Johnson down with the care he might have used in defusing a bomb. "He's clean, Sheriff."

Colby motioned to the back room with his head. The deputy escorted Johnson to Joe's cell.

"We would like some privacy, please," Johnson said.

The deputy stood still, clearly in a quandary.

"What is your name, sir? Johnson asked.

"Jason Plummer," the deputy said.

"Well, Mr. Plummer, do you think I brought my client all the way from Ebenezer to be locked up so I could break him out five minutes later?"

The deputy considered this. Then he turned and walked out of the cellblock.

"How're you doing?" Johnson asked.

"When I heard that cell door slam behind me, I got a might nervous, but I'm all right now. What's next?"

"The sheriff is going to contact the district judge and arrange for an initial hearing. Hopefully, that can happen fairly quickly. At the hearing, you will be arraigned and enter a not guilty plea, and the judge will set a trial date. The district attorney will be at the trial representing the state. He may do something to try to slow the process down."

"Why?"

"Just to give you more time in jail in hopes that it will work on your nerves and make you more likely to make a mistake."

"What kind of mistake?" Joe said.

"Well, like admitting you're guilty in exchange for a more favorable sentence or trying to break out of jail. You won't do either of those things, so eventually we will go to trial. Until that happens, you talk to no one but me about this matter, understood?"

Joe nodded.

"Good. This is going to be a test of wills that may lead you to regret turning yourself in, but if you can hold out, we've got a fighting chance. I will come to see you every day. If you need me, tell the sheriff to fetch me. I'll let him know where to find me. Do you have any questions?"

"Yeah, what if somethin' happens to you? What do I do then?"

"If I'm still alive, you wait for me to recover and we proceed. If I'm not, you ask for an immediate hearing with the district judge and request another lawyer. Here are the names of two men I trust. One practices in Memphis, the other in Nashville."

Joe was impressed that Johnson had thought about this contingency and prepared for it as meticulously as he had for everything else.

Joe lowered his voice. "Watch your back. Some of these crackers may want to hurt you for sidin' with me. Keep a Colt handy and sleep with one eye open."

"Joseph, are you familiar with the twenty-third chapter of Psalms?"

"The Lord is my shepherd, I shall not want . . .?"

"That's the one. This isn't the first time either of us has walked through the valley of the shadow of death. To get to me, they have to go through the Lord, so I'm not afraid. Now is there anything else you need?"

"Yeah, could you bring me my Bible and some hard candy?"

Johnson smiled and nodded. "With pleasure. See you soon," he said.

He rejoined Deputy Plummer, who was seated in a chair immediately outside the cellblock. Sheriff Colby was gone. Joe overheard their conversation from his cell.

"Who feeds the prisoners?" Johnson asked.

"We get their meals from the boarding house across the street."

"Is that the one owned by Mr. Washington?"

"Yeah, that's the one," the deputy said, registering surprise that Johnson knew who owned what in Benton.

"Do they deliver the meals or do you pick them up?"

"They deliver 'em."

"Well, I want to inspect every meal my client eats."

"You ain't got no right—"

"I have every right to ensure my client's safety while he is in your custody. Unless you or the sheriff want to taste his food in my presence, I will inspect his meals. So when are meal times?"

"They bring breakfast around eight and lunch at noon. Supper's at five. You gon' have to run this by Sheriff Colby," Plummer said.

"I intend to. See you at five."

55

Joe's right to a speedy trial was realized due to fortuitous circumstances. The fact that the trial was taking place in the Polk County seat, despite Johnson's denied motion for a change of venue, was a factor. Judge Richard C. Carstairs was already in residence so he did not have to travel a great distance to preside over the proceedings.

Johnson had thoroughly researched Judge Carstairs. He had been born and raised in Massachusetts. At the age of nineteen, he entered West Point and graduated three years later at the top of his class. He entered the army as a first lieutenant and served for fifteen years, rising to the rank of lieutenant colonel. Early on in his military career, he matriculated at Harvard Law School at the behest of the army and earned a law degree. He subsequently served in the Judge Advocate General's Corps, piling up an impressive list of courtroom victories.

During the war, he served in the 116th Regiment under Colonel William Woodward. He was wounded at Gettysburg and received the Medal of Honor for meritorious service. Significantly, he had commanded a troop of colored soldiers in the latter days of the war.

After the Civil War, Carstairs was appointed to the Circuit Court of Polk County by Governor William G. Brownlow as part of the Reconstruction effort. He was widely known as a man of honor and scrupulous adherence to the law. Johnson told Joe they could not have picked a better jurist under the circumstances.

The district attorney, Jonathon Kilroy, was another matter. He was a seasoned prosecutor educated at the University of Virginia who had managed to hold onto his government position after the war by swearing fealty to the United States. He was rumored to be in line for the post of attorney general and had switched his allegiance to the Republican Party to improve his chances.

Johnson was unimpressed by Kilroy's "shot gun" patriotism. A thorough perusal of the man's writings and conviction record revealed that, despite his seeming conversion, he was still a believer in white supremacy and the failed system that supported it. The lines were drawn. The battle waited.

One week after his incarceration, Joe found himself even further enmeshed in the gears of the white judicial system. After Joe entered his plea and the trial's location was decided, the process moved to the byzantine task of jury selection.

Johnson was determined to seat as many Negro jurors as possible to ensure Joe received a trial by a jury of his peers. Kilroy was just as determined to seat white jurors who would empathize with the victims.

Jury duty was a novelty for Negroes in the South. Until the war ended, they were property, completely devoid of rights. Johnson had spent his free time visiting churches and homes, encouraging the people to respond to the summons for jury duty. He spoke with the passion and eloquence honed in the pulpit.

"If we don't use our rights, there's no guarantee we will keep them. God has brought us to the 'Promise Land' but we must earn our place here. The Bible says, 'Come into my vineyard and work.' Brothers and sisters, we've got so much work to do in freedom's vineyard."

He would have to wait to see the effect of his own labors. During voir dire, the thin veneer of civility was removed from the Benton community and a generation of race-based hostility reared its ugly head.

Many white families in Benton had lost loved ones during the war.

Afterward, the town had been practically picked clean by Yankee "carpet-baggers" who stole property and bought businesses for pennies on the dollar. As a result, former slaves who had nowhere to go were gradually experiencing the benefits of freedom and their numerical majority. The Negroes' emancipated presence was perceived by longtime white residents as an affront to established cultural norms.

The trial was the first real test of the delicate post-war balance between blacks and whites. White hard-liners resorted to familiar tactics to reassert their dominance. Two potential black jurors had their homes set on fire. A white man had been set upon for merely opining that Joe should get a fair trial before his guilt or innocence was determined. Johnson found an envelope slipped under his door one evening with a cryptic message inside.

If the nigger walks, you will die in his place.

Johnson told Joe he had shown the note to Judge Carstairs to renew his request for a change of venue, but his plea had fallen on deaf ears. The trial proceeded in Benton.

56

Both Johnson and Kilroy exhausted their peremptory strikes in short order and proceeded to striking jurors for cause. The victims, Caleb Swenson and his two confederates, Billy Ray Rogers and Homer Watson, had a host of relatives and friends still living in and around Benton. These relationships were not always apparent, so Johnson had to be on guard lest a guaranteed "guilty" vote slip past his scrutiny. He typically began his questioning by asking, "Did you know any of the deceased men?" and proceeded from there.

Kilroy, for his part, understood his opponent's desire to seat black jurors. Realizing he could not strike a juror based solely upon his race, Kilroy attempted to discover the servility and pliability of potential black jurors. He particularly gravitated to black men over fifty with little or no education. These "cotton heads" would go along with anything a white man said out of force of habit.

Jury selection took three days. When all was said and done, the jury consisted of eight whites and four blacks. Johnson would have preferred a more even split, but he had an ace in the hole: one of the black jurors was Shelby Washington. He had been seated by Judge Carstairs over the DA's objection.

The courtroom was packed the day the trial began. The case had drawn interest from newspapers as far north as Chicago because of its sensational elements. A Negro lawyer representing a Negro client accused of murdering three white men in the deep South was fodder for headlines on both sides of the Mason-Dixon Line. The publicity coincided with Johnson's desire to shine as much light on the case as possible in hopes of keeping all the participants honest.

Joe was led into the courtroom shackled hand and foot. His discomfort was enhanced by the new suit and shoes Johnson had purchased for him. He was neatly shaved and shorn. Under more pedestrian circumstances, he could have been mistaken for a student or a clerk.

The shackles emphasized to Joe how helpless and dependent he was. His fate was in the hands of twelve strangers. The prospect blew through him like a chill wind.

The courtroom was capacious. The public gallery consisted of a dozen wooden benches on either side of a central aisle. The audience section was separated from the attorneys' tables by a low wooden rail. The judge's elevated bench was flanked on the left by a witness stand behind a restraining rail. To the right of the judge's bench was a door leading to his chambers. The jury box was along the wall to the judge's left.

There was a balcony for additional seating. As if by prior arrangement, the black people of Benton were seated on the right side of the courtroom and the white people were seated on the left. The seating arrangement was maintained in the balcony.

Judge Carstairs entered the packed courtroom to the bailiff's incantation of "All rise!" His purposeful stride and stern expression indicated to all that he planned to run a tight ship. Joe glanced at the jury and noticed Shelby Washington seated in the front row in a three-piece fawn gray suit. A gold watch chain adorned his waistcoat. He was the picture of decorum and was clearly aware that he was representing the Negro community in this unfolding drama.

The other three Negro men on the jury were likewise dressed in their Sunday suits and ties. The whites were less uniform in their attire but no less serious in their intent, judging by their faces.

At the judge's invitation, Jonathon Kilroy rose and made his opening remarks to the jury. "Gentlemen of the jury, the State intends to prove beyond the shadow of a doubt that the defendant, Joseph Walker, murdered Caleb Swanson, Billy Ray Rogers, and Homer Watson on or about June 18, 1865. That he subsequently buried their bodies to hide his nefarious deed and fled for parts unknown. For the past six years he has lived as a free man, enjoying the fruits of life while the family and friends of his victims have suffered the daily scourge of grief, regret, and uncertainty. Joseph Walker's motive for this heinous act was simple— revenge. He blamed the people of Benton for the loss of his own family. He was a trained killer whose hatred had been stoked by his service in the Union army during the recent War Between the States. When we have fully presented to you our compelling and incontrovertible evidence, you will have but one verdict to deliver—guilty. Thank you."

The judge turned to Johnson and said, "Counselor," as an indication for him to make his opening remarks. Johnson rose and walked to within a few feet of the jury. He was dressed in his freshly pressed black suit, white shirt, and black tie. On his lapel, he wore an American flag pin. Joe noticed a slight tremor in his hand as he pushed his notes to the side. A rawboned white man with a weather-beaten face in the front row regarded him with open hostility.

"Gentleman of the jury, Mr. Kilroy has used a lot of big strong words to support a small weak case. My client committed no murder. Instead he acted in self-defense. We will prove this. When my client learned of the false charges against him, he voluntarily surrendered himself to the authorities in order to clear his name. Is this the act of a guilty man?

"Joe Walker came to Benton after the war in search of reunion, not revenge. He and his family were victims of the cruel institution of slavery that separated him from them at the age of nine. He spent the better part of a decade trying to get back home. The Poteet plantation, formerly the Walker plantation, was the place his family called home. He went there in 1865 only to find it abandoned. While grieving the loss of his people for the second time, he was set upon by three men who followed him to exact their own revenge for his efforts to seek and secure his freedom and the freedom of all colored people. Joe Walker is an innocent man who believes in Justice enough to put his life in her hands. Gentlemen of the jury, in this courtroom, *you* represent the hands of Justice. Thank you."

Johnson turned and walked back to his seat. There was a growing murmur undulating through the crowd.

"Order in the court!" Judge Carstairs said, rapping his gavel.

The murmur represented the realization by the people that this was not going to be a ritual slaughter because Joe Walker was represented by a formidable advocate capable of giving as good as he got. The battle was joined and they could not wait to see it unfold.

After the attorneys' opening remarks, Judge Carstairs gave the jury its instructions. He reminded them that Joe Walker was innocent until proven guilty. Thus, the burden of proof was upon the prosecution. The defense only had to establish a "reasonable doubt" in their minds that the defendant committed the crime, in which case they must acquit. Finally, he told them that murder was a capital crime punishable by death.

Having established the ground rules, the judge returned to the business of the trial. "Mr. Kilroy, the prosecution may call its first witness."

"Your Honor, the prosecution calls Ben Staley." Ben Staley rose from the crowd and came to the witness stand. The years had not been kind to the ex-lawman. He walked slowly, bent over a cane. His head contained a few wisps of white hair, and his big hands were knobbed with arthritis. Only his eyes retained the hostile glint that Walker had observed upon his first encounter with the man.

The bailiff swore Staley in, and he lowered himself slowly into the witness chair.

Kilroy wasted no time. "Mr. Staley what was your occupation during the summer of 1865?"

"I was the sheriff of Polk County." Staley's voice was hoarse from years of smoking and drinking hard liquor.

"And in that capacity, did you have occasion to meet the defendant, Joseph Walker?"

"Yes, I did. He rode into town and stopped by my office. He said he was lookin' for his family who used to be slaves on the Walker plantation. He wanted to know where the Walker place was. I tried to tell 'em that the Walker plantation was deserted, but he was set on goin' out there to see for himself. So I gave him directions and he left town."

"How long were you the sheriff of Polk County, sir?"

"A little over eleven years."

"Did you deal with a lot of criminals in that time?"

"Yessuh, quite a few."

"What was your impression of Mr. Walker?"

"Objection, Your Honor!" Johnson said. "The prosecution is trying to create a false equivalence in the jury's mind based on the witness's subjective opinion."

"Overruled," Carstairs said.

Kilroy smiled and repeated his question. "So, as a seasoned lawman, what was your impression of Mr. Walker?"

"He looked like a troublemaker to me. He wore his Colt strapped down, and he looked you hard in the eye when he talked to you. He seemed full of himself. Not at all like your av'rage Nigra."

"Did Mr. Walker leave town without incident?"

"No, sir, he got into an argument with Caleb Swenson outside my office."

"Caleb Swenson, one of the murdered men?"

"Objection! The crime of murder has not been established."

"Sustained."

Kilroy rephrased his question. "Caleb Swenson, one of the men whose bodies were found on the Poteet plantation?"

"The very one."

"Do you know what they argued about?"

"I believe Caleb accused Walker of stealing the horse he was ridin'."

"And what did Mr. Walker say to that?"

"I don't recollect him sayin' anythin'. Before they could have further words, I told 'em to get on about their business. So Walker mounted up and rode outta town. That was the last I seen of 'im until two days ago."

"Now, Sheriff Staley, can you tell us what took place in the days following your first meeting Mr. Walker?"

"Yessuh . . ." Staley broke into a fit of coughing that turned his face beet red. He held up his hand to excuse himself, took a dirty white handkerchief from his pocket, and covered his mouth with it until the paroxysm passed.

"Would you care for a glass of water, sir?" Kilroy asked.

"No thanks, I'm all right. Like I was sayin', Caleb Swenson's family reported him missin' the day after he had his run-in with Walker. Billy Ray Rogers and Homer Watson also turned up missing at the same time. The last anybody seen 'em, they were ridin' out of town together. Somethin' told me to check the Poteet plantation, so me and my deputy rode out there to have a look around. Well, we found their horses but no sign of them. I suspected foul play so I sent my deputy for reinforcements and we formed a search party. After three days, we found 'em buried in the cornfield."

"Found who?"

"Caleb Swenson, Billy Ray Rogers, and Homer Watson. They'd been murdered."

"Objection, Your Honor," Johnson said.

"Sustained. The jury will disregard the witness's use of the word *murdered*."

"What was their condition when you found them, Sheriff?"

"They were dead, all three of 'em—shot dead."

This elicited a wave of murmurs through the courtroom punctuated by a shout from the back of the room. "Kill that nigger!"

Judge Carstairs banged his gavel hard and spoke with all his authority. "Order! Order in the court! If there is another such outburst, I will clear this courtroom!"

Johnson placed his arm around Joe's shoulder and spoke into his ear. "Don't let 'em shake you, brotha. God is on *our* side."

Joe nodded and maintained his composure, albeit with difficulty. He looked into the audience and by chance found Mrs. Washington, who clasped her hands and shook them in front of her breast and mouthed the words, "Stay strong." He noticed other black people in the crowd were also sending him silent support with nods, hand gestures, and smiles. Joe realized he and Johnson were not alone. The fellowship that had sustained the black race through uproot, bondage, and torture was alive and well in Judge Carstair's courtroom. His flagging hope was revived.

Kilroy resumed his questioning. "Sheriff Staley, what did you do after you discovered the bodies?"

"I formed a posse and went lookin' for Walker. I knew chances were slim that he was still in the county or the state, but I had to try, for the sake of the victims' families and the townfolks' peace of mind. Sure 'nough, he was long gone. After a week, I called off the search. But I filed a murder charge with the district court. Some citizens put up a one thousand dollar bounty, and I saw to it that reward posters were circulated. It was one of my biggest regrets that I didn't bring that killer in before I left office. Now, I'm finally gonna get the chance to see justice done."

"The prosecution has no further questions of this witness at this time, Your Honor," Kilroy said. He turned, smirked at Johnson, and took his seat.

"Your witness, Mr. Johnson," the judge said. Carstairs was a tall man whose head was crowned by a thatch of prematurely white hair. His elevated seat on the bench gave him a dignity and eminence that were augmented by his military bearing.

Johnson paused at his table and reviewed a final document. Joe noticed his hands were steady now. Johnson rose and walked to a point about five feet in front of Ben Staley.

"Mr. Staley, you testified that you could see that my client was a 'troublemaker' by the way he wore his gun and the way he looked at you. Is that correct?"

"Those were a coupla ways."

"When you were sheriff, did you wear your gun tied down?"

"Yeah."

"And did you look people in the eye when you talked to them?"

"Yes, I did."

"Did that make you a troublemaker?"

"Objection! Your Honor, the defense is trying to impugn the character of a fine public servant," Kilroy said.

"Your Honor, the prosecution has implied that Mr. Staley possesses a talent that enables him to predict who is or is not a troublemaker. I would like the jury to hear what that ability is based upon."

"Sustained. I'll give you a little leeway here, Mr. Johnson, but don't stray too far."

"Thank you, Your Honor. Mr. Staley, the other indicator that you mentioned was that Mr. Walker is a Negro who didn't act like your 'average' Negro. Please enlighten us on how one distinguishes between an 'average' Negro and an atypical one?"

"Before I became a lawman, I was an overseer. When you grew up around 'em and had to manage 'em your whole life, you get to know the ones you can trust and the ones you can't."

"Please explain."

"Well, the ones you can't trust are shiftless and lazy and they'll lie or steal at the drop of a hat. If you want to know if they're lyin,' make 'em look you in the eye. They'll start breathin' hard and drop their eyes. Those kind, you don't let outta your sight."

"And what about the Negroes you can trust?"

"Your 'good' Nigra works hard, minds his manners, and obeys the law. Generally, you don't have no trouble with 'em because they're God fearin' and they know their place. But even a good Nigra can go bad without proper instruction and proper discipline."

"So I presume that you determined that Mr. Walker was a 'bad Negro'? Even though he came to you in your capacity as sheriff to tell you his business in your county, looked you in the eye, and told you the truth?"

"He almost got into a fight with a man in the street right after he left my office."

"Caleb Swenson, who accused him of stealing the horse he had ridden in the US cavalry while serving his country. But then you knew that because Mr. Walker told you. Didn't he?"

"He might have. I don't remember."

"Mr. Swenson was a veteran, too, wasn't he?"

"Objection! Relevance?"

"Mr. Staley knew Mr. Swenson and might be able to give us some insight into why he and my client had their initial altercation."

"I'll allow it. Proceed," the judge said.

"Mr. Staley, should I repeat the question?"

"No, I got it. Caleb served in the Thirty-Seventh Tennessee Infantry. Helluva outfit."

"So was Mr. Swenson a friend of yours?"

"Yes, he was."

"Did you ever have to arrest him?"

"Objection, Your Honor! Mr. Swenson is not on trial here!"

"Sustained."

"Mr. Staley, could you share with us your theory of what happened at the Poteet plantation on June 18, 1865?" Johnson asked.

"I figure Swenson, Rogers, and Watson followed Walker out to the plantation to keep an eye on 'im. When they got there, he was waitin' for 'em and shot 'em from ambush. He buried 'em and run off their horses. Then he got in the wind."

"How long after my client left town did the three men leave?"

"Near as we can piece together, it was about an hour later."

"And how did they know where to go?"

"Whatcha mean?"

"I mean that you were the only person that Mr. Walker told where he was going."

Staley looked puzzled then wary. "He must've mentioned it to them."

"Why would he tell Swenson where he was going after arguing with him in the street?"

"Maybe he wanted to set him up for an ambush," Staley said, looking around with a smug expression.

"But my client thought he was going to a place where there would be people. Hardly a suitable setting for an ambush."

"You'd have to ask him about that."

"I intend to."

"Once you had exhumed the three bodies, did you have them examined by a doctor or medical person?"

"Yes, I did. Doc Samuels looked at the bodies."

"What did he find?"

"They were shot with a Navy Colt. Just like the one Walker was wearin' when he came to my office."

"Did you examine their weapons?"

"I was a lawman for eleven years. I know how to police a crime scene. Caleb's gun had been fired four times. The other two had full chambers. That's how I knew they was ambushed."

"Please explain."

"One man don't take on three without givin' himself an advantage. The only reason Swenson got off four shots was because he was very handy with a gun."

"I see," Johnson said. "One other thing—did you find any other fresh graves on the property?"

"No, of course not."

Johnson turned and stared at the jury with a surprised look on his face. "No further questions, Your Honor. The defense reserves the right to recall this witness at a later time."

"You may step down, Sheriff Staley."

Judge Carstairs adjourned the court for the day after Johnson's cross-examination of Ben Staley. Johnson accompanied Joe back to jail for a post-trial debriefing.

57

There was a tunnel between the courthouse and the jail through which prisoners were transferred. As Joe walked back between Sheriff Colby and Deputy Plummer, he reviewed the day's events. Johnson was holding his own, but it might not make any difference, considering the race of the judge and most of the jurors. In the back of his mind he began forming an escape plan, just in case.

Johnson was waiting at the jail and asked to confer with his client. Joe had been moved to the upstairs block of cells. Once they were alone, he asked Joe, "How're you doing?"

"Holdin' my own. It's been a while since I've been around this many white people. They smell different."

Johnson smiled. "You'll get used to it. What did you think of Staley's testimony?"

"Either his memory is failin' or he's outright lyin'. He's the one who sicced them boys on me, and he knew they'd be up to no good. And I don't see how they coulda missed Unca Jim's grave if they went over that plantation with a fine-toothed comb."

"Very good, Joseph. You would have made an excellent lawyer."

"Uh-uh. Too much talkin', not enough doin'."

"I know its difficult sitting through all this, but your turn is coming, and I think the jury will be impressed with what you have to say."

"How will they know I'm tellin' the truth instead of Staley?"

"The Bible says, 'You shall know the truth and the truth shall make you free.' To most people, the truth sounds and feels different than a lie. We're going to use the truth to bend these bars and set you free."

"Amen, brotha! Hearin' you say it makes me think it could happen."

"Keep thinking that way. Get some rest. Big day tomorrow."

"You too."

Joe tried to follow his lawyer's advice. He ate his supper and read his Bible before wrapping himself in his bunk's musky blanket and closing his eyes. To lull himself, he thought about the times he and Martha shared before she died. He finally drifted off.

His sleep was disturbed several hours later by the sound of loud voices outside in the street. Looking out the window of his cell, he saw a torch-waving crowd gathered in front of the jail.

Sheriff Colby heard the mob and instantly knew their intention. He and Jason had been playing checkers to pass the time. He grabbed a shotgun from the gun rack and loaded it, putting extra shells in his pocket. He tossed a second shotgun to his deputy. "Get back there with the prisoner and don't let anybody take him out of here. Understand?"

"Yessuh!" Plummer's eyes were wide and he had to swallow the lump in his throat, but he did as he was told.

Joe was on his feet and at the bars when the deputy came to his cell. "What's goin' on?"

"Nothin' for you to worry about. Just some townfolk here to parlay with the sheriff. Sit down and stay away from that winda."

Ignoring the deputy, Joe went back to the window and watched the drama in the street.

Out front, Colby faced a crowd of twenty-five to thirty hooded men. "What's this about?"

"We come for your prisoner. He's got a date with the hangman," a man in the front of the crowd said.

"Nobody takes a prisoner out of my jail without my say-so," Colby said.

"We ain't got no beef with you, Sheriff. Just step aside and let us take care of our business." The man to his right held a coiled rope with a noose at the end over his forearm.

"You men better think about what you're doin'. Those who don't die tonight will hang tomorrow. I promise you," Colby said.

"You cain't hang who you don't know," the spokesman said.

"I know you, Ben Rutherford. You can hide your ugly face but you can't hide that cracker voice that I been listening to practically every day of my life. And I know you, Hector Reams, with your bow legs and monkey arms."

Rutherford said, "You may have just signed your own death warrant, John."

Samuel Johnson came across the street in his shirtsleeves, holding his Bible. "Wait a minute, men. We are all Christians here, aren't we? Jesus said those who live by the sword shall die by the sword and that we should love our enemies. If you do what you came here to do, you risk losing your immortal souls for the sake of vengeance. Let the law decide Joe Walker's fate and you will be able to stand before God on Judgment Day with clean hands."

From the back of the crowd, a voice said, "Save it for Sunday mornin', Reverend."

The man Colby had identified as Ben Rutherford said, "Looks like we might get ourselves two niggers for the price of one tonight. Boy, if you don't want to hang with your client, you best skedaddle."

Johnson stood his ground.

"Suit yourself."

The crowd began to surge forward. Suddenly a shotgun blast split the night. The men in the mob turned to see Judge Carstairs reloading his still-smoking weapon. He was dressed in his nightshirt, robe, and house slippers. His white hair stood up in spikes and his eyes were still rheumy with sleep.

"What the hell is this business?" The judge elbowed his way roughly through the crowd. When he arrived at Colby's side, he repeated his question. "Sheriff, what's going on here?"

"These men came to take my prisoner. We were just discussin' how much it was gonna cost 'em."

"You don't mean to tell me that these slack-jawed, snuff-dippin' peckerwoods have the audacity to try to lynch a man who is under the protection of my court?"

"Yessuh."

"Listen to me, you silly sonsabitches. If you so much as disturb a hair on Joe Walker's head, I'll call in federal troops so fast it'll make your heads swim. Then I will take great pleasure in trying and hanging every last one of you. If you think I'm bluffing, try me."

The mob turned into a headless snake in that instant. The men began to mill and murmur. Carstairs gave them the out they needed. "I'm only going to say this once. Get the hell out of here!"

The crowd dispersed like a sand painting in a windstorm. Judge Carstairs turned to his two companions. "We dodged a bullet tonight, gentlemen. Tomorrow I intend to send for federal troops to stand watch during the remainder of the trial just so the vigilante element in town knows I mean business."

"Your Honor, I can protect my prisoner without federal help," Colby said.

"I'm sure you can, Sheriff. But these hooligans didn't just threaten you tonight. They threatened the entire justice system, and I can't let that pass. I'll send for troops from Fort Marr in the morning, and we'll see what's what. Now I'm going to get back to bed. I'd advise you to do the same." Carstairs strode away, his military bearing intact despite his incongruous outfit.

Colby turned to Johnson and held out his hand. "I apologize for my treatment of you and your client the other day. It appears I misjudged you."

"It appears I also misjudged you, Sheriff." Johnson shook his hand. He checked on Joe and they discussed the events of the evening, including the judge's decision to bring troops. Then he went back to his room to get what sleep he could before returning to the courtroom.

58

The day after the aborted lynching, an air of expectant dread hung over the courtroom. Several people who had occupied front row seats from the trial's inception were missing. When Judge Carstairs entered the courtroom, his jaw was set and there was fire in his eyes. In his opening remarks, he got right to the point of his upset.

"After last night's shenanigans, I seriously considered declaring a mistrial and allowing Mr. Walker to go free. But I've decided to give this community a chance to redeem itself. So these proceedings will continue. However, if there is another threat to Mr. Walker or his attorney, the court will be merciless in its prosecution of the perpetrators. Sheriff Colby has provided me with a list of suspects based upon his observations last night. I will determine shortly whether to pursue criminal charges in this matter. Lest the vigilantes among you think this is an empty threat, I have sent for federal troops to help maintain law and order for the duration of this trial."

He swept the audience with his burning gaze, daring anyone to dispute his authority. No one obliged.

"Mr. Kilroy, please call your next witness," the judge said.

"Your Honor, the people call Dr. Raymond Samuels."

Dr. Samuels was a tall, stoop-shouldered man with black hair, a lantern jaw, and deep-set brown eyes. In fact, he bore a striking resemblance to the late President Lincoln. His loosely knotted tie hung from an open collar beneath a wrinkled suit coat whose sleeves were inches too short. He took the oath and settled into the witness chair, crossing his long legs.

"Dr. Samuels, what is your current occupation?"

"Ah'm the county's medical examiner," Dr. Samuels replied in a voice that confirmed his southern gentry roots.

"And did you hold this position in the summer of 1865?"

"Yessuh."

"In the course of your duties, did you have occasion to do autopsies on the bodies of Caleb Swenson, Billy Ray Rogers, and Homer Watson?"

"Yessuh, I did."

"And what were your findings?"

"Each man had been shot in the heart with a Colt pistol, which I determined to be the cause of death in each case."

"How many assailants would you say there were?"

"Judging from the bullets in their bodies, I would say there was a single assailant."

"Could you determine if they were shot from ambush?"

""No, suh, I could not. Their wounds were in the front."

"What are the chances that one man could kill three armed men in a fair fight?"

"Objection! This calls for speculation on the part of the witness in an area completely outside his area of expertise," Johnson said.

"Sustained."

"Withdrawn," Kilroy said.

"Did you share your findings with Sheriff Staley?"

"Yessuh, I did."

"And what conclusions did he draw?"

"He concluded that the three men had been ambushed and buried to hide the crime."

"Did you have any reservations about this conclusion?"

"None."

"No further questions, Your Honor," Kilroy said.

"Your witness, Mr. Johnson," the judge said.

Johnson rose from his seat and went to stand directly in front of the witness. He paused to rearrange several papers in his hand. "Dr. Samuels, how long have you been the county's medical examiner?"

"Going on seven and a half years."

"And where did you receive your medical degree?"

"Shelby Medical College."

"And what did you do before accepting your current position?"

"I was a combat surgeon with the Twenty-Seventh Virginia Infantry."

"The Bloody Twenty-Seventh?"

"Yessuh."

There was a murmur of approval from the crowd.

"How many autopsies would you say you have done since becoming medical examiner?"

"About a dozen."

"Concerning the three men in question, did you discover any other wounds on their bodies besides the gunshot wounds?"

"No, suh, I did not."

"How long did you determine they had been dead?"

"Three or four days."

"I'm going to show you a document." Johnson handed the doctor several pieces of paper. "Are these copies of your reports on your findings in the autopsies of Swenson, Rogers, and Watson?"

The doctor put on a pair of rimless reading glasses and proceeded to peruse the documents. He looked up, removed his glasses, and looked at Johnson. "Yessuh."

"And what is the date on these reports?"

"June 22, 1865."

"So by your assessment, they were shot on or around June 18?"

"Yessuh, I'd say so."

"Your Honor, I submit these reports as Exhibit A for the defense."

Johnson turned back to the witness. "Three shots to the heart from pistol range. How did you figure that that was an ambush?"

"Objection! Calls for speculation," Kilroy said.

"Sustained."

Johnson and Kilroy exchanged nods. *Touché.*

"Doctor, I ask you this question as a war veteran. What kind of marksman would it take to hit those men in their hearts from concealment with a sidearm?"

"An exceptional marksman."

Joe noticed two white men conferring animatedly in the front row of the audience.

"I have no further questions at this time, Your Honor."

"Your next witness, Mr. Kilroy?"

Kilroy proceeded to call a series of character witnesses for the three deceased men.

Johnson let them pass with token cross-examinations. When Swenson's sister took the stand, Johnson was able to establish that Swenson was a leader by dint of aggression and a fiercely loyal ex-Confederate soldier.

By midafternoon, Kilroy had called his last witness and rested his case. Judge Carstairs adjourned for the day. The defense would begin its presentation the following day.

After lunch, Johnson came to the jail to see Joe. Joe was eager to see him, and they spent a half hour together discussing their strategy. At the end of this session, Joe looked at Johnson with quiet admiration.

"You got some balls on you, son. You think this'll work?"

"If I can get the sheriff's and the court's cooperation. The most important piece is your testimony."

They went over possible gambits Kilroy might use in his cross-examination. Then, they devised a way to communicate at a distance in case of need.

"Kilroy is going to try to cause you to lose your composure in front of the jury—make you look like a man capable of murder. If you start to lose your temper, take a breath and look at me."

After Johnson left Joe, he went to make his request of Sheriff Colby. Colby was sitting at his desk cleaning his gun.

"Everything all right, Counselor?"

"Yes, sir." Johnson paused then forged ahead.

"Sheriff, I have an official request to make of you that has significant bearing on this case. Would you accompany me to the Washington farm to view a crucial piece of evidence?"

"What evidence?"

"Evidence that will help me to establish my client's innocence. I'm not prepared to say more at this time. But trust me, it will be worth your while. I apologize for the secrecy but until you consent, I cannot say more."

The sheriff pondered Johnson's request. He was under no obligation to accede to it without a court order, but Johnson's actions on the night of the raid on his jail had indebted him to the man. And he was a man who paid his debts. "All right, Counselor. Let's take a ride. We'll leave as soon as Jason gets back from lunch."

"Thank you, Sheriff. I am in your debt."

"Now, what's this all about?" Colby asked.

Johnson told the sheriff the story Joe would tell the court.

59

The following morning, a troop of soldiers from Fort Marr arrived. Their leader, Captain Richard Logan, reported to Sheriff Colby, who directed him to Judge Carstairs's house. So it was that when court convened at midday, there were armed soldiers in the room and standing guard outside. It was in this supercharged atmosphere that Samuel Johnson began his defense of Joseph Walker.

"Is the defense ready to begin its presentation, Mr. Johnson?" Judge Carstairs asked.

"Yes, Your Honor."

"Please call your first witness."

"The defense calls Joseph Walker to the stand."

There was a murmur in the courtroom as people in the back rows craned to get a look at the man who was the cause of so much past and present drama in their community.

Joe rose and walked to the witness stand, his stride hampered by the shackles on his ankles. Before Joe took the oath, Judge Carstairs ordered his handcuffs removed. Joe looked out on the sea of avid faces, took a deep breath, and prepared himself for battle.

"Mr. Walker, can you tell us why you are here today?"

"I'm here to clear my name."

"Is that why you voluntarily turned yourself in to Sheriff John Colby fourteen days ago?"

"Yessuh."

"You are accused of murder, correct?"

"Yessuh."

"And you know that the penalty for murder is death, do you not?"

"Yessuh, I do."

"And yet you are here of your own free will."

"Yessuh."

"Mr. Walker, the crime of which you are accused took place over six years ago, correct?

"Yessuh. June 18, 1865."

"And why are you just now surrendering?"

"I didn't know I was wanted for murder until I saw a reward poster with my name on it. I first decided to run 'cause I didn't believe I'd get a fair trial in this county, but the longer I thought about it, the more I figured I didn't fight to get free of slavery just to become a outlaw."

"You fought in the Civil War?"

"Yessuh. Fifth Colored Cavalry," Joe's back straightened and his voice resonated with pride.

"What did you do before the war?"

"Objection! Relevance?" Kilroy said.

"Your Honor, Mr. Walker's life before the war is the only reason he came back to Benton after the war."

"Overruled," Judge Carstairs said.

"So, Mr. Walker, what did you do before the war?"

"I was a slave, suh. I was born on the Walker plantation, which became the Poteet plantation and is now the Washington plantation. When I was nine years years old, my master sold me to a man named Jackson Budreau, who owned a plantation in Louisiana. I was separated from my family for the next ten years. I did everything I could to get back to 'em. When I was growed, I ran away from my master and joined the Union army. After the war, I come back to Benton to find my family."

"And what did you do when you came back to Benton?"

"First, I went to Sheriff Staley and told him who I was and who I was lookin' for. He directed me to the Poteet place even though he knew it was deserted."

"Objection! This claim is in dispute."

"Your Honor, it would have been impossible for Sheriff Staley *not* to know the Poteet plantation was deserted. Yet he sent my client out there anyway."

"Objection sustained. The jury will disregard Mr. Walker's statement that Sheriff Staley knew the Poteet plantation was deserted."

"Did you go to the Poteet plantation?"

"Yessuh."

"And what did you find?"

"The big house was empty and covered with lichen and trailing vines. The grounds and the fields was weeded over."

"So the plantation was deserted?"

"I thought so at first."

"What do you mean?"

"I found my Unca Jim Walker living there."

There was a gasp from the crowd.

"Objection, Your Honor! The prosecution has heard nothing of this fictitious 'Uncle Jim Walker.'"

"Your Honor, the defense was not obligated to share this information with the prosecution, as it is part of my client's testimony and we do not intend to call Jim Walker as a witness."

"The objection is overruled."

"Thank you, Your Honor. Please continue, Mr. Walker."

"Unca Jim was not 'blood family,' but he was the closest thing to family I had left. He had been hiding out on the property for about six months, living off the land. He told me what happened to the rest of my family—how my mama and sister Lillian died of the flu and my daddy died when a horse kicked 'im in the head. He told me how Mr. Poteet's overseer killed my other sister, Rosemary, when the Union army raided the plantation and how the army hung Mr. Poteet from a tree in the front yard. He said he was part of a group of slaves that run off after the soldiers left. He said my older brother, Amos, run off too."

"What happened next?"

"Unca" Jim left me alone with my people's graves in the colored cemetery and went back to his cabin. I was headed back that way when I heard shots. When I came into the clearin', I seen the man who had braced me earlier in town."

"Caleb Swenson?"

"Yessuh. I didn't know his name at the time. He was standing over Unca Jim with a gun in his hand. There was two other men standing behind him. When he saw me, Swenson raised his gun, so I shot him. The other two went for they guns, so I shot them too. Then I went to Unca Jim. He was shot several times and bleedin' bad. He died in my arms. I buried him in the colored cemetery with the rest of my family. I didn't figure I'd stand much of a chance turning myself in for killin' three white men when the town didn't know me from Adam, so I buried them in the cornfield and lit out."

"So, you shot all three men in self-defense."

"Yessuh."

"Before they could get off a shot?"

"Yessuh"

"Liar!" someone yelled from the crowd.

"Order in the court!" Judge Carstairs said, banging his gavel for emphasis.

"That's a remarkable feat of speed and accuracy with a handgun. Where did you learn to shoot like that?"

"In the army, suh. My sergeant taught us, don't draw your gun unless you intend to use it, and when you shoot, shoot to kill."

"Why didn't you turn yourself in at the time?"

"I once saw a colored man get hung for stealing a chicken. I saw a colored girl get brained with a skillet for knockin' over her mastuh's birthday cake. From what I knew at the time, white justice wasn't meant for colored people."

"And yet you turned yourself in."

"Yessuh, I did—for my family's sake. I won't let the Walker name carry the stain of murder here in the place where they lived and died."

"No further questions, Your Honor."

"Your witness, Mr. Kilroy," the judge said.

"I'm confused, Mr. Walker. Did you turn yourself in for your family's honor or to save your own skin?" Kilroy asked.

"I turned myself in for my family's honor *and* for my honor," Walker said, looking the prosecutor in the eye.

"So it took you six years to find your conscience?"

"No, suh. It took me six years to trust a system that sent men to kill me, who ended up murderin' the closest thing to a father I had left in this world."

"So you would have us believe that Sheriff Staley and the white men you killed are the villains here?"

"Sheriff Staley didn't tell me the Poteet place was deserted. If he hada, I wouldna gone out there. And he told Caleb Swenson where I was goin' in front of a crowd outside his office. Why? You tell me."

Kilroy changed tactics. "Mr. Walker, you said you were a soldier in the Union army, did you not?"

"Yessuh."

"Did you see much combat?"

"Too much."

"One would think that you would have relished getting back at the white man for what he had done to you, you being born a slave and all."

"I was killin' mad at first, but once you've seen death up close, you lose your appetite for it. Toward the end, what we wanted—and, I expect, what the Rebs wanted, too—was for the killin' to be over."

"But I imagine you got used to killing white men in the army, right?"

"The only thing I got used to in the army was stayin' alive. Any man here who served will tell you that."

There were murmurs of assent from the audience.

Kilroy changed tactics again. "Let's talk about this mysterious Uncle Jim. Kind of convenient that he was there to fill in all the gaps for you, wasn't it?"

"That was the Lord's doin'."

"Was Uncle Jim armed?"

"He had a skinning knife. No pistol."

"Did you witness his shooting?"

"No."

"Why did you take time to bury him?"

"He was family."

"Did you mark his grave?"

"Yessuh, I did."

"So if we were to go out to that cemetery today, that grave should still be there?" Kilroy said with a flourish.

"Yessuh, it should."

His look of triumph faded at Joe's response. "Mr. Walker, where did you go after you left Tennessee?"

"I went west to Kansas."

"And what did you do there?"

"I was a farmer."

"How long were you a farmer in Kansas?"

"About four years."

"Why did you leave Kansas?"

"A bounty hunter came for me."

"And what happened to that bounty hunter?"

"He got killed." This caused a stir in the audience.

"Did you kill him?"

"No."

"Mr. Walker, I would remind you that you are under oath."

"I didn't kill'im."

"How did he die?"

"I couldn't say for sure. He was dead when I found 'im. I found a wanted poster for me on his body, and I decided I should move on before others come lookin' for me."

"People seem to have a habit of dying around you, Mr. Walker. Let me get this straight—you kill three men known to be crack shots in a straight-up gunfight and then a bounty hunter who is trailing you ends up dead at the hands of an unknown benefactor. Is that about right."

"Yessuh."

"You expect us to believe this string of lies. It's a blessing that your mama and daddy are dead and buried. You say you want to honor them and Uncle Jim and all the rest, but you dishonor them with your crooked tongue and your crooked ways. You went to the army and they taught you to kill, but you learned nothing of courage and honor. Despite the best efforts of your family, your elders, and the Union army, you still are nothin' but a low down, back-shootin' swamp nigger!"

Kilroy's trap was sprung. Joe felt the tiger preparing to spring and there was nothing he could do to stop it. His jaw clenched and then his fists. Just before he went for Kilroy's throat, he looked over at Johnson.

Johnson was sitting at their table with his head in his hands, frantically tapping his temples—two fingers on the right side and two fingers on the left side. Joe got the signal and the message. As prearranged, his lawyer was reminding him to remember the fourth verse of the twenty-third chapter of Psalms: "Yea, though I walk through the valley of the shadow of death: I will fear no evil for thou art with me: thy rod and thy staff, they comfort me."

Joe unclenched his fists and took a deep, measured breath. He looked at Kilroy and spoke with a voice that, despite its calmness, penetrated to the back of the room. "My parents taught me to trust in the Lord, the army taught me to spot a ambush, and my elders taught me that niggas come in all colors."

"A-A-Amen!" An elderly black woman was standing with her hand raised above her head. Shouts and grunts of approval washed the black section of the courtroom like coastal waves.

"Order! Order in the court!" Carstairs shouted. The crowd reluctantly settled into silence.

Kilroy found himself no longer able to meet Joe's eyes. "I have no further questions, Your Honor." He turned and walked to his seat, the confidence in his stride and his air of command recently departed familiars.

Before Joe could leave the witness stand, Johnson said, "I have one more question for this witness, Your Honor."

"Proceed. Mr. Walker, I remind you that you are still under oath."

Joe sat back down.

"Mr. Walker, when you buried your Uncle Jim, did you put up any kind of marker on his grave?"

"Yessuh. He gave his life for mine. I wasn't gon' put 'im in an unmarked grave."

"Do you remember what you wrote on his marker?"

"Till the day I die. I wrote, 'James Walker—Born a Slave—Died Free.' At the bottom I put the date. It was in June of 1865."

"No further questions, Your Honor."

"You may step down, Mr. Walker."

Joe stood up. Sheriff Colby approached to replace his handcuffs.

"That won't be necessary, Sheriff. Please remove the shackles as well," Judge Carstairs said.

Joe walked back to his seat unencumbered.

When he sat down next to Johnson, the latter grabbed his bicep and squeezed it appreciatively, whispering, "Well done, son. Well done!"

"Please call your next witness, Mr. Johnson."

"Yes, Your Honor. The defense calls Sheriff John Colby."

Sheriff Colby took the stand and was sworn in amidst more murmurs from the crowd.

"Sheriff Colby, what is your current occupation?"

There were a few snickers from the crowd.

"I'm the sheriff of Polk County."

"And in that capacity, did you have occasion to accompany me to the plantation owned by Mr. Shelby Washington yesterday?"

"Yes, I did."

"And what did you and I do there?"

"We visited the colored cemetery on the property."

"And what did you observe there?"

"I saw a marker for James Walker with a date of death on it."

"What was that date?"

"June 18, 1865."

There was a gasp from the crowd followed by the outbreak of a dozen muted conversations.

"Order in the court!" Carstairs said.

Johnson pulled a page from his notebook and handed it to Colby. "Is this an accurate depiction of the inscription on the marker?"

"Yes, it is."

"Would you please read what is written on that paper?"

"James Walker—Born a Slave—Died Free—June 18, 1865."

This elicited another outburst from the crowd. People were talking openly as though they were discussing the case in their parlors.

"Order! Order! I will clear this courtroom!" Judge Carstairs pounded his gavel with such force that Joe feared that it would break in two. The crowd quieted under the threat of being removed at this critical juncture.

"Please continue, Mr. Johnson," the judge said.

"I would ask that this drawing be placed into evidence as Defense Exhibit B. Sheriff Colby, in your opinion, could this marker have been placed in recent days?"

"No. I'd say it had been there for many years."

"No further questions, Your Honor."

"Your witness, Mr. Kilroy."

"No questions, Your Honor."

"You may call your next witness, Mr. Johnson."

"Your Honor, may I approach the bench?"

"Yes, you may." Johnson and Kilroy went to the judge's bench for a private conversation.

"Your Honor, Sheriff Colby's testimony corroborates my client's version of events on June 18, 1865. If my client is right, four men died on that day, but only one of them was murdered—Jim Walker. I would like to request that Mr. Walker's body be exhumed and examined by Dr. Samuel for signs of foul play. This could prove exculpatory for my client," Johnson said.

"Do you have any objections to this request, Mr. Kilroy?"

Kilroy had awakened from his state of chagrin. "I strongly disagree that this would absolve Mr. Walker of guilt, but I have no objections to Mr. Johnson's request."

"Step back, please."

The two lawyers returned to their seats.

Judge Carstairs addressed the jury. "Mr. Johnson has requested that the body of Mr. James Walker be exhumed for examination to support his client's testimony. The prosecution concurs, so I am placing the court in recess until this process is completed. Sheriff, please proceed with all due haste to execute this order. Until then, we are in recess."

60

The exhumation and examination took three days. In the interim, Johnson told Joe he was spending his time reviewing court records and old newspaper articles. Joe spent his time reading his Bible and pacing his cell. He would prefer death to life in prison. A man wasn't made to be caged.

On the second day of the recess, Joe heard the front door of the sheriff's office open, followed by a voice he thought he would never hear again. He sprang to the bars, gripping them in anticipation.

"I'm lookin' for Joseph Walker."

"And who might you be?" Deputy Plummer asked.

"I'm Amos Walker, his brotha."

"Amos! Amos! Is that you?" Joe called out from his cell.

"Yeah, Jaybird. It's me!"

"Hold it right there, mister. Walker don't get no visitors without the sheriff's say-so."

"If you gon' use that gun, you better shoot straight, buckra," Amos said.

At that point, the front door bell sounded again. Sheriff Colby's voice cut through the tension. "What's goin' on here, Jason?"

"Sheriff, this gent wants to see the prisoner. Says he's his brother. I told 'im nobody goes back there without your say so."

"What's your story, mistuh?"

"I'm Amos Walker. That's my brotha back there and I intend to see 'im."

"You got any identification?"

"I got this letter he sent to me a while back, and I got my word."

There was a pause and Joe heard papers rustling.

"All right, I'm gonna let you see your brother, but you've got to give up your gun and let yo'self be searched or it's no go. Agreed?"

"Agreed."

A minute later, Joe heard Plummer say, "He's clean now, Sheriff."

"Take him back to see the prisoner but keep your eye on 'em."

"Yessuh!"

Amos literally ran through the door to the cellblock and grabbed his brother by the shoulders through the bars.

"Damn, it's good to see you. Damn!"

His eyes were brimming with tears, and Joe felt his own dam breaking. He hadn't been fully aware of how alone he felt, despite Johnson's support, until now.

Amos's relief gave way to anger. "You blame fool, why'd you come back here by yourself? They coulda lynched you without so much as a howdy do."

"I got me a lawyer."

"A lawyer! A lawyer! When push comes to shove, these white folks always stick together. Your lawyer will watch you hang and spend your fee on office furniture."

"Brotha, my lawyer is as black as you and as smart as me. His name is Samuel Johnson, and he's a man you can believe in. Crazy as it sounds, together we might beat this thing."

Amos leaned close and said under his breath, "Believe me, one way or the otha, you gon' beat this thing."

Despite the implications for their future, Joe was heartened to know that his brother would not stand idly by and watch him hang for a crime he didn't commit. That was the primary reason he had decided to walk this path alone.

"So how'd you know when to come here?"

"I didn't. As soon as I got your letter, I headed for Benton. It took me a month by train, stagecoach, and horseback to get here. I was prayin' I wouldn't be too late. I guess God's still holdin' us in the palm of His hand, Jaybird."

"Who's mindin' the farm?" Joe asked.

"Ethan's got that covered. I had to threaten to nail one foot to the floor to keep him from comin' with me. I told him you would go up in the air and come down stiff-legged if we left the women and children to fend for themselves. That settled it. I swear Joe he's turned into such a fine young man. I couldn't be prouder of 'im if he was my own flesh and blood."

Their conversation was interrupted by another chime of the doorbell. This time, Joe heard Johnson's familiar voice in the outer room.

"That's my lawyer. He stops by every day about this time."

Sheriff Colby came to the cellblock with Johnson in tow.

Joe sensed a difference in the relationship between the two men. Something hard had softened.

"Do you want to see your lawyer now or keep talkin' to your kinfolk?" Colby asked.

Joe said, "Sheriff, could I just have a minute to introduce 'em?"

"All right, but make it quick."

"Reverend Johnson, this is my brotha, Amos, who I told you about. Amos, this is my lawyer, Samuel L. Johnson."

Johnson stepped forward with his hand outstretched. Amos ignored the man's hand and lifted him off the floor in one of his spontaneous bear hugs. When he set him back down, Johnson looked as flustered as Joe had ever seen him.

"Reverend Johnson, I want to thank you for takin' my brotha's case. He tells me that you have been a friend and a couns'lor to him these last few weeks. I am forever in your debt."

Johnson had regained his composure and responded in a way that was designed to highlight his sincerity, his commitment, and his ability.

"Mr. Walker, your brother has been, and continues to be, a man of honor. It has been my privilege to make his acquaintance and to represent him in this matter. I'm sure the sight of you has brought him a sense of well being that no words of mine could convey. I have both worked and prayed for our ultimate success. I believe that your presence at this juncture is, in part, an answer to those prayers."

Amos stared at Johnson in amazement.

"I'll be damned, Jaybird. If this is the man you chose to speak for you, you hit the jackpot."

"He doesn't just speak for me. He believes in me and vouches for me. The way you did back on the wagon train, remember," Joe said.

"Yeah, like a brotha," Amos said.

"Exactly."

"All right, somebody's got to go. It's getting' too crowded in here," Sheriff Colby said from his place by the door.

"Mr. Walker, I'm staying at the Benton Boarding House across the street. Room Nine. It would be my pleasure to treat you to supper this evening—say around six?"

"You got yourself a date, Reverend. They got any rooms at your place?

"I believe they do."

"Good. You may not have to go far to find me this evenin'." With that, Amos gave his brother a final pat on the back and left him to consult with his attorney.

As soon as they were alone, Johnson said, "Well, this is a surprising turn of events. Did you know your brother was coming?"

"No. But I'm glad he's here."

"Me too. We're going to need all the support we can get down the stretch."

He then proceeded to outline his strategy to Joe for the remainder of the trial. When he was finished, Joe gave his assessment.

"It's a long shot, but I've played long shots before. I can read the crowd better'n I can the jury. They're playing it close to the vest like they was told to. That bastard Staley is the key. How do you break a man who ain't got nothin' to lose?"

"You take him back to the thing that he regrets losing most," Johnson said.

61

When the trial resumed, Johnson wasted no time putting Doctor Samuels on the witness stand. The physician was dressed much the same as during his previous testimony, but now he sported several days worth of beard stubble, further enhancing his resemblance to the late President Lincoln.

"Doctor Samuels, have you examined the body that was exhumed from the colored cemetery on the Washington plantation?"

"Yes, I have."

"And what did you find?"

The doctor began a recitation that was as practiced as ordering breakfast. "The corpse was that of a Negro male in his sixties. Judging by the condition of his muscles and bones, he had been a laborer most, if not all, of his life. He was suffering from kidney disease and cancer of the prostate, but neither of these illnesses were the cause of death."

"What was the cause of death?"

"He was shot to death. He had bullet wounds in his right hand, shoulder, abdomen and chest, causing him to die of a combination of blood loss and organ failure."

"Were you able to retrieve the bullets?"

"Yes, they were all still lodged in the body."

"Are you able to determine what kind of weapon fired the bullets?"

"Yessuh. The rounds came from a Remington army pistol."

"Doctor, you said that there was a wound in the decedent's hand."

"Yessuh. A single bullet passed through his palm and lodged in his shoulder. This is what is called a 'defensive wound.'"

"Please explain."

"Apparently, the victim held up his hand or hands in a 'warding off' gesture and received a wound in his right hand as a result."

"I see. Did the victim have a weapon of any kind?"

"There was a knife in his belt."

"A skinning knife?"

"Yessuh."

"How long would you say the body had been interred?"

"I'd say between five and ten years based on the degree of decomposition."

"Based on your extensive experience in examining crime victims, would you say that Mr. Walker died in a fair fight?"

"Objection, Your Honor! Calls for speculation on the part of the witness."

"Overruled."

"Doctor?"

"I would say Mr. Walker was shot down in cold blood."

There were quiet murmurs among the crowd. One voice rang out. "That's right!"

Joe recognized his brother's voice and suppressed a smile.

"No further questions, Your Honor," Johnson said.

"Your witness, Mr. Kilroy," the judge said.

"Thank you, Your Honor. Doctor Samuels, can you say with absolute certainty that the decedent was murdered?" Kilroy asked.

"No, suh, but . . ."

"No further questions, Your Honor."

"The witness is excused. Mr. Johnson, please call your next witness," the judge said.

"Your Honor, the defense recalls Sheriff Ben Staley."

Staley rose from a front row seat and walked slowly to the witness stand. In the middle of the oath, he was seized by a fit of coughing. He took out his handkerchief and covered his mouth. When he removed it, Joe saw that it was flecked with blood.

"Sheriff Staley, you heard Dr. Samuels' testimony?"

"Yes. I heard it."

"And you stand by your earlier testimony that you did not discover Mr. James Walker's grave during your search of the Poteet property?"

"We were lookin' for dead white men, not dead Nigras."

"Did you examine the pistols from the bodies of Mr. Swenson, Mr. Rogers, and Mr. Watson for evidentiary purposes?"

"Yes, I did."

"You testified earlier that Mr. Swenson's gun had been fired four times."

"Yeah."

"What kind of weapon did Mr. Swenson carry?"

Staley looked at Johnson with ill-concealed hatred.

"Shall I repeat the question?"

Staley spat out the words. "A Remington army pistol."

"Objection, Your Honor! Mr. Swenson is not on trial here," Kilroy said.

"Your Honor, my client is the only witness to the events of that day and he has told us his story. I am trying to provide corroborating evidence," Johnson said.

"Overruled," Judge Carstairs said.

"Sheriff Staley, how did you know to search for the missing men on the Poteet plantation?"

"That's where Walker went."

"But why would they go there? They knew it was deserted."

"What are you gittin' at?"

"Isn't the reason they went to the Poteet place because you told them to?"

"No!"

"You sent them after Joe Walker with instructions to do him harm."

"That's a goddamn lie! Your nigger client laid in ambush and killed them boys because he was a low-down Yankee murderer. He didn't get his fill of killin' during the war, so he come here lookin' for more good southern boys to butcher."

"Just like they butchered your son Eric?" Johnson said.

"You keep his name out of your lyin' nigger mouth!" Staley shouted.

"I did some research in the archives of the Benton Herald, and I came across an obituary describing how Eric, your only boy, was killed at Fort Wagner in 1863 by members of the Fifty-Fourth Massachusetts, a unit of colored soldiers."

Staley took the bait like a hungry catfish. "Yeah, they killed my boy. The low-down, bloodthirsty field monkeys! He was nineteen years old. His mama never got over it. She left me. Said she couldn't stand the sight of me after I sent our boy off to die. She took my daughter and went north. I ain't seen 'em since. I wanted to go join up myself, but the Confederacy was on its last legs by then. So I stayed on as sheriff and bided my time."

Johnson stoked the fire he had started. "And then Joe Walker came to town."

"Yeah, he rode in on his fancy horse with his fancy clothes and his uppity ways, and I knew he was just like them that killed my boy."

"Your Honor, this is highly irregular. The defense is badgering the witness!" Kilroy interjected, sensing where this was leading.

Before the judge could respond, Staley screamed at Kilroy. "Shut up and sit down, you! I ain't got much time left, and I want everybody to know what I did and why."

The room was transfixed.

Staley continued in a voice as raspy as death. "I sent your boy out to the Poteet plantation. I waited till he got a head start, and then I grabbed Caleb Swenson and told him to take a coupla boys who could keep their mouths shut and put that uppity nigger down. When Caleb and the other two didn't come back to town by dark, I just figured they'd gone home after finishin' their business. The next day, their families reported 'em missin'. That worried me. I rode out to the Poteet place on my own and looked around, but I didn't find nothin' so I went back to town and raised a search"—he coughed loudly, took out his ruined handkerchief, and spat bloody phlegm into it—"party. After we found the bodies, I raised a posse. We rode all the way to the Kentucky border but didn't see hide nor hair of Walker. I charged him with murder and talked the white men in town into puttin' up a reward."

"Sheriff, did you believe my client murdered those men?"

"It didn't matter to me. I wanted him dead. Just like my boy." Having bared his soul, Staley sank in on himself like a deflated balloon.

"No further questions, Your Honor."

"Would you like to question this witness, Mr. Kilroy?" the judge asked.

"No questions, Your Honor."

"Your Honor, I ask that Ben Staley be taken into custody immediately on charges of being an accessory to the crime of attempted murder," Johnson said.

There were a few feeble cries of protest from the white side of the crowd, but they were drowned out by shouts of joy and applause from the black side.

"Order! Bailiff, please take Mr. Staley into custody and escort him to the county jail," Judge Carstairs said.

The bailiff came forward and placed Staley in handcuffs. He allowed himself to be led away, shuffling with his head down. The ravening cancer inside him would not allow him to make it to trial.

Johnson wasn't finished. "Your Honor, based on Mr. Staley's testimony, I would ask that you submit a judgment of acquittal and allow my client to go free."

"Objection, Your Honor," Kilroy said as if by rote.

"Overruled."

"Mr. Johnson, I will take your request under advisement and render my decision tomorrow," Judge Carstairs said. "Court dismissed!" The judge left the bench and entered the side door to his chambers.

Joe was still digesting Staley's testimony. He had only scratched the surface of the man's hatred during their brief encounter. He looked at the jury and met the eyes of Shelby Washington, who gave him a nod of encouragement. Seated next to Washington was the rawboned farmer who had glared at him since the trial began. The man made a gun out of his thumb and forefinger, pointed it at Joe, and mimed pulling the trigger.

62

Joe Walker slept little that night. Ben Staley was in the cell two doors down from him and hurled a constant stream of invective at Joe until he collapsed into a fevered sleep, interrupted by fits of coughing.

Johnson prepared himself mentally for either of two outcomes the next day. He spent most of the night reviewing his notes and reading his Bible. He was up, shaved, and dressed by first light.

He went down to the dining room for breakfast and was surprised when the staff gave him a standing ovation. Miss Irene, the cook, had prepared him a repast that could have graced the richest table in the county—coffee, scrambled eggs, honey-cured ham, blueberry muffins, fresh orange juice, and strawberries with cream. Due to his anxiety, Johnson could not do justice to the meal. Amos, who had also taken a room at the house, made up for his reticence. After breakfast, the two of them walked to the courthouse together.

When they reached the courthouse, Amos took his seat in the colored section of the gallery and Johnson proceeded to the defense's table.

Joe was led in by the bailiff. He was dressed in his court finery, but he was on edge and bleary-eyed. He knew his fate would be decided one way or another that day. The courtroom was full of people who either wanted him dead, wanted him free, or were merely curious.

He had prayed for a positive result. But his sins, real and imagined, weighed heavily on him. He longed for God's mercy but feared he would receive His judgment instead.

The bailiff said, "All rise!"

Judge Carstairs entered the room and took his seat. "Please be seated." He surveyed the room before beginning his discourse. "The thing that causes this country's system of justice to be envied around the world is our jury system. It ensures that the common man will understand and appreciate the laws that govern him. It is a bulwark against abuse of power by the state or wealthy interests. For this reason, I regard a request to abrogate the role of the jury in any case, let alone a capital case, with skepticism.

"During this trial, however, I have seen the worst of Polk County in the form of the mob that tried to take the law into their own hands a few nights ago and the best of Polk County in the form of the brave men who stood in their way. Their bravery and belief in the rule of law is indeed laudatory, but it pales in comparison to the bravery of Joseph Walker.

"The defendant voluntarily returned to Benton to surrender himself to a justice system that first branded him a slave and then an outlaw. He was willing to stake his life on the wisdom and fairness of the people of Polk County. But the implications of this case stretch far beyond Polk County and the state of Tennessee. It is a test of whether a Negro can receive a fair trial in the former Confederacy.

"I look out on this crowd and I see clearly that the Civil War united us in name only. After hearing the facts of this case, I am appalled that the sheriff who was charged with protecting Mr. Walker's rights deliberately set out to abuse them. I am appalled that Mr. Walker has been forced to live the last six years under the constant threat of being killed by a random bounty hunter, and I am most appalled by the fact that, despite overwhelming evidence of his innocence, there are still people in this audience who desire to see him executed, apparently for no other reason than the color of his skin.

"Mr. Walker has been willing to risk his liberty, his reputation, and his life in the pursuit of justice. I think he has risked enough. Therefore, I am granting the defense's request for a judgment of acquittal and order that Mr. Walker be released from custody immediately with the apologies of the county of Polk and the state of Tennessee. Court is dismissed."

His last words were drowned out by the roar of the audience as understanding dawned upon them. People in the black section were jumping up and down, hugging each other and shouting, "Hallelujah!" and "Thank you, Jesus!" Men and women were crying tears of joy, and someone started singing "The Battle Hymn of the Republic," which the crowd took up with gusto. People in the white section were shouting and gesticulating, voicing their disgust or disbelief at the judge's ruling. Ben Rutherford stood in the middle of a knot of angry white men and roared his disapproval. Judge Carstairs calmly folded his hands and surveyed the chaos his pronouncement had caused, for the first time making no attempt to reestablish order.

And what of the subject of all this calamity? Joe Walker sat at the defendant's table with his head buried in his hands, trying to hide his emotions. The noises around him seemed to be filtered through a layer of cotton. Sam Johnson was hugging him from the side, his lips moving in silent prayer.

Joe wiped the tears from his face and turned to his lawyer. He placed his palm on the nape of Johnson's neck and drew him close. He spoke into Johnson's ear the only two words his brain could summon, but they came from the bottom of his heart. "Thank you! Thank you!"

Johnson responded with two words of his own. "Thank God." And then, "We did it!"

As the bailiff was leading Joe away, he heard Amos yelling his name. "Jaybird! We won! Praise the Lord! We won!" Amos was trying to push past the soldiers who were guarding the courtroom, but they stood resolutely in his path. "I'll see you in a minute," he said and turned to make his way through the crowd.

As the courtroom cleared, Jonathon Kilroy sat at the prosecutor's table in a state of shock. How could this have happened? He had had his ducks in a row—his chickens counted. This was to have been the next step on his steady ascent up the state's political ladder. Next stop—attorney general. Instead, it had turned into a quagmire from which he might never rise. He could appeal the ruling, of course, but he wouldn't. He had no desire to face Samuel Johnson again.

Back at the jail, Sheriff Colby uncuffed Joe and returned his possessions. Joe put on his belt and hat and pocketed his wallet.

"I apologize for Ben Staley. He's a disgrace to the badge," Sheriff Colby said.

"I'm glad the town chose better the next time," Joe said.

Colby extended his hand and Joe took it. "Don't worry about them wanted posters. I'll see to it that they get pulled," Colby said.

"Much obliged," Walker said.

"Godspeed, Mr. Walker."

"The same to you, Sheriff."

Amos Walker burst through the door and grabbed his brother, lifting him off the floor.

"Put me down, Amos!" Joe said, laughing.

His brother reluctantly complied, grinning like a twelve-year-old. "You're free, boy! When that judge started usin' all them big words, I thought he was layin' a smoke screen. My heart sunk to my boots. But then the 'Man upstairs' stepped in and everything turned out just fine. Ain't God good?"

Johnson came through the door, having been delayed at the courthouse. Amos went to the lawyer and repeated his demonstration with Joe. Having played this scene before, Johnson just smiled and waited for Amos's enthusiasm to subside.

"Reverend, you're somethin' else. Watchin' you in that courtroom reminded me of watchin' Joe workin' a horse. If you ever need a man to stand for you, I'm him. Even if I have to swim the Mississippi to do it."

"Thank you, Amos. I'll hold you to that."

"You betta."

Johnson turned to Sheriff Colby. "Is he free to go?"

"Yessuh."

Johnson went to the sheriff and extended his hand. "It has been an honor to meet you, sir."

"The honor was mine, suh. Come back to see us when you can. You like to fish?"

"I do."

"I know a spot where the catfish are so thick you can snag 'em with a bare hook," Colby said.

"We'll have to see," Johnson said, smiling. He went to Jason Plummer and shook his hand. "Thanks for your help, Deputy."

"You're welcome, Your Honor," Plummer said, using the highest title he knew to show his respect for the Negro attorney.

Johnson excused himself and returned to the boarding house to pack for the trip back to Ebenezer. There was a knock at his door. He opened it to discover Shelby Washington.

Washington said, "I couldn't let you get away without paying my respects. You did the whole race proud during this trial. Just so you know, they would have had to kill me to keep me from declaring that boy was innocent."

"Thank you for your hospitality and your support. I am forever in your debt," Johnson said.

"To the contrary," Washington said. He handed Johnson an envelope.

"What's this?"

"That is your rent refund." Johnson started to protest but Shelby interrupted him. "I won't take no for an answer. I will take great pride in telling my grandchildren about this."

"Thank you kindly," Johnson said, placing the envelope in his jacket pocket.

"One other thing. I would be honored to come and speak to your students at anytime that is convenient. Let me know when," Shelby said.

The two men parted with promises to stay in touch, which they did, eventually forming one of the more successful black business ventures of the era.

Johnson and the Walker brothers rode back to Ebenezer with an Army escort, by order of Judge Carstairs. News of their recent triumph had preceded them, and they were given a hero's welcome by the people of Johnson's hometown.

Despite being surrounded by new friends and well-wishers in Ebenezer, Joe and Amos were eager to be off. So it was that one early Monday morning, roughly a month and a half after Joe had sat in Johnson's church and took his measure, the Walkers said their good-byes. Amos gave the reverend a bone-crushing hug and mounted his horse. Joe stood self-consciously in front of the man to whom he owed his freedom and his life.

"Those boys from the Ninth Artillery pegged you right. You are the Lord's shepherd. You certainly led me through death's valley."

"I'd say the Lord did the leading and we both followed," Johnson said.

"Amen to that." Joe reached into his pocket. "Since we already settled your fee, I got a gift for you." He pressed into Johnson's palm the Black Hills gold nugget that Two Lances had given him.

Johnson looked at the nugget. "Is this gold?"

"Yessuh."

"I can't accept this. It's too much."

"Among my Indian brothers, refusin' a gift is one of the worst insults. It usually leads to bloodshed. But since you are a man of peace, I would just have to settle for never speakin' to you again. Is that the note you want to part on?"

"No, of course not. I didn't mean to offend you. I don't know what to say. I will treasure this for the rest of my life."

"That'll do," Joe said, smiling.

Johnson was true to his word. He later had the nugget smelted and formed into a gold cross that he habitually wore around his neck. In fact, he was wearing it the day he argued his first case before the United States Supreme Court. On that day in 1871, though, he merely put it in his pocket.

Joe went to Dice and mounted. He and Amos waved to the reverend one last time. Joe looked at his brother and said the words he had longed to say for what seemed like an eternity. "Let's go home."

PART 7
Man Hunter

63

Joe Walker pulled his hat down low on his brow and burrowed into the saddle. His left hand gripped the reins firmly, and his right hand grasped the saddle's pommel. He nodded at the cowboy standing beside his mount. The man whipped the blindfold from the bronc's eyes and stepped back quickly. The horse took a second to get his bearings and then began to imitate a large fish out of water, twisting and turning violently to free himself of the unfamiliar burden on his back. Joe gripped with his knees and rocked in rhythm with the animal's gyrations. His comrades, who surrounded the corral, yelled words of encouragement or mock ridicule.

"Bust 'im, Joe. Come on, boy!"

"Is that the best you can do? Let *me* at that broomtail."

Joe stuck to the saddle like a burr. This was his second go-round with the big sorrel, and he knew most of his moves. Gradually the horse began to tire. Before giving in, he tried one more desperate maneuver.

Rearing up, he fell straight back to the ground, hoping to crush Joe underneath him. Joe leapt nimbly out of the saddle, maintaining his grip on the reins. When the horse rose to his knees, Joe jumped back into the saddle and maintained his seat as the animal regained his feet.

The sorrel knew the contest was over. He gave a few more desultory bucks and then settled into a resigned trot around the enclosure. Joe put him through his paces to the cheers of the watching cowboys and then dismounted, handing the reins to a rangy blond puncher named Pete Hopper.

"I thought he was gonna scramble your eggs on that last deal there, Joe," Hopper said.

"He's got spirit and smarts. I just might add 'im to my string," Joe said.

"Lord knows you like'em tall and sassy."

"Are we still talkin' about hosses?" Joe asked straight-faced.

Hopper snorted at this bit of unexpected humor from his fellow.

Joe was into his second year as a wrangler on the Comstock spread in west Texas, north of El Paso just outside the town of Lone Tree. The Comstock ranch was five hundred acres of rangeland and pasture. The owner ran about 275 head of cattle on this spread, employing fifteen to twenty ranch hands.

William Comstock was a second-generation American. His father, Richard, and his mother, Elizabeth, had immigrated to the United States from England in 1823. His father had been a captain in the Royal Dragoons. When he retired, he took his pension and his family inheritance and booked passage for the New World in search of unfettered opportunity and elbowroom.

William was ten years old when he came to America. He was the only child so his parents gave him their full attention. His mother taught him etiquette and shared her love of literature and horticulture, and his father taught him discipline, self-defense, and business.

When William turned eighteen, he went away to college at Columbia University where he majored in business and minored in English. While in New York, he met Jennifer Angstrom, the daughter of his English professor. For William, it was love at first sight. The two were married shortly after he graduated.

Richard Comstock's birthplace, accent, and English manners initially alienated him from his neighbors. Consequently, he was unable to hire white men to help him work his ranch. He ended up hiring vaqueros from a small Mexican village whose loyalty, hardiness, and horsemanship became legendary. The sons of his original vaqueros were still working for "Captain" Comstock a generation later.

William's father systematically went about earning the respect of the men in the community. If a neighbor needed a hand after a patch of bad luck, Richard Comstock was one of the first ones in line. He helped raise barns, round up cattle, and track down rustlers. He discreetly gave loans to men in financial trouble and was patient about repayment. In five years, he was the most popular man in the county.

Richard Comstock died in a cattle stampede in 1856. His wife passed peacefully in her sleep three years later. William took over the ranch and ran it with his father's competence and his mother's compassion.

His values were put to the test when the war broke out. He had been raised to believe that slavery was a sin, but he could not bring himself to take up arms against his friends and neighbors, so he did not take a side in the war. Instead, he spent his time fighting renegade Indians and outlaws who sought to take advantage of the menfolk's absence by killing and looting. He and his vaqueros defended not only his family but the families of his neighbors as well. After the war, Comstock had no trouble finding ranch hands of any stripe.

Romilio Estéban, a well-built, handsome vaquero, approached Joe and Hopper, smiling.

"How many is that for you, amigo?" he asked Joe.

"I believe that's number seven, Rom," Joe said.

"Sorry, I broke eight today. I guess the drinks are on you, my friend."

"I guess so, but this one heah should count for two."

"That's because *you* drew him and not me, amigo." This sibling-like rivalry was a staple of their friendship. The cowboys walked to the bunkhouse together, satisfied with a job well done.

Two years after his acquittal, Joe had left his brother's farm in Kansas in search of his own calling. Amos had begged him to stay, reminding him of the long years they had spent apart, uncertain of each other's existence. But Joe had been wrestling with a growing certainty that his destiny was not to be a farmer, even a rich one. In the end, he could only promise to return to the Walker homestead when he had discovered the thing that made him as satisfied as farming and raising a family had made Amos.

The harder chore was conveying his decision to Ethan. The boy worshipped the ground Joe walked on and patterned his behavior, speech, and demeanor after his adopted uncle. The only thing that kept him from tailing Joe was his budding love of Amy Taylor, the daughter of Ezekiel Taylor, who owned the place next to Amos's. Joe made the decision easier by telling Ethan it would be the height of selfishness to lure Amy away from her home and family for a life on the move with two wandering trail hands. The boy reluctantly agreed with this logic.

So Joe had left his family in Kansas one hot summer day with the promise to return when he had made his fortune. That had been a difficult but liberating decision that led Joe to the life of a working cowboy, a life he thouroughly enjoyed. He got to work with horses and cattle, and the men he associated with, for the most part, were more concerned with the skill in his hands than their color.

That evening, Joe and the other ranch hands gathered around the table in the bunkhouse for a supper of pork and beans, cornbread, and fried fruit pies washed down with sweet tea.

The bunkhouse was a two-story building with a peaked roof about thirty yards from the main house. On the first floor was a living room furnished with couches, overstuffed chairs, and two card tables. A large stone fireplace took up most of one wall. The living room was flanked by a dining room containing a long oak table with chairs along both sides and a four-by-six-foot cabinet for dishes and cutlery. The third room was the kitchen, containing a large wood stove, a carving/cooling table, and a sink.

The second floor consisted of three large bedrooms furnished with bunk beds and footlockers. The bunkhouse's walls were decorated with skins and pelts of bear, wolf, bobcat, and deer, and the wood floors were bleached from many scrubbings and scarred by the rowels of countless spurs.

The bunkhouse was "home" to the fifteen to twenty cowhands who typically worked the Comstock ranch. Indeed, it was nicer than the homes most of them had left behind. Like his father before him, Bill Comstock treated his men like family.

The ranch cook, Zeke "Slowpoke" Grayson, was a seasoned hand who transformed from cowboy to cook following an accident that left him unable to spend long days in the saddle, so the fare was simple but satisfying. Cowboy banter and tall tales helped season the meal.

A bowlegged cowboy named Tom Perkins paid the old cook a dubious compliment. "Slowpoke, if you was a woman, I'd marry you, good as these pies are."

"What makes you think I'd have you?" the old man said. This brought a burst of laughter from the crew.

"Well, I'm strong and good lookin' and got all my teeth. Which is more than I can say for you."

"You could if you wanted to keep on lyin'," Slowpoke said, pretending to be annoyed.

"'Sides, I already been married."

"What woman was desperate enough to marry you?" Perkins asked.

Slowpoke paused for effect and then delivered the coup de grace. "Yo' motha," he said. Joe almost spit up his tea.

Perkins couldn't help but smile at his own comeuppance. "You got me good, you ol' bastard," Perkins said.

Grayson smiled, revealing the missing teeth Perkins had alluded to. "Don't go after a grizzly on your first hunt, son," he said.

Perkins' riposte was interrupted by William Comstock's entrance to the room. Though he was the richest man in the county, he was dressed like a cowpoke in worn jeans, scuffed boots, a striped vest, and a faded blue work shirt. His one indulgence was a gold pocket watch and fob handed down to him from his father, who had received it from his mother.

The men greeted him with familiarity. "Howdy, boss. You come down to see how the other half lives?" a cowboy named Chuck Wheeler asked.

Comstock, now in his fifties, had piercing blue eyes, wide shoulders, and a mane of salt and pepper hair he wore cowboy style. He eased into the banter as though he had been there from the start. "No, Chuck, I heard Slowpoke was serving fried pies, and I wanted to get here before the platter was clean."

"You was almost too late," Slowpoke said, passing a plate to Comstock with two pies on it.

Comstock took the plate and sat down at the table. He cut open the pastries and savored their aroma. Then, like a man enjoying his last meal, he placed a forkful in his mouth and chewed contentedly. "Slowpoke, I believe you outdid yourself this time. If you put one of these pies on a man's forehead, his tongue would slap his brains out."

The crew laughed appreciatively at this old saw.

"That's my mama's recipe. She taught me how to cook and sew. Said a man needed to know how to take care of hisself without a woman."

"Well, blessings on her and the son she raised," Comstock said.

The old cook grew a shade ruddier beneath his beard and turned back to his pots and pans, flummoxed for the first time that evening. Bill Comstock had a way of making a man feel noticed and appreciated at the same time. It was one of the reasons cowboys rode past other spreads to seek a job on his.

"Well, there's only one way to finish a meal like this," Comstock said. He stood up and walked to the door and out into the night. The men regarded each other with puzzlement. It wasn't like the boss to depart so abruptly after breaking bread with them. He usually stayed around to chew the fat and play a hand or two of poker. Before they could unravel the mystery, there was a knock on the door.

What the . . . ? Joe thought.

Tom Perkins went to the door and opened it to reveal the boss standing there with a jug under each arm and a mischievous grin on his face. "Thought you boys might like some corn liquor to wash down that first-rate supper."

The men voiced their approval and quickly relieved Comstock of his burdens. Cups were filled all around. Comstock raised his. "A toast—to the best bunch in Texas!"

They drank the first of many drafts and settled in for some cards, laughter, and lying. In the bitter days ahead, Joe would remember this cheerful evening with considerable longing.

64

Two days later, Joe and Rom were rounding up stray cattle on the north forty, a broken stretch of arroyos filled with rattlesnakes, thornbushes, and cacti, having finished breaking the current crop of mustangs.

The strays seemed to relish their independence and retreated into the gullies bordered by steep sides and choked with thornbushes. If not for their leather chaps, Joe and Rom would have been cut to ribbons. They drove some cattle out of their hiding places with shouts and whistles and roped others and dragged them out. It was hot, thirsty work and by midday, their throats were dry and their shirts wet.

"Juro por dios, amigo. I would rather break broncs bareback with my cojones hanging out than have to do this every day," Rom said.

"They say God hears every prayer, compadre. So you might want to keep that one to yo'self," Joe said, wiping his face with his bandanna. "Besides, this beats mending fence or cleaning stables by a fair piece."

They were driving the twenty head they rescued back to the herd when Pete Hopper approached at a gallop. The dour expression on the cowboy's face announced that he was not the bearer of good news.

"Mr. Comstock's dead—shot in a bank robbery in Lone Tree this mornin'," Hopper said, his words tumbling out.

The news made Joe's physical discomfort fade into the background, replaced by a sense of loss and rising anger. Mr. Comstock was his model for running one's own place, and he still had much to learn. Plus, the man had treated him with dignity and respect from their first meeting. This was rare behavior from a wealthy white man.

"Diablos dices! Who kill him?" Rom said.

"It was the Bill Connor gang."

"Bad Bill?" Joe asked. "Bad Bill" Connor was an ex-marauder who turned to outlawry after the Civil War. He was notoriously bloodthirsty, particularly toward members of the Negro race, whom he shot, tortured, and lynched without provocation.

His specialty was robbing banks, but he also engaged in rustling and highway robbery. He had assembled a gang of ex-Confederate soldiers and ne'er-do-wells who shared his avarice and his hatred.

"One in the same. They say they killed him for his daddy's watch. I come for y'all 'cause they're formin' a posse and I thought you would wanna join," Hopper said.

Joe looked at Rom and the vaquero nodded. "Can you bring these strays in by yo'self?" Joe asked Hopper.

"Yep."

"See to it that the boss is taken care of. We'll pay our respects when we git back," Joe said. With that, Joe and Rom turned their horses and rode hard for Lone Tree.

Lone Tree, Texas, was a cow town of about one hundred residents located in the Texas Hill Country. It served as a supply hub and gathering place for the ranchers and farmers who owned places in the surrounding countryside. It had a post office/telegraph office, stagecoach station, a saloon, a livery, a Catholic mission, a bank, and a general store. The majority of the buildings were adobe. The population was a mixture of whites, Mexicans, blacks, and Mestizos. The town's name was derived from a towering Spanish oak that grew in the town square.

When they reached town, people were in the streets and everyone was talking about the morning's events. They rode to the undertaker's parlor where they found William Comstock's body laid out on a table covered with a sheet. When the undertaker lifted the sheet, Joe saw half a dozen bullet holes in his boss's body. The thing he had tried to deny all morning was gruesomely affirmed. He took a deep breath, choking back tears.

Rom stood over the body and crossed himself, his lips moving silently. He turned to Joe with tears in his eyes. "We must find the men who did this and make them pay," he said.

Joe was of a like mind. Looking back, he recalled the first time he had met Bill Comstock. It was the summer of 1873. Joe was on the verge of giving up hope of finding ranch work on any spread that would pay decent wages. Despite his riding, roping, and horse-breaking skills, one ranch owner after another had rejected him. Some were forthright in telling him it was because of his race. William Comstock was probably his last bet in the area.

After Joe had introduced himself to Comstock and quoted his qualifications for the job, Comstock had had his men cut out a twelve-hundred-pound keg of dynamite that they called "Sidewinder" because of his unorthodox bucking style and his venomous disposition.

"Think you can ride that horse?" Comstock asked, his blue eyes twinkling.

Joe marked the trace of an unfamiliar accent. "Yessuh," he said without hesitation.

"Give it a go, then," Comstock said.

Joe walked into the corral where the big chestnut was rearing and neighing like fury. His nostrils flared and his eyes rolled back in his head. It took four men to saddle the mustang. Two grasped him around the neck and "eared him down." The third roped his foreleg and pulled it back. The fourth put on the saddle. Finally, they all wrestled him to the ground using brute force. Joe mounted him in the prone position and the cowboys ran for the fence rails.

The stallion stood up as though he were on springs and began bucking with all the strength and fury in his body. Joe felt like his head was going to snap off his shoulders. He tried to make himself one with the tornado beneath him, but he lacked the time or the savagery. After ten seconds in the saddle, Joe's hand was cramping, his head was throbbing, and his spine felt like a wet dishrag. He steeled himself and prayed for the bronc to tire.

Sidewinder ran along the corral fence and tried to scrape Joe off. Joe jerked his foot out of the stirrup to avoid a broken leg. The chestnut whirled like a dervish and Joe lost his stirrup for good. At that point the game was all but over. With a savage twisting buck, Sidewinder flung Joe in the air like a rag doll. He landed on his left side and rolled instinctively toward the edge of the corral. The horse charged him with teeth bared.

The only thing that saved Joe from a probably fatal stomping was a cowhand who jumped into the stallion's path, shouting and swinging his coiled lariat. Joe would learn later it was Romilio Estéban. Two men helped Joe up and ushered him to safety outside the corral. Joe felt like he had been stretched on a rack. His entire body was one knot of pain. His vision was blurred and his forehead was bleeding.

Mr. Comstock approached Joe, a look of concern on his face. "Are you all right, cowboy?"

"Yessuh. Just need to catch my breath," Joe said.

"Well, you gave it your best shot. No shame in walking away from certain calamity."

"No, suh. We ain't through. That was just the first round where he got to introduce hisself. The next round, I get to introduce myself," Joe said, squaring his shoulders.

Comstock looked at Joe with an expression that said, "Did I hear you right?" A ranch hand came over with Joe's hat in his hand and handed it to him. Joe reached for his hat and felt the grate of bone on bone in his ribcage. He grimaced and involuntarily clutched his left side.

Comstock saw Joe's obvious distress. "Looks like we're going to have to postpone that second round for now. But he'll be waiting for you when you're ready," he said.

Joe wasn't sure what Mr. Comstock was saying to him. "Do you want me to come back, suh?"

"No, I want you to stay. Nobody has lasted more than ten seconds on that hell-raiser since he set foot on the property. You're hired. We'll find something for you to do until you mend."

So it was that Joe spent his first six weeks on the Comstock ranch recovering from two broken ribs. Even so, Mr. Comstock paid Joe full wages. He did everything in his power to justify the Englishman's vote of confidence. He hauled water, washed dishes, and fed livestock. He was the first one up in the morning and the last one in bed at night. He never complained about any task assigned to him and tried to maintain his sense of humor and his dignity throughout. During his recovery, Joe fed and talked to Sidewinder every day. Two months to the day after he was hired, Joe rode the chestnut to a standstill.

Joe ran his hand over his eyes. The man on the undertaker's table was more than Joe's benefactor; he was a symbol of a new covenant between black and white men in the South, and his death damaged that covenant and scarred Joe's heart once again.

From the undertaker's, they went to the sheriff's office, where a group of men were already gathered, their expressions grim. The men turned to regard Joe and Rom. They were the first of many of Comstock's men who would come seeking answers and revenge.

A potbellied Mexican with a horseshoe mustache approached Rom and spoke to him in Spanish. The man ended their conversation by roughly patting Rom's shoulder. Rom turned to Joe. "He used to work for Señor Comstock. He offered his prayers and his help with the manhunt."

They went into the marshal's office.

He greeted them and said, "I wish I coulda spared you this bloody business." Marshal Sam Valdez was a medium-size man in his early fifties with a bald head fringed by grey hair. His dusky skin and blue-gray eyes suggested mixed parentage.

When they entered the office, Valdez had been talking to the tallest man Joe had ever seen, easily six and a half feet tall with shoulder-length salt-and-pepper hair, piercing blue eyes, and a neatly trimmed mustache and beard in the Van Dyke style.

"Hola, Samuel. This is mi amigo, Joe Walker. He also works for Señor Comstock. We are here for the posse," Rom said.

"Gracias. This is Captain Buck Taylor. He's with the Texas Rangers, and he's here to help us with this manhunt. He's been trailing Connor's bunch since they held up a stage and shot one of the passengers up Waco way. Our luck, he was close by when they hit us."

The ranger nodded to Joe and Rom, his cold eyes measuring them.

"Sam, can you tell us how Señor Comstock died?" Rom said.

"I was going over the eyewitness accounts with Captain Taylor when y'all came in. It seems Mr. Comstock was in the bank making a deposit when the robbers came in. They were wearin' masks, but everyone knew it was Bill Connor and his bunch on accounta them pearl-handled pistols he wears and that scratchy voice of his. They cleaned out the teller's cages and the safe with no trouble. But when they was leavin', one of Bill's men noticed Mr. Comstock's gold watch and told him to hand it over.

"Mr. Comstock said no, and the bastard clubbed him with his gun barrel and took the watch off him. They left, and Mr. Comstock got up off the floor and followed 'em into the street. He shot one and the rest gunned 'im down. Their lookouts pinned me and my deputy down in here while the rest of 'em hightailed it outta town. We lit out after 'em, but they split up about five miles outta town and there weren't enough of us to follow 'em. The thievin', murderin' bastards!"

Joe spoke for the first time. "Marshal, being this close to the border, they bound to be headed for Mexico. Their wounded man will slow 'em some, but if we don't get after 'em soon, they gon' be outta reach of the law."

Before the marshal could answer, the ranger spoke up. "The cowboy's right. I've heard all I need to hear. I'm headed out. Marshal, form your posse and follow me as quick as you can." He rose and started toward the door.

"Mind some company?" Joe asked.

Taylor looked at Joe and Rom intently and made up his mind.

"Ya'll are under my orders, understand?" he said.

"Yessuh," Joe said.

"Let's go then," Taylor said.

The three men left the office, mounted their horses, and rode out of town. Each was immersed in his own thoughts, and each was determined to finally end Bad Bill Connor's bloody career.

65

As Joe and his companions left Lone Tree, Bill Connor was still twenty miles from the Mexican border. According to plan, after leaving Lone Tree, they had split up to confuse any pursuers. His gang was now four groups headed in four different directions. Once they crossed the border, they would meet up in the town of Socorra and divide their spoils. The saddlebag with the loot in it was with Connor, also according to plan.

Connor was accompanied by Jim Garvey and Brace McKinnon, two trusted lieutenants who could hold their own in a fight and keep their mouths shut if apprehended. The wounded man, Frank Wittlock, was shot cleanly through the shoulder and would recover. All and all, it had been a successful venture. The life of an outlaw had more than its share of risks, but the rewards were commensurate.

After the war, Bill Connor chose this life rather than be subjugated by niggers and Yankees. During the war, he had fought and bled for a way of life that kept things as God had intended. Just because his superiors had surrendered to the devil, he was not about to follow suit. Since the war ended, he had raped, rustled, and robbed his way from one end of Texas to the other. He intended to live and die as a free white man.

He and his cohorts crossed the Rio Grande at midafternoon and Bill relaxed his guard, knowing that once again he had eluded capture by his so-called countrymen. He would lay low in Mexico until his cash ran low, and then he would return to the United States to partake of its bounty.

Everything, with one exception, had gone as planned. He was the master of his own fate, and as long as the sovereignty of Mexico held sway over the behavior of US lawmen, he would continue to prosper. As he privately gloated, Connor had no idea that fate had joined three men who were prepared to walk through hell to bring him to justice.

66

Joe and his two companions arrived at the border about two hours after Connor had crossed. They found the tracks where Connor and his men had crossed the Rio Grande and sat their horses, staring across the river into Mexico.

Captain Taylor couldn't hide his frustration.

"One day I'm gonna be in the right place at the right time, and I'm gonna end Mr. Connor. I swear it."

"He's right across the river," Joe said, nodding in the direction of Mexico.

"Yeah, but like you said, hombre, that puts him outside the jurisdiction of US law. He might as well be on the other side of the moon."

Having been a fugitive, Joe was reminded again of how easy it was to cross a border and elude the law.

"I reckon I'll ride over there and see if I can find 'im. Mr. Comstock deserves at least that much."

"I ride with you, amigo. Connor is a curse on both my countries," Rom said.

"Hold up, men. I know how you feel, but I can't let you take the law into your own hands without authorization," Taylor said.

"If we don't go after him while the scent is hot, he'll be back to take more lives. You can count on it. I couldn't live with that," Joe said. He looked at the ranger, and the set of his jaw and the look in his eyes said he would not be dissuaded.

Taylor said, "Maybe there is a way to get around this. Have you men heard of warrant officers, also known as bounty hunters?" Both men nodded. "It's within my authority to make you warrant officers on a temporary basis. Every man in Connor's gang is wanted dead or alive. As bounty hunters, you can chase 'em to the ends of the earth. If you've a mind to."

Joe said, "Sign us up."

The ranger took the appropriate papers from his saddlebags, signed them, and had Joe and Rom do likewise. He gave each man a copy of his written authorization to track down fugitives from the law.

"If the federales stop you, show 'em these papers. They may give you some slack. I plan to go back to Laredo and wait for you and whoever you bring back with you, sittin' in the saddle or lyin' across it. If you bring Connor or any of his hellhounds back to the States alive, I promise you they'll hang."

Joe rode forward and extended his hand.

Taylor took it and said, "Luck."

Rom pulled his horse abreast of the ranger, said, "Vaya con Dios," and offered his hand in turn.

"Tú también, amigo," Taylor said and shook Rom's hand.

Taylor rode toward Laredo and Joe and Rom headed for Mexico. Rom knew the border country like the back of his hand, having been raised there. If Connor and his men had gone to ground, he would root them out. The rest would be in the hands of God.

67

Joe and Rom crossed the Rio Grande and headed for Socorra, Mexico, one of Bill Connor's known haunts. Located fifty miles below the border, Socorra was a virtual outlaw's dream because of its lack of local law enforcement and the no-questions-asked attitude of its residents.

Their plan of attack was simple. They would ride in separately to give themselves some element of surprise. If Connor were in town, they would tail him until he went to bed then sneak into his room, hogtie him, and take him out of town under cover of darkness. The next stop would be Laredo and a long-delayed trial. There were half a dozen things that could go wrong with this plan, but it seemed the best way to avoid a shootout with multiple enemies.

Rom rode in first, having donned a poncho to complement his sombrero and hide his weapons. Joe would wait an hour and follow suit.

Joe rode into town at sundown. Socorra was a cluster of adobe buildings along either side of a dusty main street. The people he passed took pains to conceal their curiosity, but he noted their furtive glances and whispered conversations. He saw Rom's gray roan tied to the hitching rail outside the cantina. He hitched Dice next to Rom's horse, scanning the street in both directions before entering the saloon.

The bar was cool inside after the heat of the sun. A rough-hewn bar ran along one side of the room. Mexicans and a few Americans stood along its length drinking alcohol. Joe saw Rom at the end of the bar standing where he could survey the whole room.

Captain Taylor had provided them with wanted posters on Connor and six of his known henchmen to help identify them. Joe saw Connor seated at a table in back of the room playing cards. He was a swarthy, big-shouldered man with bushy eyebrows, pockmarked skin, and a beaked nose. Looking at him, Joe was reminded of a vulture. He was dressed in a jacket and waistcoat with a white shirt underneath, as if fancy clothes could hide the coarseness of the man who wore them. His mouth sported a perpetual sneer and his tablemates seemed to hang on every word that came out of it.

"Can I help you, señor?" The bartender was standing in front of Joe wiping a glass with a rag.

"Tequila," Joe said. The bartender turned and retrieved a bottle of cloudy liquor from the shelf behind him and poured Joe three fingers in the glass he had been polishing.

"Two pesos."

"Do you take US money?"

"Sí, señor."

Joe placed four bits on the bar and went back to scanning the room. There was a second floor with individual rooms along a hallway. Joe suspected this was where the bar girls plied their trade. One of them approached him.

She had tired eyes, her dress was frayed at the hem, and her shoes were missing some of their spangles, but she gave Joe her best smile and said, "It's not good for the stomach to drink alone, señor."

"Sorry, I'm waitin' for a friend," Joe said. Her smile faded and she moved off in search of another prospect. Joe noticed Bill Connor staring at him across the barroom.

"What's that nigger doin' in here?" Connor said in his sandpaper voice. "The only thing I hate worse than the smell of a nigger is the sight of one. Get to steppin', monkey, and don't stop till you're outta my sight."

Jim Garvey and Brace McKinnon sat on either side of Connor. Joe turned to leave, not wanting to provoke a fight in this worst of settings. As he moved toward the door, Connor threw another barb.

"Is that coon wearin' a gun?"

"'Pears to be," McKinnon said.

"Well, I'll be damned. He must think he's a man," Connor said.

Garvey took a hunting knife from his belt and stuck it in the table. "Maybe we should fix 'im so he don't make that mistake again. It's been way too long since I nutted a nigger."

"Why don't you give me that iron, boy, before you hurt yourself with it," Connor said, sensing an opportunity to indulge his consuming hatred of Negroes in front of an appreciative audience.

"I don't want no trouble. I'll leave you to your game," Joe said.

"What you want don't make no difference, boy. I said come here!"

Two men got up and left the table, sensing trouble. Joe noticed that one of them was wearing a sling. The entitlement and contempt in Connor's voice took Joe back to the time he had been treated like an animal instead of a man by his erstwhile masters. The outlaw had crossed a line without knowing it. The tiger was awake and with it, Joe's sense of justice.

He turned and walked toward the table where the three men were seated. "You want my gun? I'ma give it to you, Bad Bill." A look of surprise crossed the outlaw's face. "Yeah, I know who you are. Three days ago you and your pack of coyotes robbed the bank in Lone Tree and killed a good man for his pocket watch. So you can come back north with me and face the law or pull your pistols and face the devil. You decide."

"You black—" Bill Connor stood up, reaching for his guns. Joe shot him through the body and his gun discharged into the tabletop. McKinnon and Garvey made their moves at the same time. Joe shot them both and turned to deal with the man at the bar whose draw had tickled his peripheral vision. He shot the man in the heart and the outlaw's bullet went wide.

Joe walked over to Connor. The outlaw was shot through the lung and coughing blood. Joe put a bullet between his eyes. He whirled as a shot rang out behind him and saw a man tumble down the stairs. Rom was standing behind him, his gun barrel still smoking. They nodded to each other. Rom covered the room while Joe reloaded.

"Nobody move! Nadie se mueva!" Rom shouted, drawing a second gun from beneath his poncho.

Joe checked McKinnon and Garvey. Both men were dead. He turned to the crowd who regarded him as they would have a werewolf in their midst and said the lines Captain Taylor had told him to recite under these circumstances. "I'm Joe Walker and this is Romilio Estéban. We are duly appointed warrant officers from the state of Texas. These men are wanted for bank robbery and murder in the United States. We're taking them into custody under the authority of Captain John Taylor of the Texas Rangers."

He noticed the man in the sling trying to hide behind another man. "You with your arm in the sling. Step out here where I can see you." The man edged forward. "Wittlock? Frank Wittlock? Is that you? I believe it is. I recognize you from your wanted poster. Unbuckle that gun belt and kick it over here."

The outlaw unbuckled his gun belt, let it fall to the floor, and kicked it toward Joe.

"Now get rid of the gun in your sling," Joe said. Wittlock reached into his sling and hesitated, debating his next move. "My boss already put a bullet in you. You won't walk away from mine," Joe said.

Wittlock pulled a derringer from his sling and dropped it on the floor.

"Now come to me." Once the outlaw stood in front of him, Joe noticed the gold chain across his waistcoat. He removed the chain and the watch it was attached to. He opened the watch and read the inscription. *"To my beloved husband, Richard. Always, Elizabeth."*

For a moment, Joe was seized by the urge to smash Wittlock's face in with the barrel of his gun. Instead, he grabbed him by his shirtfront and pulled him close. "You'll hang for what you done. I swear it," Joe said. He pushed the outlaw over to Rom, who kept him covered.

They had the patrons pile the bodies in front of the saloon. Then, while Joe stood guard, Rom went to the livery and bought a wagon to transport the corpses in. They hitched Dice and Rom's roan, Chico, to it and drove out of town. After seeing Joe and Rom in action, none of the townspeople were inclined to stop them.

68

Joe and Rom rode into Laredo three days after they parted with Captain Taylor at the border. They had a wagon full of corpses and Frank Wittlock between them.

Captain Taylor was seated in a rocking chair on the sidewalk in front of the ranger's office. "You boys are a sight for sore eyes. I was about to send out a search party. I see you got one," Taylor said.

"More than one," Joe said stepping down from wagon. He led the ranger to the back of the wagon and pulled back a tarp, revealing Bill Connor's body and those of four of his men.

"I'll be damned! You got the sumbitch and a good share of his gang. Jeff, come here and look at this."

His deputy, Jeff Parsons, a young man about Joe's age with blond hair, rounded shoulders, and facial hair patterned after his captain's, joined them and emitted a low whistle at the wagon's grisly contents. "Is that Bad Bill Connor?" The deputy asked.

"What's left of him," Taylor said. "Take the prisoner inside and lock him up. Then take this bunch to the undertaker's and make the usual arrangements." He turned to Joe and Rom. "I imagine you boys got a story to tell, and I can't wait to hear it. Come on in. Coffee's on the stove."

He turned and walked into the ranger's station. Joe and Rom grabbed their gear and followed him. They told him their story, periodically interrupted by his requests for clarification. Deputy Parsons returned during their recitation and sat quietly in the corner.

When they had finished talking, Taylor looked at them with frank admiration. "There ain't but two or three men in Texas who could've done what you did, and they're all rangers. I would've given a month's pay to see the look on Connor's face when he realized that he was on a fast train to hell and you were the conductor. To come out of a fracas like that without a scratch must mean you're faster 'n greased lightning with a shooter."

"I wouldn't want that gittin' around. Folks hear somethin' like that and they wanna see for themselves," Joe said.

The ranger realized anew how badly he had misjudged the man in front of him. "They won't hear it from me," Taylor said. He opened his desk drawer and took out a pint of whiskey and two glasses. He poured drinks for Joe and Rom and kept the bottle for himself. "To Romilio Estéban and *slow* Joe Walker, two hombres to back your play anytime, anywhere."

They drank, grateful their lives had been spared and that, this time, right had prevailed over wrong.

"There's one more thing, Cap'n," Joe said. "Every one of those men had a money belt or a wallet on 'im stuffed with cash." He retrieved his saddlebags from the coat hook where he had hung them and dumped the contents, bulging money belts and wallets, on the desk.

"We figure it's the cash from the Lone Tree bank robbery. Could you get it back to them?" Rom said.

"I sure can. And I'll make sure they know who turned it in. Speaking of money, you men have a reward coming and if you'll walk over to the bank with me, I'll see that you get it," the captain said.

They went to the bank with Captain Taylor. The bounty on Connor and his confederates amounted to $5,500. On his own authority, Captain Taylor added a $500 finder's fee for the return of the bank money. It was more money than Joe and Rom could have made in a decade cow punching.

After a hearty meal paid for by Captain Taylor, they prepared to head back to Lone Tree. As they sat their horses in front of the ranger's station, the ranger imparted a last piece of advice. "You two might find that it's not so easy to slip back into being dollar-a-day ranch hands once the news gets out about what you did in Socorra. For better or worse, you will have a reputation following you around. If you should ever decide to float your stick in a different direction, look me up. The Texas Rangers can always use men of your caliber."

"Thank you, Cap'n, but I reckon people will forget about us soon as we get back to herdin' cows and breakin' hosses full time. Rangers keep the peace but ranchers make the peace. And that suits me and Rom just fine."

"I understand. But if you ever change your minds, you know where to find me," the ranger said.

"Yessuh, we do. You take care, suh," Joe said.

"You too, Mr. Walker."

Joe noted the honorific and nodded his appreciation.

"Adios, Capitán," Rom said, doffing his sombrero and swinging it in an arc while bowing his head.

"Adios, Señor Estéban," Captain Taylor said, touching the brim of his Stetson.

They rode out of Laredo not knowing they had made a friend for life.

69

They arrived at the Comstock ranch after two and a half days on the trail. They had one more thing to do before they could rest. They went to the family cemetery and paid their final respects to their employer and friend. Afterward, Joe and Rom went to the ranch house to tell their story to Comstock's wife in hopes it would provide her some solace.

Jennifer Comstock was a woman in her early forties with auburn hair, green eyes, and a flawless complexion. She was as big a favorite with the men as her husband. She would mend their torn clothing, remember their birthdays, and tend them when they were sick. They would have wrestled a grizzly to keep her from harm. Despite her stunning looks, she was as unassuming as a schoolmarm. With the death of her husband, she had invested all her emotional capital in her nine-year-old son, Matthew.

Joe and Rom told her their story, downplaying their courage and perseverance and emphasizing that justice had been done. Joe concluded by returning Mr. Comstock's heirloom to her, hoping it would, somehow, ease her pain. "Miss Jenny, we was able to get Mr. Comstock's watch back, and I know he would want you and Matthew to have it," Joe said.

Jenny Comstock accepted the watch and took one of Joe and Rom's hands in each of hers. "You were his favorites. He said you both reminded him of himself when he was young. Men like you and my husband were made for this country. It knocks you down and you get back up smiling. Until the day you don't get back up. This country's taken my father-in-law and now my husband. I won't let it take my son. I want Matthew to have a chance to see his children grown. So I've decided to sell the ranch and move back east. Don't worry about your jobs. Keeping you and the rest of the men on will be part of my asking price."

Mrs. Comstock's decision set Joe and Rom on a new course. They decided to use their reward money to buy a spread of their own. Rom had a wife and family in Mexico whom he longed to bring north. After life on the plantation and in the cavalry, Joe looked forward to being his own boss. But before they could strike out on their own, there was one more task to see to.

Frank Wittlock's trial lasted three days. Joe and Rom testified for the state. In the end, Wittlock was sentenced to death by hanging. After the sentence was carried out, the duo felt they had discharged their last duty to the Comstock family. It was time to attend to their own affairs.

Having decided to leave the Comstock ranch, they were eager to be away. They collected their last paycheck, said "so long" to their friends and ranch mates, and hit the trail. Joe had the sense that this was another watershed moment in his life. They rode east toward the Gulf of Mexico and a town called Corpus Christi. It sounded like a good place to put down roots.

PART 8

Home

70

Joe Walker sat astride Brandy, looking down into the valley that sheltered the Spanish Rose, his 250-acre spread in the so-called "wild horse desert" of southern Texas. From this base, Joe operated all over the territories. His work as a bounty hunter kept him on the trail for weeks, sometimes months, at a time, but this was the place he always returned to. Here he bred and broke horses for sale to the army. Here he could step outside without a gun on his hip. Here he could sleep with both eyes closed.

During this trip Joe had ended the murderous career of the outlaw Jim Slocum. On his way home, he had reviewed the journey on which life had taken him from slavery to freedom to fame. Along the way, he had found his biological brother and made lifelong friends, but there were also scars from wounds that would never fully heal.

Brandy, his bay gelding, gave a loud whinny at the sight and smell of home. He did a little sideways dance, eager to cover the last mile of this long journey.

Joe patted his neck. "All right, I know you're anxious to get home, but give a man a minute to look at what he's been working for."

The ranch house, corral, and outbuildings sat beside a stream that flowed through the center of the verdant valley. This was an offshoot of a tributary of the Nuéces River. There was a copse of birch trees a quarter of a mile beyond the ranch house that provided timber and firewood. The country was full of wild mustangs that could be caught and broken for working and riding, if a man had the skills to do so. Joe looked on all of this with a sense of contentment that few other things in life provided him. His reverie complete, he pointed the bay toward the ranch house, a purring hum rumbling in his chest.

As Joe covered the last hundred yards to the house, a man came out the front door offering a wave and a smile of welcome. Romilio Estéban was Joe's partner who minded the ranch during his frequent absences. Romilio greeted him with warmth and familiarity. "Hola, mi amigo! It is good to see you safe and well. Gracias a Dios."

Joe and Romilio had established an unbreakable bond while moving from ranch hands to ranch owners. Both were men of honor, expert wranglers and hard workers. At five foot ten and 165 pounds, Romilio was all muscle, sinew, and bone. He moved with the effortless grace of a cat. He was darkly handsome and could have had his pick of the women he encountered during his forced bachelorhood before reuniting his family in North America, but his heart unquestionably belonged to his wife, Consuélo.

Joe stepped down and greeted his friend. "Well, I see you didn't burn the place down while I was gone."

"That's because you weren't gone long enough, cofrade." They both smiled at this oft-repeated exchange. A raven-haired, strikingly beautiful woman came out the front door, still drying her hands on a dishtowel. Consuélo was followed by a miniature version of herself, six-year-old Rosita. The child ran across the yard and flung herself into Joe's arms.

"Tio José! Tio José! You're back! Where did you go? What did you do? What did you bring me?"

Joe could not hide his pleasure at the sight of the child. He smiled broadly and the countenance that emerged would have been unrecognizable to his adversaries.

"Well, darlin', I went to look for just the right gift for my little sobrinita. It took a while to find it."

"Let me see! Let me see! Oh, please!"

Consuélo intervened. "Rosita, at least let your tio get in the house before you start pestering him with a bunch of foolish questions," she said, concealing a smile.

"Tio José!" Two boys came running from the barn. These were the twins, Miguel and Manuel. At twelve years old, they were beginning to shed the awkwardness of boyhood and assume their father's grace.

Walker turned to greet them. "Mornin', muchachos. Consuélo, what you been feedin' these boys? I swear they musta grown a foot since I left."

"They *do* eat like los lobos," she said shaking her head. "Speaking of food, I can fix you some breakfast if you're hungry."

"A man would have to be a fool to turn down your cookin'," Walker said. With that, the family went into the house, Rosita still perched on Walker's arm and the boys trying to behave as if they weren't as excited as their sister by his return from the wide world.

Over breakfast, Joe told Rom about his latest manhunt. Rom sat shaking his head upon hearing about the close call with Slocum. "José, you are pushing your luck too far. You have paid back any debt you owe to the law. Come home and let's train and breed horses together. It's what you love and it won't kill you."

"To tell you the truth, I'm tired and I've been thinking about hanging up my guns, but I got a feeling that there's still something left for me to do."

Rom was silent. His worried look spoke volumes.

At midday, Romilio and Consuélo's oldest son, Ramón, and the ranch's only hired hand, Jesse Brady, returned from checking on a herd of mustangs that they were planning to drive into a box canyon for culling later that week. At eighteen, Ramón fit the Estéban mold: handsome, hardy, and horse savvy. He greeted Walker with a nod and a firm handshake, a man's greeting. He took some pain in describing the herd they were scouting, led by a black stallion that was as wary as a roadrunner.

"There's about thirty in the herd . . . prime stock. But we're gonna have to work to outfox that broom tail that's leadin' em. It's good you're back, Tio, because it's probably gonna take all of us to box him in."

Jesse, though ten years older than Ramón, had no problem deferring to the younger man. He was a rangy, good-natured Irishman who had attached himself to Walker after the latter saved his life five years earlier when three outlaws tried to rob him after a profitable night of poker in an El Paso saloon.

Jesse had been drunk from celebrating his good fortune and would have been easy prey. He still carried the scar from the knife stroke of one of his assailants. Joe stepped in because the affable Irishman had bought him a drink earlier over the objections of his companions. He shot the man who knifed Jesse and his two friends fled, leaving him alone in the alley behind the saloon. He took Jesse to the town doctor and waited for him to recover sufficiently to fend for himself.

Walker sought no reward for his actions but, as a result, he gained a lifelong friend. Not knowing what else to do with Jesse, he put him to work on his ranch. It had turned out well for all involved. The Estébans saw him more as a family member than an employee, and he would have laid down his life for any one of them.

Romilio said, "Tomorrow, we'll start to build the blind at the head of the canyon and then do the drive when we've finished." He was proud of Ramón's assessment of the situation but kept that to himself.

Rosita could wait no longer. "Tio, what did you bring me?"

"Was I supposed to bring you something?" Joe asked, feigning puzzlement.

"Tio! You said . . ."

"Oh yeah, that's right." Walker stroked his chin, "Let me see . . . Rosita's present . . . Rosita's present. Where did I put it?" He walked over to his saddlebags and retrieved a package with a ribbon around it. He gave it to the little girl, who was now dancing like a bug on a hot rock.

She tore open the package and discovered a doll in a blue and white gingham dress complete with shoe button eyes and long black braids.

Rosita screamed, "A doll! A doll!" She ran to Walker and threw her arms around his neck. "Thank you, Tio! Thank you so much!" She turned to Consuélo. "Mama, look, a doll—and she looks just like me!" The doll's cinnamon-colored skin was due to Joe having coated her with a café con leche mixture after buying her at a mercantile in Nebraska.

"I'm going to call her Angelina," the little girl declared. Rosita did not lose sight of the doll for the rest of the day and went to sleep with it clasped firmly to her breast.

After the little one went to sleep, Joe gave the boys the gifts he had picked up for them during his trip. There were leather gloves and socks for the twins. He surprised Ramón with a pair of silver spurs. The young man's reaction brought tears to Consuélo's eyes and a nod of appreciation from Rom. He gave Jesse a flask to hold the "toddy" he used to warm his bones in the winter and, truth be told, in the summer as well.

The big Irishman responded instinctively. "I'll be damned! Oh, excuse me, ma'am," he said to Consuélo, turning almost as red as his neckerchief. Her laughter absolved him instantly. Walker also brought a briar pipe for Rom and some dressmaking cloth for Consuélo.

When the others had retired, Walker sat at the table with Consuélo and Rom and produced the roll of bills he had earned bounty hunting. He passed the money to Consuélo, who retrieved a lockbox from under a loose floorboard beneath the rug. She took a key that hung from a chain around her neck and opened the strong box. It was filled with cash.

Walker said, "It won't be long before we have enough to buy that fifty-acre plot next to us. Then we can run some cattle and produce our own beef for sale."

Consuélo touched his arm. "José, no amount of land is worth the risk you take. Why don't you come home and stay? We already have everything we need."

The fact that she shared Rom's concern moved Joe and made him mentally examine his motives for staying on the bounty trail. Life had taught him that there were men who believed they could take whatever they wanted, including human life. One of those men had taken him away from his family at age nine. They were wolves among sheep. To stop a wolf, you needed a tiger, so he had become a tiger. But even a tiger needed a home, and that was what the money was for.

Instead of trying to articulate his thoughts, Joe said, "It's sure good to be home. And it's gettin' harder to leave every time. I got a feelin' the Lord's about to take my hand, and wherever he leads me, I'll follow. Right now, he's leadin' me to that bed upstairs." Following this evasive maneuver, he rose from the table and went up to the loft for his first fully restful night's sleep in some time.

71

Walker tried to give Brandy a rest when he was at home, so the next morning he saddled a dappled gray mare named Twilight, one of Dice's many offspring, and rode with the men to the work site. Ramón and Jesse had found a winding box canyon about one hundred yards long. The canyon had a narrow entrance, steep walls, and a pond at the far end, making it ideal for their purposes.

Walker savored being part of a team again. These men were good hands, and the prospect of working with them again pleased him as it always did. He especially enjoyed following a plan that he hadn't devised and that wouldn't end in violence or bloodshed. He spent the day chopping down trees and hauling them to the head of the canyon where they would use them to make a gate to trap the mustangs once they drove them into the cul-de-sac. Gratefully, he fell into the healing rhythm and banter of ranch work.

It took two days to get the canyon ready. It had been chosen for its narrow width and shallow length. Wild mustangs survived by their wits and their speed, so to catch them, *you* had to be smart and fast. Each man had a role to play. Joe, Ramón, Rom, and Jesse would be drivers. Their job was to get the herd moving in the right direction and keep them running. That basically meant outmaneuvering the stallion that led them. Under stress, the herd would follow him instinctively. The twins would man the canyon gate. First, the drivers would follow the herd at a distance until they were positioned downwind. Next, Rom would approach the bunch walking behind his stallion, Salvaje. Then nature would take its course.

An hour later, the herd was in the right location. Rom had circled them and was approaching downwind. The other riders were concealed in a grove to the east parallel to the herd. Salvaje fairly whistled at the smell of the mares in the black stallion's harem. The black saw what appeared to be a rival approaching and rapidly separated himself from the group to face down the interloper. He came on swiftly, paying no attention to the man in the stallion's wake. Ten feet away he paused and neighed suspiciously, but by then it was too late.

Rom leaped into the saddle and rushed the stallion, who turned and fled this new threat. At the same time, the other drivers broke cover and moved to place themselves between the stallion and his mares. The mustang instinctively wheeled away from the yelling riders and signaled his herd to follow him in the direction of the box canyon. The herd turned as one and followed their leader. Joe and his companions flanked them and kept them moving in panicked retreat toward the waiting cul-de-sac. As they approached the canyon, Joe and the other drivers began firing their guns in the air to add to the herd's frenzy. The herd swept through the mouth of the canyon and the twins ran home the rails of the recently built gate behind them, trapping them in a canyon where there was water and grass but no egress.

"Well, that went off slicker 'n lard on a hot griddle!" Jesse exclaimed.

Joe was relieved the drive had gone smoothly. Phase one of the operation was indeed a success. The herd had pulled up at the back of the canyon and were milling around restlessly taking equine inventory. Seeing his pursuers had abandoned the chase, the stallion headed back toward the mouth of the canyon and the open range.

When he got there, he encountered the men and the gate. Neither discovery pleased him. He pawed the ground and then reared and pawed the air, loudly trumpeting his disgust with this turn of events. When the men approached the gate and his herd, he turned and retreated into the canyon.

"Well, nothin' unknots until we deal with that rascal," Walker said.

"Amigo, let's give them some time to settle down. Anyway, I could use a lunch break," Rom said with a smile.

They pulled out the lunch basket Consuélo had packed for them and enjoyed a meal of tamales, rice, and beans. After lunch, the men mounted, uncoiled their lariats, and lined up in front of the canyon's entrance. The twins opened the gate and they proceeded abreast into the canyon. As they approached, the herd retreated. Finally, they were backed up to the edge of the pool that abutted the wall of the canyon. The stallion paced in front of his mares, feinting at the line of riders. Savalje's presence was driving him crazy.

Rom rode forward and the stallion charged. The vaquero was ready. He swung his rope expertly and dropped the loop around the animal's neck. The stallion reared but Savalje was already balancing his weight against the wild leader's, and it was a temporary stalemate. Joe moved in from the right and Jesse from the left. Each dropped a loop over the stallion's head. With three lariats on him, the stallion abandoned the idea of retreat. Instead he charged his adversaries, but they triangulated his momentum and rendered his effort ineffective. From this vantage point, Joe could see what a truly magnificent animal he was. Muscles rippled under his gleaming coat. His mane whipped like a battle flag and his eyes were on fire.

Slowly, they began to move the struggling horse toward the hitching post they had sunk at the edge of the canyon. While Walker and Jesse kept tension on their ropes, Rom dismounted and tied him to the post. With the stallion tethered, they rounded up the others and drove them to the mouth of the canyon to start the drive back to the ranch. With the black restrained, the rest would follow Salvaje now.

The drive home was uneventful. All and all, it had been a successful undertaking. They would break some horses for sale, add others to their herd, and release the rest. As for the stallion, Joe and Rom would ride back to the canyon and release him to the life for which he was born.

72

About the time Joe and Rom were setting up camp on their way back to the canyon, the stranger arrived at the ranch house. He watched smoke rise lazily from the chimney and saw the bay gelding in the corral next to the barn. His prey was close. It was dusk, which suited his purpose precisely.

He cradled the Sharps rifle next to his cheek. This weapon would eliminate any advantage Walker might have in a gunfight. Yes, he had fantasized about staring into Walker's dying eyes and watching as recognition dawned there. But he had waited too long for this moment to have it spoiled by hubris. He had dreamed of this day while picking maggots out of his food, while wrapping his rotting feet in homemade poultices, and while enduring the daily abuse of men whose hatred of him was compounded by the wretchedness of their own lives. The only way for him to regain some semblance of peace in his life was to end Walker's.

Jesse had finished supper and was looking forward to a chew. Though she had never said a thing, he knew that Consuélo found the sight of his habit unpleasant. So he would wait to indulge himself until he got to the barn. A light rain had begun to fall, so he grabbed his hat and slicker.

"Ma'am, I'm goin' to feed the hosses then I 'spect I'll turn in early."

"All right, Jesse. Buenas noches."

"You need some help?" Ramón asked from the kitchen.

"No, I got it. Put the kids to bed."

When the tall man stepped out on the front porch, only his silhouette was visible. The stranger held his breath and squeezed the trigger. The Sharps's load blew his target back against the door and he fell face down, motionless. There was a scream from inside the cabin and the door flew open to reveal a woman who knelt beside the bounty hunter and tried to roll him over. The stranger drew a bead on her—best not to leave any witnesses.

The sound of shattered glass was followed by the barrel of a rifle protruding from the front window. An instant later a bullet slammed into the tree he was using for cover. The next shot whined over his head. He quickly retreated, mounted his horse, and fled the scene of his revenge. The only man he had to worry about was dead. Anyone who pursued him would pay the same price. The ledger was finally closed. A thin smile spread across his lips, a smile that made him look reptilian.

73

Riding up to the ranch house the next day, Walker suddenly had an uneasy feeling. He unstrapped the gun in his holster and searched the familiar grounds with a hunter's eyes.

"Qué pasa, amigo?" Rom asked, noticing his posture.

"Ain't sure. Keep your eyes peeled."

When they drew within fifty yards of the cabin, Ramón exited the front door and came toward them at a dead run. Walker noticed he was wearing his sidearm.

"Papa, Tio, somebody shot Jesse!" By the look on his face, they knew the news was going to get worse.

"How bad is he, mijo?" Romilio asked.

"He's dead, Papa. He's dead." Then the emotion he had held in check overnight while guarding his family spilled over in hot tears. Rom dismounted and took his son in his arms. As Joe watched them, his thoughts were hot even as his blood turned cold.

He rode on to the cabin and dismounted. At the sound of his step on the porch, Consuélo came out the front door. She was carrying Rosita in her arms, and the twins followed closely behind. Her lovely face bore the ravages of fresh grief. Walker embraced them both.

"José, he's gone. Our Jesse is gone. They gave him no chance. There was nothing we could do." She began to sob. Walker had no words. He could only hold her and pat her back until Rom arrived to take his place.

He turned to Ramón. "Where's Jesse?" The boy took him to the root cellar. There wrapped in a blanket was his faithful friend and trail mate. Walker removed the blanket and saw the fist-sized hole in Jesse's chest. His first response was rage so overwhelming that his vision blurred and there was a roaring in his ears. Someone had attacked his family in the sanctuary of their home, and they had done it in the most cowardly way imaginable. Whoever he was, he was as good as dead. He realized that Ramón had been speaking to him. "Say what?" he asked.

"I was saying that I only saw one man and I shot at him, but I think I missed. I wanted to go after him but Mama wouldn't let me. She said there might be others."

"She was right. When did this happen?"

"Just after sundown. Jesse was going out to bed down the horses. Tio, who would do this thing? He must pay for what he did. We will make him pay." There was a resolve in the boy's voice that belied his years.

"Ramón, you've been a straight-up man here. I'm right proud of you for keepin' the family safe. Now here's what happens next. We gon' bury our brother Jesse. Then I'm goin' after the cur that killed him. I need you and your father here so I can rest easy knowing Consuélo and the children are safe. You need to do what you know how to do and let me do what I know how to do."

"Your tio is right, mijo," Romilio said.

They turned to see him standing in the doorway.

"Nothing would give me greater pleasure than gutting the coyoté that killed Jesse and leaving him for the buzzards, but our first duty is to see that your mother and the children are safe. I will not lose another member of mi familia to a coward's attack. So sí, we will follow José's plan."

They laid Jesse to rest in a plot behind the house. Walker carved a wooden marker on which he wrote the following epitaph:

JESSE CHRISTOPHER BRADY
FEBRUARY 12, 1852–SEPTEMBER 17, 1880
BELOVED FRIEND AND BROTHER
FAITHFUL TO THE END
YOU WILL LIVE ON IN OUR HEARTS

Walker had thoroughly searched the area where the shooter concealed himself. He found a spent Sharps rifle shell and boot prints in the dirt. The shooter was probably a bit below average height given the size of his feet. He also found dark wool threads in the bark of the tree where the assassin had rested his shoulder. The killer's horse had been tied to a tree ten feet behind him. Walker memorized the hoofprints. Time to hunt.

After the funeral, Walker impatiently ate the ceremonial meal Consuélo had prepared. As soon as practical, he pulled away from the table and went to his room in the loft. There was a locked six-by-six-foot cabinet on the wall across from his bed. He opened it with a key from the dresser. Inside there were rows of pistols, knives, and long guns. From the pistol rack, he took a Colt .44 and the shoulder holster that accompanied it. He took his Henry from the rifle rack. Finally, he retrieved ammunition for both weapons from a footlocker beneath the bed.

Back in the main room, he said simply, "Time to go."

Consuélo came and hugged him tightly. "Vaya con Dios, José."

Rom and Ramón followed him to the barn. He saddled Brandy in silence and led the big bay into the yard.

"Rom, you take care of the place. I'll be back when this is finished."

"Sí, hermano. Stay safe."

From the saddle, Walker leaned down and shook Ramón's hand. Then he wheeled the bay and rode away, his mind already on the task ahead.

74

Jacob Budreau was breathing easier having crossed the border into Mexico. Apparently, there was no one from the Walker place on his back trail. He was a free man and his nemesis was dead. Life had turned out a lot better than he could have expected while rotting away in a Missouri prison courtesy of Joe Walker.

Walker stopped at the ranger station in Laredo. He planned to report Jesse's murder and obtain authorization to pursue his killer into Mexico. This was a formality the outcome of which would not deter him from his mission.

When he walked into the ranger station, he went to the wanted poster wall from force of habit. On one of the posters under the caption "Escaped From Prison" was Jacob Budreau's likeness. The flyer gave his physical description along with the information that he had escaped from the Missouri State Prison in March of that year. The state was offering $5,000 for his recapture.

The truth hit Walker with the force of a physical blow. Budreau had fulfilled his deadly promise, as far as he knew, and planned now to hide out below the border until the heat died down.

"What's up, ol' hoss? You lookin' for work?"

Walker turned to face Major John "Buck" Taylor, the OIC of the ranger station. Over the years, Joe and the ranger had become fast friends due to working together numerous times to bring outlaws to justice.

Taylor paused with his hand extended and a welcoming smile still on his lips. His look turned to one of concern. "Are you all right, Joseph? You look like you just saw a ghost."

"I just did," Walker replied. "Major, I'm here to report the murder of my ramrod, Jesse Brady." He went on to describe the circumstances of Jesse's death. Taylor's jaw tightened as he heard the details, and a dangerous glint came into his blue eyes.

"I been trailing the man who killed him for the last ten days. I reckon he's in Mexico by now," Walker said.

"Any idea who the varmint is?" Taylor asked.

"Not until five minutes ago." He went to the wall, retrieved Budreau's poster, and handed it to the ranger. "I put that son of a bitch away nine years ago. He swore he'd kill me when he got out. Jesse and me are about the same height and build. In the dark, in the rain, I figure he made a mistake. It's the last one he's ever gon' make," Walker said with a matter-of-factness that caused Taylor to nod unconsciously.

"So what can I do for you?" Taylor asked.

"Suh, I need you to swear out a warrant for Budreau's arrest on the charge of murder and I'll enforce it or die tryin'."

"Done," the lawman said. "Joseph, If you're goin' below the border, you're gonna need more than your southern charm to maneuver down there." He reached into his desk drawer, retrieved a badge, and slid it across the desk.

Walker had worn a ranger's badge before on temporary assignment. In fact, the second time Walker saved the life of one of his ranger partners, then-Captain Taylor had practically insisted he join the force, but Walker had declined, preferring to remain his own boss. He paused. "Before you offer me that badge, Major, you need to know that it ain't likely that I'm gon' be bringin' Budreau back alive. We promised each other that our next meetin' would be our last."

"You plan on givin' him a fair shake?" the ranger asked.

"Yessuh, I do. Which is more than he gave Jesse."

"Raise your right hand," the major said and swore Walker in.

After filling out the warrant for Budreau's arrest for murder and giving it to Walker, the major asked, "You got a plan?"

"Start in Socorra and move on from there," Walker said.

"Socorra," the Major snorted. "Keep your eyes peeled in that vipers' nest. You know, if you wait a week, I can send a man with ya."

"T'ain't necessary, Major," Walker said, placing the badge in his vest pocket. "Like they say, 'One riot, one ranger.'"

75

Jacob Budreau stopped running in Socorra, Mexico. Socorra was a tiny village fifty miles below the US border with a reputation for being a haven for men from the States on the run from the law. There was no law in the town, a man didn't need much Spanish to get by, and both the women and the whiskey were cheap. Budreau had heard about it in prison and had decided to make it his base of operations if he succeeded in breaking out.

Nine years of hard labor had physically and mentally transformed Budreau. He had gained twenty-five pounds of corded muscle. His skin was the color of saddle leather after years of laboring in the sun. He walked with a limp from having his left foot broken by a sadistic prison guard who didn't like the way he responded to an order. Most significantly, he trusted no one, and his ruthlessness had been honed to the edge of insanity.

He dismounted and walked into the local cantina. All eyes turned in his direction as he walked to the bar.

"Si, señor?" the bartender said.

"Whiskey," Budreau said.

The bartender filled a hastily wiped glass with three fingers of rye and set it down in front of Budreau. "Two pesos," he said, eyeing the stranger suspiciously.

Budreau fished a coin from his pocket and threw it on the bar. He downed the drink in one gulp.

A voice behind him said, "You better break that glass, Pedro. It ain't fit for a white man to drink outta now."

Budreau turned to see a pocked-faced white man with missing front teeth seated with several cronies at a table opposite the bar. He walked over to the table carrying his empty glass. He set the glass on the table. "Why don't you break it, hoss?"

The American stood up. He was a head taller than Budreau and outweighed him by at least forty pounds. "How 'bout I just break you, boy?"

With the speed of a striking rattlesnake, Budreau backhanded the big man across the eyes. This both stunned and temporarily blinded him. Budreau followed up with a blow to the outlaw's throat. Then, grabbing him by his shirtfront and his belt, he hurled him across the room like a sack of grain. The man landed on his right shoulder and an involuntary scream escaped his lips. Before he could get his bearings, Budreau was on him like a rabid wolf. He stomped the man repeatedly, ignoring the sounds of bones breaking. His last kick was to the side of the man's head, and he went limp.

Budreau grabbed the man by the back of his collar and dragged him back to the table where he retrieved his shot glass and jammed it into his adversary's mouth. He slammed the outlaw's chin on the table and the glass exploded into shards, piercing his tongue, cheeks, and lips sending forth gouts of blood. He looked at the man's stunned tablemates, his eyes like storm clouds.

"Anybody else got somethin' to say?" he asked. Receiving no response, he returned to the bar. He said to the shocked bartender, "Another whiskey, por favor, and another glass."

76

Joe rode into Socorra three days later. The town hadn't changed much in the ten years since he was last there in pursuit of Bad Bill Connor—same dusty street, same sunbaked buildings, same wary inhabitants. He dismounted in front of the cantina where the events had unfolded that set him on course to become a bounty hunter.

He walked into the cantina and approached the bar. He did not recognize the man behind the bar, a narrow shouldered, potbellied Mexican with a handlebar mustache and a dirty apron.

"Si, señor?" the barman said.

"Tequila," Walker said.

The bartender poured the drink and set it in front of Walker, who downed it in one swallow.

"Another," he said.

They repeated the ritual.

Walker said, "I'm lookin' for a friend o' mine, a short, light-skinned fella with gray eyes. Me and him was s'posed to meet up heah last week, but I got held up. You seen 'im?"

"No, señor. I have not seen him. Maybe he got held up too," the barkeep said.

Walker suspected the man was lying. His job and his life probably depended upon his discretion. Besides, he was just a little too unfazed by the sight of a heavily armed black man in his establishment.

"Mebbe so," he said. "I think I'll hang out awhile. See if he shows up. How much for the bottle?"

"Six pesos, señor," the bartender replied. He seemed suddenly uneasy.

Walker placed the money on the bar and moved to a table in the corner from which he could view all the exits. The bartender came from behind the bar with a tray containing a bottle and several glasses. He went over to a group of men at a table diagonal to Walker's. He made a show of putting down the tray and then, with his back to Walker, said something to one of the men who glanced briefly in his direction. Then the bartender returned to the bar. Shortly afterwards, one of the men got up from the table and left the bar.

This is about to get interesting, Walker thought. He had not flashed his badge because he thought it would be more of a liability than an asset in this situation. He suddenly stood up and walked to the back door of the saloon.

"Señor, a dónde vas?" the bartender asked in alarm. Walker kept walking through the back door and into the backyard. He walked behind several more buildings and then crossed the street. He needed a high vantage point.

There was a chapel at the end of the street. He proceeded to the church and stepped inside. The interior was cool and quiet. He climbed into the bell tower, which commanded a view of the entire street. *This'll do,* he thought. He checked his loads and waited.

Ten minutes later, the man who left the bar returned with two others. The squat bull in the middle was Jacob Budreau. The physique was drastically altered but the face was still the same. Walker resisted the momentary urge to pop up the sight on the Henry and end this episode before it began. Budreau paused and stared at Brandy before drawing his gun and entering the bar.

As soon as the street was clear, Walker whistled for Brandy, who came on the run for the church. He climbed down from the bell tower and exited the church just as Budreau and his confederates ran out of the cantina. Walker vaulted into the saddle and fled the town. There was a volley of shots behind him. He leaned low over Brandy's neck and was soon out of range. The outlaws caught up their horses and set out in pursuit of the stranger. Presently, Budreau and his men realized the futility of trying to catch the bay and headed back to town. When the outlaws broke off their pursuit, Walker made a wide circle and headed back the way he had come. Now that he knew where his quarry was, he was not about to abandon the hunt.

77

Jacob Budreau was worried. He was incredulous that his enemy was alive and on his doorstep. All of his calculations and plans had to be revised in light of those two facts. After nearly beating a man to death who insulted him on his first day in town, Jacob correctly surmised that the leadership of the local thugs would be his for the taking. His plan was to mold this raggedy group into a first-class gang that would allow him to continue his life of crime.

His paranoia was running rampant. He felt Walker's eyes on him from behind every bush and tree. He had no doubt the bounty hunter would shoot him from ambush without hesitation as he had tried to do to Walker. He couldn't wait to get behind closed doors so he could figure out his next move. His gang escorted him all the way to his door. He placed two men on guard outside his quarters and plotted his next move.

Walker followed the crowd right to Budreau's lair, a two-story adobe dwelling about a mile out of town. He hid Brandy in the trees and watched the bulk of Budreau's gang leave to go back to town. Two men were left out front on guard duty.

A little after sundown, a Mexican woman came to the house, spoke to the men, and entered. Thirty minutes later, she called them into the house, presumably for supper. Walker took this opportunity to move closer to the dwelling.

After supper, the men resumed their posts. The Mexican woman left, having completed her domestic chores. The men sat and smoked, occasionally walking the perimeter of the building. The taller of the two pulled a flask from his pocket and they passed it back and forth.

Walker began to formulate a plan. Under the cover of darkness, he circled the building and found the privy out back. He slipped inside and waited. After a while, the taller man came to the outhouse to do his business. He stepped into the enclosure, already unbuckling his pants. Walker tapped him with his blackjack before he could utter a sound and caught the sagging figure in his arms. He bound and gagged the outlaw and left him in the outhouse. He had taken the man's serape and hat, and he donned these now and headed back to the front of the house.

He walked toward the other guard, who was dozing in his chair. Walker kept his head down with his hat pulled low over his eyes. The shorter man roused himself at Walker's approach.

"I thought you fell in."

Walker came close enough for his face to be seen.

"Hey, what the—"

Walker tapped him with the blackjack and he slumped sideways to the ground. He threw the man over his shoulder and carried him to the backyard where he bound and gagged him and put him in the privy next to his partner.

Walker returned to the front of the house, tried the door, and, to his surprise, found it unlocked. He slipped inside on noiseless feet. He paused to let his eyes adjust to the darkness. The front room was empty. He saw the door to a second room and glided to it. This was the kitchen. It, too, was empty. Walker ascended the stairs and went to the bedroom across from them. Peering around the corner, he saw a figure lying on the bed covered by a blanket. He took out his blackjack and advanced to the bed. Once he got Budreau out of Socorra, they would settle up.

When he got next to the bed, Walker discovered that it contained not a person but a simulacrum made of rolled blankets and a large gourd. Realizing his mistake, he turned instinctively, resulting in his taking Budreau's knife stroke along his ribs instead of in the back. The outlaw had been hiding behind a wardrobe in the corner. Walker grabbed Budreau's wrist and tried to twist the knife out of his hand, but the man's wrist was like an iron bar. He wrenched free of Walker's grasp and slashed at his face. Walker ducked away from the thrust and drew his own knife. The two men circled each other, their breathing the only sound in the room.

"I knew you'd come for me, so I left you a trail of bread crumbs," Budreau said.

Walker drew his Colt and Budreau's smile froze. Never taking his eyes off Budreau, Walker put the gun on the floor and kicked it behind him. "Come on, you backstabbin' son of a bitch," he said.

Budreau lunged and feinted with his knife. When Walker ducked away from the feint, Budreau clubbed him on the side of the head with his fist. Walker staggered to the side and slashed Budreau's tricep.

They circled again, slashing and feinting. Budreau rushed forward and slashed from right to left. Walker leaped to his left, but the outlaw's knife caught him on the backstroke, drawing blood.

Walker noticed that Budreau had a limp, so he began circling to his left. Budreau could not match Walker's speed, so he tried to grab him and use his bulk as a battering ram. Throwing caution to the wind, he lunged and grabbed Walker's blade in his bare hand. Walker sliced through tendons, but Budreau drove him backward to the edge of the bed and fell on top of him.

Walker grabbed Budreau's right wrist and kept his knife from piercing his eye. But he knew Budreau's superior strength would soon be his undoing.

"I told ya I was gon' kill ya," Budreau hissed.

Walker used his remaining strength to bring his knee up into Budreau's groin. The outlaw's breath came out in a whoosh and his lower body went limp. Walker rolled and they both landed on the floor, positions reversed.

Walker wrenched Budreau's knife from his hand and plunged it into his chest once then twice. He poised for a third strike but saw that it was unnecessary. The outlaw shuddered and lay still. The knife still in his hand, Walker rolled off Budreau and lay at his side, gasping. Slowly, his breathing slowed and the bloodlust cooled. He rose to his knees and looked into Budreau's dead face.

This was the face of the man whom he had either feared or hated for most of his life, the face he associated with so much anger, pain, and loss, the face that was the last remnant of his blighted childhood. He reached over and closed Budreau's eyes and then, to his surprise, he began to cry.

He cried for his lost family members, his lost childhood, and his lost friend, Jesse. His tears were hot, as though their purpose was to cauterize his psychic wounds. He let the tears flow without restraint until, as suddenly as they began, they stopped.

For the first time in his life, he felt completely free. He gave a soul-cleansing sigh and wiped his eyes with the back of his hand. There was still work to do. He wrapped Budreau's body in the blanket from the bed then cleaned and dressed his own wounds. Next he went to the stable behind the house and saddled Budreau's horse, lashed the outlaw's body to the animal, and led him to the place where Brandy was waiting.

Walker went to the outhouse and found the two outlaws conscious but still restrained. He freed their feet and motioned them toward the house. In passing, they noticed Budreau's horse and its grisly burden. Once inside, he made them sit at the kitchen table and bound them to their chairs. Finally, Walker removed their gags.

The shorter man blurted out, "This ain't over, mistuh."

"Shut up, Reggie," his partner said sharply.

Walker pulled back his coat lapel and showed them the badge pinned there. "I'm Joseph Walker, Texas Ranger," he said.

The tall man said, "Budreau told us you was a bounty hunter."

"Used to be," Walker said. "Jacob Budreau's an escaped prisoner who's wanted for murder in the state of Texas. I'm takin' his body back to the States to satisfy the law. Budreau's the only one o' this Socorra bunch that the Rangers are concerned about right now. But that could change in a hurry if you fellas decide to keep stickin' your noses into ranger business. Comprendé?"

The two outlaws nodded. Walker stood up to leave.

"Ain't you gonna untie us, Ranger?" Reggie asked.

"Nope, your pards'll be along to do that directly," Walker said. "Tell 'em what I told you. If any of y'all do decide to come after me, I plan to shoot first and ask questions later. Let's hope we don't meet again. Adiós." With that, he left the outlaws to their own devices.

He mounted Brandy and headed north. The sun was rising as he rode out of Socorra. The trail ahead might get rocky, but his heart lifted knowing he was headed home where he would complete his transition from gunman to stockman. For all intents and purposes, Slow Joe Walker was dead. He was killed in a knife fight below the border.

Epilogue

When the outlaw band discovered their bound companions and heard from them Budreau's fate, they debated following Walker and exacting revenge. But, in the end, their loyalty was as anemic as their morality and they concluded that Budreau's loss was probably a blessing in disguise.

Walker took Budreau's body to Laredo, gave his statement, and turned in his badge. After bringing Budreau to justice, Walker abandoned the bounty hunting life and became a full-time rancher. The demon inside him was finally laid to rest.

He saw his adopted family grow and prosper. He met and married a widow who worked in a boarding house in Corpus Christi and, in his forties, started a family of his own. When Joe held his son, Jesse, in his arms for the first time, he vowed that the boy would always have a family and a home to return to, come hell or high water.

Acknowledgments

There are many people who helped make this book possible, starting with all my English and writing teachers from elementary school to university who encouraged me to put down my thoughts and feelings on paper and then try to learn what I could from the results. Most notably, Mrs. Janet Fishbain, my high school English teacher, who contacted me recently to comment upon the writing talent I demonstrated while taking her class over fifty years ago.

A heart felt thanks to my editors, Katherine Don and Kim Bookless, who helped me turn a series of dramatic episodes into a coherent novel. The book's successes in language, character, and plot development are a result of our joint efforts. Any missteps in those areas are mine alone.

Also, thanks to Bethany Brown and her colleagues at The Cadence Group for advising and educating a novice author on the finer points of designing, marketing, and publishing his first novel.

Thank you to Brother Richard Scott, my artistic mentor, who showed me how to bring a project and a partnership to fruition.

Thank you to Terri Pellitteri, my dear friend and test reader. You encouraged me to keep writing even when it was just for my own amusement and then supported wholeheartedly my plans to craft a book from the first fruits of my imagination.

Thanks to my daughters, Brenna and Sarah. You were role models in successfully pursuing a dream and have encouraged me to follow suit. You come from a line of strong black women who were, in many ways, the anchors of their families and their communities.

Thanks to my son, Nathan. You were the inspiration for this book wherein a black man achieves hero status merely by being true to himself and to those he loves. Watching you love and provide for your family against all odds makes me extremely proud.

Thank you to Luther Byles, my "brother from another mother," for your lifelong friendship. Most of the insights about male bonding in this novel are drawn from our sixty-plus-year relationship.

Thanks to my sister, Joyce and my niece, Yvette, for your unconditional love and support and your abiding belief that I can do anything that I set my mind to—even write a book in my eighth decade.

Thank you to Margaret Sleeper, my partner in this project and in life. Thank you for lending your remarkable talents as proofreader, consultant, and critic to this book. Without you, my dream would never have taken wing. I love you for who you are and for who you help me to be.

And finally, thanks to my parents, William and Marie, to whom I owe my life, my education, and whatever natural gifts I possess. I hope that this story of family, faith, and perseverance will help to preserve your memory and in some small way demonstrate my lasting love and respect for you.

William Greer
March 25, 2020